# FIXIN' VIXEN

# Fixin' Vixen

Cat Collins

Dramatic Tuba Books

# OTHER BOOKS BY CAT COLLINS

*The Diminishing Magic Series*
Jewels of Clay
Flames of Gold
Guardian of Whispers

*Reindeer Games series*
Fixin' Vixen

COMING SOON BY CAT COLLINS

Book 4 of the Diminishing Magic series – early 2024
A dark fantasy Fae pirate series – Spring 2024
Reindeer Games Book 2
featuring another one of Santa's naughty reindeer – Christmas 2024

For the real Mandy
&
The real Santa

Thanks for all the merry.
May your suspenders cross, your snow fall
gently, and your bells jingle all the freaking
way.

# REINDEER GAMES #1

# STORY CONTENT EXPECTATIONS

This book is a "Why Choose" romance, which means the main character, Vixen, will be hooking up with more than one love interest. Sometimes at once. In addition, it's MMFM, meaning two of the male characters will be together in that capacity too.

If that sounds appropriately naughty and/or nice, please continue reading. If that's not for you, I understand. Thanks.
Check out my other paranormal romance books for more traditional pairings.

*Vixen*

# CHAPTER 1

Santa was a real dumbass if he thought his little trick would work. You couldn't just stuff Christmas spirit into someone like you were Gordon Ramsey making holiday turkey. No. Christmas spirit was born of love and magic and both of those had been obliterated in my heart roughly six seconds after I found my boyfriend of two years recently 'fixed' nose between the thighs of his ex.

Fucking Clari—

Wait. She rebranded when he did. Lost a couple of letters.

Fucking *Clare*.

I hoisted my bag over my shoulder and trudged toward the Holidays Inn. No, not that one. The one at the South Pole, designed for magical species, with small idyllic cabins, huge evergreen trees, and a picturesque setting that looked like it was ripped out of every Hallmark Christmas movie ever made. It wouldn't have surprised me if Santa had some boring, but handsome man who just happened to be here to run these cabins for his dear old ailing auntie locked and loaded for me to fall in love with behind these doors.

The joke was on Santa. I was finished with romance for a while.

Maybe forever.

Heartbreak would do that to a girl. Er, reindeer shifter.

When I reached the porch, I stomped all the snow off my boots that I could and took a deep breath. Even after shifting back to my human form, my body ached from the long flight from North to South. I craved a gallon of alcohol and a nice warm bed to wallow in. At least I would get those here on my little forced vacation. I just had to get through the long weekend.

I'd play nice, plaster on a fake smile, and "chillax" as Santa put it. I'd bide my time until I was allowed back at the North Pole again because I'd be damned if I let that asshole Rudy ruin my place on the fleet. I was Vixen. *The* Vixen and I'd been one of the leaders of the fleet for centuries. Way before he ever showed his formerly crimson nose.

Christmas was a couple of weeks away and Santa was going to ground me if I didn't have an attitude adjustment, so adjust my attitude, I would. At least externally. Though if you asked me, Rudy was the one who needed to change.

Or maybe die.

The wooden door squeaked as I opened it and the second my toes stepped over the threshold of the cabin facility's main lobby, warmth penetrated my bones, and the ache of flying melted. This place wasn't going to make my heartache go away, but at least my body was more comfortable out of the frigid air and on the ground.

I pulled off my hat and my red mane tumbled down over my shoulders.

Rudy had said my hair was what drew him away from Clare at first. He'd run his fingers through it every chance he got. I should've known then. It should've hit me like a blinking red warning light. He pursued me before they broke up. I didn't act on it until after they'd called it quits, but the old saying was true: once a cheater, always a cheater. He had only her short brown pixie cut to play with now. Sucker.

I shook my head to dislodge the spiral I was taking. I did not need to think about him anymore. He will go down in history as the worst boyfriend, the most despicable reindeer, the embarrassment of Santa's fleet. He had to. The pain in my heart demanded it.

I slid out of my coat and trudged over to the counter, passing several people who were sitting by the huge fireplace chatting and sipping drinks. A man caught my eye on the way over. He was dressed in a black suit, though his red tie had been loosened around his collar. He seemed very out of place for that kind of establishment. His dark hair was slicked in carefully controlled way that made his cheekbones even sharper. A fleeting thought of what he would look like with bed head swirled in my mind, but I tucked that away in the darkest recesses where it belonged.

The way he was poised in the chair closest to the door said he was all about refinement and control. He wasn't relaxed, but he didn't look uncomfortable either. His back was straight, jaw tight his cold-as-ice eyes seemed to drink me in. The coolest shiver spread through me; goosebumps erupted over my spine.

I looked away, unable to hold his gaze for very long. Something about him was magnetic, but I didn't need any warning bells this time. He was the lethal kind of gorgeous that signaled trouble. It practically drizzled from him like melting icicles dripping on the snow.

I dropped my bag on the floor and picked up the—Santa help me—set of jingle bells lying on the counter, ringing them to call someone over to check me in. A woman's voice called from beyond a swinging door. "Ho, ho! I'll be just a minute. Make yoursElf at home!"

Leaning against the counter, I turned to face the fireplace. A man drinking a beer sat beside a young girl, probably around eleven or twelve. He stared at her numbly while her thumbs flew over the phone in her hand. She sighed and looked up. "OK Boomer, the Wi-Fi in this place sucks. You hauled my ass all the way here in the middle of a crisis and then cut me off from the world so I couldn't keep up with what was going on. SMH. Dad of the damn year."

The man frowned. "Language, Cherish." She huffed at him and went back to flicking her phone. "I told you this trip was to help us become closer. We can't do that if you don't try to. Love is a two-way street."

Cherish kept one hand on her phone and twirled her long black braids with the other, never even looking up. "I'll get that printed on a t-shirt." Then she raised her voice to punctuate her point. "If we ever get out of this hellhole!"

I couldn't help but laugh. She was my kind of kid, and I instantly felt a connection to her and her brazen sassiness. Her father's dark eyes fell as he took another long sip of beer. I could read the anguish on his face. It made me feel for him. He was clearly trying to connect with her. I knew from experience that sometimes trying wasn't enough.

"Ho ho, here I am! Let's get you all checked in and decked out, shall we?" I turned and found a woman striding through the swinging doors backward, carrying a tray of cookies. Her hair was a piled-up mess of salt and pepper curls tied with a huge red velvet bow and two literal candy canes hung from her ears. It looked like Christmas had exploded all over her.

At the North Pole, we liked to call them Festivers. They're the ones who start listening to Christmas music on Halloween and leave their tree up until Valentine's Day. They're so full of Christmas spirit, it erupts out of them like volcanoes all the time.

I shuddered. They were the worst, and I swore if she tried to put me in an ugly Christmas sweater with kittens on it, I would've bolted. Flown right back to the North Pole.

"Hello there. I'm Holly." Of course, she was. "I'm assuming you're Vixen. It's quite an honor to have such an esteemed member of Santa's fleet here with us this week! Please, have a cookie."

I took a cookie because it had Rudy's face on it. I bit into it with extreme force, chomping and chewing out my frustrations at the asshole reindeer. It would probably give me indigestion later, but I didn't care. It felt good to grind him between my teeth. "Thank you, but can we keep the reindeer shifter thing on the DL? I'm trying to be lowkey here if that's okay with you. Just a little chillaxing time to myself." I cringed at the words coming out of my mouth. Who still said chillax? That would be Santa.

She tapped her finger on the side of her nose. "Of course. Mum's the word." She rummaged around behind the counter and produced a key. "You're in cabin twelve. I'll just check you in under the name Vicki Klaus with a K." She winked, thinking she was being so stealthy, and handed me the key. "We have drinks here in the lobby at five each evening. Breakfast is from seven to nine, lunch from twelve to one, and dinner from six to eight. The Wi-Fi doesn't always work," she said in a hushed tone as she glanced at Cherish. "But the password is Jolly with a capital J, twelve, twenty-five. Anything else you need, just jingle the bells in your cabin, and one of my staff or I will come running. Santa gives us a little magic to use here and there."

I didn't plan to jingle the bells. I'd planned on a three-day drunk that ended with me flying back North to claim my spot on the team. I fiddled with the collar around my neck, a touchstone, and symbol that Santa hadn't given up on me completely.

Okay, big guy, I'll play your little game.

# CHAPTER 2

A fit of giggles erupted behind me. I turned to find three women crushed together on the couch with shot glasses in their hands and the look of being buzzed in their eyes. They had on what I liked to call the college-girl winter uniform: black leggings and boots with different-colored oversized sweaters on top. They looked at the same time, interchangeable and unique. They had the same messy buns in differing shades of hair, the same perfect makeup with long fake eyelashes of various lengths plastered on, and three different cloying scents of perfume wafting through the air.

The blonde one raised her glass. "To passing our last exams and graduating!"

The brunette clinked her glass with her friend's. "And to the start of our illustrious careers!"

The redhead completed the trio. "And to finding hot husbands to fund us so we don't have to work!" They drank their shots and slammed their glasses upside down on the coffee table, shrieking together at their brilliant idea.

I took another survey around the room. They were in for a real surprise if they wanted to find husband material in the resort. Unless some available men were hiding in their cabins, the dashing dark businessman perched near the door was the only viable option. And the way he was looking at them, with his lip curled in disgust, I didn't think any of them stood a chance with him. However, he did seem to fit the rich criteria given his name-brand shoes and expensive diamond snowflake cufflinks.

Holly appeared at my side, shoving a red drink I hadn't ordered in my hand. "My special holiday recipe. I call it Jingle Juice. I think you'll like it." I had no idea what it was, but I didn't care. I took a sniff, picking up notes of apple and cranberries with Prosecco and mint too.

I took a sip and the flavor burst along my tongue. Downed the whole thing in a matter of seconds. "Would be trouble to get another one?" She nodded and tittered back to the kitchen, delighted that I loved her concoction. She appeared at my side again with a fresh glass of Jingle Juice and I was well on my way to squeaking what small amount of enjoyment out of the vacation as I could. That juice packed a punch.

Holly placed a hand on my arm, the jingle bell rings on her fingers chiming. "Someone's preparing your cabin. I'm a little short-staffed at the moment, so it should be ready in about an hour if you want to hang out here and mingle until then."

Great. Mingling is *just* what I wanted to do. I painted on my fake smile. "Sure thing. Thanks."

I glanced around the room, searching for a single chair in a quiet spot, but there appeared to be precious few of those around. There was a cozy double-sized chair across from where Cherish and her dad were seated. A couple sat in it; their legs wrapped together in union as they sipped champagne. They tried to do that stupid thing where they entwined their arms together and sipped from their flutes, but they botched it, tangling in a mess of limbs and spilled champagne. Which they ignored as they shared a super-hot kiss that was pretty much all tongue.

Ugh. Honeymooners.

They finally untangled when they realized I was looking. The man extended his hand to me. "Hi, I'm Aaron with an Aa. This is my wife, Erin with an E, adorable right? We just got married."

I gulped my Jingle Juice. "You don't say."

The businessman by the door made a little half-smirk, but quickly righted himself into a respectable mature adult before anyone could catch on.

Aaron with an Aa nodded. "Yes! A little over twenty-four hours ago. We've only just come up for air."

He wiggled his eyebrows, and his wife smacked his arm playfully. "No one needs to know that, Aaron. Sheesh. I mean, it's implied, but you didn't have to say it out loud." I smiled, searching for an escape plan. I didn't want to hear lovey-dovey talk for the next hour or so, for sure.

I was seconds away from waiting outside in the snow when a deep, sensual voice drew my attention. "Here, take my seat."

I turned and found the businessman scooting his chair across the floor with a screechy scrape of wood against wood, offering me his chair. Was this a polite gesture or a calculated one? I wasn't sure. What I was sure of was that

I didn't want to wade any deeper into the honeymooners' personal lives, the bickering father and child, or the roaring drunks with failed Mrs. degrees, so I took the seat and pulled it away from the door, closer to the fire. "Thank you."

He leaned back against the wall, folding his arms and looking down at me with cool interest. His voice was like velvet in my ears, rich, decadent, sinful. "If you'll allow me, you are a stunning creature. A shifter of some kind, no?"

While it was commonplace to be asked the species question, especially in a place built for magical beings, it took me as a bit of a surprise. Maybe because I was trying to ignore what I was, take a mental vacation in the middle of this forced one. I took a sip of my drink and nodded, confirming his suspicion without answering the obvious *what are you* question.

I wondered what he was, in turn. He seemed to pick up on my unspoken thoughts. "I'm Jack. Frost King of the Winter Court, at your service." The way he drew the s out in the last word slid into my veins like chilling ice water.

He extended his hand. His palm was cool against mine, but not in the way that reminded me of death. His touch was fresh, alive, bursting with vibrancy. A zing rippled inside my heart like I'd been jolted with electricity. "Vicki."

He stared at the leather collar with the shimmering diamond V at my throat. I scrambled to cover it with my hot pink scarf, because of course, the King of the Winter Court was tight with Santa. I tried to deflect it so he wouldn't figure out my identity. "I have to say, you don't see many people vacationing in expensive suits."

Jack chuckled and it rumbled deep inside me, somewhere nearing the Southern region. "I'm here on business.

I have meetings with the Sun King of the Summer Court. He's a rival, so I insisted we come to the coldest place on Earth to conduct our business. It gives me the upper hand in negotiations."

I looked out the window at the freshly falling snow. There were mountains of it already, piled up and begging to be played in. I had no such desire in me. At all. "So, you're responsible for this snow, then?"

"No, this is natural. I could supplement it if I wanted, but I see no need for that now. I'm content to let it be as it is until I feel like it's needed. Do you enjoy the snow?"

My mind went straight to the first day I decided to let Rudy into my life. He'd dumped Clare and was hanging around outside my door, practically begging me to let him in. I went around to the back of my house gathered up a bunch of snowballs and took them upstairs to my second floor. The next time Rudy whinnied to get my attention it rained snowballs on his head.

Then I let him in, and things got physical very quickly. The rest, as they say, is history. Or it will be if I can manage to tame my mind into submission and stop thinking about what he did to me twenty-four, seven. "Not particularly."

"That's a shame. Maybe I can change your mind before you leave."

"I doubt it."

He raised his eyebrow in a challenge, then wrapped his hand around my glass, grazing my fingers and causing my pulse to kick up a notch. My Jingle Juice chilled in my hand, a crisp white frost covering the glass and turning the contents inside it into a frosty slush. He didn't let go until I started raising my glass to my lips, smirking as he watched me drink like it was the most entertaining thing he'd ever seen. Damn, it was good too. The little touch of frost was the kicker on an already delicious drink. "I guess it pays to know the Frost King, huh?"

He took my free hand and turned it over, pressing a light kiss against my knuckles, his cool breath skating over my flesh and crawling inside me like it was searching out my soul. "It does."

I took my hand away, anxious to put some distance between this mysterious Fae and myself, but still preferring his company over the others in the room. "Is your appearance another tool in your arsenal of dominance over your business competitor? I mean, you're wearing a tie during cocktail hour."

Before I could take another sip of my drink, Jack whipped his tie from his neck with a pop of fabric that had my pulse racing in a way it hadn't in ages. He slung it over my neck like he was claiming me and slid out of his jacket slinging it over the back of my chair before he stepped around and placed himself right in front of me. Being that close, the color of his eyes was dazzling. Steely gray. They lasered in on my own as he slowly, and I mean S.L.O.W.L.Y, unbuttoned the top three buttons of his shirt, revealing a sliver of olive skin at his throat that just begged for attention. "Does this make you feel more comfortable?"

Nope. Not really. It made me feel something though.

I chugged the rest of my Jingle Juice just to keep from staring at him and his alluring beauty.

A loud thump came from outside the door and everyone in the room jumped. Well, everyone but Cherish. She kept her eyes glued to her phone and the scowl on her face while the rest of us turned to the door to see who or what was there.

Jack flicked his fingers. It was subtle, but I caught it. A second later, a roaring gust of wind and snow slammed against the cabin and a deep male voice cursed outside. "Well, shit." The door flew open, bouncing back against the wall and then closing shut. A huge man stood there taking up the entire frame of the door. "I think it was frozen shut. Good thing I'm a Yeti, huh?" He winked at no one in particular and strode inside.

The three women on the couch all screeched at the same time and began shooting each other looks that silently indicated *I saw him first* to the others. I could see why they were acting that way. The Yeti man was...hot. No other word would work to describe him. He wasn't cute or handsome or gorgeous like Jack. He was hot in a way that made you clench your thighs together in response to his presence.

He looked like the lumberjack dudes on NickTock: buffalo plaid shirt with low-hung suspenders that cradled his perfectly formed and muscular ass. His brown hair was nearing his ears and lighter on top, like he'd been kissed by the sun, and he just radiated masculinity like he was made to model for nature magazines or camping stores with bulging biceps and square shoulders.

I'd known a few Yetis in my time and heard some rumors about things they were particularly skilled in, but looking at this guy, I could tell none of those rumors did him justice. He was walking sex in a plaid shirt. And when his eyes glazed over the three bimbos on the couch and found mine, I had to force down the yelp that was building in my throat. And the worst part was he knew it.

Behind me, Jack snickered.

I ignored him.

"Yeager! Oh, my jingle bells, Yeager, I forgot you were coming!" Holly squeaked as she appeared from the kitchen carrying yet another batch of cookies, these shaped like stars and bells. He scooped one up and put it in his mouth as she fussed around him, brushing off the snow that still clung to his shoulders and hair.

He smiled warmly and let her dote on him. "Am I that forgettable?" A trio of no's wrang out from the couch. Man, I hated to agree with the bimbos, but they were right. No one who ever saw this guy would forget him.

Yeager dropped his bag and picked up another cookie as Holly scrambled around the counter muttering "Oh dear" about a hundred times.

He shot her an endearing smile. "What's wrong?"

Holly sighed. "It's just that I boo-booed and gave your normal cabin away to Vix—" she stopped herself from revealing my secret identity. "Vicki over there. It was an emergency request from—" Again, she paused. At least I had to give her credit for trying to conceal my identity. "The highest authority this time of year."

So much for staying on the down-low.

Yeager peered over at me, a glimmer of amusement in his eyes. "Is that right?" Holly nodded. "That's okay. I can bunk with Karl for a couple of days."

Holly tutted. "Um, Jasper is visiting."

"Got it. I don't want to interrupt their alone time, do I? Crystal *probably* wouldn't mind sharing with me." The way the grin broke over his face and the emphasis on the word *probably* told me he had shared more than a cabin with this Crystal in the past.

"Sorry, Sugarplum, she has the flu. And with the repairs needed in cabin eight, the other employees are stuffed in one spot."

"What about you, Holl?" He batted his eyelashes.

She'd have been clutching pearls if she had any on. "Goodness, no. The scandal! I couldn't insult the memory of my dear departed Cornelius like that and invite a virile young man into my personal space."

Yeager seemed unfazed by his lack of accommodations. "I guess I'll just shift and camp out in my Yeti form, then." He shrugged and Holly looked like she was going to come unglued at the suggestion.

The three bimbos jumped up at once, practically running over to him. The blonde gripped his bicep. "You could stay with us. We can make room in cabin five. And if it helps, we're nymphs."

Ah. Mystery solved.

"Thank you for the kind offer, ladies, but cabin five is one of the smallest and you're already overbooked with three in it. I couldn't impose." He released himself from her grip and strode over to me with purpose, cocky swagger guiding his steps.

He stuck his hand out and I reluctantly shook it. His grip was firm and warm and the way he drew his fingers over my palm as he released my hand triggered an avalanche of feelings rushing through me. "Hello, *Vicki*. I'm Yeager and you're in my cabin, but I'd be willing to share."

# CHAPTER 3

I removed my hand. "Holly just said it was my cabin and I'm not willing to share, thanks. You should shift and stay outside tonight. Not a big deal for a Yeti, right?" It shouldn't be. We reindeer stayed shifted pretty much twenty-four-seven at this time of year. Of course, I was missing out on that little tradition thanks to the maddening situation Santa had shoved me into.

I turned to get around the Yeti, but he blocked my path with his massive frame. "I could, sure. But now that I think about it, there could be problems with that. I'm here to help Holly with some heavy lifting and wood chopping and a lot of physical things and if I sleep all night shifted, I'll lose some of my strength. Could be dangerous to me or others when I start slinging wood around."

Double entendre delivered and understood.

Huffing, I turned back the other way and found Jack leaning against the wall with his tight white dress shirt clinging to his lithe body, smirking. Watching me trying to squirm and get away from Yeager. The look in his eyes was curious. And ravenous.

Yeager stepped around me. "I won't be any trouble. I don't snore and I get up early. Plus, I'm so tidy it's nearly OCD. And I have sisters. I know to leave the toilet seat down."

"What a glowing resume," I replied with a droll tone. I was eager to get away from him, so I took a step toward the door, my cabin key clutched in my hand. Holly was suddenly there with another Jingle Juice. She shoved it in my hand, and I didn't even pause long enough to let Jack frost it up for me before I downed the whole thing.

There was not enough alcohol in the world to help me face the crazy my night had become. Smirking hot guy on the left and, forward hot guy on the right.

Yeager stepped behind me, pressing his hard body into my back as the warmth of him overtook me. "I have other talents besides leaving the seat down." He took a huge step back, giving me space and looking down at me to make sure I understood what he meant. Just as I was about to shout at him, he shrugged. "Or we could just sleep. Up to you."

Nothing in the damn world was up to me. Not my life, not my job, least of all, sharing a bed with a smoke show who was putting it all out there under the tree for me. Worse still, he'd already decided I was going to share my cabin with him.

I hadn't.

Jack launched away from the wall and prowled over, offering his two cents. "You know, it's the time of year for giving. What better way to imbue the Christmas spirit than to offer your room for the night? It's a cliché, for certain, but true all the same."

I tried not to react, but a growling snort rolled from my lips, my reindeer almost escaping without my consent.

First, don't try to tell me about spreading Christmas cheer. I knew how to do that. Well, I used to know. And secondly, it couldn't count as spreading cheer if I was forced to do it, now could it? "Then why don't you invite Yeager to stay with you then? You know, to show your Christmas spirit and help the poor guy out."

As soon as I suggested it the very thought of it amused me. Those two could not have been more opposite if they tried. One cool and calculating, the other hot and imposing. A twisted grin crawled across Jack's face. "I would, of course, but I travel with the crown jewels of Winter. No one outside my court is allowed in the same room with them. The rule isn't mine, but one handed down millennia to millennia."

I huffed. "So, put them away in a trunk or something. I'm sure Holly could loan you one."

Holly shoved another drink in my hand. I was up to, what, four? "Of course, I could, but the only trunk I have is full of my dear departed Cornelius' belongings. It would take hours, if not days to bring out the contents and store them somewhere else safe."

At this point, the Jingle Juice wasn't even burning as I chugged it. My throat was numb to its effects. My nose was also numb. And my fingers and toes too if I thought about it.

The whole thing was nonsense. I scanned the room again landing on every person I could see, trying to come up with reasons for them to house the handsome Yeti. Cherish and her father were obviously out. The newlyweds were going to be banging all night. I strode over to the dark corner beyond the fireplace where four people sat, their heads down as they played a card game. They were all wearing black and huddled in the corner like they were trying to hide from every source of light in the room.

"Excuse me. Would any of you happen to have a little room for the Yeti to stay tonight? He's tidy, gets up early, and doesn't snore. Or so he says anyway." I silently cursed myself as Yeager chuckled behind me, amused that I used his stupid list of reasons.

All four heads jerked up in an entirely unnatural way. Both in speed and angle. They hissed in my direction, and I jumped back as fangs descended along their canines. The tallest one of them spoke, his voice thin and whispery. "It wouldn't be advisable to have a warm-blooded person near us at night. We have our supply with us, but sometimes blood lust is hard to resist."

The blonde man across from him played a card that made the rest groan. I guess he won. "Our sleep schedule is off due to our need to train and nocturnal proclivities. If you don't mind, we have a big day tomorrow and we're relaxing."

Vampires. Just what we needed to add to this little merry band of inn guests.

I marched back to the center of the room, clenching my teeth so hard I was going to need the Elf dentist to replace some fillings as soon as I got back to the North Pole. Luckily, Holly was there in the clutch, serving me yet another Jingle Juice on the night that seemed to never end. When I'd taken care of it down the last drop, I grabbed the hot Yeti by the elbow, yanking him toward the door. "Come on then. Count this as your one and only Christmas miracle. One night. You keep to your side of the bed and say nothing. Do nothing. We will be sleeping and parting ways in the morning."

Yeager laughed like he didn't believe a word I'd said, but he followed me dutifully out the door to the sound of Jack telling us to have a good night.

# CHAPTER 4

By he time we got to cabin twelve, my buzz was operating at level eleven. I wasn't in the passing out stage, which was good, but I was quietly hovering near the bad decision stage.

I shouldn't have agreed to the cabin sharing.

Swinging the door open with a big sigh, I walked into the cabin, and like I did every time I entered a room, I hopped a step as soon as I got over the threshold. It was a stupid habit that I hated but it was so ingrained in me, I couldn't get rid of it. Especially when I was teetering on tipsy.

Yeager chuckled. "You hop like a cute little bunny."

I grunted.

He threw his bag down on the bed, then stretched, peering down at me through dark sinful lashes that likely had caused many hearts to flutter and pine. "I'm usually on the left side, but since you're being kind enough to share, I'll let you choose the position."

Definitely shouldn't have agreed to cabin sharing.

He licked his lips and I had to turn away from him. That man was sex personified. Yetified? I mumbled something about not caring which position and he replied with a low tone that set my blood on fire. "Good. I like to switch it up. Makes things interesting."

I took a deep breath to calmmyself. "I meant sleeping positions. We will not be engaging in any other kind of positioning," I spat. He shrugged and smirked like he didn't believe me. And damn my traitorous thumping heart if I didn't find that a smidge attractive.

That was me: always drawn to the confident swagger.

It's what attracted me to Rudy.

*Nope, brain. Not going there.*

Instead of traveling down that particularly painful rabbit hole, I took a moment to look around the cabin. As had been pointed out in the lobby, it was big with a king-sized bed complete with fluffy red and white plaid comforter, two small wooden chests for clothes, and a couple of cozy red chairs flanked the fireplace, draped in quilts. The fire was already roaring, casting a golden glow across the cabin.

Yeager used his sleeve to grab a metal pitcher that was sitting near the fireplace. The staff must have left it for me. He poured the steaming liquid into two cups and handed me one. I took a deep whiff. Spiced apple cider. Yum. One sip told me the spicy part was definitely rum and there was a lot of it in the drink.

I felt Yeager's eyes on me as I sipped my beverage, so I stepped toward the door between the two chests which I assumed was the bathroom. Up close I could read the red and green script on the sign hunt there.

'Tinkle All the Way.'

*Kill me now.*

Unamused, I flipped the sign around and found another equally festive 'Ho, Ho, Hold On. Occupied' on the reverse. Santa would've freaking loved it. Especially because it had a drawing of him with his legs crossed trying to hold his urine.

I removed the sign and tossed it in one of the drawers.

When I turned back around, Yeager was right up in my personal space, unhooking his suspenders. As they fell to the ground, I backed into the door trying to keep a respectable distance from his simmering hotness. But he stepped closer and took the tie Jack had hung around my neck earlier between his fingers. "This tie doesn't go with your sweater." He tugged on the tie, and it slowly slithered from around my neck. Goosebumps followed in its wake. It was like the Frost King was there touching me. Yeager frowned. "Or was the guy in the suit trying to mark you as his by literally putting a collar around your neck?"

I wrenched the tie from his grasp and threw it into the drawer with the sign. "What? No. He just..." I didn't know why he'd done it, so I shrugged.

Yeager spied my collar then and kept his eyes glued to my throat as he traced his finger over it, then down to the diamond V hanging from it. "V for Vixen? You belong to Santa then."

It wasn't too hard for him to figure out my identity given Holly's ridiculous attempts at stealth. I opened my mouth to deny it, but I suddenly stilled as his finger dipped lower, making a V in the hollow of my throat, then another one further down my chest, then another that skimmed the swell of my breasts. I sucked in a breath, eager for him to stop touching me and even more eager for him to keep going.

Damn me for wearing a V-neck sweater.

And damn, damn, damn that Jingle Juice.

"Santa doesn't own me. My collar is a symbol of loyalty. A badge of honor for my job. No different than a general's chest being decorated or a human pilot wearing wings on their lapel." A wave of anguish rolled through me. I really did love my job, and I loved that well-intentioned big guy for trying to help me, but there was a hollow cavity in my chest and Rudy had detonated the bomb that made it. No matter how loyal I was or how much respect I had for Santa, this little trip wouldn't fill the void inside me. Nothing would.

Yeager swallowed, his Adam's apple bobbing in the most tempting way. "Good. I don't want that collar, as sexy as it is, to stand in my way when I take you on that massive comfy bed over there."

Damn.

Hot. Cocky. Alpha—the holy trinity that would lead to my ruin.

"We aren't going to have sex." I tried to sound firm, but I knew my words were a little too slurry from the Jingle Juice and the hot toddy. There was too much falseness in them. Because, man, did what he suggested sound good.

Great.

Spectacular.

"Why not? We're adults. I think you're beautiful and you can't take your eyes off me either."

I set my empty cup on the chest and growled. "Because there's nowhere else to look. You're right on top of me."

He chuckled. "Not yet, but I will be soon."

I shoved him, moving him a few inches at most, then poked his solid chest as I spoke. "Look. I just got out of a long-term relationship with an asshole who cheated on me for months with his ex. My broken heart is bleeding all over my life, so I can't handle any more complications. Can't take any more painful reminders of what he did to me." My throat started to close at the mere mention of Rudy's betrayal. I hated myself for being so affected by him. Still. "Yeah, you're tasty, and under any other circumstances, I might be inclined to..." I trailed off before I could talk myself into it.

He tucked a strand of hair behind my ear, his large warm hand grazing my cheek. "Understood, Bunny." He leaned in close, his breath skating over my ear and I trembled at the sensation. "Tell you what. I had a long day, so I'm going to go take a shower now. You put on your PJs and think about this while I'm gone: What better fucking way to get over someone than to get under someone else?"

He grabbed his bag and slipped into the bathroom, leaving the door open just a crack.

I knew that move.

I'd *made* that move.

He was hoping I'd be so turned on at the thought of him showering all naked with his glorious, tanned skin on display, soap lathering over his body, and steam slipping over his skin. He wanted me to join him.

And for a few seconds, I sure thought about it.

# CHAPTER 5

As the steam rose around me all I could do was clench my fists to keep from hitting the shower tiles. I'd be the one Holly asked to fix them, so no point in making it hard on myself by obliterating them.

But damn, did I want to smash something to bits.

The look of pain in her eyes was enough to bring me to my damn knees.

Whomever this dickhead of a guy was that hurt her, he was a fucking fool. She was as perfect a woman as I'd ever seen. I wanted to run my hands through her deep auburn hair and press my hard body against the soft curve of her hips. I wanted to taste every inch of her creamy skin. I wanted to bury myself in her and never come back out. All of that within a matter of minutes of meeting her.

I took a deep breath and soaped up, trying to scrub away the awful itching feeling under my skin. She was already firmly inside me and the depth at which I wanted her was difficult for even me to understand. And it wasn't just physical either. Sure, I wanted to fuck her every way I could imagine and then more I'd make up along the way, but that wasn't all. I wanted to possess her, to hold her heart in mine and erase every hurt she'd ever experienced until she only ever smiled that beautiful smile for the rest of her days. The one she accidentally let slip out when she read the cheesy tinkle sign on the bathroom door.

I was in too fucking deep already.

I reached for my special Yeti shampoo because thinking about her and slathering my dick in soap was not going to end well. Because damned if I was going to jerk off thinking about her when she was feet away. Nope. If I were going to get off, she'd be right there with me while I did, and she was going to experience release like she'd never known before at the same time.

I let the hot water run over my body. It helped to ease some of the tension in my muscles. I wasn't lying to her when I said I'd had a long trip, though the journey to Holly's itself was nothing. It was the unending phone calls from my parents, my sister, and the elders of my flurry of Yetis, each taking turns berating me for running out and shirking my responsibilities.

I hadn't run out. I'd left to think about what they expected of me. Holly needed me and it was the perfect time to get some distance from the shitstorm brewing in my life. A shitstorm I was absolutely not going to let anywhere near Vixen.

I had time to figure it out. The mating ritual wasn't going to take place until the Spring equinox, so I had over three months to find a way to avoid spending the rest of my life with a nice, adequate, unspectacular woman whom I could never love, popping out special little Yeti babies forever and ever.

When the shower started to run cool, I got out and found my thoughts drifting back to Vixen. I dried my hair with a towel, and then wiped the condensation from the mirror. I took a second to look at myself. Who was I deep down in there under that muscular and tattooed body? Was I the kind of guy who took advantage of drunk women just to get a piece of them or was I the type of guy who respected boundaries, no matter how much he wanted someone?

Fuck, if I knew.

Maybe I was the kind of guy who was a little bit of both.

I had a way to have her. Or at least take the problem of her being too drunk to decide to sleep with me of her own volition off the table. It was forbidden. If my father found out, he'd disown me.

Shit, maybe that was a way to get out of the mating thing too.

I wasn't going to force myself on her. Even though it was obvious she needed an escape from her pain. I could deliver it to her. I was certain of it. I just had to forfeit the one secret my flurry had guarded for centuries to do it.

It took about five seconds for me to decide she was worth it.

Fuck, but I was in deep. Never, ever had I felt this way before. It was like every nerve ending in my body was on fire like I was alive in the best way possible.

I pulled my gray sweats on and left my shirt and underwear in the bag. It would make undressing easier. Just one little tug, then boom, boner. Then I paused at the door to run my hands through my hair before I entered. A skitter of unease coiled through me. Was I nervous?

I didn't get nervous around women. Around anyone.

Shaking it off, I strolled back into the main room of the cabin. Vixen was reclined in one of the chairs sipping more cider. She'd taken her reindeer collar off and wore black and gray plaid pajamas that almost swallowed her whole. They were at least two sizes big. Her hair was piled high in a clip and her eyes unfocused from all the alcohol. She looked damned adorable and utterly fuckable.

I strode over and took the cup from her hands. She groaned at the loss of her alcohol, and it went straight to my dick. "You've had enough for one night, don't you think?"

"That's the whole point: not to think." She glanced up through her lashes and her eyes went wide like she was seeing me for the first time. "Oh no. You don't get to do that."

"Do what? Take your drink?"

"No. You don't get to walk out here looking like that." She pointed at me, waving her hand from my head down my body and back up again, her eyes spinning with motion. Man, she was drunk. "With that hair and those tattoos on that..." she sucked a breath through her teeth, and it was the sexiest thing I'd ever heard. "...body. Damn you for having a body like that. And those deep green eyes looking at me like you want to devour me. You look sexy and I look and feel like a plaid trash heap. It's not fair."

She stuck her lower lip out and it took all I had in me not to take it between my teeth. "Well, Bunny, it's not my fault you failed to pack your sexy jammies."

I paused as she momentarily looked pissed, but her expression changed into longing when her gaze snagged on my low-slung sweats. "I could help you sex up your look if you want. Make some adjustments to lessen the garbage pile aesthetic." I decided that instant I wasn't going to cross the line. But I was damn sure going to strut right up to within a millimeter of it. "Stand up."

She did as I asked though her knees wobbled a bit before she got herself fully upright. I unbuttoned the bottom button on her pajama top. "The guy who cheated, what's his name?" She looked up and seemed to ask why with her big blue eyes, so I gave her the truthful answer. "I need to know who I'm going to kill. Or at least punch in the throat for hurting you."

Vixen snorted, amused with my declaration. Damn, that smile. "Rudy."

Of course, it was the most famous fucker of all who'd done this. I wasn't troubled by some imagined competition for her, I was bothered by the fact that he'd done this and remained the guy everyone loved. It wasn't right. He needed to be outed for what he'd done. No, he needed to be forgotten.

My fingers grazed her stomach as I unbuttoned more buttons on her top, she gasped with the contact, the alcohol loosening her lips. "These were his pajamas. I don't know why I do this to myself. It's like I can't tear him out of my heart no matter what I do."

My heart thumped in my chest. Like it was physically reacting to her sadness and pain. "I'll tell you what. Let's make them yours now." I grasped the hem of her top and ripped it, tearing the bottom half off and throwing it into the fire. It left her stomach exposed and, if I'm honest, a bit of underboob that made my cock spring to attention.

She gaped at the fabric burning in the fire and directed a real genuine smile at me for the first time. I fucking melted.

It didn't take much encouragement for me to continue. I took the collar and tore it from her top in one long tear. The top fell, exposing the soft flesh of her shoulders and I almost came apart from sheer desire. There was nothing but one button holding the top together across her breasts. It would take so little to pop it right off.

But I wasn't going to do that to her. She deserved better.

I kneeled in front of her to rip the fabric of her pants. I wanted to pull them down completely, but I managed to suppress the urge and turn them into shorts. Short shorts. Short enough to see the black lace panties she wore underneath. I'd never shown as much restraint in my life as when I ignored all of her beauty and turned her to face the fire as it consumed the fabric that once belonged to the man who'd broken her. "Watch it burn, Bunny. Think about what a dumb fucker he is and watch it burn."

# CHAPTER 6

My face glowed with the warmth of the fire as I watched a small piece of Rudy turn to ash. I was warm on the inside too, thanks to the alcohol and the man standing behind me who so easily delivered me a tiny victory over my demons.

I was overwhelmed with gratitude. I had a hunch that the newfound fire surging in my heart in that moment would fade, but in that moment, I reveled in the feeling of empowerment. Yeager had given me a small sliver of my heart back. One that Rudy had stolen from me.

I whirled around and launched myself into his arms, wrapping my legs around his waist. He grunted in surprise, then slid his hands under my ass to support me. Not that it was difficult. He was strong enough to rip flannel into shreds with no effort at all. His cock hardened at my core and while I knew it was a hasty decision I would regret in the morning; I kissed him.

He'd told me to think about sleeping with him and I had. After what he'd done for me, how could I not, right? He was so hot, and I needed something to help me burn the rest of Rudy from my mind.

"Hold it, "he murmured against my lips. Then shock wove through me when he suddenly set me back down in the chair. I looked up in confusion, my heart stuttering with his rejection. Though it made sense that he'd decided I wasn't worth the effort since I was standing there in what was left of my ex's pajamas. Still, it was a surprise. I fumbled with an apology for botching everything. "I'm sorry. I shouldn't have... let's just go to sleep now."

I tried to go to bed and bury myself under the covers, but he placed his hand on my chest and gently pressed me back into the chair. "No, you should've, but not like this. I'm not going to sleep with you when you're drunk. That would be a dick move. One like Rusty would make, I'd bet."

"You mean Rudy?"

"Whatever. He's nothing." He blew his breath out as he placed his large hands across my stomach, inching toward my sides, and curling his fingers over my hips. "I'm about to do something here and I'm trusting you to keep it to yourself. I can't let this get out. It would put my flurry in danger and cause all kinds of chaos. Understand?"

I didn't really, but my head was swimming and I wanted, no I needed him to keep his hands on me in some way, so I nodded. He moved his hands across my stomach as he spoke. "Every generation certain Yetis are born with extraordinary gifts. These chosen ones are responsible for the survival of the species. Not even the elders know why this happens, but that's not important. What is important is I'm one of them—the only male this generation—and I can use my gifts to heal, to draw off unwanted or unhealthy impurities in the bodies of not only Yetis but other super-natural creatures too."

"Like demonic possession?"

"Yes, and more. I cured my grandmother's emphysema, helped loads of Yetis get over their colds. I even rid the neighboring flurry of a banshee possession, which was more fun than it sounds like. It's complicated and a coveted power among my people. I'm not supposed to let anyone outside the flurry know that I'm gifted like this. It could be disastrous if other species found out. I'd be hunted. Used. Who knows what else?"

The thought of that made me uneasy. "You're using this gift on me? Why?"

My skin began to heat under his hands and that seemed to travel to other places on my body. "To dispel the alcohol. Because, Bunny, in case you haven't figured it out yet, I want you. I am fucking mad with the need to be inside you, but you're drunk and hurting and I'm not going to take advantage of you. I want you to decide you want me with a clear head. And I want you to remember every salacious thing I do to you in the morning."

The swirling tattoos on his shoulders, biceps, and back seemed to come alive, shifting and morphing, curling tendrils of black rippling along his arms. I was drawn in by their beauty, captured by the heady feeling of the alcohol that had been clouding my brain dissipated. I gasped as the tattoos turned into black smoke skating across his bronzed skin then wafting away in a cloud. I looked into his shimmering green eyes and bit my lip, desire swelling in me in the fiercest way.

He removed his hands, and the tattoos went back to normal. I was suddenly very sober. And very turned on. "Now that your head's back on straight, what do you say, Bunny? Want to get naughty with me?" I didn't answer him. Instead, I launched myself at him like a rocket, pressing him down on the bed and straddling him. He laughed in surprise. "I'll take that as a yes."

I nodded and he groaned as he lifted his hips, letting me feel the hard line of his cock against my core. A rush of memories surged through me and caught me off guard. I froze. Utterly froze. I went from one hundred degrees to negative twenty between two heartbeats. Panic clawed its way up my throat.

"What's wrong?" he asked. "Did you change your mind?"

"No. It's just…" I paused. Why did I think this was a good idea? I should've made me keep the alcohol inside me. It would be easier than facing this. "Could we just change positions?"

I made a move to lift my leg, but he flipped us over before I could, positioning himself over me. The feeling of him on top of me as he settled down helped ease some of the raw emotion inside me. I tried to kiss him, but he leaned away. "What just happened? You're not feeling pressured, are you?"

Shit.

"No. It's embarrassing, and I'd rather not talk about it. Can you just…kiss me?"

He shifted his weight to his elbows, focusing on my eyes and ignoring my request. "This is about Randolph."

"No." I paused, unsure of how to tell him. But he was nice and respectful of my boundaries. He deserved the truth. "A little bit, yes."

"Out with it."

"I'm fine now. Can we just get back to it?"

"I don't think we can, Bunny. I'm not letting that fucker in this bed with us, so tell me and we can move on."

I didn't want to talk about it, but he was right. Rudy was a ghost hanging over my entire existence. I needed to exorcise him. "He just always wanted me on top. I think he liked my tits or something. I don't know. He ruined that position for me, that's all." My cheeks flushed with heat. How would a man like Yeager understand my dumb insecurities? I was the one who'd jumped on top of him anyway. I did it to myself.

"Say no more. I told you. I like to switch it up. This will work for now." He pressed down, rolling his hips and leaning in and whispering in my ear in his sinfully deep voice. "Do you feel how hard I am for you?" I nodded, breathless, as I gripped his shoulders and raised my hips to meet him. "I bet Richard never made you feel like this, did he?"

"No." If he had, I certainly didn't remember it, at least at that moment.

My heart hammered in my chest as he finally kissed me, his full mouth moving against mine in the most languid way. He devoured me, sliding his tongue over mine and claiming more than just my mouth, he was claiming a little piece of my soul. He kissed me like it was an all-consuming need and I writhed under him, relishing the feel of his lips against mine.

They felt new. Different. Worth exploring.

He spoke as he nibbled and licked his way along my jaw and back against my mouth with hot breath that mingled with my own. "Here's another thing you should know about Yetis. It isn't a secret like the other, but something I think you'll appreciate."

He pulled back and the smirk on his face made me clench in anticipation as he popped the remaining button on my pajamas. I gasped when he dragged his tongue between my breasts in a long stroke. Oh, my soul, his tongue was long. I mean, not grotesque, but longer than any I'd seen. And I swear it had tiny bumps on the surface of it. He licked across both of my nipples, and a chill scattered through me as they pebbled in response. The sensation was incredible. Not rough like a cat's tongue but textured enough to make everything he did with it feel extra pleasurable.

None of those rumors did this justice.

"The scientific term is retractable corpuscles, but you probably don't care about that right now." He ran his devilish tongue over my neck and behind my ear, drawing elicit moans from my lips. "No, you want me to stop explaining and move my tongue down to your pussy, don't you, Bunny?"

My hips bucked in response to his words. "Yes."

He chuckled, then made good on it. I squirmed under him as he slowly licked my breasts, tasting my skin and trailing along my stomach until he reached the waistband of my pants. I was a panting, needy bundle of fire begging for him to drench me with his tongue. He looked up at me, smirking as he yanked down the fabric that stood between us. I buckled and shifted forward, unable to tamp down my desire and the promise he'd laid out in front of me.

I bit my lip. Damn, he needed to hurry up and get on with it or I was going to explode. "Spread your legs. I'll make you forget Ronald ever existed." I eased mt legs apart, and he wasted no more time, leaning in and licking my center with his long tongue. I cried out and took his head in my hands, bucking my hips as he devoured me. He spoke between strokes of his tongue. "You taste divine. Cranberries and apple cider and rum."

I had to laugh. It was pretty much everything in my system from the past few hours. "You're just saying what you knew I drank."

He raised his head, pure lust in his emerald eyes. "Another scientific Yeti thing. We have extreme sensitivity to taste. And your pussy is the best thing I've ever eaten." He went back to licking my clit and I almost lost my mind at his relentless pace as he licked and sucked me, desire and passion igniting between us like nothing I had ever experienced in my life. He was Skilled with a capital S, and I would never get the textured feel of his tongue out of my mind.

"Yeager. Please."

"Please what? Fuck you with my tongue? Okay." The manly lust erupting from him as shoved his tongue inside me made me scream in ecstasy. It was more than I was ready for, and I threw my head back, gripping the covers as I came for him.

He kept his head buried between my legs, sucking my clit as I rode out the orgasm. When I finally collapsed underneath him, he pressed soft whispering kisses back across my body and breasts, my throat, and my jaw, and then he kissed my mouth with lustful abandon. I tasted myself on his lips and it lit a new fire inside me. Within moments of having the best orgasm in my life, I was ready for more. Yeager purred into my ear. "I'm certain Rasputin never made you come like that."

# CHAPTER 7

This woman would be the end of me. I didn't normally get attached so quickly, but one taste of her, and I knew one night was never going to be enough.

She shuddered underneath me, coming down from her orgasm. I tore my sweats off and went right back into position above her, rolling my hips and pressing my cock against her soaking soft depths. The feminine sigh that came out of her mouth at the contact made me feel like I was going to lose my cool and come all over her before I got inside her.

Vixen was an accurate moniker. To the fucking tenth degree.

"You want more, Bunny?" I took my cock in my hand, rubbing it over her pussy, groaning at the velvety feel of her. She lifted her hips, finally opening her eyes and locking onto mine. Her pupils were blown out, invading the flecks of gray in her baby blues. She was still in that blissful post-orgasm state, and I was about to make her come all over again. She nodded, finally realizing I'd asked the question. "If it helps, it would be impossible for me to have any STIs because of my gift. I've got some condoms in my bag though if that makes you more comfortable."

I was hovering above her. My hard chest pressing against her soft one. Her diamond-sharp nipples made me ache for more. But I wasn't going to go further until she gave me the okay. Did I want to put on a glove? No fucking way. Would I? For her, yes.

She ran her hand down my chest, over my stomach. My muscles clenched. "No, it's fine." That was the green light if I ever heard it. I pushed inside her. Just the tip. She hissed in pleasure.

Here's the thing: was I bigger than most dudes? Yep. Not unnaturally so, just big enough to know better than to ram into a woman with no warning. Taking it slow was about to kill me fucking dead, but I needed to do this right. So, I inched in, pressing her legs further apart with my knees. "There you go, Bunny. Let me in."

She groaned. "Why are you going so damn slow? Please get to it." The pleading tone of her words was music to my ears.

Okay then.

I thrust inside her, burying my cock as deep as it could go. She bucked off the bed, arching her back and huffing, "Yes."

This woman. She was wet, warm and responsive. All the best things in the world.

I pulled all the way out and slammed in again. She laughed and thrust her hips, meeting me with as much enthusiasm as I was feeling. Leaning down as I set a slow steady pace, I licked my way across her breasts, pulling a taut nipple in to suck on it as she bucked beneath me. She gripped my hair in her hands, pulling me from one nipple to the other. I was an equal opportunity licker, so I went willingly. "Fuck me," I breathed into her chest.

"I am," she mumbled back.

Funny. That was the icing on an already perfect cake.

I picked up my pace, pushing inside and rolling my hips up to hit the right spot that always made women see stars. Her response was immediate. Her eyes glazed and she gripped my shoulders as I hit it over and over and over again. "You like that, don't you, Bunny?" Her response was a whimper as her nails sliced into my shoulders.

Bleeding had never felt so fucking good.

Her pussy was squeezing my hard cock like it was designed to cradle it. The more I gave her, the harder she moaned and the harder she moaned, the harder I gave it to her.

Yeah. This was definitely not going to be a one-time event. It wasn't even going to be a once tonight event. How in the shit had that dickweed cheated on her? What was so fundamentally wrong with him that he'd willingly walk away from this? He had to be the dumbest asshole in the North Pole.

North America.

Earth.

Was she fucking him out of her system? Probably. I gave zero fucks about being her rebound or whatever this was. I was consumed by the way she spoke and moved, and the way her eyes lit up as she narrowed in on me, her breath hitching.

She was almost there. I reached down between us and circled my fingers along her swollen clit. The sensation of her soft skin against mine coupled with the sight of my hand wedged between us brought everything into sharp focus. She wrapped her hands around my neck, pulling me down, kissing me with her juicy lips. I licked along the seam of her mouth, and she opened willingly for me, groaning in the tangle of our tongues. She threw her head back against the pillow, giving me access to her slender throat, so I trailed my tongue along her collarbone, making my way up to her ear. "Let me hear you come. I want to watch you fall fucking apart for me."

Her core squeezed, release coming at my command. Making a sound I'd never heard come out of my own throat before, I groaned. It was long and low and deep as I followed her into that oblivious space that magically appeared when people came together.

Yeah, I could be a romantic poet as well as a lumberjack.

She was still beneath me, closing her eyes and nearly panting instead of breathing. I left my cock inside her, giving myself an unfettered seconds to memorize the look of bliss on her face. Because once I left this place and went back to the life I had in store for me—*if* I went back to the life I had in store for me—I would live in the memory of this moment for a long damn time.

She ran into the bathroom as soon as I pulled out of her. I didn't think she was ashamed of it or regretted it, but I assumed it was the first time she'd been with anyone since Rupert, and it was a lot for her to process. I let her have her space, cleaning myself up and slogging on my sweats as the tap ran in the bathroom.

When she came back out, she'd brushed her teeth, put her hair in a messy bun, and changed into some more plaid pajamas. Message received. No seconds of her supremely tasty cake. At least the pajamas were her size. Progress? Maybe.

I slid into the bed on the left side, throwing the covers back and patting the space next to me. There was a millisecond of hesitation before she gave in and joined me. Determined to get as much of her as I could, I pulled her close, wrapping her in my arms. She turned over and put her back to me.

Spooning, it was.

Undeterred, I put both my arm and leg around her. "Is this okay?"

Fuck, if she said no, I didn't know what I was going to do. Definitely didn't want to let her go. That hadn't happened since...it had never happened.

She didn't answer for a long time. So long that I thought maybe she'd drifted off to sleep. Finally, she put me out of my misery. "Yeah."

A hundred and one different things went through my mind as I breathed in the flowery smell of her shampoo and the warm spicy scent of her skin. That's what she was: sweet and spicy at the same time. I couldn't stop running scenarios where this, us, happened again. Even if she was over him—she wasn't—the odds of a woman like her wanting me long-term were slim. But I'd be damned if that's where my head went.

My father would've called me a pussy.

Maybe it was the utter terror of the life that had been lined out for me from the minute I came into this world. Or maybe it had been too long since any woman had piqued my interest. Yetis were pack creatures. We often took several lovers at a time, within our flurry and outside it. I'd slept through my share of them, sometimes at the same time, but I never found one of them appealing on the level that I had Vixen. And I'd known her four fucking hours, at most.

I didn't know what that said about me. Probably said more about her.

Didn't matter. I was determined to make sure her broken heart was put back together piece by piece so I could have another taste of it.

# CHAPTER 8

Yeager, thankfully, was up and out the door before I woke. I'd been so out of it, I hadn't even heard him, though remnants of his clothes were strewn all over the floor. He'd started a fire for me, which put him on the nice list.

As did the double O the night before.

Still, unease fluttered through my heart. I couldn't believe I'd been so needy. Because that's what it was. Utter need to erase the void in my heart. Yeager wasn't just outrageously attractive with cut muscles, an astounding tongue, and a dirty gravel of a voice. He was tangible contact. I'd had none since Rudy gave me the worst Valentine's gift ever—his dick in Clare.

*Fucking Clare.*

Yeah, it had been ten months. Should've been over it.

Whatever happened between Yeager and me couldn't happen again, though. It was reckless. Hooking up with the first hot guy who'd asked? Amateurish. Immature. Emotionally damning. I wasn't ready, even for something casual.

Still though. The sex had been mind-blowing.

*Not happening again.*

If I said it to myself enough, maybe I would manifest it into being. Santa always says that if you can dream it, you can do it. Yes, that was his phrase. Ugh.

Needing to load some serious calories after last night's Yeti-mounting, I threw on a pastel plaid shirt over my white thermal, then added jeans, thick socks, and boots. The finishing touch was my pink beanie, scarf coat combo. Once I was adequately prepared as a human—cold didn't trouble me in reindeer form— I headed out to the lodge, not bothering to make the bed first.

I was bombarded, in the face, with a frigid blast of Winter wind as I stepped outside. The clouds above were dark and heavy, signaling an impending snow. Though Santa magic kept the climate around the cabins comfortable, it didn't mean snow-free. Maybe I could hole up in the cabin with the smutty book I found recommended on NickTock, the North Pole's number one app. As long as I had some more of that cider, it would be an ideal way to wait out the weekend.

Had to get food first.

Wrapping my scarf over my face, I broke for the lodge. It wasn't that far away, but the snow was already deep, well over the top of my ankle boots. I took two steps and sunk into the drift, yelping in surprise. Behind me, a low masculine voice uttered, "Allow me."

I was pulled up by my shoulders, then set right, wobbling more than I would've liked. I should've just shifted, but it would've been embarrassing to show up for pancakes naked. I didn't want syrup in my— "Here. I can assist." I was about to tell the guy he couldn't do anything about the fifty yards of snow, at least a foot deep between me and the coffee, but I swung around just in time for him to raise his hand in front of him and flick his wrist. The snow in front of me melted, creating a path of hard frozen dirt straight to the lodge.

Jack, the Frost King.

He was dressed in a navy suit with a white shirt and powder blue tie. Dress shoes. No coat whatsoever. My eyes widened and he shot me a sheepish, sexy grin that held zero apology. "Frost King. The cold doesn't affect me," he offered in explanation. He held out his elbow and I took it, and we walked in comfortable silence to the lodge. I mean, what did I have to say to a Fae King? He was powerful, impressive, a little bit scary. But I guess my silence didn't bother him, since he said nothing to me either.

When we entered the lodge, he took my coat and hung it on the hook by the fireplace. Now that we were inside facing each other, I got uncomfortable with the lack of words. So, like I did sometimes, I filled the silence with verbal graffiti. Meaning, loud and inappropriately bright. "So, the King of the Frost Court. I guess you're used to it, but it's cold enough out there to shrink your balls, isn't it?"

My cheeks reddened. Why in the world did I ask him that? He was so intimidating. "I mean, can you not do something about the weather? Make it warmer maybe?"

He grinned and I hoped it meant I hadn't offended him. His smile though, was alarming in a way that made me hear bells in my head. So disarming. "Making it warmer would be my counterpart, John's purview." He dipped his head to the man sitting on the couch with his feet propped on the table. He was wearing a Hawaiian shirt and board shorts. At. The. South. Pole.

John, the Sun King of the Summer Court. Even though I was a Winter kind of gal due to my species and job, I'd heard stories about the Sun King. He had a reputation for shady business and even shadier pursuits. It didn't mesh with the vibe he was giving off. John tipped his head toward Jack, locking his lazy gaze on his rival. Jack met him with a steely look of his own before he refocused on me.

When he raked his eyes over my body, all the way down, then back up again, chills popped up in the wake of his perusal.

I took a step, edging toward the fireplace, putting some distance between us so that his unnerving gaze wouldn't feel so cold. It didn't bother him. "Coffee?"

"Yes, please. Fill half the cup with any kind of creamer they have."

Jack arched an eyebrow at my request but disappeared into the kitchen door to retrieve my warm beverage without comment. I sunk into the cozy chair the newlyweds had occupied last night. They weren't up yet. Probably sleeping off their night of carnal activities.

As if he picked up my thoughts about my own carnal mistakes the prior night, Yeager stepped in through the side door, his arms filled with freshly cut logs. He stomped his boots to remove the snow, then sauntered over to the fire-place to unload the wood. I couldn't help but gawk at him, feeling a sliver of disappointment that I didn't get to watch him split the logs.

He walked like he knew every eye in the room was on him. I couldn't tell if the only other ones in the place—

Cherish and her dad—were looking because I couldn't tear my own eyes away from him to check.

Even though he was layered up for the weather, I could still appreciate his bulging biceps as he worked, setting the logs in a pyramid stack. Remembering how they felt wrapped around me, sent a flicker of heat straight to my center. Damn, he was fine, and he had the moves to back up that swagger.

Someone beside me cleared their throat to get my attention. "Your coffee, Flame."

"Huh?"

"I don't believe your name is Vicki and your hair reminds me of fire."

I lifted my hand to receive said coffee, still unable to tear my eyes off Yeager, due to the fact he was leaning over stoking the fire, his hot ass occupying some very tight jeans. He turned his head and smirked and I knew I'd been caught ogling his backside. "Can't get enough of my wood, huh?"

Holy Fruitcake.

Snapping myself out of it, I swung away and took my coffee from Jack, knowing the blush on my cheeks was likely as red as my hair. The corner of his mouth kicked up. Just a little. It wasn't even a grin. It was like half a grin. One-quarter of a grin really. His eyes flicked to Yeager, then back to me. "You two have fun last night?"

Yeager stood upright, brushing his hands together to clean them off. "Look at her, man. What do you think?"

I did a spit take. "No, we didn't..." Except that we did. We definitely did.

And to make matters worse, my sputtering landed all over Jack's pretty navy jacket. "Oh, my soul. I'm so sorry.

Let me help you." I handed my cup over to Yeager, who took a sip for himself and frowned. Then I proceeded to paw at Jack's lapel with my hands. It didn't help at all, so I pulled my sleeve down and used it to wipe at the coffee spill.

I wasn't normally this big of a klutz, nor did I feel shame over sleeping with a guy. But I wasn't myself. Not since February. Maybe Santa had been right to send me on this little vacation. If I spazzed like this on the Christmas Eve run, the results would be disastrous. We're talking about kids waking up and getting a glimpse of Santa, elves falling out of the sleigh, toys everywhere. Total shitshow.

Jack wrapped his hand around my wrist, halting my furious wiping. "Let me." He pulled a crisp white handkerchief from his pocket and sopped up what was left of my blunder. The jacket was dark, so it didn't show too badly, but still. I tried to formulate more words of apology, but he reached out with his hankie, attempting to dab my mouth. "You have a little white chocolate creamer on your lips."

Yeager's massive hand zipped between us, snagging Jack's arm to keep him from wiping my face. Jack's gaze snapped to Yeager, leveling him with a look. There may have been a soft snarl escaping his throat too. Yeager didn't even flinch. He simply stepped behind Jack and fixed his eyes on me. After he stared at me with a sinfully heated look that I felt in the depth of my being, he released Jack's arm, leaning in and fake whispering in his ear. "I just wanted to see what she looked like with white cream dripping from her luscious lips." He shot me a wink and mouthed 'later' and then strolled over to the kitchen—with *my* coffee—like he hadn't just offered up a graphic innuendo before seven a.m.

All I could do was blink.

Jack didn't even acknowledge Yeager. "You didn't what, exactly?"

I slumped into the chair, making sure to wipe my lips before I looked up. "Hm?"

There was that quarter-grin again. "Never mind."

"Thanks for the coffee, by the way. I'm sorry I spit it on your jacket. I have no excuse for that."

"No worries." He pulled the same wooden chair he sat in the night before over. Instead of sitting in it properly, he spun it on one leg, then straddled it. I gulped. It was the juxtaposition—manspread and expensive suit—that got me. Where Yeager was hot, Jack was completely cool. Everything he did, said, probably even thought, was calculated. He was sitting in that chair in that way for a reason. "Are you going to share your name or keep me guessing? Not a Vicki and you don't look like a Matilda."

If he only knew.

"I thought you heard last night. I'm Vixen. Yes, *that* Vixen. No sense keeping it under wraps now."

A shrieking squeal made both of us jump. "Uhmahsoul! I can't believe that skank! She didn't. She. Did. Not. Dad, I'm dead, D.E.D. You can bury me under the big tree out there. Tell Mom I loved her." Cherish was gaping at her phone and freaking out.

Her father let out an exasperated sigh, his exhaustion, and patience plainly at their limits. "You're being a little dramatic, Honey. What happened?"

"What happened? Well, Sophie G. told Sophie R. that I wanted to go out with Aiden. I told her that *in confidence.*"

"Well, at least she didn't tell Aiden, right? By the way, you're too young to go out with anyone."

Cherish rolled her eyes like a professional eye-roller. "Da-ad. You don't get it. Sophie R. likes Aiden too, so she went and told Max to tell Jackson to tell Aiden that I liked Caden instead. Aiden and Caden are best friends! And now Aiden is trying to set me up with Caden because he thinks I like him, and Lilly is over here slinging words on me because Aiden dumped her last week, and she likes Caden now. And all this is happening while my ass is sitting in Tim-buck-freezing-too!"

"Language, Cherish." She ignored her Dad's warning, typing furiously on her phone, fingers flying faster than I could track.

A deep voice wafted from behind me. Yeager had re-appeared, and he was leaning in close enough that I smelled his soap or cologne or whatever made him smell fucking edible. Nope. Can't do that. "Riveting," he purred into my ear, then he shouted over to Cherish. "Why not go out with Aiden and Caden both? Show them all not to mess with you."

Both Cherish and her father whipped their heads in our direction. Cherish looked like a light bulb was literally hanging over her head. Her father swiped her phone from her hands, looking up to Yeager. "Can we not encourage her, please?"

I turned around and smacked Yeager in the head, giving him the stink eye. He chuckled at my meager attempt to knock sense into him. "Sorry. I'm incorrigible." He stuck out his hand. "I'm Yeager. This is Vixen." He'd said it like we were a couple.

We were not a couple.

"Isaac. Cherish. Age eleven." Cherish waved a hand in our vague direction but was more focused on the phone she'd wrestled back than her father's explanation introduction. "Divorced. Mother remarried. He's the one who bought her a phone more expensive than my car." He sighed again, muttering 'Fucking Bruce' under his breath.

Never had felt something more deeply.

The door banged open. The newlyweds and Mrs-ers rushed inside, shaking off the snow and chattering their teeth. Aaron and Erin shared a sweet kiss and the others spied John on the couch and made a beeline, chattering and primping on the way there. Was it redundant to say the Sun King was hot? Probably. But he was.

Not as hot as the Frost King though.

Before I could ask for the breakfast I could smell wafting through the air, Holly burst from the kitchen carrying a pitcher of orange juice. "Oh good. The gang's all here. Well, except for the vampires. We'll see them later, I s'pose. Anyway, breakfast is up. Join me in the dining room."

We filed into the side room which held a large table with rustic picnic benches. I ran my finger over the dark wood, admiring its charm. It seemed old, and weirdly, loved.

"I knew you liked my wood." Yeager stepped over the bench, angling his fly at my face for a second as he stepped over the bench, then sat like a civilized person.

"You made this? The table too?" He nodded, shooting a glance across the table where Jack was taking his seat directly across from me. "It's beautiful."

He ran his hand down my spine. I hated myself for it, but I shivered when he tugged on the length of my hair, just a bit, but it hit right in that spot between pain and pleasure. I liked it. "You're beautiful."

*Not as beautiful as your hard cock was last night.*

I reached for my glass of OJ, ready to drown the words before they leapt out of my mouth. I yelped. Jack had taken my glass in his hands and chilled it so that ice crystals formed on the rim. He smirked as I took a sip and groaned at how perfect the temperature was.

"Show off. He does that all the time and it's annoying." John Sun reached across the table and snagged the massive plate of waffles. For a second, I thought he was going to eat them all, but he politely doled out some to the Mrs.ers before serving himself and eye-fucking each of them as he slid the syrupy fork into his mouth.

Jack sneered in his direction. "Not as annoying as I will be at ten o'clock. I hope you brought you're A-game because I will wipe the floor with you if you didn't." He snapped his steely gray eyes back to Yeager. "Vixen's right. Your crafts-manship is astounding. I should hire you to make furniture for my palace. My dining table seats forty. Do you think you could handle making something that size?" The 'astound-ing' remark was a backhanded compliment. The size of his table was simultaneous dick-waving and shoving his wealth and status in Yeager's face. To his credit, the Yeti didn't take the bait.

But I'd be damned if Jack's biting marks and murderous glare at John didn't get me a little hot.

# CHAPTER 9

I couldn't care less if I'd insulted the lumberjack. My words were for John, the Sun King. My palace was bigger, I had a larger staff to manage and thousands more subjects to appease than that buffoon. I could barely keep track of the days inside my kingdom due to the relentless schedule I kept. This was not a humble brag, but a fact, plain and simple. John needed to get it through his sun-drenched skull. I was a force, and he would reckon with me whether he liked it or not.

What interested me most in the moments that followed my comment was Vixen's reaction. I couldn't help but notice the way her cheeks flushed as she glanced in my direction, the way her nostrils flared, and her pupils dilated. She was aroused by my tone. What I wouldn't give to use my voice and tell her exactly where I wanted her—on her knees with her mouth wide open for me.

I knew she'd slept with Yeager. Even before he'd crudely confirmed it. I couldn't care less about that either. I was a King. I didn't do attachments and relationships. See the aforementioned schedule. What I *did* do was take the occasional lover to file down the sharp edges of my mind.

Vixen was the kind of woman who would make me forget who I was. I craved that feeling more than I craved the feel of her lips on my manhood.

Of course, I couldn't truly pursue her. Not even for a tryst. I was here to do one thing and if I didn't focus on it, my kingdom would be at stake. So, no, as tempting as she was, Vixen was out of reach.

That didn't mean I couldn't watch from afar, however.

She sucked in a breath as she lifted the fork to her lips, reveling in the syrupy aroma. When she inserted the fork into her mouth and groaned, a single zip went straight to my cock. When she swallowed, I had to subtly shift my position on the bench to hide my growing erection.

She was a flaming vision.

A clanking sound disrupted my revelry. Yeager's fork had hit his plate. When I looked over, he was practically glaring a hole into my skull. He'd done it on purpose. To draw my attention away from Vixen. "Oops. Sorry. Slippery fingers." He whispered something in Vixen's ear and her sweet blush spread from her cheeks down her neck. While I loathed how he interrupted me, I couldn't begrudge him for giving her that rosy glow.

Truly. A vision.

For the rest of our breakfast, I was engaged in a mundane conversation with Aaron and Erin, learning that they'd met on Christmas day in a tiny town in Maine called Arundel. Yes, Aaron and Erin are from Arundel. The unequivocal coincidence of it all!

By the time Holly shooed us away to clear the plates, my head was pounding with a dull throb. Thankfully, everyone cleared out of the lodge shortly after. John went to prepare for our meeting. Yeager went to fix something broken in the triad of nymphs' cabin—I'd wondered if they made the whole thing up just to get him alone—the father and daughter set out to ride snowmobiles and the newlyweds went off, I presume, to make baby Aeryn with an Aer.

This left me alone with Vixen.

Maybe luck was on my side. I'd need it for the meeting.

I approached Vixen. She'd pulled up the chair I'd come to think of as mine to look out the window at the gently falling snow. I didn't mind. I could share with her. I flicked my wrist, forcing the snow to swirl in front of the window, forming into a dove for a moment, then dissipating on the wind.

Her gasp was everything.

Her smile when she turned to me was even more than that. "Are you flexing on me right now?"

"Simply giving you an occasion to smile."

I pulled another chair over beside her, straddling it because I'd noticed how it drew her eyes downward before. This chair didn't have the same feel as *mine*, but I'd suffer through it to be closer to her.

She turned back to the view and curiosity overwhelmed me. It's true she was a beauty, but the longing in her eyes told me volumes about her. She was lonely. I was deeply acquainted with that condition. "What brings you here so close to Christmas? I assumed you'd be prepping for the big night."

"Normally yes, but Santa had other plans. Seems I needed an attitude adjustment, so he sent me here to 'chillax' and get my mind straight."

I tipped my chair on the front legs, angling toward her. "What made your mind crooked?"

She bristled at my closeness. Not because she didn't like it, but because she *did*. "A guy. My ex. Rudy. Yes, I know, cliché to date someone so famous and have my heart broken when he went on to someone else. Trust me, I've punished myself for being so stupid. It won't happen again." She sighed and her breath fogged the window.

I assumed the voice I usually reserved for my business meetings or subjects who've wronged others. The one she liked earlier. "Do you presume to think for me, Flame?"

"Huh? What do you mean?" she gasped. Surprised by my forcefulness.

"You told me what happened with Rudy, then promptly decided I would judge and condemn you for it. I don't. Maybe you shouldn't do that to yourself either." Blowing on my fingertips, I sent my magic out, using ice crystals to etch a picture of Rudy, and then I drew a circle with a line through it. The prohibition symbol or the cancellation symbol is probably more accurate in modern terms. Hard for me to keep up, being so ancient. "I *do* judge *him*, though."

She laughed. It sounded like the Winter wind whipping through the ice-laden willows in the Frost Forest back home. I don't know what possessed me, perhaps it was her laugh or her sudden freeness, but I couldn't hold myself back. I leaned in and captured her lips. I registered her shock, briefly, then it morphed into something more. Something deeper, as she moved her lips against mine.

I wrapped my hand behind her neck to pull her close. She gasped and leaned away, leaving me wanting. Her voice was breathy, full of lust, when she spoke. "Your hand is so cold against my neck."

"I'm the Frost King, Flame. What did you expect when I touched you?"

"I d-don't know..." She was stuttering, hoping she hadn't offended me as she probed with her blue-grey eyes. "I didn't hate it."

I took that as the signal to continue. I cupped her face, running my cool thumbs along the warm skin of her cheeks, and then I dove for her lips because one kiss between us wasn't adequate. I wanted more. Needed more. I ran my tongue along her lower lip, and she whimpered. The sound wound through my body straight to my cock. When she opened her mouth and allowed me to sweep inside with my tongue, I lost myself to the taste of her.

The more heated our kisses became, the more my Fae power surged within me. It was a side effect of my kind and one I had to dispel before I froze her to death. I broke away, slapping my hand against the window and trailing my tongue along her throat. The chill sent goosebumps across her creamy flesh. Splinters of ice crawled across the pane, crackling as I released some of the power I'd built up.

I couldn't remember a time when a woman brought me to this state so quickly.

She flipped her head, examining the results of my power and grinning at the sight. She opened her mouth to speak, but a thwacking sound hit the window. She jumped up from her chair, abandoning me, as the snowball outside slid down the panes.

A moment later Yeager lumbered inside, taking up most of the doorway and looking like the monster he was. "Oops. I meant to hit the hole in the wreath." He pointed to the wreath hanging on the outside of the door and smirked. "Guess I need to work on throwing my balls."

Vixen laughed. I couldn't help but notice her stepping away from me and toward him. It was only a step, but I hated every inch of it. I raised my hand and sent a chilly gust of wind to slam the door. The lumberjack seemed determined to thwart me at every turn.

The alarm on my watch went off, signaling it was fifteen minutes until my meeting with John. I needed time to prepare, and get in the right state of mind, so I'd have to let everything else lie until later. Once my meeting was done, I intended to take care of Mr. Oops. Because I knew he'd seen Vixen kissing me through the window and purposely threw that snowball to interrupt us. They may have slept together, but they weren't in an exclusive relationship after one night.

I rested my hand on Vixen's arm. "If you'll excuse me, it's nearly time for my meeting." She nodded politely. The next moment, the door burst back open, and everyone filed inside. The Sun King, the trio of nymps, Aaron and Erin, the father and daughter, and one other bringing up the rear. I could not believe my eyes when he stepped over the threshold.

# CHAPTER 10

olly came rushing from the kitchen. The squeal she let out at the sight of Santa nearly blew the windows out. "Oh mercy! You're here! It's Santa everyone. Santa is here!" He lifted his red mitten to wave at her and she promptly wilted to the floor.

She fainted at the sight of Santa.

Fainted.

He shook his head, rushing over to check on her. In the few minutes it took her to wake up, the rest of us collectively side-eyed each other. That is, all of us but Cherish. Isaac wrapped his arm around her and pointed to Santa like she should've been as excited to see him as Holly. Her response was to roll her eyes and declare, "Santa, Dad? Do you really think I still believe in that nonsense? I don't even care." Only the way she dragged that last word out sounded like she'd said 'care-uhh.'

It was at that moment that my uterus shriveled and died.

Santa's booming voice carried over the huddle of employees who were trying to revive their poor vexed boss.

"How many times have I told you, Holly? There's no need for such fanfare when I'm here. I'm just a regular guy." Liar. He was not a regular guy, and he had a reason for appearing here less than a day after he'd sent me.

He helped the poor fangirl to her feet and strolled over to me. "Hey, Boss. Come to check up on me? Look, I'm chillaxing." I plopped down in the cushy chair and propped my feet on the coffee table. And as if I'd willed it into being, a mug of hot coffee appeared in front of my face. Yeager. He'd poured me another cup and delivered it just in time to provide visual evidence of said chillaxation.

Okay, he got points for that.

Santa looked down with a twinkle in his eye. "I'm not checking up, I'm here to help you."

I took a long slurp. But it was too hot, and I almost burned my tongue. The thought of Santa hanging out with me the next few days made me want to puke, so I'd had to do *something* to keep from it. Apparently, I winced or had some sort of reaction, because Jack placed a finger on the side of my mug and the coffee cooled just enough to be drinkable.

Points.

The action seemed to startle Santa, based on his look that said 'eep.' He turned back to me. "I'm going to provide you—and all those staying here—with a fun distraction designed to raise your Christmas spirits. I spent all night designing these tasks and I believe everyone is going to enjoy them and come out more festive than before."

"What?" Only it came out like "wrt" because my teeth were clenched. Santa was notorious for his ridiculous Reindeer Games. Every year before Christmas he created a contest or assignment for one, some, or all of us. They always ended in chaos, confusion, and nightmares.

Literally.

Last year he gave us all sleeping potions with the idea that we wake up and create artwork for hospitals based on our dreams. Sounded great. Let's give the sick and bed-bound folks something beautiful to look at. Only every single one of us had paralyzing nightmares so our paintings looked like psychopathic killers had made them with the blood of their victims. Talk about a nightmare before Christmas.

To this day, Donner is still seeing a therapist for his trauma-induced fear of pine needles.

Yet, Santa carries on.

And he'd brought several innocent people into this time.

"Don't look so glum, Vixen. Everyone gather 'round. Let me explain how this is going to work. Wait, where are the vampires?"

I pointed to the window. "Sun."

"Of course, well you can explain to them later."

Yeager perched on the arm of my chair, throwing his arm around the back. It was casual, but also predatory. And damn it if it didn't give me a little tingle. Especially when I noticed Jack boring a hole in him with his steel gaze. Did I want them to fight over me? No, but I was woman enough to admit it would be all kinds of panty-melting. I'd kissed Jack hours after I'd slept with Yeager. Some would say that made me a slut, but I didn't much care about what others thought of me. Each of the men had their great qualities. And yes, I was attracted to both.

However, I needed to back burner that while Santa was standing in front of the fireplace lecturing like a professor.

"I call this the Twelve Games of Christmas. You'll form teams of four and do a challenge per day for the next twelve days."

"Hold up," I bellowed. "I'm only here for the long week-end. That's what you said."

"I spoke with Cupid, and everything is covered for you back at the Pole." I opened my mouth to scream about the fact that he was likely going to let Fucking Clare do my job. Cupid was my best friend, but if Santa deemed it, she'd have no choice. Thankfully, Santa seemed to remember I had a mortal enemy at the last second. "Cupid's bringing Mariah up to speed on your work."

Thank my soul. I liked Mariah. She was fun, made great NickTocks and most importantly, she never slept with Rudy.

Seeing I was satisfied, Santa droned on. "I've already arranged for all the guests to have extended time away. I've emailed bosses and spoken to families. Everything is taken care of financially and otherwise. The only task left is to shackle the Fae."

Yeager chuckled. "Together? That would be fun to watch."

Jack ignored him and arched a perfect eyebrow. "How so?"

"Simple, my friend. Neither of you can touch the weather. No trickery or crafty Fae workarounds in the games either. If you can't agree to this condition, I'll ask you to leave."

Jack didn't like the idea of that. I could tell by the icy frown on his face. I knew what he was thinking: if they didn't agree, they'd be asked to leave and forced to reschedule their important business meeting. I could see their wheels turning as they considered their option. Finally, they both huffed "fine" at the same time.

There was a lot of history between those two. And it appeared that John was as interested in their business deal as Jack was.

Santa continued with his rules. "Each team gets a candy cane that will serve as one vote. You can't cast your cane for your team. Holly, Karl, Jasper, and Frank, the custodian will get votes as well. The team with the most candy canes in their stockings at the end will receive a special Christmas present from me. And, of course, bragging rights."

The Mrs.ers executed a triple high five in perfect co-ordination. They must have been practicing that skill. Their competitive nature was already taking over. They were into this idea.

Me? Not even a little.

I loved Santa and respected his authority, but he knew I didn't like his silly games and he'd done this anyway. He lowered a look on me that made me scrunch in my chair. I had no choice in this. "We'll begin this afternoon. Choose your teams and come up with names now. I'll send an Elf shortly to make up for the deficit in numbers so that all the teams are fair and even. He can be on your team, Vixen."

Yeager swished my hair over my shoulder, leaning in close. "I'm on your team too."

"As am I," Jack stated rather matter-of-factly. Yeager growled and it hit me right below the belt, specifically my lady bits. Jack shrugged in response, whispering to Yeager. "Do you really think I'd be on a team with the Sun King? Or the college nymphs?"

He didn't have that vibe at all. I patted his arm. "That's fine. You can be on my team and the lumberjack can deal with it."

"And I'll deal with you later, Bunny," Yeager crooned. Why did that sound so appealing? I was losing control over my libido, sitting there between the two of them. I shouldn't be thinking naughty thoughts about either of them. I had to play these dumb games now. I couldn't lose sight of why I was there in the first place.

Santa clapped his hands together and all the bells in the place rang in response. He had weird powers like that. "I wish I could stay, but as you know, I have work to do up North. My Elf will be here soon with the first contest. I'll magically send instruction cards for the rest of the games to Holly." She swooned again. But hey, she stayed upright this time. "I expect everyone to play nice and have fun!" He glared down, making sure I knew he meant me.

A half-hour later, John Sun had predictably teamed up with the Mrs.ers. They announced their team name by each of the women pointing to themselves and saying "Ho!" and then pointing to John and saying "Hot." So, *Ho, Ho, Ho, Hot.* Cue, eye-roll.

Isaac and Cherish had teamed up with the newlyweds and they debated over the team's name. Aaron/Erin wanted to include some version of their names but Cherish was not having it. "Bor-inguh," she snipped, but when her father glared her into submission, she whispered, "No offense."

"How about the Fearsome Foursome?" Isaac suggested. I swear I heard Cherish's groan before it came out of her mouth.

"Thank you, next."

Erin was massaging Aaron's temples, but managed to offer up, "Cherished Gifts?" She didn't even respond to that one.

A few moments later she snapped her fingers. "Hot chocolate..." Her dad frowned, looking over to the very Caucasian couple, then back to Cherish, scolding with a look for bringing race into it. But she held up her finger, dramatically. "...With Marshmallows!"

The was an uncomfortable beat before both Aaron and Erin burst into laughter, declaring at the same time, "We love it!"

Hot Chocolate with Marshmallows was born. All that was left was for Yeager, Jack, and I to decide our team's name.

# CHAPTER 11

I swear on the highest mountain peak that I will never be on a team called Frostbite." Yeager was pacing in front of the chair, glaring at Jack and waving his hands. He was not a fan of Jack's obvious nod to himself with that suggestion. "If anything, we should be called the Lumberjacks. At least that includes both of us, Jack." The way he said his name sounded *so* sarcastic.

"You're a clown. Lumberjacks has nothing to do with Vixen. She's on the team too."

"Okay, fine. We can be called Vixen's...Valiants?"

Cherish leaned over the couch. "That one is cringe A.F." She peered up at Yeager and shook her head. "Cheugy. You're doin' too much." Isaac opened his mouth to say something about her comments but gave up. Probably because he didn't understand a word she just said. Like all of us. She wasn't done either. She whipped her head toward Jack. "And you over there tryin' to be Daddy."

That last one I got. He *did* give that vibe.

Isaac put his arm around her and pulled her down, so she was sitting back on the couch properly. He whispered something in her ear, and she scoffed, folding her arms across her chest and declaring, "I literally don't even care-uh."

Yeager looked amused, but Jack clearly didn't understand. "Daddy? Was that a compliment or derision?"

I shrugged. "Depends on who you ask."

He put his finger under my chin, directing me where he wanted me to look. Which was right at him and his silvery eyes. "I'm asking you."

Keeping his chilly finger where it was, he raised a single eyebrow. I licked my lips and he stared like he was enraptured with the simple biological function. Then he shifted on the armrest. It was a tiny change of position, but when his leg brushed against mine, a groan escaped him. It made my nipples perk right up. And boy oh boy, did he notice. Before I could respond to any of it, he slung his legs over mine, trapping me underneath him. Though, I didn't care to move away at all.

Yup. He was definitely Daddy. "Yes, it's a compliment." He gave me that quarter of a grin and even though his cool finger was still under my chin, I melted. I was a total puddle, literal and figurative.

There was a distinct tug on my hair. Yeager was standing behind me, grasping onto the long length to grab my attention away from Jack. Even sideways and slightly upside down, he was a sight. I expected him to be jealous at Jack's obvious move toward me—they'd been going back and forth all morning—but his emerald eyes were full of mirth instead. "We still don't have a team name, Bunny."

"We could be Vixen and the Studs."

Did I mean to say that out loud? Nope. Did I expect both men to look like it meant something? No again. Did it get me a little hot to think about them, both of them? Maybe.

Nah, I wasn't in a place to have anyone else. Casual sex and kissing aside.

Just when I'd convinced myself I wasn't interested in either of them, a loud pop reverberated around the room. Everyone looked up in surprise. Not me. I knew that sound. It was a tell-tale signal that an Elf was about to appear by way of magic. Before I could explain what would happen, an engine sound echoed through the lodge, and—boom— an Elf riding on a sleek black motorcycle appeared just inside the door. The bike skidded across the wooden floor, then rocketed toward the counter where Holly stood. She shrieked and the driver swung the bike around, swerving to a stop sideways at the counter.

No one said a word.

Or even moved.

The driver slung his leg over the motorcycle and removed his black helmet. He was wearing dark aviators with a black leather jacket and pants. He had a bright red scarf draped over his neck that made him look like he didn't give a shit about being put together but looked one-hundred percent put together anyway. He looked at Holly and lowered his sunglasses. "Sorry about that Holl. I'll clean up the skid marks."

She put her hand to her chest. It made the jingle bells on her sweater ring. "You most certainly will, young man."

He smiled at her and that was all it took to make the anger dissipate. "I'm definitely a man, but the young part is debatable." She giggled. Really, it was a cackling hyena sound. Like she couldn't control the outburst coming from her mouth. The Elf slid his shades off and turned to face the room.

Oh. Got it.

That was why Holly instantly went ga-ga.

"Vixen!" he roared. He took three long strides and promptly liberated me from Jack's legs and Yeager's grasp by lifting me off the chair. "How's my favorite ginger?" He kept me in his embrace for what seemed like minutes. I was standing there with my feet dangling, breathing in the fresh peppermint and vanilla scent of this Elf who'd for some unknown reason, considered me a friend.

I wasn't. Not really.

I'd met him a few times with Rudy. They used to hang out together a lot, but something came between them. Something Rudy refused to discuss with me at the time. Every time I saw the Elf, he acted like we were best buddies. He was always nice to me, but he had a bit of a reputation at the Pole. For several reasons. One of which was his meandering hands. Like the ones gliding way too close to my ass at the moment.

I wiggled. Not that I really wanted to stop his roaming hands. The guy was a smoke show. But it wasn't the time, nor the place as I was wedged there between two other men. "I'm good. How are you, Hart?"

He finally dropped me and took my hands. "Well, I had to murder a few Elves to get the honor of being the one who came here to help out your team, but I'm better now that I'm here."

Several people in the room snickered. What they didn't realize was that it was just as likely true as it wasn't. Like I said, reputation. "Introduce me to your..." he paused to take in both Yeager and Jack with curious eyes. "...friends?"

I took a deep breath. "This is Yeager and Jack Frost. They're on the team with us, I guess."

Yeager shook his hand. "Yeager Hanson. I'm a Yeti." A threat, maybe? Yetis were fierce and while Elves weren't usually known for being intimidating, this one certainly was, not just by his muscular frame, but by the big dick energy he gave off. "That was some entrance."

"Thanks. You only get one first impression, am I right? Here, have a candy cane. Made it myself this morning." He pulled a small candy cane from his pocket and shoved it at Yeager, who looked amused, and dubious. He shot a glance at me, asking if it was okay to eat. I nodded and he unwrapped the package around it.

Hart was the head of the candy cane department. His canes were divine. As Yeager took a lick with his sinful tongue, I looked away, knowing I was a tick on the clock away from blushing at the memory of it between my legs. "Tell me, Yeager, how do you feel about being on a team with our ginger dream here?"

Yeager stuck the pointy end of the cane in his mouth, then took his blessed time dragging it back out again. Of course, he was eye-fucking me the whole time. Didn't hate it. "I'm fucking thrilled to be on Vixen's team. She can confirm I'm a team player."

Team player, as in helping me have two astronomical orgasms and him being satisfied with one himself? Yeppers. Team player. Go fight, win!

I nodded but I don't think anyone caught it. Jack was at my side, too busy extending a hand and sizing up my Elf friend. "Jack Frost, King of the Fae Winter court." He gave a curt nod that spoke volumes. He wasn't giving an inch more than was polite. Not letting anything out of his mouth he didn't want. It was attractive on a level I didn't understand. He also got a candy cane and the same question. To which he replied, "Pleased."

Okay then.

Needing to get the rest over with, I gestured around the room. "Everyone, this is Hart Brandywine. Hart, this is everyone, and by that, I mean Isaac and his daughter Cherish, newlyweds Erin and Aaron, John Sun of the Fae Summer court, and...?" I stalled on the names of the Mrs.ers. Thankfully they provided the necessary information.

"I'm Mindy." The blonde.

"I'm Mandy." Brunette.

"And I'm Vanessa, but I was born on a Monday, so call me Monday. It better fits our brand."

Oh, my soul. Mindy, Mandy, Monday. Kill me now.

They giggled in Hart's direction, but his stone-faced reaction to their silliness shut them up. He used his long black leather-clad—seriously—legs to stride across the room, checking out everyone as he went. He finally arrived in front of Cherish. Her mouth was gaping open and for once, her thumbs were completely still. Yeah, he was that gorgeous. The title of "Sexiest Elf at the North Pole" for three years in a row was earned.

*Earned.*

Even an eleven-year-old recognized. True she was mature for her age, but still.

Hart leaned down, putting his hands on the back of the couch, basically caging her in between his arms. It wasn't a sexual move—she was a child—but was meant to give her his full attention, which she ate up with a spoon. He handed her a candy cane, then nodded his head back toward me, Jack, and Yeager. "Spill the tea on those three?"

Her face lit up like a Christmas tree. It was the first time I'd seen her react with anything but disdain for everyone around her. Hart had that effect. She even put down her damn phone to answer him. "Well, Ok Boomers over there are simpin' for sis, but IDK if they've smashed or not. Probably, because lumberjack is sharing a cabin with her which is totally sus if you ask me. Zaddy, OTOH, can't stop looking at her. He has high-key goals."

Hart smirked. "No cap?"

Her face was as straight as a razor, her eyes large as she gave her reply. "No cap."

"And what about that snack between them?" He was asking all these questions about us with a stage whisper. And she was replying loudly. Everyone in the room was catching it all. Though most of them probably didn't understand what they were talking about. I didn't.

"Bruh, she's Gucci, but IDK about her feels. I can't say if she's vibing on either of them. SMH"

Satisfied he'd gotten his intel, he gave her a second candy cane. "You're the GOAT, girl."

She sighed and melted into the couch. As Hart strolled back over to us, she looked at her bewildered dad and said, "Hart has that rizz."

Isaac's eyes went wide. I got it. Rizz sounded way too much like jizz for anyone's liking. I was sure it didn't mean that exactly. Well, I hoped it didn't. "So, you can talk like a pubescent teen girl, huh? That on your resume?"

He chuckled. "Yeah. I can communicate with kids, part of the job. But it's not my best kind of talking. No cap." Got it. No cap meant you were telling the truth.

"What's your best way of talking?" Yeager chimed in. I slapped his solid arm because I knew what Hart's answer would be. He'd set him up for it.

Hart wiggled his eyebrows. "Dirty talking."

Pegged that one. I could only imagine.

And I had once. Imagined Hart and I...

After Rudy moved out and I happened to pass Hart as I went to the stables one morning and he was coming from the underground MMA fights Santa knew nothing about. He had that dangerous vibe coming off his win. He looked ready to tear anyone apart in the best way possible. My brain, and various other places on my person, just went there and imagined a scenario of him backing me against some wall and just getting at it.

Of course, I felt guilty after I'd thought about him. Even though I'd kicked Rudy out, I was still a slave to the feelings I'd had for him.

Hart clapped his hands together. "Let's play the first game."

He went back and collected a duffle bag from his motor-cycle, rummaging through it until he produced four plain white stockings. He handed one to each group and left one on the counter for the vampires to collect later.

"Now that you have team names, you're going to decorate this stocking to fit the name and vibe of your team. The caveat is that you must use only what's on your person or in any purses bags or pockets to decorate the stocking. We're talking about clothes and shoes, underwear...whatever you have. And you can use the scissors, glue, and thread that Holly will bring out in a moment to secure the decorations on your stocking."

He turned to her, and she jumped up and ran down the hall while he kept talking. "Once they're all done—assuming we have to wait until the morning for the vamps to finish theirs—we'll cast our votes in secret. Remember teams get one vote and they must agree on who they choose to give their candy cane to. Any questions? Nope. Let's get going."

# CHAPTER 12

Vixen was everything I'd remembered and more. I wasn't fucking prepared for the sight of her. Did I murder other elves to get the job? Nah. I just maimed them a little bit. I mean, shit, dislocated shoulders heal in no time. And, Santa's next-in-line elf, Cream Bunderclatch would've been an awful team player. His fractured nose would probably heal and make him look less boring to the ladies and/or men he wanted to screw. I was doing him a favor.

But I was going to get involved in Santa's contest for Vixen.

And there she was, squeezed in between two assholes basically begging them both to fuck her with her eyes alone.

I wanted in on that action.

Had for a long time.

Rudy had been my friend forever. But that night after one of my more violent takedowns, I found him fingering Clare in the alley behind the old toy warehouse we had converted into our MMA ring. He hadn't even had the decency to do her inside the building. He just had her leaned against the filthy wall and poked his fingers on her pussy like he deserved to take something from her. The guy had no technique. None. He didn't even kiss her. Just went straight in like he was a fucking gynecologist doing an exam.

I appointed myself as his judge, jury, and executioner that night. Not just for the horrendous way he was pumping his fingers into Clare, but for the way it would make Vixen feel when she found out.

They always find out.

What was that human phrase? Been there, done that.

I couldn't stand for any of it, friend or not, so I went over and dislodged his hand from Clare's cunt and beat the ever-loving shit out of him, being careful to avoid his trademark face. So yeah, the bruises he had the next day were all internal. And deserved. I bet he had trouble holding his dick to piss for days.

Never spoke to him again. Asswipe. Vixen was a woman who deserved so much more than that. Any woman did, really, but looking at her now in that tight sweater and smelling like the fresh sunrise at dawn, I had to admit, I was in the fucking game. Though I wasn't used to being in the position to pursue a woman. They came to me with dripping pussies and promises every day. Every night. It's what came with the title, North Pole's sexiest elf. That title had a hold over me. I carried that thing everywhere I went, and I couldn't get away from it. That's why I hated it.

Though I didn't hate the pussy it got me.

None of them could compare to Vixen, though. I was sure of it. And I was going to do what it took to have her and give her what she deserved. I didn't give any fucks about the other two guys wanting the same thing.

I plopped down on the coffee table facing the three of them, running my hand over the stocking we were supposed to decorate, then subtly sticking my fingers inside the cuff, drawing them in and out while Vixen tracked each movement. "Let's start decorating so we can go do some fun things. What's our team's name?"

Vixen ripped her gaze from my hand which was basically fingering the stocking, locking on my eyes. Couldn't help but notice the dilation in her crystal blue peepers. *Oh, you have no idea what I can do, my little ginger minx.* She crossed her legs. A sure sign that there was some throbbing going on down under. "We were debating when you showed up. We've thrown out Frostbite, Lumberjacks, and Vixen's Valiants. Got any ideas?"

"I have several ideas. All of them naughty, but that's another discussion."

Jack Frost finally broke his silence. "I'll agree on that." He angled toward Vixen, attempting to ignore me and failing. That guy was like a hawk, taking in every move she made as well as any of us around her. The Yeti was oblivious to it, but there was pure need in his eyes, and he was looking at Vixen to quell it. Couldn't blame him for that. "We need to find something we all have in common."

"That makes sense," she replied. "Though I highly doubt we'll find that. Not with a lumberjack Yeti, The Frost King, and an Elf? Then you add a reindeer shifter in the mix and it's a hodgepodge of crazy personalities and favorite things."

The Yeti laughed. "I like crazy." I'm sure he did. I'd been to North Pole orgies with Yetis. Their tongues? Fuck me, they were outstanding. Yetis were down for anything. At least the females were, in my experience. "I don't know about likes, but what I *don't* like is that Reginald character who hurt Vixen. I would love to punch him in the face."

I was warming up on the Yeti. Respect for not using his actual name. "Trust me, pal. It is so fucking satisfying. He's a bit of a pussy. Can't take a punch for shit." Vixen gasped. The shape of her open mouth sent a signal to my cock. Wake up and party. "What? He didn't ever tell you what happened between us?"

"No. I just thought...well, I didn't know what I thought."

"I thought he deserved a smackdown for cheating on you and that's what he got. I know he used to be my friend, but I agree with the Yeti. I hate that reindeer."

Jack grinned. It looked weird on his stoic face. "That appears to be our common ground: hate for Rudy."

Vixen was quiet. Deathly quiet. I could see she was trying to keep her face schooled into the perfect façade, but I knew her. Well, enough to know she was about to break. Grief and loss could sneak up on you at the worst time. She wasn't in the 'over him' stage just yet. I could help with that. Just like I could help her in that moment. "How about Rage Against Rudy?"

"Yes. That's it," Yeager shouted. "I love it. Rar." That came out as a bit of a growl. Vixen approved of the sound. I could tell because she'd angled toward him and ran her luscious pink tongue over her lower lip. The lips I had a huge desire to snack on.

Jack nodded his agreement, then looked to Vixen. Her eyes were brimming with tears, but she sucked in a deep breath, wiped them away, and sat up straighter. "That's perfect. We need a brown face. Does anyone need to take a shit? We could use it on our stocking."

# CHAPTER 13

I didn't *really* want to apply shit to our stocking. We were discussing Rudy and my brain went there. I waffled between anger and sadness quickly and I never knew when the switch in my head was going to flip. I tried to refocus on the job at hand instead, asking the guys to come up with things we could use and making a pile on the coffee table.

For the face, we decided on the beige emergency thermal socks Yeager pulled from his jacket pocket. They were clean and dry and would work better than anything else we had on us. I took the scissors from the bucket Holly provided us and went to work cutting scraps to piece together in Rudy's head. "I have to admit, it feels pretty good to hack on this sock thinking about Rudy."

Yeager nodded. "I imagine it's cathartic. Like burning his clothes."

That *had* been fun.

"Yeah, something like that." I made a big snip. "What do we use to make the label with the team's name?"

Hart was already using his scarf to cut a red prohibition circle and slash to go around Rudy's head and some candy canes for antlers. Yeager had popped two buttons from his plaid shirt to use for eyes. I was a bit distracted by the sliver of skin peeking through now. I probably wasn't going to sleep with him again, but I could enjoy the view anyway.

To answer my question, Jack took a light blue silk handkerchief from his pocket and whipped it open in the air. "We can use this for the name."

"Um, I would feel awful about cutting that up. It looks way too expensive."

His response was to reach for another pair of scissors and start cutting. "I need to contribute something, and I have drawers full of handkerchiefs in my Kingdom." After he'd made a pretty nice-looking R, he looked down at me. "This will make you happy, won't it?" I nodded, because yeah, it was silly, but I did want us all to donate to the stocking and also make something worth voting for. "Then this is what I'll do."

Hart whistled at Jack's commitment to the team. No idea why.

After I'd made the face shape, I went to check out the competition.

*Damn it Santa, I was one contest in and already at peak competitiveness. Crafty bastard.*

The Ho Ho Ho Hot team girls had used their red, yellow, and orange sweaters to make a patchwork sun. It looked fairly good, though each of them was showing too much skin and racy bras now that they'd mangled their clothes. Isaac was actively trying to keep Cherish from seeing them.

Probably fearing her cutting up her clothes as a fashion statement.

John Sun was attaching a pair of his sunglasses to the sun on the stocking. According to Jack, he had about thirty pairs on him at any given time. He said they were the keys to his kingdom, but I didn't ask what that meant. Figured it was a Summer King thing.

Meanwhile, over at the Hot Chocolate with Marshmallows team, there was some creative thinking happening. Isaac had torn the tail of his blue shirt to fashion it into a mug. He'd allowed Cherish—or perhaps hadn't been looking when she did it—to cut one of her lower braids off. She swirled it into the mug, making the hot chocolate with her hair. I got up to get a closer look at the marshmallows they were gluing in the mug.

Could not believe it.

Erin had pulled a couple of tampons out of her purse and snipped up the insides to form the little marshmallows that rested in the cup. I had to comment. "Wow, that's some ingenuity right there."

Aaron beamed. "That's why I love her. But she's not on her period now. In case you're wondering. We planned the wedding and honeymoon around her cycle."

I was *not* wondering in any way. Thanks for the TMI, Aaron.

I vaguely smiled at him as he glued one of their red wedding napkins, also taken from Erin's purse, under the mug to make it look like it was resting on it. He wrote the team's name and did a fancy little swirl underneath. Okay.

Determined to make sure we could compete with all that, I wandered back over to my team just as Jack was gluing on the last R. "I'm loving this, but we have some competition."

Yeager glanced over his shoulder. "Nah. We're good. We just have the issue of the nose. Maybe we can ball up some more of Hart's scarf?"

Hart scoffed. "That won't work. After the vain bastard got his nose fixed, it's much smaller. With no distinguishing features. Anything would do now."

We all started cleaning our pockets. I had a wad of unused tissues in my jacket that I carried for the sneak attacks my tears liked to pull on me. Other than that, I had a couple of hair ties and a penny. "This would work for a regular reindeer nose, I guess."

We glued it on, but Hart didn't think we were finished just yet. He took a tissue and ripped it up. I opened my mouth to ask why, but he reached out and put his finger to my lips, keeping it in place way longer than necessary. I had to squelch the urge I had to lick it. He seemed to pick up my thought because he swiped his finger, just a little, across my lower lip and smirked. "Watch."

He took a switchblade from his pocket, flicked it open, and sliced through the palm of his hand. Just like they did in movies. I always wondered why when people needed blood in movies, they went for the hand. Why not the arm or leg? You needed your hand. Especially Hart, who had candy canes to make once he was done with the nonsense of the competition. He did not seem to care about any of that. He simply held his hand out, letting the blood drip onto the tissue as he smiled.

When he was done, he glued it underneath the penny, like it was stuck up a nostril, making our reindeer look like someone had clocked him in his brand new nose. He gave me a sly grin. "If I ever see him again, this is how he'll end up. No cap."

Beside me, Yeager whispered, "Baller."

I'm sure my mouth was gaping open because my words just tumbled out of it. "I'm not sure if that was hot or gross."

A trio of voices in the corner of the room all declared "hot" at once. There was also a very enthusiastic nod of the head from Erin.

Hot, it was.

Once he glued the bloodied tissue onto our stocking, he leaned in close, and I was hit with his yummy scent. "A little blood's appropriate for the situation, don't you think?" I wasn't sure about that, but I was sure that my nether regions tingled at his action.

Maybe I needed professional help. Being desperately attracted to three men at once time was not normal. It had to be the rebound effect going bonkers in my body and mind.

The teams all hung their stockings over the fireplace with the hooks that had come from somewhere when we were all distracted with our creations. Santa likely. Hart walked around his motorcycle to go behind the desk and pulled a sticky note and pen out from behind it, scribbling a note. When he was finished, he strolled back over and stuck the note to the top of our stocking.

*Dearest Vamps,*

*Don't even think about touching this blood. If you lay so much as one fang on it, I will come to you in the middle of the day and drag you out into the sun and watch you burn. Then I'll piss all over your ashes and laugh at your demise.*

*Love,*

*Hart Brandywine*

I raised an eyebrow and my gaze landed on Yeager. He seemed impressed with Hart's direction. Jack, on the other hand, sighed. "That's not how you deliver a threat. You're sending a mixed message."

Hart shrugged. "Exactly. It keeps the enemy off-balance. They'll be wondering if I'm serious or if it was a joke and eventually rule on the side of caution and choose not to do it just in case I was serious. Spoiler alert: I wasn't joking."

Holly interrupted the deadly silence that Hart had created when she burst into the room carrying a tray and declaring lunch was served. We all shuffled into the dining room. Hart slid in as the head of the table, and I took the bench next to him with Jack on my left. Yeager was across from me, tearing into the turkey croissant sandwiches before the rest of the group had settled in and was completely unapologetic about it.

John Sun sat next to Yeager, eyeing Jack the whole time. Jack did his best to ignore him, but I could tell it was bothering him. I needed to distract him. "I guess you missed your meeting time with all the stocking decorating. You can reschedule, right?"

"Yes. Tomorrow, an hour after we've finished whatever game comes next."

The way he delivered the line—glaring at John with a raised eyebrow—said he was taking charge, dominating the terms of their meeting before John had a chance to do it first.

John took a big swig of his drink before responding. Stalling. Their relationship was strange. Finally, he used his napkin to wipe his face and said, "Agreed." Jack snorted. It wasn't loud enough for anyone to hear but me, but I caught the meaning. He'd won the strange showdown between them.

All they were doing was talking about a meeting time.

There was a lot I didn't know about Fae Kings.

A pop sound caught everyone's attention. The second afterward, an envelope appeared on the table next to Hart. His name was written in red glitter with beautifully scrolled strokes. He picked it up, rolling his eyes. "Love note from Santa."

He ripped open the envelope and read the contents of the letter, then sighed. It sounded a lot like Cherish, to be honest. He muttered 'fuck' under his breath, then turned his attention to me. "Appears there's a candy cane emergency. That shit-for-brains Drake Bellbottom got his arm stuck in the extruder. Blood and bone everywhere. It gummed up all the cogs and I'm the only one who can fix it."

Erin's hand flew to her mouth. "That sounds awful. I hope he's okay."

Hart grunted. I don't think he shared her sentiments because he ignored her and stood up. "I've got to go take care of this. I'll pop back here as soon as I can. Definitely before the next game." He leaned down and kissed the top of my head. Like it was a normal thing to do. I mean it wasn't like it was sexual, but the way he ran his hand down my spine, reaching far enough for the tips of his fingers to graze my ass told me it wasn't a friendly kiss from a buddy.

That was the trouble with Hart. Everything he did seemed sexual.

Didn't hate that about him.

He reached out, slapping Jack on the back. "While I'm gone, don't do anyone I wouldn't do."

Aaron shook his head. It seemed to hurt as he did. Probably a sex injury. "I think the phrase is don't do any*thing* I wouldn't do."

Hart winked at Jack. "Nah. Meant what I said, didn't I, Jackie boy?" He grabbed his half-eaten sandwich and popped out of sight.

I turned to Jack. "What did he mean by that?"

Jack lowered that steely gaze at me, taking his sweet time to answer. When he finally did, goosebumps erupted all over my flesh, just at his tone and the look he served. "He meant you."

I had no idea how to respond to that. None.

Across the table, Yeager chuckled. "Something tells me we may be playing more than one game here. Okay, okay. I'm good at games. Challenged accepted." He wet his lips and I got a glimpse of that miraculous tongue. Just the tip of it, but it was enough to melt those frost goosebumps.

The room seemed to spiral around me. Were the three of them talking about me like they were going to compete for me too? And if that was the case, how did I feel about it?

I didn't know.

I spent the rest of the lunchtime pondering each of the men, then berating myself for even going down that road. Had I learned nothing from the failure that was my experience with Rudy? More than two people in a relationship was trouble. And painful. Even though all three of them were peak-level attractive, I couldn't imagine what it would look like to date all three at once.

No, I had to stop the madness.

No men.

None.

However.

I guess it wouldn't hurt to let them flirt. I could be nice to them without jumping into bed with them all. We *were* on the same team, and I had to get through eleven more games with them. Yeah, I could do it. I could keep them at arm's length.

Maybe.

Yeager stood abruptly from the table and yanked his phone out of his pocket. He grumbled something unintelligible after one glance at the screen. He gave a forlorn look and then turned to Holly. "Hey Holl. Pops needs me to take care of some important flurry shit. Are you going to be okay without me for a while?"

"Oh sure thing, Hon. We've got enough wood for another day at least. Take your time and give your Dads and Moms my love."

Had she just said, 'Dads and Moms,' as in plural? I guess I knew as little about Yetis as I did Fae kings. I must have had a shocked look on my face because Yeager chuckled. "Long story. I'll tell you tonight." He made a point to walk around the table to go in the direction of the door, leaning in and whispering on the way. "Right after I take you again. This time we can try the shower. You know, getting dirty and clean at the same time." Then he stood up and cleared his throat. "In case I don't get back in time to vote in the stockings game, you have my proxy, Bunny." He winked at Jack and strolled out the door.

Oh, my soul. What had I gotten myself into with him?

I turned to find Jack studying me intently. He didn't look disturbed from having heard every word Yeager had whispered in my ear. He looked intrigued. Suddenly, he placed a cool hand on my leg. "If you'll excuse me, I need to go and prepare for the new meeting time. I'll see you later in the day. We can have a drink if you like."

"Sure. That sounds nice, Jack." And I wasn't just being polite. Jack was mysterious and I hadn't forgotten the way he'd kissed me earlier. I wasn't sure it would happen again, but I wasn't discounting it either.

Like I wasn't discounting Yeager or Hart.

Yep, I was in trouble.

# CHAPTER 14

With all three of the attractive distractions away for the afternoon, the rest of the guests meandered in and out of the lodge and I nestled in by the fire with a spicy book Cupid had recommended to me. I was just getting to the good parts when Cherish plopped into the chair beside me. "Whatchya reading?"

"Um. It's an adult story. You wouldn't be interested."

She snatched the book out of my hands, then catapulted over the couch so I couldn't easily get it back from her. "Greyrock grabbed me by the throat, shoving me against the tree as his form went from human to beast. I whimpered. His claws ripped the bodice of my dress, and I was exposed to the dampness of the night, aching for him to let me go, but yearning to stay pinned against the tree. The growl that escaped his throat went straight to my core, and within moments I was dripping for the one man—one wolf—who was my utter destruction. The fur on his arms rippled and smooth taut skin appeared in its place. Need pulsed—"

Isaac came out of nowhere and knocked the book out of her hand and it went flying across the room, skidding to a stop at Erin's feet. She picked it up, taking more than a few seconds to note the title and author before she handed it back to me.

Cherish laughed. "Werewolf smut? Really, Vixen, I expected better from you. They never get wolves right in those books."

I was a little mortified I'd been called out by a child for reading werewolf smut in front of the whole group. "How would you know anything about werewolves or smut? You're like five years old."

She snarled at me. Literally snarled. "I may not know much about either of those things yet, but my day's coming." Her canines elongated for a split second, then went back to normal.

Isaac tucked her under his arm. "I apologize. She does know a bit about wolves, but she's not had her first shift yet. I'm wondering if it's a bad idea to be here right now, considering how hormonal and emotional she's been lately."

"Ugh. Dad, stop being so extra. I'm not going to shift yet. Even though every single one of my friends has already gone through it. I'm damaged, periodt."

"Honey, you're not damaged. You're exactly as you should be. Now maybe we should leave Vixen to her book, huh? And apologize for giving everyone the wrong impression about our species?"

"Fine. I'm sorry Vixen. I'm a little gassed about my first shift. It's hard not knowing exactly when you're going to turn into another being. It could be right now. Or now." She made a big dramatic pause. "Or now." When that didn't work to turn her, she finally apologized like her father had said. "I didn't mean to go all ragey. Or swipe your romance book. Though I can tell you for certain wolves can't switch so fast like that. It's not realistic."

I turned to Isaac who nodded his head to confirm it. I didn't care about the reality of werewolf shifting, as long as it was hot in my escape mechanism, which it was. But I remember going through puberty and shifting for the first time. True I didn't have fangs and claws, but it was harrowing, nonetheless. "It's fine Cherish. I'm sure your shift will go smoothly, whenever it arrives."

Erin had slid onto Aaron's lap, reaching up and stroking his temple. "I can't imagine what that's like for you guys. Our shifts are a lot more subtle."

Aaron nodded. "We're merpeople. In case you were wondering, no, we don't have sex in mer form. It's too complicated and not nearly as much fun."

No, Aaron, I was not wondering. Cherish rolled her eyes and put earbuds in as I questioned him. "How are you two standing the cold, then?"

"Oh, we do fine in icy waters. Our scales protect us, but we stay in human form throughout the winter. Kind of like hibernation, I guess you could say. We can stay out of the ocean for months at a time if we must. No big deal."

Okay then. Learn something new every day.

The door to the lodge flew open with a gust of wind. Four people clad in black snow suits, ski masks, and hoodies slinked into the room. One of them made fast work drawing all the curtains shut as the others pulled the four-seater table into the corner where Holly had a huge hutch covering the windows.

Well, hello there vampires.

Once they'd all stripped out of their ski suits, they were all wearing tight black catsuits with skulls on the back. What in the world was their story? We all stood there gaping at them—even Cherish looked up from her phone—until they noticed. The tallest one—I decided to call him Lestat in my head for fun—waved his hand in our direction. "It was a thrilling run today. Almost beat our record time. I'm sure we'll be victorious in the end. Whenever we get a real rig." The rest nodded at him like he was making sense.

Isaac made the first attempt to communicate with them. "Hello, I'm Isaac. This is Cherish, Vixen, Aaron, and Erin. What kind of record are you trying to beat?" His voice was a little shaky, because let's be honest, we were all hoping that record had nothing to do with sucking the most blood in one minute.

The vampire who'd drawn the curtains—Edward in my opinion because they never gave us their names—slinked over to the table. "Bobsledding, of course."

Not that made any sense at all.

Dracula next to him added the next bit. "Four-man team, as you can see. Under the Transylvanian flag."

Okayyyy. That was a head-scratcher.

"Isn't Transylvania part of Romania? And don't they already have a bobsled team?" Aaron asked. They all nodded in the affirmative. "Then why not try out for the Romanian bobsled team?"

The last vampire, Spike for funsies, gave a perplexed look. "We're hoping to make Transylvania independent. And we thought winning a gold medal would hold more weight and help our coup."

We all exchanged looks. We had questions. Many, but I asked the most important one. I mean, outside of geopolitical posturing. "Is there a bobsled track nearby?"

Lestat tutted. "Oh no. We're not ready for that just yet. We're just practicing on sleds on the giant hill out there, getting ourselves used to the cold at this stage. It could take a few years to have success, but we're committed to our goal. Mark my words, one day…" The rest of the vampires hissed and clapped, but Lestat quieted them. "Now we're given to understand we have a stocking to decorate. Can someone provide us with the details?"

Isaac, very bravely I might add, approached the table of black catsuit-wearing vamps and explained the rules and specifics to them. He also took the note Hart had left from our stocking and slid it across the table at them. I noted Spike looking over at the bloody tissue, but none of them made a move toward it.

I guess they were training and watching their diets.

After a few tense moments, everyone went back to what they'd been doing before the vampires swept in. And they set about making their stocking. I personally couldn't wait to see it.

Hours later, after a lazy afternoon, we were helping Holly clean up the dinner she'd made us. While the vampires abstained from eating, they did sit with us. And never gave us their names.

Jack, John, and the ho's had come back for our meal, but Yeager hadn't made it back from his trip to see his family yet. I was starting to worry a bit about him because the look on his face when he got that text did not scream 'I'm going home for a fun time.' Just when I was about to nonchalantly ask Holly questions about the wayward Yeti, a big pop resounded in the room. Hart appeared holding a basket full of candy canes and a sexy smile which he lowered on me. "Miss me?"

"Hardly."

"Liar."

Cherish strolled over and snagged a candy cane from the basket, not even waiting for a second to rip open the package and start eating it. After a second, she pulled it out of her mouth slowly. "Wait. Do these have Drake Bellbottom guts in them? If so, I am shook."

"Of course not." Hart pulled a black bag out of his pocket, big enough to hold four candy canes. "These are the ones with Drake Bellbottom's guts in them. Bon appetite. Yeet!" He tossed the bag at the vampires and Spike reached up and grabbed it from the air. The vamps devoured those canes within seconds. Cherish giggled at Hart like eating blood-laden candy canes was a thing people did.

Hart set the basket down on the coffee table. "Alright. Since we're almost all here, let's start."

He handed a card to Holly. She did her best to keep her squeal about getting a direct communique from Santa, but it was obvious on her face. While she regained her composure Hart leaned over, tugging on the end of my hair. "Where's the Yeti?"

"Family business of some kind. He said he'd be back later."

"Oh, okay, well if you need someone to bunk with tonight, I'm your guy." He shot a predatory grin at Jack, who froze him out with an icy eyebrow raise. It seemed like they were threatening each other, but I could've been mistaken.

If I'd been able to read 'male' better, maybe I wouldn't have had my heart ripped out.

Holly rang the jingle bells around her wrists—both of them— to get our attention. "Each team gets one cane and one vote. You'll wait in the dining room as the votes are cast. No peeking at any time, which goes for the rest of the games. I'll tally up the canes at the very end of the contest. Take five minutes to deliberate with your team now about your vote, then we'll begin. I mean, as soon as the vampires hang their stocking."

Lestat took the stocking they'd created and sauntered over to hang it. It was...well, it was something. Beside me Jack cursed. "I told the damn Yeti that Frostbite was a good team name."

Hart cocked his head. "For vampires, yeah. I like our name better." He snaked his arm around my waist, pulling me in and squeezing me. His vanilla peppermint scent floated by me, and I had to take a step away. He was showing me support and I appreciated it, but I didn't need to get entangled with yet another man. What was it that Cherish had said? Periodt. With a t.

There was a collective gasp as Lestat stepped away. The entire vampire stocking was covered in black. When Spike turned around, it was clear they'd cut the fabric from the ass of his bobsled catsuit. Two pale cheeks were peeping out at us. Cherish commented "Ok, Boomer," which he ignored.

They'd used the white tablecloth—which was probably a violation of Santa's rules, but I wasn't going to be the one to mention it—to fashion a snowman. Then Dracula, because he seemed to be the craziest one of the bunch, had ripped his own fangs out of his mouth and placed them at the snowman's neck, simulating a vamp bite. Their team's name was red checkered, possibly underwear, and so were the tiny drips of blood on the fangs.

The whole thing was macabre but oddly cool-looking.

Erin paled. "Did you really rip out your fangs for this? That's commitment."

Dracula shrugged. "They'll grow back eventually."

Okay then. All the teams turned to discuss their votes. Hart, naturally, was the first to speak up. "I like the vampire one, honestly. It's ingenuous, subtle."

I laughed. "You think ripping out your teeth is subtle? Nope. I like Hot Chocolate with Marshmallows, it's the more creative one. It's the tampon usage for me. Seriously, we should vote for them. And I get two votes because Yeager gave me his proxy." I wiggled my fingers at Hart. He leaned over and bit at them. Like he was switching to the vampire team. Luckily, I jerked them away too quickly for him to make contact. He looked sad about it.

Ignoring us, Jack strolled over the fireplace, literally stroking his stubbled jaw as he walked back and forth, eyeing the stockings. He stood there for nearly three of our five minutes debating, then came back over, looking smug. It was a good look on him. "We should anticipate who others will vote for and act accordingly. For example, Erin was freaked out by the vampires, so they won't get her vote. On the other hand, John Sun would never vote for anything I was involved with and vice versa. No matter what the nymphs said or did to steer him along. I also know he's got an affinity for merpeople, due to being the Sun King, so my best guess is Ho, Ho, Ho, Hot will vote for Hot Chocolate. Frostbite, while they're a wild card we don't yet know how to predict, I think they'll vote for us, thanks to Hart's blood on our stocking."

"Wow. I'm impressed. What else?" I asked.

"Hot chocolate will vote for us too. For several reasons: Isaac's embarrassed by Cherish's outbursts and though we may not like it, out of those of us here, we're the most closely related to Santa. He'll deflect to us because of it. The monogamous and over-sharing merpeople have been eyeing the nymphs with disdain, likely due to their overt sexual natures, so they won't vote for their team. Then there's Cherish's crush on Hart to add to the mix. We'll sweep this round, no matter what. But I say vote for Frostbite now because they're the least likely to score points in future games."

Hart shook his head. "Damn, that was genius. I didn't know you had it in you. I guess I won't kill you now for eyeing the hot reindeer we both want to bang." He gestured to me with his thumb, unabashedly. "Unless you let me down in the next contest."

Jack shrugged. "I'm starting to understand the nuance of the mixed signal."

Was that mutual respect? I had no idea. And I didn't want to stick around to discover the answer. Because something about the exchange between them made me feel unbalanced. The room started to cave in around me. Not really, of course, but I couldn't stop thinking about how Rudy had spoken, loudly, about his intention to date me. It was all over NickTock at the time, for goodness' sake. And as far as I knew, he was still with Clare when he started telling any and everyone, he wanted me. I'd never been in that position before and I'd felt so wanted and so seen.

But knowing how it turned out, I didn't think I could go through with that kind of thing again. So, I did what I'd done since Valentine's Day when I walked in and discovered my boyfriend on top of Clare. I fled.

# CHAPTER 15

The entire day with my family had been too much. My father, as alpha of the flurry, was a standup kind of guy. Normally, we got along fine. But he'd tricked me by texting that there was a big emergency that needed my 'gifts,' and I'd run out and left Vixen because of it.

When I got home, I discovered it was nothing but a lie.

Worse than that, he'd pitted the entire flurry against me and staged an intervention.

They were all there reminding me of my duties as the chosen one.

Their words, not mine.

I wasn't *chosen*, I was trapped. And as far as I could figure, the only way out of it was to leave it—them—all behind. I didn't want to do it, but if they didn't stop the nonsense and leave me the fuck alone about it, I would.

They'd even gotten Camilla, my supposed intended to come play along too.

She didn't want me any more than I wanted her. She was a great woman, but kind of boring for my taste. And most importantly, she was into my sister, Nadia. Never once looked in my direction sexually after they hooked up. As far as I was concerned, it was a wonderful thing. I wanted them both to be happy.

However, I'd been born with the gifts of my family, so I was the one who needed to pass that trait along. And I looked, I fucking looked everywhere, but to my knowledge, Camilla was the only gift-born female in all of the South Pole and I was the only male. It was us or nothing.

My father wouldn't stand for nothing.

And he wouldn't have stood for me impregnating Camilla and going on my merry way either. No. It was one of the points I brought up with him the most. Camilla and I agreed we could stand sleeping together once or twice, long enough to plant the seed, then get out. But Dad was a diehard traditionalist. Camilla and I were born with gifts; therefore, we'd be the ones to raise our gifted Yeti just like he and Mom had raised me.

Circle of life and all that bullshit.

I just wanted to get out of there and back to the Holidays Inn.

"That's me you're trying to play footsie with, Milla. Nadia's a little to the left," I whispered to her across the table. Her eyes widened, but sure enough, she twisted in her chair and the next thing I knew, Nadia was doing a spit take with her wine. Bullseye, Camilla.

Mom directed Dad where to lay the next in the never-ending platters of food she'd prepared for our very civilized intervention. "Thanks, Dear. Listen, Yeager, hear your father out. We're not sentencing you and Camilla to a life shackled together. You both can take other lovers as you need. You've grown up in a house full of love. Why would you not want that for your own child?"

"I don't have a child, Mother. That's the point. You're asking me to plan my future with hypothetical people yet unknown. What if I find a partner who doesn't want to share in this lifestyle, then what? Rule them out completely no matter how I feel about them?"

She tutted, taking her seat next to Dad, and then grabbing his hand. "I don't see why you'd want someone like that, but I'm sure it could be worked out. Right, Camilla? You don't mind him having other lovers, do you? You could have other men too." Ha. She was clueless about Camilla and Nadia.

Camilla looked dumbstruck. Possibly because she hadn't been paying attention at all. She was too busy trying to give my sister a clandestine orgasm under the table. "I don't know. I guess?"

My sister, seeing her girlfriend in distress, piped up. "I don't know why this has to be decided today anyway. They're young for Yeti. It'll be centuries before Camilla's too old to bear children. Can't we table this for now?"

I raised my glass. She was my favorite sister out of the four I had. "I'll drink to that."

We clinked glasses and my father glowered. "Come walk with me, son."

Oh, my soul. We were taking this away from the table. That meant it was ultimatum time once again. It was a cycle with my Dad. Not only was he traditional, but he was also predictable.

Once we were out of the house, pacing toward the ice caves at the back of our property, he started in on all the things he would give me if I would just marry and knock up Camilla. That list included wealth untold, everlasting fame in the Yeti community, happiness beyond measure, and anything else I wanted.

The trouble was, I didn't know what I wanted.

I just knew what I didn't want: Camilla and being chained to a child who'd also have a life in chains.

How could I do that to him or her?

Still, as I looked into my father's earnest eyes, I got why he was this way. The Yeti gifts dying out was just as unthinkable to me. How many had I alone saved? Thousands, if not more. Camilla too. We did have a responsibility to the species, as much as it was a burden.

I should've cured Crystal of her flu, but I'd been too afraid my family would find out I'd used my gifts on a human. Then again, I'd gone right ahead and used them on Vixen an hour later. I guess she was the line I didn't realize I had.

By the time I managed to extricate myself from my family's well-intentioned interference, it was well beyond midnight. I'd missed the voting in the first game. And I'd missed Vixen even more. Absurd as it was. I'd only known her for a day. Yet, there was something about her.

I crept as quietly as I could into our cabin. She was curled up in bed, asleep already. The fire had died down, so I took a little time to stoke it before I shucked out of my clothes, leaving on my boxers, and crawled in beside her, intent on waking her up and driving inside her to chase my family demons out of my mind.

When she stirred awake at my movement, she looked up with sleepy eyes. "Oh, there you are. Is everything okay with your family? We missed you. I think we won the first game." She reached out, trailing a finger over my chest as she spoke in that groggy sleep voice. I don't even know if she was aware of it. It was like she just had to touch me.

And I had to touch her. So, I brushed the back of my hand against her soft cheek. "Yes, everything's okay at home. Go back to sleep now, Bunny."

I had no idea where that thought had come from. I didn't want to sleep. I wanted to be inside her. My cock was already up and raring to go, but I'd missed the chance because she'd closed her eyes and cuddled against my chest and was back asleep within seconds.

Maybe my father had gotten in my head about my responsibilities. Way to go Dad, cock-blocking me from miles away.

Whatever had made me pass on primo sex with a goddess, I tucked it inside myself and pulled her closer, reveling in the warmth of her skin and the soft curves of her body. I was asleep within moments, my family long forgotten.

~~~~~~~~~~~~~~~~~~~~~~~~~~~~~~~~~~~~

I left her sleeping the next day. Not that I wanted to, but I knew Holly would be up cooking breakfast and asking for this or that from me. I loved the work Holly gave me. It was a great physical distraction if nothing else. I couldn't think
~~~~~~~~~~~~~~~~~~~~~~~~~~~~~~~~~~~~

of another place on the planet where I was more at home. Other than my flurry, which was questionable at the time, as much as I hated to admit it. Holly was like another parent to me. To everyone.

She was draped in tinsel when she came out of the kitchen carrying scrambled eggs and toast for the group. My stomach rumbled; my mom's Yeti feast went mostly uneaten the night before.

Hart popped in from wherever the hell he'd been. His knuckles were split, and blood was dripping from a gash on his mouth. He had a wild look in his eyes that said not to fuck with him.

So, of course, I fucked with him. "What happened to you? Another candy cane extruder emergency? Oh, my soul, did the red and white sugar combine to make pink? How did you cope?"

He wiped the blood from his mouth. "Yeager, Meister! Glad you could join us today."

I rolled my eyes. "Never heard that one before. Seriously, why are you bleeding all over Holly's floor?" At that, Holly came over with a towel and started wiping up his blood, muttering something about the vampires.

Hart shook his head. "Damn polar bear got the jump on me. I handled it."

I was as immediately surprised as I was offended. "You wrestled a polar bear without me? Rude. Call me next time, asshole. I love a good arctic throwdown."

Cherish had been taking our conversation in with wide eyes. She set her phone down on the table, then shuffled up to Hart. "Is that true? You wrestled a polar bear?"

"No cap. There's a celebration of non-shifter polar bears not far out from here. We need to be on our toes when we go out, especially after dark, for real, for real."

Cherish nodded. "Bet."

It would've been easier for me to understand the vampires speaking Transylvanian. But it appeared he got the warning across to the youngster. She stood there googly-eyed as the rest of our group filed in for breakfast.

Jack had foregone his suit for a turtleneck and dark jeans with a swoop of orange scarf around his neck. He looked at once different, but the same. Still formal and restrained, but somehow put together with casual aloofness. And his eyes were shifting all around the room, searching for Vixen. His body was tense and rigid until she stepped into the lodge.

She hung her coat up on the hook, then swung around, her hair flipping over her shoulder. She was wearing a deep blue sweater cardigan with a white thermal under it. That thermal was very acquainted with her perfect tits. The second Jack clocked it, an infinitesimal grin crawled across his face.

He would have to do better than that if he wanted her attention.

I took it upon myself to show him.

I ran over and picked her up, throwing her over my shoulder like Santa did his sack. She yelped as I swirled her around and deposited her into the plush chair next to the fireplace. Once her ass was in it, I tipped it back until she was horizontal. She looked up at me flushed and blinking. "What are you doing?"

"Is this not how you say good morning at the North Pole?" I leaned down and licked her neck, all the way up to her ear. Her immediate response was to groan at the feel and clutch my shirt by the collar.

The chair tipped forward, backing me up. On the other side was Hart. "No, we generally say good morning with our words, not our tongues. Although, I could get behind how you think." He leaned in himself, but she swatted us both away, jumping up from the chair and strolling to take Jack's arm as he escorted her into the dining room.

Both Hart and I watched them go. "We're playing with fire, aren't we?" he sighed.

"Possibly."

"Well, let the games begin, then." He stuck out his hand and I took it. It seemed more like a moment of camaraderie than a challenge. I couldn't get a good read on him like I had Jack Frost. He was certainly up to no good when it came to Vixen. Who was I to blame him? There was something about him that made me feel okay with the strange way things were playing out. He didn't feel like competition, he felt like an ally.

After breakfast was all cleared up, Holly got another card from Santa. "Your second game entails a fun Christmas tradition: putting up the Christmas tree. We're taking it outside this time.

"Each team will choose the perfect tree from the forest behind the cabins. You'll bring it back here to the garden area behind the lodge to set them up. Santa will send us stands." She paused to fan herself. "Isn't he just awesome? Anyway, use whatever you wish to decorate your trees, as long as the owner of the items is okay with it. You're welcome to use whatever is in the shed out near the garden, though there aren't many Christmas things in there.

"This evening's votes should be cast on theme and execution of concept. Good luck."

That was the best news I'd heard since Vixen said yes. Trees were my fucking specialty. I was going to kill this challenge.

# CHAPTER 16

Yeager had refused upward of fifteen trees since we'd set out on our trek to find the perfect one. "What's wrong with this one again?" Hart called to him from yards away, shaking the tree while he spoke. "Too green or too symmetrical?"

Jack snickered. "Stand down. I don't think he's going to be happy unless we let him choose the tree."

I didn't even understand how there were trees at the South Pole to start with, but Yeager made a big point about how magic overrode the permafrost and what would've been a distinct lack of animal life. But thanks to Santa, we had trees and polar bears. Vicious ones that elves enjoyed taking down, I'd heard. Knowing Santa, I would bet my life penguins were running around somewhere too.

"Exactly, Iceman, I'll let you handle it if we need to make snow. For this challenge, we need a lumberjack. I'm looking for the perfect cedar. It needs to..." He trailed ahead shouting things about trees that none of us understood, snow whipping around him as he swished through another clearing in search of the holy grail of trees.

I decided to pick Jack's brain while he was occupied, and Hart was off doing whatever he was doing. Didn't want to know. "What should our theme be? I'm all for using what's left of the polar bear Hart slayed earlier to symbolize Rudy's guts."

Jack's eyebrow went up. "That seems violent."

It was. And as soon as it came out of my mouth, I regretted saying it. First shit, then guts. My mind wasn't very Christmasy at all. I guess that's why I was there. "I know. I'm sorry. It's just…"

I wasn't sure how to express it to him, much less to myself. It had been a constant struggle for months. One I should've been able to control. "Do you ever have a moment where everything's normal in your existence, then bam, you're hit with something so overwhelming, it nearly knocks you out?"

He nodded but stayed mum, allowing me to continue. "That's how it is when I think about what happened with Rudy. I can be fine, just enjoying the company I'm in, living my life, then out of nowhere, something he did or said pops into my head, and I'm lost in memories, and I can't get find my way through them, no matter how hard I want to."

"You were with him for a while. It's natural for things to haunt you sometimes. It doesn't mean you're not moving on. It means you're processing what happened to you."

"Well, I'm tired of processing."

"I can understand that." He gripped my gloved hand with his bare one. It was still weird to see him out there with no coat or hat. Though he looked handsome in his turtleneck,

I wasn't going to be mad about it. There was something so magnetic about Jack. With his flinty attention focused on me, I was charged and serene at the same time, like the snow at our feet.

"I've found it!" Yeager shouted. "Come check it out."

To his credit, the cedar tree truly was a sight. It wasn't too big or small and was perfectly symmetrical. We gathered around it, gazing up and admiring it. "It's beautiful, Yeager. Well done."

He gave me a lopsided grin that melted me a little. "You're beautiful. I'll start chopping while you handle the decorating. After, we can troll the competition."

"Now that's a promising idea. Maybe we can sabotage a little." Hart declared as he joined us. He was always up for chaos, that guy. "What's our theme?"

Everyone turned to me, but I was hesitant to throw out the idea about the polar bear guts. Thankfully I didn't have to. Jack came in with the clutch idea. "What if we went with the theme of Christmas memories? For example, in my kingdom it's customary to hang ribbons from the prior year's gifts, showing a continual cycle of love among friends and family. I could grab some from my palace easily."

Even though I was drowning in memories of a douchebag reindeer, I liked the sound of Jack's traditions. Maybe hanging ribbons with him and the others would relieve some of the building pressure in my chest. "That sounds nice, but what about the rest of us? We should all take part."

Hart cocked his head. "Okay. Obviously, in my family, we do candy canes. I can pop away and get as many as you like."

Jack grabbed his arm to stop him from disappearing. "The decorations have to mean something. You can just throw your candy canes on the tree and call it a day."

"That's not what I'm doing Jackie. In my family, for every candy cane we place, we have to say something nice about someone. It sucked growing up having to be nice to my baby sister, but now I mean the things I say each year. Mostly anyway. We could do that for our tree. If you're not too chicken to share the feelings you keep so tightly bottled up in your designer suits." He leered at Jack. It was a taunt, a dare to make Jack say something he might not normally.

It didn't work. Jack gave a single nod, then Hart popped away to get the candy canes. As he did so, Jack strolled away, citing the need to be alone to get to his Kingdom. He didn't leave us much choice in it, so we left him to it. "What about you, Yeager? Any family memories or traditions?"

He ran his hand through his hair. It was the first time I'd seen him act uncomfortable in any way. Something had happened the day before with his family. While he hadn't shared what, I could tell he was concerned. What troubled me about it was that I'd picked that up so quickly and I didn't much like the feeling of him hurting. "I'm sorry. If you don't want to talk about it, you don't have to. I'm sure we'll have enough ribbons and candy canes without adding more items."

"No worries, Bunny. It's all good." He moved away from what I was already calling our tree and headed back into the denser forest. "Be back in a second."

When he'd gone, I was left to think about the memories that still haunted me.

Sure, I'd had a lovely home with parents who'd loved me before they passed. Reindeer shifters lived a long time, but not forever. We'd had great Christmas trees growing up and I was loved, but those memories were overshadowed by my recent past. The one where Rudy and I sipped champagne and hung plaid balls on the tree we picked out together. He'd made them all from scratch and each one had a unique design, meant to show all the different things he loved about me.

It was such a sweet gesture.

At the time.

All I had now was the tattered remains of those plaid balls because I'd shifted in a rage once and destroyed them with my hooves, wanting and needing to erase all existence of him out of my life.

It's not like I could put them on this tree.

Yeager appeared just as I was wiping the tears from my eyes. He didn't say anything. Instead, he handed me several sprigs of berries. "In my family, we only use natural things that can be consumed by animals or repurposed in some way."

"I think my heart needs to be repurposed."

I hadn't meant to say it out loud. And I instantly regretted it. The painful look in his sparkling green eyes got me. It was like he was reaching inside me and feeling my hurt right along with me. "No, Bunny. Your heart is perfect. Reginald is the one who's lacking." He leaned down to kiss me, and I welcomed it, allowed myself to get swept away in the feel of his soft lips against mine. I permitted myself to rest, just for a second, in his strong arms as he lifted me off the ground and kissed me like he wanted to erase any remains of Rudy from my life.

As much as I enjoyed how his tongue twirled around mine and the masculine groans that sprang from his chest as we got carried away, deep down somewhere I knew it was just a band-aid for the hurt Rudy had inflicted. At some point, I would have to heal myself from all the pain.

"Ahem, I don't recall giving you two permission to start without me."

I pulled away from Yeager, biting my lower lip because, dang the blood flow was strong. Reluctantly, I turned to find Hart standing behind me with a basket full of candy canes, smirking.

Yeager adjusted his fly as he chuckled. "It's adorable you think I need your permission to do anything. Here." He picked up most of the berry sprigs he'd brought out—somehow, they'd landed on the ground—and threw them into Hart's basket. "You can carry the fluff. I'll get the tree."

It took only a few minutes for Yeager to slip out of his coat and use his ax to chop down the tree. Watching his muscles bulge as he whacked at the trunk sent a tremor through my girlie bits. When he unhooked his suspenders and they fell in such a way that made a big X on his ass, it took everything in me not to shout *x marks the spot.*"

He was a force of nature with that ax. Even Hart stood watching in awe as he fell the tree and used ropes from his bag to tie it up. As soon as everything looked secure enough to suit him, he turned back with a smirk. "This'll be easier if I shift to haul the tree. Do you mind carrying my clothes for me?"

I nodded, but it wasn't like he was waiting for my answer. He simply peeled out of his plaid shirt and thermal, dropped his jeans, and shucked out of his boots. His body was a work of art. Really. Muscular and solid, like a hot wall carved out of deliciously tanned granite. And the tattoos curving over his shoulders and back only served to accent his ropey muscles and hardness even further. Sure, I'd noticed him that first night, but out here in the illuminating light of day with snow glistening around him against the backdrop of a light blue sky, he was magnificent.

Hart muttered, "Show off," under his breath.

Yeager winked at me as his skin began to slick with sweat. It was brief, but once he was glowing with it, white fur rippled along his body, and he changed before my eyes. It didn't appear to be painful, though I'd ask him about that later because he grew as the change overtook him. He was tall in his human form, probably around six-four, but he had to be seven feet as a Yeti.

His eyes stayed the same pure green color and I swear on my soul he winked at me again before he bent over and took hold of the ropes around the tree. We'd walked nearly a mile away from the cabins to find this perfect tree, but as we pulled it into the garden area, Yeti Yeager looked completely nonplussed about it.

Cherish, however, was gaping up at him with the roundest eyes. "And I oop." Her head swirled around just as Jack was strolling into the garden with his trunk of ribbons. After checking Hart next to me, she nearly fainted from shock. "Is that Yeager in beast mode?"

Hart leaned down. "Bet."

She uttered one word, then went back to decorating her tree with her team. "Goals."

Yeager had the decency to grab his clothes in his massive paws and walk away to change. He strolled back into the garden as Jack and I had begun stringing the ribbons. He took a few himself and reached up to the top of the tree to lay them on, hip-checking me as he did. "So, what did you think? Was I scary?" He bit at the air around me and it made me laugh.

"Not really, no. Though I hated not seeing your tattoos, if I'm honest."

"You can see them all tonight if you want. I'll put on a show for you."

I didn't mind the sound of that, but Hart and Jack had both stopped decorating to stare directly at us. Deflecting, I pushed his massive chest away. "Let's just get these decorations on first. It's looking like the vampires are in this to win this."

# CHAPTER 17

A few hours later, dusk had settled over the garden. All of the teams were gathered with hot apple cider and waiting for the tree reveals. The atmosphere was cozy and festive, though my heart was racing with dread. This is why Santa wanted me here: to experience all these warm cushy feelings so they'd spread within me and spark that Christmas cheer.

To use a word: humbug.

How could I feel festive when I was so broken inside?

Holly jingled her bells to get our attention. "Each team will need to explain their concept to the others. Once we're all finished, we'll head inside to cast our votes. Vixen, why don't you start us off for Team RAR."

Shit.

I glanced at my team, silently begging them for support, but Holly had put the spotlight on me. And yeah, I knew she was probably emailing Santa an hourly report on the condition of my Christmas spirit. So, I plastered a big ole smile on my face, took a long sip of cider, then stood up. "Um, our theme is Christmas memories. Each of the decorations here represents memories to one of us. The ribbons are Jack's. In his kingdom, they save their ribbons each year to show an ever-evolving circle of family and friends. Like tying everyone together."

He'd said it better when he explained it to me, but I did the best I could. And the ribbons he brought to use? They weren't of the chain superstore variety. They were silk and velvet, covered in glitter and lace and decadent details. I'd expect nothing less from Jack.

"The berries are Yeager's tradition. In Yeti culture, they use natural items that can be used by the animals or re-made into other things. It's a wonderful way to enhance the tradition of the Christmas tree in the first place, I guess. And cool that they like to recycle."

Also, better when Yeager had said it, but he was grinning at me like he was proud, so I assumed I did well enough. I was starting to sweat though. I could feel every eye on me, and I just knew they could see right through my thin veil. I was not faking it until I was making it. It was lying, pure and simple. Christmas, yay!

Hart jumped up from the stump he'd been sitting on. Never before had I been so grateful. "The candy canes are my thing. In my family, when we put a candy cane on, we have to say something nice about someone. We've already done that as a team, so I'll pass these canes out to you so you can all participate with us."

He handed one to Isaac who hung his candy cane on a branch. Cherish sat up in her seat, warning him with a death glare that he should not say anything about her. He —wisely, I think—chose someone else. "Mandy, I think you have a pretty laugh." Cherish used the blanket on her lap to bury her face. Mandy, in turn, smiled and thanked Isaac with a bewildered face.

As the others started sharing, I tuned out. I couldn't imagine a worse way to spend the next few minutes. I was seconds away from jumping off my stump and running back into my cabin, but a cool voice whispered in my ear. "You've got this. Focus on me."

I looked down as Jack removed my pink mitten and took my hand. As he threaded his fingers through mine, the chilly feel of his skin had the most calming effect on me. When he gave me that quarter-smile, my unease dissipated. "Thank you," I told him. He didn't respond, but he didn't have to. The way he squeezed my hand told me all I needed to know. He was there for me.

Holly, though I didn't blame her completely, drew me back into the fray when she innocently asked, "Which part of your tree is yours, Vixen?"

It had been Yeager's brainstorm. At the time, I'd been fine with it, but that was before I had to talk about it in front of everyone. I'd be better prepped for the next game, for sure, but I had to dive in and deal with it right then. I stood up and wiped my hands on my jeans. "The plaid star at the top of the tree is made from something that used to belong to someone else. That asshole—sorry, Cherish, person—is out of my life now and that's a good thing. So, I took what hurt me and remade it into something else, something, I don't know, nicer maybe. So, yeah, no more bad memories."

I went to sit back down but was immediately engulfed by huge biceps and the swooniest cedar scent. I landed in Yeager's lap, and he wrapped his protective arms around me as if to keep the hurt from getting back in. I gripped those biceps like they were my tether to reality.

"Well, isn't that something? Thanks for sharing, Vixen. Your tree is lovely." I was dying an agonizing death and Holly was moving the contest along like a good host." Now I'm very curious about the Frostbite team's entry."

With everyone refocused, I relaxed a little. Yeager ran his nose along my neck before nipping at my ear with his teeth. "I'm thinking I'll tie that plaid bow on my cock for you tonight. Make sure you think of nothing but me when you look at it."

I snorted. It was ridiculous.

And...intriguing.

To him too, if the bulge in his pants was an indicator.

I couldn't. I *shouldn't*.

But.

The vampires took their places in front of their tree. It was completely covered in a huge black trash bag. No decorations, no color, just a big slick black surface covering the greenery. Dracula stuck a stick into the fire, as Lestat gave their explanation. "This bag represents the oppression our kind has been under for centuries. Vampires are overlooked and undervalued in every arena in our country. This is why we wish for Transylvania to declare independence. Once we have it, there will be no stopping us."

Hart leaned in from behind, whispering between Yeager and me. "Stopping them from what, world domination? Eating kittens for breakfast? Vampire blood orgies? I'm so fucking curious."

Dracula used his magic and rose from the ground, carrying the stick he'd lit in the fire and placing it at the top of their tree. A second later, streams of light and sparkles shot out like fireworks. Everyone gasped.

At the base of the tree, Edward shrugged. "I'm a chemist."

Speechless, we all clapped. I mean, what could you say to that display?

As Jack used his magic to dump snow on one of the wayward sparks that had gotten way too close to Hot Chocolate with Marshmallows' tree, Holly cleared her throat. "Okay then, HCWM, you're up next."

Aaron stood up to talk about their tree, steadying himself on his feet, but his wife subtly pushed him back down in the chair. Probably concerned about his penchant for oversharing. Isaac gave their presentation instead. "As you see, we decorated our tree with paper products. The theme is things we no longer need. The brightly colored pieces were made from bridal magazines Erin can trash because she's happily married now. The larger white pages are from Cherish's AP history book from a class she swears she can do with her eyes closed, though I'm unsure about that. The small white ones are from a book. By the way, Vixen, I've already expressed ordered you a new copy."

"You used my smexy werewolf book?" I wasn't mad, per se, just surprised Isaac had let her. Though it was likely it was a stealth operation on her part.

Cherish cocked her head. "That thing was trash. I don't care if you like smut, just make it realistic if you're going to read about werewolves."

I had to laugh. And something told me she probably had a list of realistic wolf fiction for me to look over.

Isaac continued. "The star at the top was made from a copy of my marriage certificate. Obviously, I no longer need that."

This time his 'fucking Bruce' was a little more audible. Cherish's eyes lit up. "Language, Dad."

"Yeah. Sorry, honey." Cherish rolled her eyes and from the look on her face, I knew she was going to use that against him in the future.

With that out of the way, John Sun poured out of his chair and made a grand bow in front of team Ho, Ho, Ho, Hot's tree. It was decorated with oranges and lemons with beach towels strung as garland. On top was a glistening model of a sun that I was sure John had gathered from his kingdom. "Our theme was Summer. The best of the seasons and the kingdoms, no offense to my counterpart. His numbers are dwindling, you know, which is kind of eek, but I'm sure your Kingdom will bounce back after our meeting, right Jack?"

Jack didn't comment or respond outwardly other than to straighten his spine and cross one leg over the other. "Anyway," John went on, "because Summer is a time for relaxation and celebration, we have daiquiris for all. Even a virgin one for you, little lady." He winked at Cherish, who bristled in response, then he spread his arms wide. Mindy, Mandy, and Monday appeared carrying glasses and wearing bikinis and shades like it was ninety degrees, not twenty-nine.

Hart slung one arm around Jack and one around Yeager. "We're not voting for that asshole, right?"

# CHAPTER 18

After more speculation from Jack Frost than an Elf should have to endure in a lifetime, we ended up throwing a cane in the Hot Chocolate with Marshmallows stocking. Vixen made the point that her book had contributed to their tree, so we went with that. My money was on the vamps, but I could be a team player when necessary.

Sometimes.

I didn't know how Jack dealt with that sun moron all the time. I knew a bit about the Fae monarchy dynamics, given my network of underground Elf spies that fed me intel at the Pole, but I'd had no idea John Sun was such an overt fuckwad. I'd need to keep my eyes on him.

When I wasn't keeping them on Vixen.

She was standing in front of me in Holly's massive kitchen, wearing flannel pajama pants and an oversized white shirt that might have belonged to the Yeti. Though I didn't give two shits if they shared clothing. Probably would've given good money to see the massive beast strutting around in her pink thong.

Assuming she had one.

Yeah, she *had* to have one. Hot pink was her favorite color.

All I knew for sure though, was she looked edible, and I was going to use my time wisely so I could have a nibble.

Case in point, I had her stirring a bowl of gingerbread dough as I pulled a batch from the oven and set it on the rack to cool. Santa had sent the supplies and recipes for the next day's contest, and I'd convinced Holly she needed to put up her feet and relax, so I got the kitchen and all the privacy I needed with Vixen.

All I had to do was make a few batches of gingerbread for the next game. With the Yeti fixing some dangling shingle somewhere and Jack Frost holed up in his cabin sulking about John Sun's taunting, I could get behind the idea of gingerbreading with Vixen.

She paused to stick her finger in the dough and take a lick. My cock had an opinion on the sight of her tongue glossing over her lips. The opinion was yes. "Taste good?"

She nodded. "Delish." After a few minutes of silence, she spoke again. "Can I ask you something?"

"Sure. But we need the dough pliable. Maybe a little more stirring?" So, I could watch her tits bobbing under the thin white shirt, not because I wanted the gingerbread houses to turn out well. They could fall during the game, and I would've been cool with it.

"Got it." She paused, doubting herself before she even got to her query. I nodded for her to go on. There was something on her mind and it had nothing to do with decorating Christmas trees or making gingerbread.

I hated to see that cloud hanging over her like that. She was made for light and happiness. Rudy the ass-nosed reindeer had stolen those things from her and anyone with eyes could see she was struggling to get them back. To get herself back.

"You knew him well once. Was I...I don't know... stupid to date him in the first place? I just thought...I mean, everyone has exes, right? He'd broken it off with her when we got together. I thought I was doing the right thing, but now that I'm on the other side of it, I feel like shit. I should've never said yes to him. Look what he did with my heart and it's all my fault. I did this to myself."

I pulled Holly's stocking oven mitts off so I could take her face in my hands. She was flushed from the heavy stirring and heat of the oven beside her. "You did what everyone does when they enter a relationship, you took a chance. That's the point of dating, to find out if you're compatible. Don't you dare give him the power to hurt you anymore. To cause you to question yourself. *He's* the one who blew it. The next guy you date might be the quote, unquote one. Or the guy after that. You don't know. None of us do. But in the end, if choose to hole up without taking any more chances, that's the real tragedy of this situation."

Dropping her beautiful face, I raised my shirt, revealing the tattoo I had on my ribcage. My father's last words. Creepy AF to have them on my chest, I knew, but it was a reminder of both him and what he wanted for me. What I wanted for myself.

Vixen put down the bowl long enough to trace over the words on my ribs as she read them aloud. "The greatest risk in life is not taking one at all."

The feel of her fingertips alone gave me goosebumps. And I wanted way more than the tips of her fingers on my body. So, I grabbed her hand and trailed it over my pecs, down the ridges of my abs as she watched the slow progression I made across my body with desire.

I had to drop her hand to remove my shirt so she could see my other tat. Her breath hitched.

You better fucking believe she reacted.

I was the North Pole's sexiest Elf, after all.

I earn that damned title every year. Not that I ever, *ever*, wanted it, but I used it to my advantage at times. Like this one, with her heaving chest and pink lips parting like she wanted—needed— to taste me.

I was vibrating with the need to lay myself out and let her do it.

I had to go slowly though. Rudy had robbed her of her spirit too and I couldn't go in too hard or fast without spooking her. Though the way she was staring at my chest, my rippled stomach, that deep v that I knew drove women wild, I got the overwhelming thought that maybe slow wasn't the right way to play it.

I turned so she could get a good look. The quote between my shoulder blades was my mother's. I had the words memorized. "With perseverance and a strong heart, anything is possible."

Vixen pressed her other hand against my back while she mindlessly stroked my ribs with the one she'd kept on me. It would've tickled if I hadn't been so turned on. "I could learn a thing or two about taking risks and making my heart strong."

I turned back around, and her eyes flicked to mine. Something sparked between us, like the flick of fire when I lit the gas stove earlier.

Not something. Lust. Pure, rabid, aching passion. She was milliseconds away from taking her hands off me. I could sense her brain working through the two different scenarios. Back away or bring her hands down to the bulge that had formed against my zipper the second she touched me. The one she was eyeing like it was a juicy steak and she was starving.

What she wanted—me—and what she thought she deserved—nothing—were warring in her mind. For me, it was a thrilling fucking precipice to be on.

But what she'd probably label as *better judgment* won out in the end.

She drew her hands away, grabbing the bowl to dump the contents into the cooking pan we'd prepped earlier.

So close.

But I was not one to give up. Not with a quote about perseverance tattooed on my back.

I let her work in silence, getting a clean metal bowl and then throwing more ingredients in like we'd been doing. I had no damn clue how many batches of gingerbread we needed to make for the game, but I was content to hang out in the kitchen with her all night.

Sure, some of my thoughts on her were primal and yes, I was checking her pert ass as she worked at the sink, but not everything I felt for her was sexual. She was fun and smart and just easy to be around. At least she was before Rudy wrecked her life. She needed to believe those things about hersElf again.

"I have another tattoo you didn't see."

She swung around, clutching the bowl as she stirred. "I know. I didn't think it was wise to explore that one. What does it say?"

Interesting. If she knew the location of my third tattoo, then she would've had to have watched the Sexiest Elf competition at least once. It was my largest tat, and it was always out there on display when I was forced to strut my ass across the stage and sling around that damn candy cane pole. "I'll tell you after you tell me how many times you voted for me to win."

She shook her head. "What? No. I don't vote in that contest."

"Really?" The rosy blush of her cheeks was insanely sexy. I took a certain candy cane from my pocket. One with a tiny green ribbon laced among the red and white. Taking a lick first, I ran it over her lips. I didn't even need her to taste it to get what I wanted out of the exchange: the truth. This magic cane would get it for me. "You didn't throw me one single vote? Are you telling me you're a Buck Marigold gal? I'm shocked and offended." I wasn't either of those things. I hoped and prayed and begged for anyone else to win that stupid medal each year. Even hum.

"Buck? He's not even close to your league. Your belly button lint is sexier than he is. I just think the whole contest is dumb."

Odd compliment, but I'd take that and file it away. Probably jerkoff to it later. "You can say that again. I fucking hate it, but I know you voted for me." I lowered my gaze, looking through my lashes. I'd been told they were sexy, but I failed to see how eyelashes equated to sex. Just using my arsenal.

She used the spatula to fold the gingerbread in the bowl, looking down as she did so. Avoiding eye contact. Gotcha. She pursed her lips. So sexy. "The votes are anonymous. At least according to the hosts on NickTock. You'll just have to take my word on it. I didn't vote for you, but I'm glad you always win anyway."

Satisfied I had the truthful answer—yes, she voted and more than once— shrugged. "The tattoo on my thigh are lyrics to a song my baby sister wrote. *One is for getting to know me, two is for showing you who I am; Three is growing our winter tree, don't let four leave me out in the snow.*"

Thank fuck she'd picked up the metal bowl because she dropped it as she squealed. And I mean, squealed. "Brandy Bliss is your sister? Are you kidding me? Brandyyyy! Bliss!"

Yep. My sister was more famous than I was.

"Bliss Brandywine is my sister. Brandy Bliss is some bullshit stage name she came up with. I guess it keeps her real or some nonsense. She's just my bratty little kid sister to me, even now that she's got billions of dollars and all the fame she could ever want."

"She's a beautiful goddess with the voice of an angel." She declared and strolled over to me, her eyes squinting as she took my face in her hands and examined it. "You look nothing alike."

"Um, thanks for that, but we aren't biological siblings. She was adopted by my parents when she wasn't even a year old. My mom's best friend was her mother and when her parents died in a ski accident, she didn't even hesitate to step in. I know it will sound silly, but I fell in brotherly love with that girl the day my mom brought her home. I'm telling you, *in love.* I used to bounce her on this very leg to make her laugh." I slapped my thigh. "It's why I chose that spot for the lyrics."

I couldn't help but notice that Vixen had pressed closer to me, her leg brushing between mine. I shifted, pulling her closer so that she was basically riding the thigh we'd been discussing. I knew then it was Yeager's shirt. I could smell the warm cedar scent on it. "You know, most people think it's a sad song about love going wrong, but it's really about our relationship growing up together as close siblings.

"I had a habit of locking her outside when she annoyed me, but before you yell at me, it was never more than a few minutes and I told you, I love her more than anything. And she's obviously fine because the entire North Pole loves her and her first big hit. The rest is, blah, blah, history."

She went over the lyrics in her mind, and her face lit up when she realized they could mean more than one thing.

It was getting very warm in that kitchen. And it wasn't because of the massive ovens. I traced my finger along her jaw because I was compelled to do so. It reminded me a little bit of how I was just dumbstruck with love for my infant sister that day. So sudden. So unexpected. "It's funny how looking at things from a different angle can change your whole worldview, huh?"

"Yeah." She was close, our breaths mingled together with the scent of gingerbread. I was certain she was going to go in for the kiss, but I was wrong. Instead, she picked up the gingerbread-laden spatula and flicked a mound of dough at me. It hit my face, then slid down to the V-neck of my t-shirt.

I gaped at her, and she smirked. My cock practically stood up and waved. "That's for locking the most divine woman ever created outside in the snow."

I gripped her wrist, stopping her from throwing more dough and forcing the spatula out of her hand. It landed somewhere close to the sink. I think. Didn't care where. I was a breath away from throwing her on the table in the middle of the gingerbread trays, when she did the unexpected: she leaned down and licked the gingerbread off my chest, groaning as her tongue played along my skin.

# CHAPTER 19

I didn't stop to think. I mean, why would I have started using common sense at this stage of my life? I was so surprised by the essence of Hart, I threw myself into him headfirst. Or rather, lady bits first. Because there was something so rock-solid about him, the way he loved his family. And how he just owned who he was with zero apology.

There was a lot more to him than his sex appeal.

Though his sex appeal was next level.

And I was content to leave the part of my brain that was telling me the way to happiness—the way to get over Rudy—would be to either have no contact with another male again or to have a safe monogamous relationship with a boring, predictable guy.

Hart was neither.

He was danger and chaos and unfettered abandon rolled into one heart-pounding package and the part of me that had died was aching to live in that world, if only for a moment. I wanted to feel alive. I wanted to feel his kind of alive.

His stormy blue eyes took me in with curiosity when I ran my tongue over my lower lip, taking care of the remaining dough in one lick, while I stared—unabashedly—at his arousal. His voice purred. "So Ginger, is this what we're doing now?"

I put down the bowl I was still clutching. It seemed like I was breaking down a barrier between us. One I'd built to protect myself. Though I didn't need protection from Hart. I was sure that what I was about to do with him was equal parts safe and unguarded. "Yeah, I think so."

He stood up, shirking his tight white t-shirt. Sexy was such an understatement. "I'm one hundred percent in, but first..." He popped out of the kitchen, then fifteen seconds later, popped back again. "...all doors are locked. Not that I'm against voyeurism, but because I'm about to show you how you should've been taken care of by that loser. I want you focused on me, so let's take the Yeti's shirt off for now. It smells like him."

He started unbuttoning the buttons on Yeager's shirt. Why I'd worn it, I didn't know. I'd gotten out of the shower, and he'd gone to fix something for Holly. His shirt was just sitting there on the bed, so I'd put it on. It was like he was lingering there with me, but Hart was looking at me like I was the only woman on the planet like he didn't care about me having another man's shirt on. It was simply an obstacle to my nakedness, not a statement.

It was liberating.

By the time he'd gotten it off me, I was trembling with the need to be touched. He seemed to get that because he ran a single finger between my breasts. I arched when it grazed one nipple, then the other. "I should've told you about Rudy and Clare when I first spied them together. I'm not a man who normally has regrets, but that's my biggest one. Now I'm going to make it up to you by proving just how fucking lacking he was."

The promise of his words settled inside me, and I bit my lip as he took my shoulders and pressed me against the wall. "I want you right here."

I nodded because I truly didn't care where or how. I just *wanted*. Him. This. "The first time I witnessed them together he had her pressed against a dirty wall. Her panties were down around her ankles, and he was railing her with his fingers, grunting like a pig while she yawned."

I didn't want to hear the gory details of Rudy's betrayal, but the smoky sound of his voice, the light touch of his fingertips as he eased my pants down was arousing in a way I couldn't define. He ran a knuckle over my damp panties, barely grazing my core. I gasped and angled toward him. "To be honest, she looked fucking bored out of her skull. She definitely wasn't getting off on it."

He snaked his hand inside my panties, slowly running the backs of his fingers over my throbbing clit, confirming what he already knew. I was soaked. Because of him. "There was no way she was wet for him; not like you are now." He turned his hand in the other direction and without warning, he pushed two fingers inside me, then pulled them back out slowly. I whimpered and shook my head. The feel of the three silver rings he always wore as he buried them inside my wetness had me clutching his wrist and panting in no time. "Nah, Clare was dry as a bone and he was fumbling around down there like he was pushing elevator buttons instead of fingering her like he wanted her to come."

I threw my head back against the wall as he curled his fingers to reach the spot that made me twist and writhe. "Oh, my soul, Hart. That's..."

"Good?" I bit my lip because I couldn't even form a word. "Of course, it's good because I know how to make a woman come." That was no brag. It was true. I could feel it as deeply as I felt the brush of those rings against my skin. "Did you ever get this fucking wet for him?"

Hart took the candy cane sitting on the table next to us and ran it over my collarbone, then circled one of my nipples with it, eyeing them as they pebbled in response. "It's okay to be honest. My ego can take it. Plus, there is no denying how much you're enjoying this."

To prove his point, he grazed my clit with his thumb as he pressed deeper inside me. He took one nipple into his mouth, circling it with his tongue, then sucking it so hard it made a soft pop when he let go. The sound, the sight of his tongue circling the other nipple, the sensations had me reeling and I blurted out the answer he was demanding from me without knowing where it had come from. "Everything with him had something attached to it. Even if it was temporarily good, it was never just about me. So, no. Never this good."

It was as undeniable as the desire pumping through me: Hart was taking nothing from our exchange. This was all for me. Every thrust of his fingers ever stroke on my clit, every lick and kiss and sigh.

I wasn't sure what to do with that notion.

He, however, did.

I groaned as he pressed his greedy mouth against mine. His lips were hot and wet and the way he ran his tongue over the seam before he thrust it inside, sent shivers through me. All the while he kissed me with brazen desire, he was pumping his fingers and circling my throbbing clit. It was an incredible feeling to be pinned against someone like him. To hear his moaning grunts as he drove his fingers in and out, kissing me hard and with so much abandon I had to hang on. I clutched at him, running my hands over his taut skin, tracing his sinewy muscles, and enjoying the way they tightened as he moved.

"Do you want to know something else?" He licked his way over my throat from one side to the other, stopping long enough to nibble on my earlobe with his teeth. I sucked in a breath. "I think she faked her orgasm." I laughed. Because, yeah, I'd done that with Rudy on more than one occasion. Wouldn't need to do that with Hart though. That was for certain.

I was close to the edge, and he knew it. Bathed in it. That smug look on his face only added to the tide coiling inside me. Oh, my soul, I wanted to come undone, but I wanted to live in the moment right before that release too. He growled against my ear, placing a soft kiss on the tender spot behind it before sucking on my earlobe. "I know because one, she sounded like a cat dying, and two, he only used one fucking hand."

His rings clinked together as he drove harder inside me. At the same moment, he moved his other hand over my hip, taking a second to squeeze my ass cheek, then angling inward. He paused, just for a second, and when I didn't protest his obvious movement, he used his middle finger to trace my crack, then grazed lightly over my hole. Not deep, but just enough to brush the nerves inside.

A strange—not unwelcome—sensation rocketed through me, and I hurdled off a cliff of lust. He kept both hands as they were, lightly circling and pushing as he uttered, "That's it, Ginger. Let me feel you come all over my fingers."

The entire kitchen began to blacken and spin out of control, but only for a second. Hart kissed me again, this time, it was leisurely like he was mapping my lips with his. I bucked my hips against him and thrust my hands in his hair, tugging harder than I meant to, but his growled response let me know it was fine with him to hold on in this way as I came undeniably, unshakably, undone.

It took a little time to come down from the high of the orgasm, but after I was completely spent, I managed to lift my head and crack open an eye to look at him. His eyes were hooded and his chest heaving. I expected some sort of smart-ass comment, a brag, or a smirk, but I didn't get that. He knew what he'd done, and he was content to let me ride it out as he watched.

I would've voted a thousand more times for him.

Before he could say or do anything, I made my move, spinning him around and pressing him against the same wall. I kissed him—hard—as I fumbled with the button and fly on his pants. When I finally got them undone and down around his ankles, he took my face in his hands. "I'm good with this, great in fact, but maybe I should warn you about the next bit."

I couldn't fathom why I'd need a warning. I figured he was hung, but from the outline in his red underwear, I didn't think he was larger than Yeager.

Which was *not* the thing to be thinking about as I was descending to my knees to suck the cock of another man.

That was a troubling notion brewing in my mind. I had to block it out.

I shouldn't have been doing this with either of them, but my body wasn't listening to me at that moment.

As my knees grazed the concrete floor, he angled toward me. I would have sworn on Santa's bag that I heard a jingling bell. Dismissing it, I hooked my fingers over the waistband of his shorts, then scraped my nails lightly over his hips as I drew them down. He hissed and wrapped his hand in the length of my hair. Ready. Waiting. Stiff.

He snickered when I got the pants down. His cock sprung free of its red confinement and that's when I knew I shouldn't have dismissed the jingle sound. He tugged on my hair, pulling my gaze away from his hard, jingling—I said jingling—cock. "Surprise."

His tip was pierced.

But it wasn't the piercing that was so shocking. I'd been there and done that a long time ago when I was a wild young thing at the North Pole. Donner. It was the fact that the bar going through his hard penis had two small round Christmas bells on the ends. One on each side of the piercing. And yeah, when he moved, they jingled.

So many questions ran through my head. He must have been able to tell based on my look. "To sum up, yeah it hurt when I got it, not now; the six-week abstinence recovery was brutal; I have a rigorous cleaning routine that I never skip; And most importantly, I've never had one single complaint. Ever. Care to test that statement?"

I opened my mouth to, I don't know, say something, but he took his cock in his hand and tapped it against my lips. I'll be damned if that jingle didn't flutter through me.

There'd be plenty of time for follow-up questions, right?

He sighed as I ran my tongue over his tip, taking care to flick at each jingle. The sound was so amusing, but that flutter of excitement turned into heat real fast. "Mmm, Ginger, you look good on your knees. Like you want to take my whole cock right now."

True, true.

I took his tip into my mouth, sucking and salivating as he pushed in further. The bells scraped my tongue as I opened for him, and we both sucked in a breath. Before long, my head was bobbing and he was lifting his hips, forcing me to take him slowly down the back of my throat.

He tasted delectable and the way he rolled his hips, grinding his pelvis against my face as I took him in made me moan. And when I did, he matched me. Soon, we were lost to the passion churning between us. He liked making comments and each dirty thing he said made me wetter for him. "Yes. Open up wide for me like a good girl."

He placed a hand under my chin, helping me to take more in the back of my throat, then he pulled out of my mouth and I ran my tongue over the length of him a few times as he watched. I couldn't get enough of it. Neither could he, based on his hooded eyes. When I flicked the bells again, he mumbled, "Fuck, I love that sound. Almost as much as I loved hearing you come with my fingers inside you. Do it again. Make them ring."

I nodded as I sucked. The bells were hot. One day I might explore how and why that was, but at the moment, I just liked making them jingle with my tongue. He shuddered when I did. "I'm almost there and damn, I'm going to come so hard for you Ginger."

Something sparked in my head at his words. It was the nickname. I'd been called Ginger a lot in my life, but in his mouth, with that sexy half-tilted smirk and a voice like melted butter, it meant more. So, I gave him more.

I reached behind me and grabbed a dollop of gingerbread, slathering it down the length of him. Then I proceeded to lick and suck until it was all gone. "Fuck me. I'm never going to be able to eat gingerbread without thinking of this now."

"Good."

It would probably make the next day's game a little awkward, but I didn't care. Especially when his hips were starting to rock out of control. He threw his hand behind his head, looking down at me to watch as I bobbed on his pierced cock, reveling in the taste of him, the feel of the bells tickling my tongue. The sight of him, though, his perfect abs and muscled bicep behind his head, the way he trailed his ringed fingers over his chest while he watched me sent a wave of heat hotter than the oven.

And just as the timer went off on the last batch of gingerbread, he moaned his warning. "This gingerbread is about to get some cream." I opened my mouth and took all he had to give, slurping and swallowing as the taste and scent of gingerbread overwhelmed me.

# CHAPTER 20

I woke up to a cold drip of water on my face.

At least I hoped it was water.

With Hart, one never knew what was going to happen. I was laying on the couch in the lodge—the place he'd declared his bedroom, though he could've popped back to the Pole to sleep in his own house—and his arms and legs wrapped around me. He'd convinced me to rest there while he worked on the last batch of gingerbread. I was spent beyond belief, so I took him up on his offer and dozed off a few minutes after I laid down. The couch was comfy. And putting the clues together, I assumed he'd finished the gingerbread, then settled in behind me to sleep.

I never moved. Not that I wanted to. Much anyway. He'd made me feel alive again, but alive was a scary place to be.

After the third drip of water rolled down my face, I cracked open my eyes. Jack and Yeager were both standing there looking down at Hart and me all cuddled up together. A cold sense of dread swept through me. Jack was using his magic to wake me and the look on his face was one of cold satisfaction. Yeager looked equally amused. It was strange to see them together like that.

Yeager put his finger over his mouth and winked. I tried to wriggle from Hart's grip, but Yeager put his hand on my shoulder to keep me from it. The next second, Jack twisted his hand and a snowball formed in it. A snowball that he promptly dropped on Hart's head.

Hart cursed and leaped off the couch with me in one arm. "The fuck?" With his other fist, he reached out to the nearest person whom he assumed was the guilty party—Yeager—punching his angular jaw.

I gasped, because man, it was a solid hit. From the hand where he wore his rings. Yeager's head swung on impact, then he turned back to Hart, a devious smile creeping across his face. And yeah, blood dripping from the corner of his mouth too.

I ducked because I figured there was about to be some sort of brawl. Didn't get far because Hart was not letting me go.

There was no brawl.

Instead, Yeager laughed and wrapped his arm around Hart's neck, pulling him close as he wiped the blood from his lip. "Nice. I can see how you single-handedly took down a polar bear. Pro-tip: Yeti bones are indestructible. And maybe next time hit the guy who actually assaulted you."

He flicked his eyes to Jack, who turned his head slowly to stare down Hart. He gave him that quarter grin that sent a little shiver of pleasure down my spine, especially when he used it as a threat against Hart. "Good morning. I hope you made coffee."

Hart finally released me from his grip and glowered at Jack. "When would I have made coffee? I was a little busy making gingerbread and having my cock sucked. Then I had to get some sleep for today, so sorry, no coffee. You'll have to make your own."

Yeager let out an uproarious laugh. And I knew I was blushing beyond reason. Jack's only reaction was to adjust his pink tie, and then his snowflake cufflinks.

Holly cut the tension in the room when she burst through the kitchen door with the aforementioned coffee. Her sweater was covered in tinsel. So much so that she was leaving a stringy silver trail behind her. "Coffee's ready. Decaf in the green carafe, high-octane in the red." She set the tray on the counter, then turned to Hart. "Oh good, you're up. You can go clean up the tornado you left in my kitchen. I don't know what you got up to in there, but there is gingerbread all over the place."

Hart wiggled his eyebrows at me. "You have no idea where that stuff went, right Ginger?"

There was extra in that nickname now. And he was making sure I remembered it.

Like I could forget sucking his jingle-belled cock?

I beelined straight to the coffee and poured myself a huge cup from the caffeinated pot. Then added the only creamer she brought out. Oh, my soul, it was gingerbread.

There was no more time to consider my embarrassment or the amusement in Yeager's eyes and flinty steel glint in Jack's. The door to the lodge opened up and the rest of the guests sauntered in. Even the vampires. It took them nearly ten minutes to get all the black protective gear off, but as soon as they did, a pop carried across the room and Holly had a brand-new communique from Santa in her hands. She fanned herself before she read it aloud. "Today our teams are going to make gingerbread houses with a twist." She waved her hand in the air with a flourish.

Lost a couple of big clumps of tinsel in the process.

"Teams may use as much or as little of the gingerbread and candies provided as you want. Fresh royal icing will arrive momentarily."

The second after she said it, four elves popped into the room carrying huge plastic tubs of white royal icing. Couldn't help but notice Buck Marigold was one of them. I glanced up at Hart who nodded his head toward Buck with a 'there's your man' look.

Rolled my eyes. He was dirt compared to Hart.

After the elves placed the tubs down and popped away, Holly continued her directions. "You'll have two hours to construct the perfect gingerbread house. Here's the twist..." More tinsel. This time on her shoes. "The house you make must be a replica of one of your team members' houses. Or apartments. Or living quarters. Or...cave? Wherever you call home. We'll cast votes on creativity, representation of home, and use of materials. Good luck!"

Before our team could make any decisions, Hart popped away. He came back with a tray of gingerbread and a tub of candy. The next second, he popped across the room and got one of the tubs of icing, setting it down on the coffee table. "This is our spot to work. Approach and die."

The others smiled like they knew he was joking but kept a wide berth as they claimed work spots anyway.

Hart and Yeager sat on the couch, leaving a spot in the middle for me. Jack, on the other hand, paced back and forth on the other side of the coffee table, his brain already ticking. "My palace is out. The walls are made of glass and ice so that I can see the Winter snowfall from every angle. I don't think we could replicate it with gingerbread, nor do I think you could capture the elegant beauty of the palace."

Hart snickered. "Flexing."

Yeager nodded. "Yeah, but I don't think we want to do my home either. It's carved into the side of a mountain covered in ice. It'd be hard to make the mountain exactly right, even with tons of gingerbread. It's really like a warm, cozy cabin fused into the mountain. The physics of it would be challenging."

It was interesting to hear about where they lived. I knew Yeager had issues with his family, but the way he described his home was full of longing and love for them. Even Jack sounded wistful when he spoke of his. I turned to Hart, and he smirked. "I live in a converted loft above the sleigh garage. I love it, but it's basically a square box of metal with windows as far as the exterior goes. Not pretty enough to use as a model for our gingerbread house." He turned, looking through his long dark lashes. "So, we'll do your condo?"

Shit.

What he meant was, we'll do the condo that still belonged to both me and Rudy. Together.

I'd managed to kick him out and wanted to sell it with the intent of giving him his half and going on my merry way. Maybe moving in with Cupid or getting a cute apartment near the stables like some of the other reindeer lived in.

But I had yet to contact a realtor.

I couldn't seem to let it go. No matter how much I wanted to leave that part of my life behind. It had been mine before

Rudy bought half of it and moved in with me, yet it still felt like ours. I didn't want to recreate it in gingerbread, but it looked like I had no choice. "Okay, fine. My condo's a cute converted Victorian home and would look good in gingerbread, so yeah."

Hart grabbed a knife and started cutting a large piece. "Here, I'll do the shape since I've seen it and you two haven't."

Yeager slung his arm around my shoulder. "Look who's flexing now."

Undeterred, Hart sliced through the gingerbread while I pulled out my phone to show Jack and Yeager pictures. As I was scrolling through my camera roll, I came across a picture of Rudy and me standing in front of the condo. Yeager huffed. "Hm. So that's what Raymond looks like."

He grabbed my phone and angled it so Jack could see. His response was as subtle as I expected. Just the tick of his mouth. "The condo is nice. And you look happy in that picture."

Yeah, because I was happy then.


"Okay, I've got the three sections carved from one piece to make it sturdier. I think we need the licorice to outline the windows. I could make the steps and railing leading up to the door with candy canes."

Jack leaned over, grabbing an orange gum drop out of the bowl and flattening it in his hands. "Let's use these for shingles. It's Vixen's home so it should be colorful like she is."

I didn't feel colorful. I was anxious and annoyed about having to give up my home because of Rudy. Plus, I had another added layer of stress because of having to make one of my biggest problems in gingerbread form in front of the whole group. I mustered myself as best as I could and helped my team finish the gingerbread house. When I thought we were done, Yeager surprised me by grabbing an orange skittle from the bowl. "Which window is your bedroom?"

I pointed to the arched window on the second floor. He dipped the Skittle in the icing and then stuck it on in the window. "There's you." Then he got a green, purple, and red skittle and placed them in the window too. "Green for me, purple for Jack, and Hart is red."

Wait. Was he implying what I thought he was implying?

All the Skittles together at once?

Nah.

Hart high-fived him just as Cherish declared. "This gingerbread is bussin' bussin. I can't keep it out of my mouth."

"Neither could Vixen."

I smacked Hart on the shoulder, and he leaned close. "Don't slap me unless you want it too, Ginger. Next time..."

He left his sentence dangling which was good. There wasn't going to be next time. How dumb would I have been if I allowed that?

"Alrighty. Our time's done. Let's all take a look around and then we'll clear out to cast our votes." Holly had taken some of her missing clumps of tinsel and tied them artfully into the curls piled on her head. That woman was all in for the Christmas thing.

I'd been once too.

Rage Against Rudy ended up voting for the vampires again. Spike, apparently, lived in a motor home which they carved in detail. They even made black licorice wheels and Rolo chocolate headlights. It was much more creative than John Sun's palace, which looked like a huge hut covered in pretzels, or Aaron and Erin's starter home with a picket fence made of white chocolate bars.

"Please tell me we get to eat these eventually." Cherish was eyeing my Victorian condo with interest. It *did* look pretty amazing.

And I couldn't stop staring at the four little Skittles in the window.

Hart picked up on that little detail. "Hm, I wonder which Skittle she likes best. Red, green, or purple, Vixen?"

"Honestly, I don't care much for Skittles. They get stuck in your throat when you eat them."

"You had no problems getting things stuck in your throat last night," he challenged.

Yeager reached around me and smacked him on the back of the head. It ruffled his hair in the deadliest way. Damn him for looking so perfect. And damn Yeager for making it happen. "Don't," he snapped. "You don't want to do that. She won't eat any Skittles; then where would we be?"

Hart nodded. "You're right. I don't want to live in a world where red Skittles are not eaten."

"Then shut the fuck up about it. Be cool."

Yeager to the rescue. I think. I had no idea. They were using candy as a metaphor for sex. And while I enjoyed eating Skittles, I ate them one at a time. I had no idea what to do with three flavors at once.

Hart picked the purple Skittle off the house and plucked it in his mouth. "I don't think purple's your color, Ginger."

A sneer crossed Jack's face. It was as hot as it was menacing. He didn't say anything, but I could tell his wheels were turning as he stared down Hart. He had the deadly quiet thing down.

Thankfully, Cherish found another stray piece of gingerbread and ate it, moaning about how *bussin'* it was. Hart shot me a smirk, then dragged Yeager outside, saying something about hunting a polar bear.

# CHAPTER 21

While I wasn't planning on pursuing anything with Vixen. Even though her kiss had been nearly life-changing, I was at the Holidays Inn to work. Big kingdom work. Hart popping in with his aloof demeanor and sexy confidence, wearing leather and riding a motorcycle, no less, sparked something in me.

I'd already clocked Yeager's attraction to her, but Hart had all but challenged me, and I wasn't the type of man to walk away from a challenge. I thrived on the takedown. And the Elf had thrown down the gauntlet, so I wanted—needed— to pick it up. Having Vixen would be a very pleasant reward for winning against the guy in the room who commanded the most attention. More than Yeager even.

So, when I should've been preparing for my meeting with John, instead I plucked another purple candy out of the bowl, placing it in the window with the others. Then I allowed Vixen to snag me with nothing more than a smile and a question. "What's it like in the Winter Court?"

My response was swift. "I could tell you, Flame, but it would be much more magical if I showed you." Her eyes lit up and pulled her bottom lip between her teeth. Even those with the steeliest of spines would whimper at the sight of that. I bet she did that when she came.

Throwing my best judgment to the wind, I took her hand and pulled her outside the lodge so we could be alone. Once we were outside, she threw her arms around herself for warmth. I was so set on showing her my world, I hadn't even stopped to get her coat.

Not wanting her discomfort for a single second, I decided to move forward without explanation. Sure, it would surprise her, but I bet the look of awe on her face would be gorgeous.

I pulled the snow globe from my pocket and took her hand, uttering the magic word. "Wintertide." We whooshed away to my kingdom inside the globe within the next moment.

We landed in the foyer of my palace. I wanted her to see that first. And I wasn't wrong about her reaction. Once she steadied herself from the effects of traveling the way we had, she gasped, then let loose a squeal that vibrated inside me.

Everything was made of crystal, glass, and ice. I'd designed it so the length of the outer walls was glass, allowing a nearly three-sixty view of the cascading snow that my kingdom enjoyed year-round. Some of the supports were stone, but I made sure they were glistening white, which kept the eye from landing on them too long.

All the appointments in the room—drapes, fabrics, artwork—were navy and the furniture was either white or silver. Her eyes glinted over every surface as her face glowed with utter joy. When her gaze was drawn to the ceiling, she reached out, waving her arm around until it landed on me. She pulled me over, whispering in my direction, though her sight never left the ceiling. "This is where you live, Jack?"

"Yes. Do you like it?" She nodded, still gaping up at the large icicle chandeliers that hung from the glass ceiling. There were small ones in each of the corners and a large one in the center of the room. They stayed frozen if I deemed it, though the temperature in my palace was pleasant enough for any visitors not used to the chilly temps.

"It's astounding. I feel like we're in a snow globe."

"We are. I suppose it's a snow globe within a snow globe technically, though I'd never thought of it that way before." It was just home to me. And her awe of it took my breath away. I couldn't remember the last time I'd brought an outsider into my palace. Vixen was like an explosion of color in the foyer, not just because of the hue of her flaming hair.

It was simply her.

She ran over to the ice fountain in the center of the room. It changed daily—due to the magic I placed on it— but at that moment it was a cascade of stars. I couldn't have planned it better if I'd tried. She was heat and passion and magnificence all rolled into one beautiful package. Stars could only wish to be her.

Yes, Vixen stirred something in me: warmth. And even though I usually ran as far away from the fire as I could get, all I wanted to do was wrap her in my arms and get as close as I could. I was moments away from doing just that when we were interrupted by my butler Burl shuffling into the room. "Sir, I wasn't expecting you. What do you require? The special case?" Burl was ancient and loyal but had trouble reading rooms. Especially that moment.

Even though I'd heard him, my eyes never left Vixen. She'd moved over to the massive settee I had set in the corner so that I could witness the snow from any angle. The chair was covered in fluffy white fabric that felt like clouds with a navy throw I used when I read. She draped herself over the settee, throwing her legs over the arms, looking both seductive and at home at the same time. I waved Burl away. "Make sure no one comes in this room." I assume he nodded and scurried away. I couldn't be bothered to check.

"Aren't you going to join me?" Her voice was like a soft cascade of snow. My cock swelled in my pants, and I could think of no other thing than seeing her laid out naked on that settee.

As I approached, I lost my jacket and tie to the floor. By the time I was closer to her, my sleeves were rolled to my elbows. She tracked my movements with heady interest, her chest was heaving, and her eyes hooded with desire. I leaned against the window, delighted in the chill it gave me. And in her. "You're a vision."

She patted the seat next to her, but I shook my head.

This was the moment when I would discover who she truly was.

I wouldn't classify myself as having a problem. It was more of a condition of my genetic makeup. Yes, I'd had many lovers, but sex was complicated for a being who couldn't get overheated. Heat would eventually shut down my organs and kill me if I was exposed to too much of it. Same for John Sun, but in reverse, which was why I chose to set our meeting at the coldest place on the earth. I could stand some higher temps for a time, but I'd never been one to have sweaty sex or prolonged periods of touching.

Just kissing her had forced me to seek cold to replenish my magic. I couldn't imagine what being inside her would do to me.

Many women had been turned off by the way I enjoyed sex. I desperately wanted Vixen to be turned on.

But I wouldn't know unless I tried it.

"Take off your sweater." When I didn't go over to help her, she gave me a look that was more curious than anything but reached for the hem of her top with no hesitation. I hadn't been wrong about her attraction to me, thank my soul. "Wait. Do it slowly and keep your eyes on me."

She smiled, seeming to get what I was asking for. Then she peeled her sweater up at a laborious pace, never breaking eye contact. When she got it over her head and those flaming locks tumbled over her shoulders, I groaned. "Now your pants."

She shrugged off her boots and socks quickly. Which was fine with me, but the way she shimmied out of her jeans, her hips wiggling back and forth gradually, had my cock springing to attention. I ran my hand over my fly to rid myself of the uncomfortable, yet delicious, pain her body was causing me. She threw her jeans over the back of the settee, then sprawled across it, crossing her shapely legs, poised for what was coming next.

Her panties and bra were sheer white with red straps, like a present made for me to unwrap. A present with pert pink nipples that were hardened by desire.

I stroked myself harder. She watched the movement of my hand, her breaths coming faster. "If you come over here, I'll do that for you."

I grinned. "Thank you. But would it disturb you if we stayed where we are? And still took things further?"

An odd look of indecision crossed her face. I couldn't tell if she was apprehensive about my request or something else. Thankfully I didn't have to wait long for her to clarify. "Why would it disturb me? The sight of you rubbing yourself has me throbbing."

She twisted on the settee, and it gave me a magnificent view of her delicious skin and the white triangle between her legs. Whatever she'd thought in the moments before had dissipated. She wasn't apprehensive about anything. "Although, I want to see you too. What's under those perfectly tailored designer duds? Unbutton your shirt."

The command in her voice, the confidence, stirred me. I slowly—because I understood the art of seduction—began to unbutton my shirt. She bit her lip, her gaze focused on my chest as I revealed myself to her. When I yanked the tail of my shirt out of my pants, she gasped in delight. "In the name of Santa's bag of toys, your body is immaculate."

I ran my hand over my chest, spreading my shirt in the process. Just because I was a nearly immortal King who wore mostly suits didn't mean I failed to work on my physique. This sight in front of me, the way her body arched in my direction, would be the reason I continued to do so. "Turn around now. I want to see if the back of you matches the exquisite front." She giggled, but instead of simply standing up and jutting her ass at me like most other women in the past had done, she spun slowly and perched her knees on the settee, waiting for my next direction.

My soul.

"Hands on the back of the chair," I commanded.

She complied and if that wasn't enough to make me combust, her legs drifted apart as she slid down and back up again. Running her pussy along the seat as she gripped the chair back. I ripped my belt from my waist, throwing it down. At the clank of the silver buckle, she turned back to see, grinning like a cat when she found me unbuttoning my pants. "That's more like it. Would you like to see more too?" she purred.

I didn't even comment because she knew I did by the way I slid my hand into my ice blue boxer briefs, what my answer would be.

What it would always be if she were to ask again.

She playfully threw her hair over one shoulder and reached behind her to unclasp her bra. When she had it removed, she laid it over the wooden loop at the top of the chair. It hung there jauntily as she grabbed the navy blanket to cover her breasts before she turned back around and slid down the settee on her side.

My voice was low, intense, and full of desire. "Are you a tease, Flame?"

She gestured to the hand that was gliding along my stiff shaft. "No more than you, Frost."

I didn't think I could smile as big as I did. Being a kind and benevolent man, I removed my hand from my hard cock long enough to drop my underwear. I hadn't even stopped to step out of my pants, so I didn't bother with the boxers either. Vixen slid the blanket down her body, giving me an unfettered view of the loveliest pink pebbled nipples I'd ever seen.

I couldn't help myself. I raised a finger and melted an icicle hanging from the chandelier above the settee. One single drop of frigid water dripped down into the space between her breasts. She yelped and looked up, putting two and two together. "You did that on purpose, didn't you?"

"Yes. Do you want me to do it again?"

Her eyes went feral. "Yes, I truly do."

I flicked my fingers again, this time sending a small stream of chilly water over each breast. She arched into them, gasping and twitching. I didn't think her nipples could become harder than they were, but they did at the feel of the icicles. She was enjoying this. Whether or not she'd continue was a question I needed to be answered. "Take your panties off for me."

Without hesitation, she twisted in the chair and raised her legs straight up before she lifted her hips and slid the panties up her legs until they dangled on one toe. She flicked her foot, sending them flying at me. Surprised by the action, I still managed to catch them in the hand I didn't have my hard cock in.

I rewarded her by sending three little drips that landed right where I wanted them to go—her pussy. "Moan for me like that again, Flame. Light my fucking blood on fire." I sent another quick stream of ice water, and she lifted her hips so it hit her pussy right where she wanted it. The sound from her throat was feral.

The next thing I did was a calculated risk. But I didn't have it in me to keep from it. I put those panties straight to my nose and took a long drag of the arousal laced in them. Then I put my hand against the glass to feed on the cold outside to keep my magic from draining at the heat that blasted through me. She didn't question either move. And I didn't question how lucky I'd gotten. No, I was more turned on than I'd been in ages and hungry for more. So, I held one finger up. "Do exactly what I do. Understand?"

Nodding, she held up one finger, waiting, thirsting at the thrill of our game. I ran my finger down my throat and she matched my movement. When I slid over to my nipple, toying and circling just to watch her play with her own. Her eyes fell shut as she pinched and pulled herself, even grabbing the roundness of her breasts in her hand and squeezing. "Does that feel good Vixen?"

"Mm-hm. I wish it were you though."

As much as I liked the sound of that, she wasn't following my directions precisely. "In time." I paused, trying to slow down my heart rate at the thought of it. But I couldn't touch her. Not yet. "You're not watching me, Flame."

Her eyes popped open, and her hand stilled on her right breast as she checked my hand. I was still running it over my chest, and she looked perplexed. I decided to help her out. I cleared my throat, then took my hand off my dick long enough to wave it at her, then started pumping myself again.

She got it. Without hesitation, she put her other hand between her legs and hummed as she started to stroke her clit. Shuddering, I directed her to sit up. "I want to see what you like, where those fingers go, what makes you wild." She sat up with her back against the seat and her feet on the floor. When she spread her legs wide for me, I was the first to gasp.

Her pussy was unsettlingly beautiful. And her fingers stroking her already swollen clit had me pumping hard within a second. Not only that, but the lust in her eyes as she played with herself and watched me twist my hand over the end of my cock, then back down again, was astronomical. This was a woman who knew what she liked and wasn't ashamed of it.

For a moment I didn't think I could handle it.

I put that thought out of my head. I could handle anything she wanted. She parroted my own words back to me. "Does that feel good, Jack?"

Precum had started to bead at the tip, so I used my thumb to spread it around, then went back to my pumping. "Yes. Give me more. Put those fingers inside you and tell me how wet you are."

She inserted two fingers, not bothering to start with one, sliding them in and out a few times. "You've made me gush. I'm so drenched for you." She held them up for me. They were glistening. I don't know what sound I made—I was focusing on her—but it amused her.

Then we were both lost in the haze of pleasure as we pumped together.

"Faster," I told her. "Harder. Lift those sexy hips. I want to see you go deep."

"My soul," she panted. "You're going to kill me if you keep talking like that." There was a beat of silence before she said, "Don't stop."

Not one to disappoint a lady, I followed her order. "Keep your eyes on me, Flame. Look at me slicking up and down my hard cock. This is all you, what you do to me. When I come all over my hand it will be your design."

She threw her head back and cried out as she came. I'd like to think my words and actions had something to do with the suddenness of her release. I couldn't take my eyes off of her as she rolled her body through her orgasm as she pulled her fingers away and pinched her clit until her body fell back against the settee. She hadn't even finished panting when she opened her eyes and looked at me with hooded lids. "Don't come on your hand. Come on me."

Stunned silence.

Never before had I ever been asked in such a way.

I wouldn't be asked twice.

I strolled the few feet to her, swirling my hand around my engorged and aching cock. As soon as I was close enough to touch her, I grabbed her hand and shoved her fingers into my mouth, sucking and licking her juices as she looked on with wide eyes, enjoying every second of it. My cum spurt out of my hand, landing on her stomach. She groaned as it dripped down, inching toward her center. She angled her hips like she wanted it there. We both watched in awe as it inched toward her bare pussy.

This woman.

She was no longer the challenge or the gauntlet I must take up. She was my wildest desire, and I would have her again.

# CHAPTER 22

That had to be the hottest sex never to have been sexed. Jack hadn't even touched me until the end, yet I had the most intense orgasm I'd had in a very long time. Well, not counting the ones Yeager and Hart had given me. Honestly, they were all on an equal level with that. The experiences with them—the men themselves—were different, but all three times very satisfying.

It had been so long since I'd been craved by a man. Maybe that's why I'd overruled my own decisions to avoid sleeping with them. I didn't regret it. I couldn't. Not with Jack looking at me like he was, with adoration.

However, there was a tiny niggle of doubt running through me. That niggle had a name. It was slut. Or whore. Or bimbo. Three different men in three days. It was unconventional, for sure, but I didn't *feel* like a slut. I felt cared for. And I didn't know how to handle the idea of that, so I buried it deep.

Jack picked the navy blanket off the floor and began wiping his cum from my stomach. I yelped. "Don't you have towels in this place? I bet you do, and I bet they're white."

He half-smiled. "They are, but I don't have time to run upstairs or wait for Burl to bring one in. I'm expected by John Sun in a few minutes. Besides, I have as many blankets as I do handkerchiefs."

Was that a flex? Maybe. Didn't care.

I let him clean me off like the chivalrous person he was. Though he took his time between my legs. Didn't care about that either. Then we got redressed and it was time to go. I was bummed about it too. "I didn't even get to see your Kingdom at all. I got one room, not a tour, Frost."

"Do I detect a complaint?"

"Not in the least. A request to see more at another time."

"I would give you my Kingdom if you desired it. But, yes, next time we'll make time to explore."

I truly hoped that extended to exploring each other, but I didn't press it. I didn't get fully why he wanted us to stay apart like that. It seemed like more than a kink though. Probably something about his inability to take heat. It didn't matter though. If that was the way he wanted us to be, then I was fine with it. He was such a mysterious and alluring man. I wanted to know what made him tick and I suspected if there were more times with him, he would share them with me. Whenever he was ready.

Though if watching each other self-please was all we ever got, I was good with it. Rudy had kept the door closed to the bathroom when he'd done it. This, with Jack, had been hugely arousing. It was why I'd come so fast.

Jack took my hand, leading me toward the ice sculpture in the middle of the room. "If you'll excuse me." I was about to ask but didn't have to when he shouted for his butler. "Burl, bring me the special case."

A few seconds later, Burl came scuttling in from a side room that looked like an office carrying one of those metallic briefcases. He briefly nodded in my direction to acknowledge me, but then he handed the case to Jack. "The special case? Are you feeling lucky or out of your mind?"

Jack patted his back. "When have I ever acted out of my mind, Burl?"

Burl sighed. "There was that one time when —"

"Don't finish that sentence. We're off. See you in nine days." He pulled the snow globe out of his pocket and handed me the special case so he could take my other hand. "Macrocosm."

Seconds later we arrived at the spot we'd left from, and he was already hauling me inside the door and out of the cold. We were met with a noncommittal "Hm" from Yeager.

Though John Sun was beside himself. He strolled up to Jack, looked down at his special case, and scoffed. "Oh, really? The special case? Did she suck your dick and make you think you're invincible today?"

A massive hand reached around and grabbed the wide lapels of John's Hawaiian shirt, spinning it around so that he had to look at Yeager to see who was about to choke the life out of him.

Yeager nodded at Jack as if to say, 'I got this' before he lowered a menacing gaze on John. "Number one: in no circumstance will I let you speak like that about Vixen or any other woman in my presence. It's crude and demeaning to assume Jack's over there smiling because he was given a spectacular blowjob. Second, even if had the best head of his lifetime..." he paused to look at me. His expression said he assumed a BJ from me would invoke such a strong statement. "...it's none of your fucking concern. You've got Fae business? Fine, go do it, but don't you dare make those kinds of assumptions or declarations again. You'll regret it." He dropped John at Jack's feet, then winked at the Frost King.

So violent, then so casual in the next heartbeat. It was—my soul be damned—attractive.

John scrambled to his feet, grabbed his plain black case, and scrambled out the door. Jack passed me, running his fingers across my back as he watched John leave, presumably to go to their important meeting and not wanting to walk directly with him. Yeager spied the movement and chuckled under his breath. Once John was out of earshot, Jack turned to Yeager. "Thank you. I would've handled him, but it was nice for someone else to do it this time."

"No problem. I call it like I see it. Always. Just remember one thing though," he jutted his head toward me, zeroing in on Jack's still-moving fingers along my spine. "I had her first."

I swung around and hit him on the bicep which did nothing and Jack smirked as he walked outside. Like it didn't bother him at all to hear Yeager make that claim.

Next thing I knew Yeager had thrown himself on the couch with his feet propped up on the coffee table sipping something steamy from a mug. He took a big slurp of his drink and then looked up at me. "Fae, am I right? So, did you give him the blowjob of a lifetime or what?"

"Yeager!" I pulled back. "That's none of your concern. Just like you said."

"Technically true, but let's just say I'm invested in your sexual shenanigans."

"There were no shenanigans?"

"Really?"

"Yes, really."

"Then you want to tell me why your sweater is inside out and your hair completely disheveled." He took a long swig. "Or why you smell of sex? Because *that,* Bunny has my cock invested too."

I blew out a long breath. I had no idea how to respond. I mean, he'd caught me. And even though he didn't seem to care about what I'd done with Jack—moments ago, mind you—he was eyeing me like he wanted to take my sweater back off, only not to fix it right-side out. I opened my mouth. Nothing but stammering came out. "I, uh, we, well it wasn't, um..."

He put a finger over my mouth. "Let me help you out here. Though I'm tempted not to because that blush you're rocking has me at half-mast already. What you might not know about me, and my kind is that we're pack creatures.

"We often take more than one lover at a time. Shit, my father has three wives and a husband. The five of them raised our flurry, which is my two sisters, two-half sisters, half-bro, and myself. There are a few other arrangements among the parentage, with more kids that I call my siblings too. And while we don't sleep with siblings—gross—we're accommodating with the whole nontraditional lifestyle. I have a special place in my heart for my biological parents, but we're all one big happy flurry. That's just how Yetis are."

He paused to gauge my reaction and when I didn't give one, he continued. "I'm telling you this because I grew up with a lot of sharing in my life. Sometimes people outside our kind have trouble adjusting to our lifestyle, I guess. Truth is, I don't have a jealous bone in my body. Though I do have a hard bone in my body right now and it would like it to be inside you. I don't give a shit if he was first today. I was just messing with him."

Heat, fast and relentless, burned through me. This was... it was a lot to take in. I tended not to judge anyone for their relationship choices, but until that very moment, I had not truly considered a real relationship with Yeager. Or Jack. Or Hart, whom I hadn't forgotten about. It was just a lot to think about.

It had been three days.

And honestly, I was scared I wasn't ready for anything more than a hookup. And if said hookups kept happening—with any or all of them—was it a relationship? I didn't know.

I *did* know that Yeager's green eyes were piercing me with desire.

Maybe I was starved for good sex after I'd broken up with Rudy. Ten months was a long time of *'petting the cat'* alone.

The sound of squeaking broke the mood. We both turned and found Holly brushing in from the kitchen carrying several Christmas mice toys. Did I mention they were glued to her sweater? Yeah. "Oh, there you are Yeager. Just the man I was looking for. The windows were delivered for the repairs in cabin eight. Probably should get those in before nightfall. Then you wouldn't have to share a cabin. I mean, if you didn't want."

Yeager sighed, adjusted his fly, and then turned to Holly. "Sure thing, Holl. Just give me a couple minutes to wrap up this conversation then I'll head right out."

"Righty-oh." She disappeared from where she came, and I was left with Yeager looking less than pleased at her appearance.

"Well fuck. I should help her. She doesn't have anyone else. Karl is a great cook, but he's weak and skinny. Crystal's still sick, not that she has any skills. It's up to me if this cabin's going to be in condition to take on new guests any-time soon."

"Of course. Poor Holly. She seems a little lost sometimes. I guess she misses her husband."

"She does. He was the handyman. That's why I can't refuse her. I don't know how long it will take to get the windows in, but we always have tonight to finish what we were about to start because there is no way I'm bunking in cabin eight."

"*Were* we about to start something?"

"Oh yes, we were, Bunny."

~~~~~~~~~~~~~~~~~~~~~~~~~~~~~~~~

It was after midnight before Yeager came into the cabin. I'd dozed off waiting for him. Though I told myself nearly a hundred times that I wasn't waiting for him, specifically. I was simply choosing to stay awake. Still, I'd gone to sleep questioning myself because deep somewhere in the recess of my brain I knew I was waiting for a man hours after I'd been with another one.
~~~~~~~~~~~~~~~~~~~~~~~~~~~~~~~~

The creak as the cabin door opened is what woke me, not Yeager himself. He was trying to stay silent and it took all I had in me not to turn over and watch as his clothes rustled from getting undressed. Every so often he softly cursed, 'shit...fuck' then he'd blow out his breath, presumably upset he'd made noise. It was adorable and heart-warming to think about him trying to control his massive body's movements in the small cabin. Just so he wouldn't disturb me.

"I'm awake. You don't have to be quiet."

He sighed, then threw a couple of logs in the fireplace before coming over to the bed in only his underwear. His body was silhouetted against the light of the flames, and it made my temperature rise. The way he looked at me with affection and a glint of mirth in his eyes, any lingering thoughts I had about being with two different men in one day flittered out of me like little birds. He was so solid, muscular, and sensual, he made me feel something I hadn't in an exceptionally long time. Safe.

I traced my hand over his granite abs, then hooked a finger in his waistband. He moaned. That deep, brawny sound went straight into my bones. But when I glanced up to see the expression on his devastatingly handsome face, I didn't find my own desire mirrored there.

I found concern. And pain.

He took my hand from his waistband, then brought it to his lips, kissing my fingertips one by one before sighing. "Can we put this on pause for a few minutes? I don't want to, but I'm not in the right headspace to deliver what you deserve now."

I nodded and scooted over so he could crawl into bed beside me. "Of course. What's wrong?"

He turned to his side so he could face me. In the moments he took for him to answer, he put his hand in my hair. The tangle of his fingers mixed in with his masculine cedar scent left me reeling and wanting him on a level I hadn't before, but there was something more within me too. I wanted to ease whatever pain he was going through.

"My father just showed up. Another sneak attack. This time though..." he trailed off and my stomach clenched. I put my hand on his cheek, cradling his strong jaw. He closed his eyes. "I don't know if I can stop this anymore."

He took his hand away and held it up in the flickering firelight. A shiny gold band circled his finger. I bolted upright. "Wait. Did you get married this afternoon?"

He chuckled. "No. This isn't a wedding band, it's a binding ring. It's fused with magic, and it means there's nowhere on this planet I can go that my father can't find me. It's his insurance policy to keep me from running out on my Chosen One responsibility. I can't fucking believe he did it."

I couldn't fathom how a father could do something so vile as to force his son into a life he didn't want. "You said you had time to figure something out. Why did he do this today?"

"Don't ask questions you don't want answers to, Bunny." I *did* want answers. So, I nodded at him to answer me. "Okay, you asked for it. When I was at home for the intervention, I mentioned—in confidence—to my brother that I'd met an incredible woman who I couldn't stop thinking about. Spoiler alert: it's you. And Ivan, being the jealous bastard he is, ratted me out. Dad grew concerned about me being a flight risk, so, here we are."

That. Was a lot.

My mouth dried and my gaze bounced all over the room —at the fire, the wall with the painting of a winter cabin scene over Yeager's shoulder, the inside of my eyelids—anywhere to keep from looking at him. He couldn't be saying that he wanted to be with me, for real. Like, as in more than just sex.

Oxygen, who needed it?

He took my chin in his fingers. "Open those baby blues. I'm not saying I want to marry you. And for the record, I would never use you to get away from my situation. But I'm not going to lie here and say that I don't want you, that I haven't thought about what happens when we're done with these games. Because I do and I have. The fact is that I wasn't expecting you, but I'm grateful that you came along.

"What happens beyond us, in this bed, on the chair over there, in the shower in the morning maybe, is my burden to carry. I'll find a way out of my problem that doesn't involve you."

My muscles relaxed. A smidge. "Yeager, I'm sorry I didn't mean to freak out on you, but no matter what the calendar says, in my heart, what happened with Rudy just happened. I'm not ready for..."

I was so messed up I didn't even know what I wasn't ready for.

"I know. Roscoe did a real number on you, but don't worry. I've got another number in mind now: sixty-nine."

# CHAPTER 23

It took five seconds to recognize that Yeager and Vixen had slept together the night before. Again. They'd come into the lodge the next day chatting and smiling and it was all over them. She looked a little tired from having been up all night and he looked like a smug son-of-a-bitch who ate the canary.

Or rather, the reindeer.

That was fine. They could have their playtime. I'd been forced to pop back to the Pole to remind my network of helpers exactly how I wanted them to operate last night. They were getting too damn sloppy for my liking. Not that Santa would've cared what I was up to. He was a live-and-let-live sort of guy. I suspected he knew about the underground fight club I organized as well as my biggest operation: secret tours of the toy factory for spoiled little rich kids whose Mommies and Daddies were wrapped around their fingers.

People paid a premium for it, especially humans. And I knew Santa wouldn't care about the racketeering because I didn't keep a cent of the money for myself.

Okay, maybe a few cents here and there. The rest of the money went to places it was needed. Like the hospital and soup kitchens. Now and then, I'd throw some into improvements around the Pole. Like the ultramodern mistletoe grow-house last year and the Elf Retirement Home the year before. I was looking at upgrading the reindeer stables next. Obvious reasons.

I'd rigged the whole toy factory experience with magic and once the kids were back at home snug in their beds, they'd forget the whole thing, wake up the next morning and want to do it again because they never realized they'd already done it. Mom and Pop didn't remember either, so here they'd come for round two. Or three or four. Honestly, there were enough spoiled rich kids in the world to keep the profits rolling in even if they had remembered the experience.

As long as my helpers remembered to administer the magic memory-erasing potion.

Glove Matterhorn had forgotten the night before.

And while I was off making sure he wouldn't forget again; Yeager and Vixen were enjoying the pleasure of each other's company.

Not that it bothered me. He was a beast, but I liked my odds as far as Vixen was concerned. But really, there was no need to make it a competition. Not with him anyway. Jack, on the other hand? He seemed to thrive on the challenge. Just how far he'd take it remained to be seen. Again, I wasn't worried. My Ginger and I had a connection that formed long before she met either of them. Fucking with Jack was just for amusement.

I strolled over behind the couch where Vixen and Yeager sat sipping coffee, putting my hands on their shoulders. "You two looked like you had a good fuck last night. Care to share the juicy details?"

Vixen did a spit-take. Yeager laughed and winked at me. "A gentleman doesn't eat pussy and tell."

"You're not a gentleman."

"Mm, I think I am. Let's ask Vixen. What do you say? Keep in mind that a gentleman is very giving and makes sure his partner is taken care of first and repeatedly. That feel like it defines me, Bunny?"

The blush on her face matched her hair and I swear I felt it on a cock-level.

She yelped when Jack blustered into the room with a gust of winter wind behind him. "Jack, good morning, how are you?" She jumped up and ran over to greet him with a hug. Which he accepted and looked vaguely traumatized by for a blip of a second before he threw that icy exterior back up.

I slid into her place on the couch, leaning in so only Yeager would hear me. "What do you think the deal is there? They're into each other, yeah?"

"Mm-hm, but I don't think he's the sharing type."

I pulled one of my special canes out of my pocket and slung my arm around the couch, angling toward him so I could get a good read when I brushed the cane along the back of his neck. "What about you? Are you the sharing type?"

He didn't answer, verbally anyway. All I got was a smirk and a very loud truth bomb from my candy cane.

Oh, you dirty boy.

"Gather around everyone." Holly came out from the kitchen with a platter of cinnamon rolls in one hand and some game cards in the other. She wore a green dress shaped like a Christmas tree that had gold garland wrapped around it with huge gold star earrings dangling from her ears.

"Her clothes are killing me. Do you think she dresses like Christmas threw up on her year-round?" Vixen had come back over. She plopped on the couch next to me and Jack perched on the arm next to her. He greeted me with a raised eyebrow, which I returned.

Yeager laughed. "Yes, she does. And the weird thing is that I've known her for years and I have yet to see a repeat outfit."

Vixen rubbed her temples. Too much Christmas for her. I didn't blame her, not after what she'd been through, but at the same time, she needed to perk that spirit back up or she was going to lose a job I knew she loved.

Holly set the tray on the counter. Cherish ran over and swiped one and had half of it eaten before Holly even had her glasses on to read the cards. I liked that kid a lot. I might even give her a free tour of the toy factory if she wanted it.

"Today's game is a classic—Christmas charades."

"Kill me now," Vixen muttered under breath. Yeager reached across my lap to squeeze her thigh in support. I felt obligated to do the same. Jack and his eyebrow took more than a cursory glance at our two hands on her legs. Especially when I started rubbing a little circle that Yeager matched. Vixen shifted. It was slight, but since it had been toward us and not away, I had to assume she was into it.

The temperature in the lodge dropped significantly.

"All teams will compete at once. Each member will get one card with a Christmas song to act out for the team. Jasper, Karl, Frank, and I will keep a stopwatch for one team. We'll start the timer when the action begins and when the correct answer is guessed. Then we rotate to the next person and add the time on, and so on until all team members have had a go. The team that has the shortest time gets four candy canes in their stocking, the second shortest time gets three candy canes, and the third, two, and the last place team gets one. We'll begin after we eat. Get 'em while they're hot."

A half-hour later, Vixen, Jack, and I were wedged together on my—yes, *my*—couch, and Yeager had a card in his hand, ready to go. He looked over to Jasper, our timer, as he counted down. "On my mark. Three, two, one, go." Jasper clicked the stopwatch and Yeager swiped the red Santa hat from his head. After he put it on, he rolled his hand over his stomach in an exaggerated way. Santa obviously, but there were a lot of Santa songs. Jack was quick with the first guess. "Santa, Baby?"

"No."

"I Saw Mommy Kissing Santa Claus?" Vixen guessed.

"No."

Yeager shook his head, growing frustrated when team Frostbite cheered after having gotten Winter Wonderland. It had to have been no more than six seconds. How the fuck did they do that so fast? He made a low rumbling growl that Vixen definitely noticed and looked over toward Hot Chocolate with Marshmallows. Then he angled himself away from Cherish before he held his fist in front of his package and mimed jerking off. He even made a face I was fairly sure was his actual come face. I bellowed in laughter. "Santa Claus is *Coming* to Town!"

Jasper confirmed the win as Vixen shook her head, "Oh my Soul."

"What, it got the job done. Much like me last night."

He smirked and used his long legs to step over the coffee table. He held out his hand to pull me up since I was next. I grasped him, pulling him into my chest since Cherish's team had gotten theirs right and she was looking over in our direction. "Good one. Though, I feel like you were probably being generous to yourself there. Maybe didn't need to hold your fist so far out. Seems like you were overcompensating." I stepped over the coffee table and then turned around to gauge his reaction.

He plopped down next to Vixen. "Aw, it's cute that Hart thinks I have a tiny dick."

"Cute isn't the word I'd use." Vixen sighed. Though her eyes were pinned to his fly, so I took an innocent peep and damn, he did not have a tiny dick.

Yeager curled his hand in Vixen's hair, toying with the long strands, then focused back on me, serious as he nodded to the card Jasper handed me. "Let's do this."

I glanced at my song. Too damn easy.

Jasper counted me down. I popped to the kitchen and grabbed a piece of leftover candy, then popped over and grabbed Holly away from the Ho, Ho, Ho, Hot group and popped back in front of my team with both things in tow. I set the blue Jolly Rancher on the table, then pointed to Holly, the Jolly Rancher, then spread my hands, indicating the room and all its decorations.

Jack snapped the cuff of his sleeve dramatically. "Holly Jolly Christmas."

As soon as Jasper clicked the stopwatch, I popped Holly back in her spot just as Mandy was guessing "Oh Christmas Tree." Though when I looked over the vamps were looking on like they'd gotten theirs right hours ago.

Jack slid off the couch to take his turn. Jasper handed him the card and the expression on Jack's face morphed from casually disinterested but playing along to cold disdain in a heartbeat. "I'm not doing this one."

Yeager leaned forward. "Is it hard?"

"No. It's...I'm not doing it. Give me another." He shoved it at Jasper, who refused to take it, glancing over at Holly in fear. He didn't know how to handle Jack's refusal. And I had to admit, I didn't get what the big deal was. He was smart, he could figure it out.

Holly waved her hand. "Please play along Mr. Frost. There are a limited number of cards. Not enough to get another."

Jack pressed his lips together. The temp dropped another ten degrees. "All due respect, Holly, but we will forfeit this game if we must. This card isn't being played."

Forfeit? Woah. That seemed extreme. Even for the cold bastard.

Yeager jumped up. "What's the issue?" He stepped over the table with his long thick legs and went over to Jack, checking out the card.

Holly was beside herself now because Yeager had already seen it and it couldn't be played now. But that didn't trouble the Yeti. Nope. He took the card and ripped it into pieces. It fell to the ground like snow.

"Yeager! What am I going to do now? I'll have to check in with Santa about rules violations in his game."

"Sorry Holl, but Jack's right. We aren't doing it. We'll take last place for this one if we must."

Vixen, who had been strangely silent throughout Jack's discourse, spoke up. Though, it was more of a whisper than anything. "It's Rudy, the Famous Reindeer, isn't it?"

Jasper clicked the timer. "You got it!"

Damn Jasper, read the fucking room.

The vampires seemed to get it though, because they went back to playing with the tall blonde vamp pointing to his descended fangs and the little crazy vampire shouting, "All I Want for Christmas is my Two Front Teeth."

The two other teams finished out the round and I slung my arm around Vixen. "Are you okay, Ginger?"

She melted into me, just for a moment, then straightened her spine just as Yeager plunked down on the coffee table in front of her to take her hands. When Jack slid in next to her, she angled toward him. It was an interesting little group we had going. Each of us wanted her, each of us had been with her in some capacity or another, but that dumbass card had wrapped us together in a way that had nothing to do with sex.

"I appreciate what you were trying to do, Jack, but it's fine. I've spent over ten months hiding from him, but that didn't do me any good. In fact, it hurt me. While I was keeping myself away from him, I kept myself away from other things too. And I don't want to live like that anymore. I need to face what happened to overcome it. Step one is being able to hear his name and not falling into a puddle of tears or rage-eating raw cookie dough."

That right there is why Santa sent her to the Holidays Inn. The fact that she'd gotten to this conclusion on day four was a good sign. Now, Santa wanted me to report to him about everything. I intended to do that because I knew he loved her and wanted the best for her, but as she sat there having the epiphany, I decided to keep it to myself. The concern I'd had about her had changed. It had grown deeper and seeing Yeager and Jack sitting there with that strange mix of concern and pride on their faces too? It was intimate and I didn't want to share it with anyone else. Not even Santa.

She'd had a shift in attitude, but maybe I had too.

I hadn't stared at her tits in hours.

Vixen stood up. "It's my turn. Let's see if we can win this thing."

Yeager piled his massive frame on the couch beside me and Jack perched on his favorite armrest. I bet he'd like to bend her over it. I mean, we all would.

She took the card from Jasper, and I swear the look on her face when she read it was like lightning and pepper-mint and revving motors all rolled into one. She took my breath away.

And she looked straight at me as Jasper counted her down. When he got to one, she smirked and pointed to my cock.

I jumped up, whacking Yeager in the head unintention-ally. "Jingle Bells!"

Boom. Two seconds.

I sailed over the table picked her up and popped her back to the couch, throwing her at Yeager. Her legs knocked Jack sideways, and he fell into the heap of us too. It was a cacophony of limbs and grunts and laughter.

Yes, it was just a stupid little game—that we didn't even know if we'd won or not—but there was joy in the victory she'd had in her mindset.

It took a few minutes, but after we'd all righted ourselves, Yeager threw his arm on the back of the couch. "Wait just a damn second. I have questions. Is that what you call Hart's cock, Jingle Bells? Or are you referring to his balls? If so, do they jingle or is it figurative? And most importantly, why haven't you named my cock yet? My cock needs a name, Bunny. I'm not moving from this spot until he gets it."

Meanwhile, Isaac is ushering Cherish through the room with his hands over her ears while she grumbles that she literally doesn't care-uh what we're talking about.

Oops.

Jack shook his head. "Maybe we should table this discussion for a more private time and place."

"Did she give your cock a name too, Jack? Oh, my soul, she calls your cock Popsicle, doesn't she?"

"I do not call any part of him popsicle."

She would now. The candy cane I was running along the crook of her elbow told me she thought it was perfect for him and the Daddy vibe he rocked. Popsicle. And yeah, she wanted to lick it.

# CHAPTER 24

**I**'ll name your cock if you want, Yeager. How about Anaconda? Or maybe Beast? Ooh, Ax. You're a lumberjack. That's good, right?"

I was lounging on the couch between Yeager and Hart, who was idly running one of his candy canes along the neck of my sweater as he talked about Yeager's dick. He'd started with my arm but had wandered to other places. Everyone else had cleared out to do other things after lunch, but I'd noticed Jack being even more silent than normal. "Everything okay Jack?"

"Yes. Just running through some scenarios now that John Sun has asked to postpone our meeting for a couple more days."

Yeager was playing with my hair. I found that I liked the feel of his fingers massaging my scalp. As much as I liked the soft brush of Hart's fingers against my collarbone since he'd abandoned the candy cane. It might have looked odd to someone to let them both touch me like that, but after what I was choosing to call a breakthrough about Rudy earlier, I didn't much care. There was no one else around and Jack wasn't bothered by it. At all. I could tell he liked watching the movements of their hands as they raked them slowly over parts of me.

That man was a voyeur.

Maybe I was too, because watching him touch himself had been explosive. But it wasn't the time to think about that. Not while two other men were mapping my body with their fingertips.

"Why did John postpone your meeting again?" Yeager asked. "Was it a stall tactic to rattle you?"

"That's what I'm trying to discern. I have the upper hand, have for years, and he knows he can't stop the inevitable, so I'm unsure what he's thinking."

"I can tell you exactly what he's thinking: he's thinking about having his cock sucked by three women at the same time. I don't think his stalling is business-related at all. I think he's all about that pussy."

Jack shook his head. "Good guess, but you don't know that for sure, Hart."

"Oh, but I do." Hart picked up the candy cane he'd dropped in my lap, tapping my nose first, then slapping it—hard—at Yeager's zipper. He cursed and shoved Hart's shoulder. They wrestled back and forth for a minute with me in between them. I had to use both arms and a leg to separate them. Like they were children.

When he'd settled back down, a serious expression passed over Hart's face. "I'll tell you how I know. This is a bit of an Elf trade secret, but considering I'm head of candy canes, it's within my authority to disclose that these candy canes with the green ribbon are the ones we hand out to kids when they sit on Santa's lap. There's Elven magic within them and it allows us and Santa to read the deepest desires of the kids. All they have to do is touch the cane and we know exactly what they want.

"I've used these kinds of canes on every single person here, including John Sun. He's an asshole. He isn't prepping for your meeting because he thinks you're weak and losing your touch. So yeah, he's in his cabin banging the three very eager nymphs on his team instead. He hasn't even given one thought to your negotiations."

"Good news for you then, Jack. And the other bit...?" Yeager laughed. "That's interesting."

Hart stuck the end of the candy cane in his mouth, then drew it out again. "It truly is my Yeti friend. It truly, deeply, is."

Jack leaned forward. It was no longer about his business with John at that point. No, it became about me. "Not that I don't appreciate your perspective on John, but this feels like a violation. Especially if you've used what you gained by those candy canes to sleep with Vixen."

Oh wow. He was just diving right in there. I could see why he thought this way, but when I considered the night in the kitchen with gingerbread, I didn't feel violated. Or offended. I was flattered, in a way. And whatever he'd done, it made Hart an exceptionally good lover on top of being sinfully hot.

Maybe my thinking was skewed based on what had happened with Rudy or what seemed to be happening with all three of them, but the candy cane dragging out my deepest desires didn't give me pause. "It's okay, Jack. I don't feel violated. What I chose to do with Hart was just that—my choice. Just like with you."

I let out a breath. There *that* was out in the open.

Neither Hart nor Yeager were surprised by the revelation.

Jack folded his arms over his chest. "That's good to hear. And now I must apologize for asking this in front of you Flame, but it appears we're putting cards on the table; what do you think about this, Yeager? With the candy canes of truth, do you not feel like he has an unfair advantage when it comes to pursuing her?"

Yeager's emerald eyes twinkled as he winked at me. "Nah. The idea of jealousy or competing for her over either of you just isn't in me. I come from a pack, so I've seen how sharing can work. And here's the thing: I want her, and she knows I want her. The two of you want her too. How could I blame you? I get that it might feel messy to you, based on your personality and the life you seem to lead. But if she gets with you or Hart, as well as me, I don't see that as a problem. I see it as an incredible, sexy, confident woman making choices about who she wants to share her body with. And I thank the damned stars I'm in the mix.

"Hart using his candy canes isn't cheating. Because he's not my enemy, he's, my teammate. We both want the same thing: Vixen's screams of pleasure as she comes undone. You should think about suiting up and joining us. If that's what Vixen wants. And I'm guessing she does."

I was simultaneously hotter and colder at the same time. Jack had caused the temperature in the room to drop, yet Yeager's words had me heating up. This wasn't the first time he'd hinted at a group thing but hearing him lay it all out like that—with zero apology and no strings attached—was to use his word, interesting.

Did I want that? All of them?

Yeah, I did.

But I didn't know what that looked like. Not yet. Glancing at each one of them told me that they didn't either. Well, maybe Yeager did since he seemed to have experience with this kind of thing. And I guess Hart knew based on his candy cane discoveries.

That left me and Jack running through scenarios in our minds. And he was. I could practically see the wheels turning behind his steel eyes. My thoughts were whipping around too. Especially when Yeager leaned over and kissed my neck on the left while Hart did the same on the right. It was like they'd shared some silent communication between them to just go for it and they did.

Just like them, their kisses were different. Hart was all aggression, scraping his teeth along my neck, nibbling on my earlobe, and sending little jolts through me. While Yeager's soft warm lips gave way to the languid ministrations of his tongue as he licked the hollow of my throat and across my jaw.

At this alone, I was throbbing.

I flicked my eyes to Jack. He'd slid over to the coffee table in front of us. His hands were resting on his knees and his gaze was flicking between Hart and Yeager as they worked together to drag a soft moan from my lips. The sight of him watching them. Watching me. Made my mouth dry.

Was I going to let this happen?

I didn't get to answer my question because a pop reverberated around the room. Hart groaned as he pulled away from me and picked up the letter that had landed on his lap. Yeager pressed a kiss behind my earlobe before uttering, "Can you not, put that popping thing on do not disturb?"

I expected a smartass remark out of Hart, but I didn't get that.

He ripped open the envelope and paled as he read whatever it said. "Fuck. Fuck. Fuck me. Fuck. For the love of my ever-fucking-loving soul. Fuck. Fuuuuuck."

Jack put a hand on his arm, sensing he was about to lose it We all did. "What's wrong?"

Hart popped away, then back again. Over and over and over, screaming fuck every time he reappeared. He basically popped back and forth all over the room for five minutes. It was alarming to see him like that.

Something was not okay.

Each time he popped back, we tried to talk to him, to calm him down, but he didn't seem to hear me. Finally, Jack seemed to get a read on his pattern and pointed to the chair next to the fireplace. Yeager went over to it and when Hart popped next to it, he tackled him into the chair, throwing his legs over Hart and pinning his arms above his head to hold him in place.

For a second—and I mean just for a second because I knew Hart was in distress of some kind—the area south of my fluttering stomach twitched at the sight of Yeager straddling Hart as his chest heaved in and out.

Hot. Hawt. Hot.

But I couldn't stand there and fantasize about how mouthwatering the two of them looked like that. All strength and aggression with coiled muscles and heaving chests.

Well, I could and did, but I shouldn't have.

After an intense stare-down period where both men seemed to communicate without saying a word, Yeager released Hart's wrists. When he was satisfied Hart wasn't going to bolt again, Yeager pressed his hand on Hart's chest, specifically his heart. I could imagine how it was pounding beneath Yeager's hand. "You good now, man?"

Hart nodded. "Yeah. Thanks. I guess I went off the rails there for a minute."

"Understatement," Jack whispered.

Yeager peeled himself off Hart, sitting in front of the fireplace so he'd be close enough to get to him again if he needed it. "Look, I respect your right to privacy and all that, but the fuck was that about?"

Hart gestured to the letter on the floor. "See for yourself."

I picked it up and as soon as I spotted the subject, I knew what had happened. It made my heart heavy like it was too big for my chest. I read it out loud so Jack and Yeager could hear. "Congratulations. You've been selected to participate in Mrs. Claus' fiftieth annual Sexiest Elf of the North Pole contest. Proceeds will go towards the North Pole Children's Hospital. To celebrate fifty years, the theme this year is gold, so be sure to sparkle tonight. Arrival time is five p.m. Contest to be broadcast live on NickTock at seven. Mrs. Claus will see you there."

"Poor pitiful you, accused of being sexy." Yeager let out a belly laugh. "Is that really what upset you? That's nothing. In fact, I'm going to go ahead and say it: you *are* sexy. Own that shit, Man. Get another medal or trophy or whatever they give you for winning."

Jack ran his hand over his stubbled jaw. "I agree. I do not see the tragedy in this. Do you not want to defend your title?"

"No, I don't. I never wanted the title in the first place. I get that it's stupid to complain about this, but you don't understand what it's like."

I went over and sat next to Yeager. "Explain it to us."

He sighed, then ran his hand through his glossy dark hair. I had the biggest urge to do that myself. But it was not the time to tell him how sexy I thought his hair was. "I don't mind strutting nearly naked in front of the world. I don't mind being called sexy. I don't mind the perks of winning with the women it brings to my door. And the medal is nothing. The big prize isn't advertised and it's the most coveted thing in the world. Trust me, it's good.

"But the second I won my first title, I became a non-entity. Gone were my achievements and expertise I had from years at my job. Gone was anything I wanted to say or do outside of the sphere of sex. I had all these ideas and goals and nobody, not even Santa, would listen to them because I was *the* sexy Elf. I was supposed to stand there and look good. As Cherish would say, periodt. It's such a hollow feeling to know that all anyone sees is my body.

"And believe me Vixen, I'm aware that women go through this every day. I truly hate that and hope that you know I don't objectify you. Sure, I want us to smash in a million separate ways, but I value you as a person first. My soul, I hope you see that."

I swallowed. I didn't need his candy cane of truth to tell me he was being honest. His despair, the longing in his voice was palpable. I'd never liked the stupid contest in the first place, and this was why. He was so much more than a hot body, and everyone deserved to be seen.

I instantly regretted ever voting for him. "I see you, Hart. I do. I'm sorry I voted in the past. If I'd known—"

"Ha, I knew it. But don't worry. I'm used to this. I'd hoped being here for these games would've kept me off the radar this year. Guess not."

Jack slid around to the other side of the coffee table so he could face Hart. "There's an easy solution."

"Yeah, don't show up," Yeager offered.

"I can't do that. Tell them, Ginger."

"It's true. This thing is put on by Mrs. Claus. If he doesn't participate, it'll get ugly for him. Santa may be chill about a lot of things—ridiculous contests designed to help others achieve Christmas nirvana, notwithstanding—but he doesn't play around when it comes to the Mrs. Hart has to go." I looked over and hoped he could feel the sympathy in my voice.

Yeager stood up, reaching for my hand, then holding his other out for Hart and nodding his head at Jack. "Well, if you have to go, then let's spend the day making sure you're memorable."

# CHAPTER 25

We spent the afternoon prepping Hart for the contest. Part of me was worried Yeager's plan would backfire and get Hart into trouble with Santa and the Mrs. The other part of me, the bigger part, was hoping he'd get what he wanted out of it, which was to say, out for good.

Yeager strutted out of the kitchen with a huge bowl of popcorn he'd made, setting it in my lap so that both Jack and he could reach it. There had been no further talk about the three of them and me and I was glad about that. I needed time to figure out what I wanted. They seemed to get that. Yeager anyway. Hart was too busy getting his stuff together for the contest.

Jack was thinking about it too, I detected him running calculations in his brain during the day, mulling it over.

He'd turned out to be helpful with items from his Kingdom. Hart was going to make an impression, that was for sure. For his help, Hart had popped away and gotten him a phone to use for voting, since he didn't have one.

Cherish came unhinged when she found out about that.

She was with Holly and the employees prepping for the next day while the adults were gathering in the lodge to watch the competition. Even the vamps. Lestat had cast his phone onto the big screen TV so we could all watch comfortably and vote from our phones.

"This is very exciting," Erin said, "I never knew this competition existed."

Her husband pulled her into his lap. "I hope I don't need to be jealous." She shook her head and kissed him, groping him in the process. I'm guessing that was a no.

The screen blinked a few times, then the camera zoomed in on a gold curtain with the trademark NickTock logo on it. Nerves rang through me. "Sh. Everyone, it's starting."

Santa strolled out on the stage to uproarious applause. When everyone finally settled, he addressed the crowd and then introduced his Mrs. I didn't even hear what she said because my ears had started to ring. All of the reindeer— yep, him too—were sitting on the side of the stage, guests of honor for the fiftieth celebration. All of us had come on board before the competition had started, so I guess we— they—were there as witnesses.

I hadn't laid my eyes on Rudy in months, and I swear, my tongue started to tingle as I watched him interact with the audience.

"Are you kidding me right now? Rapscallion is throwing out finger guns? What a douche." Yeager threw his arm around me, tucking me in closer. A second later, on the other side, Jack threaded his cool fingers with mine.

Didn't expect that.

There I was encapsulated by two men who were doing everything in their power to protect me from the sight of my ex. I had a feeling some of the others in the room were staring, but I didn't care. I was going to get through this. For Hart. Yeager and Jack were going to help me. Screw everyone else who may have had a problem with me sitting there with them like that.

I managed to regain my composure as the competition began. First up, Buck Marigold. Fitting, since his name had the theme in the title. He strutted across the stage wearing a gold lame` robe with very tiny briefs. His red locks were tipped in gold, and he even had several thick gold necklaces draped around his neck.

Mindy, Mandy, and Monday declared together. "Pass."

It made me laugh. Buck didn't have that sexy vibe. He was good-looking, but it was like he didn't know what to do with it. And as soon as I had that thought, I regretted it. How dare I judge him?

Next up, an Elf I didn't recognize. Sinn. His dark skin practically glowed as he took the stage wearing even smaller gold briefs with a thong back. He wore shimmery gold eyeshadow and gold dusted his sharp cheekbones, which glistened as he did a fancy turn around the candy cane pole that Buck didn't even touch. The nymphs shouted, "Smash."

The third entry was literally wearing gold string. It was tied in complicated ways around his body and —yep—his cock with a big gold ring right at the top. It left nothing to the imagination. Noth. Ing. That guy was in it for the size of his member and nothing else. And he was sure to put it out there for everyone to see.

Hard to believe Mrs. Claus was sponsoring this even after looking at *that.*

Spike stood up and went over to the TV, squinting and John Sun laughed. "Getting a closeup?"

"Yeah. I'm trying to see what knots he used. I'm a sailor. Call it professional interest. Because cringe." He sounded so much like Cherish that the entire room laughed. Also: he's a vampire sailor from Transylvania? What?

As far as the string wrangler, the nymphs were divided. Two smashes and a "hard pass" from Mandy. Across the room, I swear Isaac let out a breath of relief.

The next contestant had a flare. I'll give him that. He wore an assless gold catsuit and carried a gold whip, which he brandished all over the stage. Cupid had to jump up and run behind her chair to keep from getting whipped. I couldn't wait to see her again. As soon as I got through this contest. I had to get through the night first. As hard as I tried to avoid it, I kept looking over to Rudy sitting in the second row of chairs behind Cupid.

He was classically handsome and though I detested the sight of him, I was unwillingly drawn to him too.

The crack of the whip pulled my attention back to the contestant. Jack huffed, "I can't believe this is supposed to help sick children."

"Yeah," Yeager agreed. "Looks like Mrs. Claus has some kinks. Or at least these guys do."

From the corner, "Pass."

When the next Elf came out covered in nothing but gold paint, I closed my eyes. Then I purposely tuned out for the next four contestants. One of them must have been good because he got a resounding smash from the nymphs. When the music stopped and Mrs. Claus stepped up to the mic to introduce the next contestant, it was like everything around me slowed down and sped up at the same time. "Our last contestant needs no introduction. The reigning three-time champion, Mr. Hart Brandywine."

Yeager and I both slid forward in our seats. Next to me, Jack crossed a leg. I think we all held our breaths as Hart stepped out from behind the curtain.

He was wearing a black hoodie and pants. He even had on gloves that covered his sexy silver rings. The hood of his sweatshirt was over his head with a sparkling gold crown on top of it. Jack's to be precise. Beyond that, he wore his dark aviators, so his amazing eyes were covered too. If anyone had seen him on the street, they'd probably pass right by him, if not for the crown.

Even still.

*Even still.*

Sensuality exuded from him.

He was literally walking sex. And I didn't mean literally in a Cherish way. I meant it in the way that every person in the lodge with us and in the audience leaned forward. Like he was pulling them in. It was in the way he led with his pelvis when he walked. And in the cut of his wide shoulders that thinned into his perfect hips. Even in sweats, his body betrayed him.

He couldn't get rid of it. And he was trying.

I'd never wanted anyone to lose so much in my life.

He pulled out the sign we'd help him make, holding it up to the camera so the whole audience could see. It read *Don't*

*Vote For Me. Buy a Gift for a Child in Need Instead. Gifts, not objects.* Then he went to the edge of the stage and stood there unmoving. Camera flashes popped, the audience was mumbling, and a frenzied rumble of energy seemed to reach out from the big screen and grip me by the heart. After a few uncomfortable minutes, he strolled over to the reindeer, saying something in Cupid's ear. She smiled and I knew he'd said something about me. Then he pulled off one glove, reached behind her, and punched Rudy in the face.

I jumped off the couch. I didn't know what to do. I couldn't *do* anything, but the sight of the blood dripping from his nose did something to me. It seemed like a spell had been broken.

How many times had I wanted to do just that?

And how many times had I convinced myself it was wrong to feel that way?

Too many. On both counts.

Yeager wrapped his arms around me from behind, whispering in my ear as he chuckled. "Rage against Rudy personified."

Jack leaned in. "I didn't think he'd go that far to throw the contest."

I knew that the punch had nothing to do with throwing the contest. That move was for me.

"Listen, I've taken one of Hart's punches. That shit is going to hurt him for a while. It was fucking epic," Yeager commented.

It was. But it didn't work.

# CHAPTER 26

We voted for over an hour. Not just our team, but the others too. Vixen had told them how much Hart hated the title and how he'd been forced to participate, so everyone was on board to help him out by voting for the idiot with the string.

The whole thing backfired, and I felt like shit over it. It had been my idea to protest by actively trying to be unsexy, but at the end of the day, Hart couldn't do it. He *was* sexy. End of.

Within minutes of the contest ending, his 'look' had gone viral and started a movement. #GiftsNotObjects trended worldwide. People were posting selfies of themselves wearing black and homemade crowns and holding presents, presumably for kids in need. However, at the same time, they were voting for him to support his protest of the outdated concept of sexy contests in the first place, causing him to win the thing again anyway.

Yeah. Explain that to me.

Vixen didn't take his win well. Neither did I. Or Jack. When Hart sent us a message that he was proud of the win and going to do a press junket as a result of it but would be back for the game the next day, we read between the lines. He was defeated and shackled into the title for another year. Probably for multiple years. While I didn't know what the spectacular prize was that he'd won, I knew it wasn't what he wanted.

And that fucking ate at me.

I didn't know what Jack did after the spectacle, but Vixen and I went to bed snuggled together discussing ways we might make things easier for Hart when he came back the next day. We didn't even have sex. Which was mind-blowing to me. I always wanted her. Always, but we'd both been too defeated. It had seemed wrong to enjoy pleasure when we knew Hart was hurting.

So, we didn't.

When he popped into the lodge the next morning, Vixen bolted at him. She wrapped her arms and legs around him, apologizing over and over for what had happened. He buried his nose in her hair and held her against him. I knew in my soul that was the best thing any of us could do for him— her. And when he slid his hands from her legs to her ass, I figured he was going to be okay.

I pressed against her back, copping my own feel, and gripping Hart's hands at the same time. "Sorry, Man. What happened last night sucks, but you're here with us now, so put it behind you. If it helps, I can tell you how ugly you are all day long."

He laughed. "Yeah, thanks, but you really don't believe that."

I didn't. It gave me zero pause to admit it.

Jack blew in the door and spotted the three of us. His eyebrow shot up. There was a lot said with that one eyebrow. I was going to make it my mission to learn to read what he was thinking when he arched it. At that moment, it appeared to be questioning if Hart was okay. I pulled Jack in by the neck, smooshing him in between us. He bristled, but just for a second, then he slapped Hart on the back. "Not the outcome we wanted, but some progress was made. You can levy the movement into something bigger next year. Perhaps take a cue from the vampires and wear a garbage bag."

Jack coming in hot with the jokes. Who knew he had it in him?

Vixen laughed and that snowballed into a big ole group chuckle.

It was nice.

Vixen wiggled out of our grasp and drug Jack over to the coffee pot. I was still gripping Hart's hands. He hesitated for a second, then pulled away. When he ran his hand over his jaw, I spotted his swollen busted knuckles. I grabbed his hand back to inspect them. "Is this from clocking the asshole reindeer?"

"This one was Rudy." He held his other hand in front of my face. "This one was something else." I lowered my gaze. And somehow I morphed into my father without consent. I was looking at him like I was certain he'd done something wrong, judging him, which was idiotic on my part. He deserved to do whatever he had to do to cope. "I had to work out some frustrations."

His hand was a shitshow. "I feel sorry for the guy."

"Wasn't a guy. It was a brick wall."

That Elf was a baller.

But my comment went unsaid when Holly sailed into the room wearing a green sweater with blinking lights and a black skirt with bells on the bottom. Going for the double sensory experience today. Behind her, Karl, Jasper, and Frank carried reams of white paper and a bucket of scissors. She jingled her skirt to get our attention. "Today teams will be making snowflakes." I wished I could replicate the sound that came from Cherish. The girl was not a fan of crafting.

"This is a two-part game. In part one, you'll get one ream of paper and make as many snowflakes as you can for one hour. Keep in mind they must resemble snowflakes. Don't just cut willy-nilly and expect it to pass muster. You owe Santa your best work.

"At one hour, the judges and I will count how many you've made and the team with the most will get four candy canes, the second place team will get three, and so on and so on. At that time, I'll explain part two."

We took our spot on the couch and all the other teams fanned out while the paper and scissors were passed out among the teams. "Good luck. Your time starts now."

We all grabbed some paper and scissors. Well, everyone but Jack. He sat there perched on the arm of the couch. This time both eyebrows were up in the stratosphere. I had to laugh. "The Frost King doesn't know how to make paper snowflakes."

Hart snorted and Vixen paused mid-cut. "Really Jack?"

"I can make real snowflakes. Why would I bother with fakes?" To prove his point, he held up his hand and wiggled his fingers. When Vixen gasped, both Hart and I swung around to find snowflakes dotting her long eyelashes and juicy lips.

That was cool. Nah, hot.

Both.

She looked amazing. Jack looked smug.

Hart passed him a pair of scissors. "When you're done flexing, we're going for quantity here. Start cutting." The nip in his voice was unmistakable. It burned inside me. We should've done something else to help him get out of the contest.

"It's easy. I'll teach you, Jack. Watch me." Vixen handed him a piece of paper and showed him how to fold it. I picked her up and put her on my lap so she could be closer to Jack as she demonstrated.

And so I could lean over to Hart. "Do you want to talk about it?"

He bit his lip. "What's there to say? I'm good."

"But you're not."

"But I have to be."

Frustration rolled off him. "What did Santa say about your stunt?" Vixen and Jack both stopped cutting.

"Who had Santa gives him a pat on the back, a raise, and streams of congratulations on your Bingo card?"

"Wait. He was happy about it?" Vixen asked. I was with her. Didn't understand.

"Yup." He popped the p on the end of the word. "Donations to the hospital tripled in one night, so he was ecstatic. On top of that, Mrs. Claus is working on a brand-new line of black athletic clothes with a gold crown logo. She's tentatively calling BeneFit. One guess who the spokesmodel will be on that. And they're thinking of making next year's

North Pole's Sexiest Elf contest bigger with women contestants to show their equality. So, outside of the hospital donations, everything that happened last night made it all worse."

"Fuck me. That's...I don't even know what that is." I didn't. It was a nightmare. "All that in one night?"

"Yeah. Things move fast at the Pole." He took a deep breath. "Can we focus on something else?"

"Sure. Let's talk about how sick my snowflake is." I held it up for the team to see.

Vixen beamed. "That's good Yeager. Now we only have four-hundred, ninety-nine to go."

Forty-five minutes later there was a pile of shredded paper at our feet. Vixen laid her scissors on the table and sighed. "My hand is cramping. I need a break."

She pulled her phone out of her pocket. Like some kind of bat signal went off at the appearance of a phone, Cherish piped up from the chair by the fireplace, "Good luck with that because the Wi-Fi is spotty again. Straight facts."

Vixen giggled but attempted the phone anyway. After a few seconds of scrolling, she paused. "Okay, my friend needs a man's opinion on these dresses for the Snow Ball tonight. Which one do you like?"

She waved her phone at Hart first, then flicked a few times for him. He smirked. "Cupid trying to go for the kill, huh? I feel qualified to say the first dress is the sexiest. Speaking from a strictly professional standpoint." He was joking about it now, but the humor wasn't hitting right. We all knew how he really felt.

Jack reached out, grabbing the phone to give his opinion. "The third one has an alluring quality. It gives off a mysterious vibe that sparks the imagination." He glanced over at Cherish to check the correct usage of the word vibe. She gave a silent thumbs-up. That girl heard more than she let on.

Vixen angled her phone toward me. Her friend Cupid was gorgeous. She had long blonde hair, full pink lips, and a cute turned-up nose. Still, she couldn't hold a candle to Vixen. I checked out the dresses. Hart was right that the first one was the sexy one because it left little to the imagination and Jack had nailed the description of the third one. It had long sleeves with a few cutouts here and there. But for my money, I liked the second one. It was strapless and short without being slutty. It hugged her great figure without being too tight. "I like the second one. It seems to bridge the gap between sexy and demure."

"Hm. I think you're right. I'll text her," Vixen agreed.

After she'd told her friend, she picked the scissors back up. Hart had since stopped his cutting and was looking at her like he wanted to say something but wasn't. I angled my head toward him and gave him a look. Telling him to get it out, whatever it was.

He seemed to get my gesture and run with it. "How are you feeling about missing the Snow Ball tonight, Ginger?"

There was a distinct horrified expression on her face before she sighed audibly. "Fine. If I'd been at the Pole, I wouldn't even be going this year anyway, so whatever."

I didn't buy it for a second. None of us did. There was a whole lot packed into that whatever.

# CHAPTER 27

Hart whistled. "That's a shame. Let me tell you, boys, she looked like a dream last year. Rudy's a cunt for making her attend the most important event of the holiday season alone."

I didn't look like a dream. I looked like a loser as I sat there in my gorgeous white dress—everyone wore white to the Snow Ball—alone waiting for my date who never showed up. "Thanks, but that's not accurate."

"Beg to differ."

Jack slid over to the coffee table facing Hart, manspread on level red for dangerously hot. "What was she wearing?"

Yeager chuckled under his breath as Hart leaned forward like he was sharing state secrets instead of describing a party outfit. "It was one of those dresses that tied behind her neck and plunged low enough so that her mouth-watering breasts were heaving out of it. It hugged her hips, then flared out at the bottom, trailing behind her when she walked. I couldn't keep my eyes off her. No one could."

Waves of crisp coolness drifted around me, emanating from Jack. "Her hair?"

"Up mostly, with a few little curls falling around her face, grazing her neck and shoulders. It was piled on the top of her head with a white shimmery ribbon running through it. For hours I sat there imagining what would happen if I just went over there and tugged on it. I pictured a cascade of red spilling down the open back of the dress."

"Fuck me." Yeager.

"Indeed." Jack.

"I don't think I'm doing a decent job of describing it, but I'll just say it jingled my bells so hard I had to go into the bathroom and jerk off. Twice."

My cheeks flushed. Not only Hart's description but also Yeager and Jack's reaction to it. They were all staring at me imagining what Hart had described and three sets of heated eyes at once was a lot to take.

I'll admit I didn't hate the way that felt, but at its root, it was wrong.

I hadn't felt beautiful at the ball at all. I'd felt abandoned. It was the first time I fully realized there was something wrong between Rudy and me. He'd sent a text saying he'd be late, then never showed. All around me, everyone was dancing and drinking and having fun while I sat there like the turd in the punchbowl. "Hart stop."

He looked at me with those soulful sexy eyes and I could taste ginger on my tongue. "Yeah, that's an effective way to describe it. My heart stopped."

Yeager growled. "Where was Ralph during all of this?" The look on his face went from lust to murder between two heartbeats.

"I don't know. When I questioned his absence the next day, he said something important came up. That's all I got out of him."

"Something like his dick inside another woman." Hart squeezed my thigh. "If you want, I can find out. I have people for that."

I considered it for a second. Sure, the curiosity was there, but what good would it have done me? He'd already hurt me as much as he possibly could. Finding out he was screwing Clare during the Snow Ball wouldn't change a thing. "No thanks. I don't want to know. It's weird. I used to love going to the Snow Ball, but I guess it's now just another thing he took from me." I went back to cutting. It was easier than looking at them and hacking something to bits felt fitting. "It doesn't matter anyway. I'm here and the Snow Ball is there, so it's a moot point. Cupid will send me pics and I can follow on NickTock maybe. I shouldn't be there."

They would be there, Rudy and Clare. That was the last thing I wanted to see. So, I plastered on a huge smile and thank all the silver bells in the land, the timer on Holly's clock went off.

Time to count snowflakes.


We only got two candy canes for the first portion of the contest. Frostbite was the winner by a long shot, then somehow Ho, Ho, Ho, Hot came in second. Then us, then Hot Chocolate. Probably because Cherish had spent most of the hour on her phone in distress about some savage trolling in her world. No idea.

Holly took a second to flick with the controller on her sweater, changing her blinking lights pattern before she read the card. "For the second portion of the snowflake-making contest, teams should select one snowflake to represent your team. Then we'll cast votes on creativity, execution, and style. You'll have five minutes to pick your snowflake."

Eager to think about anything but the Snow Ball, I started to sort through our pile. It was evident which of the guys made which snowflake. Yeager's were bigger with wide swaths of paper and smaller holes. They looked strong and sturdy like they wouldn't tear if you tried to hang them up. Hart's on the other hand, had sharp jagged edges that looked unrealistic and real at the same time. They were surprising and artistic in a way. Jack's were precise. Not only symmetrical but almost identical too. They resembled actual snowflakes with little spikes jutting from the entire stem of the snowflake.

It struck me to the core that these snowflakes did a perfectly accurate job of defining each of the three men in front of me. Fitting since mine looked like a hot mess.

"Damn Jack. You're a quick study." Hart said as he plucked a snowflake from the table.

"If I do something, I do it right."

Yeager slung an arm around him. "Included, but not limited to, say, red-haired reindeer shifters?"

Jack slipped out of Yeager's grip, but I didn't miss the smirk he gave him. He was warming up to Yeager. And to Hart. And possibly to the ideas they'd presented him.

Still unsure about how that would work.

"I say we pick this one. We good on that?" Hart was holding one of Jack's up. It was one of his first, but not his best, but I think that's what made it better somehow. It just gave off a vibe that seemed like us.

Oh, my Soul, I was losing my grip thinking a paper snowflake could give a vibe or reflect us in any way. There was no "us."

The team agreed on the choice. We voted for Frostbite again because their snowflake had been even more technical than Jack's. Who knew that bobsledding vampires seeking Transylvanian independence could craft? I didn't have that on my Bingo card.

When the voting was done, Hart slung his arm around Yeager, pulling him over into the dining room for a private conversation. They huddled together discussing something for several minutes. Yeager kept glancing at me and grinning, while Hart was using his hands dramatically.

"They're up to something." Jack pressed his cool hand on the back of my neck, then he leaned over and kissed my cheek. "I've been summoned to my Kingdom. I'm afraid I have business to conduct, so I don't think we'll be able to enjoy the visit like we did our last. I'd love to show you some more of my palace anyway."

Did not have to ask me twice.

I looked over to Yeager and Hart. They were still clustered together so I took Jack's hand. He pulled out his snow globe and said, "Wintertide." We whooshed into his palace again. This time, it was his throne room.

My Soul, I was hanging out with a man who had a throne room.

Of course, his throne was made of ice, and of course, it was magnificent.

It wasn't massive—not much larger than a regular dining chair—but it gave off such a sense of power, that I knew I was gaping at it.

"Have a seat if you like." Jack removed his black suit jacket and spread it over the seat for me. That left him in a fitted white shirt and black silk tie that shimmered when he moved. There was not one dark hair out of place, not one wrinkle in his suit. Immaculate was the only word I could use to describe him.

I sat on the throne and giggled like a schoolgirl as I gave a royal wave to my invisible subjects around the room.

The high back was solid ice with scrolling swirls carved into it that formed the arms and legs. I'd guessed an ice throne would have jagged edges and sharp icicle points, but this one wasn't anything like that. It was refined. Structured and clean, with no unnecessary details that took the eye's attention away from the person who was meant to sit on it.

That person, at that moment, was me. And Jack was staring at me with a look that I was certain would melt the throne underneath me.

"Your majesty, the Duke of Hailstone insists on seeing you now. I'm afraid he's not going to take no."

Jack grumbled at Burl's interruption, and I stood up and gave his jacket back. It was fun to play queen for a moment, but he had work to do.

"Fine, send him in." I looked around the room to find a place to disappear, but Jack took my hand, keeping me in place. "This shouldn't take long."

I nodded and he let go of my hand, allowing me to scoot a respectable distance away from him, but still on the dais. The Duke burst into the throne room, glancing in my direction, then narrowing his eyes on Jack. "You've got to do something about John Sun. The winterberry crops are dying due to his encroachment. My subjects, your subjects are losing their wages as we speak."

John Sun. Why was I not surprised?

"He's postponed our meeting again, but I assure you, Hailstone, I'm in control of the situation."

"Are you?" The Duke blustered. His big bushy beard waved as he spoke. "Because I've spoken with Dukes Glacierfloe and Winternight, as well as the Duchess from Icehaven. The kingdom is melting, Your Majesty plain and simple. Nearly one-third of the permafrost is sludge."

Jack leaned forward. "Impossible."

"Go see for yourself."

Jack shot me an apologetic look, but I wasn't going to stand in the way of his work. "You can swish me back then go do what you have to do."

"Give me a moment, then I'll go investigate." He waved Hailstone away. "This is not what I expected to hear today. Hailstone blusters about everything, but if what he's saying is true, I need to know."

He used his snow globe to deposit me back into the lodge. "If there's anything I can do to help you, please tell me." He remained calm and waiting before he planned any action, but there was worry in his posture and I didn't dig the crease between his eyebrows.

"You've already helped me, Flame. I'll see you later." He leaned in and I thought he'd give me another peck on the cheek, but instead, he took my chin and angled it so he could kiss my lips. And that kiss contained a lot of fire for someone who was always cold. He was so sure, so purposeful as his mouth moved against mine. And when he drew back, I was breathless.

No sooner than I'd had the thought that I wanted more, he'd swooshed back into his snow globe world.

"We've been waiting for you."

"We're doing a mani-pedi party."

"Let's go!"

The nymphs. I was about to refuse their invitation if it could even be called that, but no sooner than Monday had taken my hand, an envelope popped into my other. I opened it and found shimmery white paper with red foil letters.

*Go with them. Enjoy yourself and get ready. We're going on a date tonight and I'm not taking no. See you in a few hours, Ginger. You're going to love this. -Hart*

That was unexpected. A date? With Hart? I couldn't wrap my head around the idea. First of all, is elfmail the best way to ask a girl out? And secondly, what about Yeager? And Jack? Was this his way of trying to get in good with me before them? Or beyond them?

Based on the brief conversation we'd had about it, it wasn't likely,

Still, I knew Hart and he had an angle. I just couldn't figure out what it was. Before I could give it any more thought I was whisked away to the nymphs' cabin where we sipped wine and did each other's nails for a few hours.

The next time I heard the pop, the item that appeared leveled me as much as surprised me.

# CHAPTER 28

Laying on Monday's bed was a white box with a shimmery white ribbon around it. The nymphs were clapping and bouncing, begging me to open it. Yes, I wanted to know what was inside, but I couldn't help but feel that there was something more at stake than simply unwrapping a package.

My hands shook as I untied the ribbon and pulled the top off of the box. Of course, there was white tissue paper with silvery flecks that I had to open too. Elves could wrap packages. I flipped back the paper and found another note.

*Put this on and use the ribbon to tie up your hair. Text me when you're ready and I'll pop over to get you. I promise you, this will be a night you'll never forget. - Hart*

"Oh."

"My."

"Soul."

The nymphs were screaming at full tilt as I lifted the dress from the box.

It was stunning.

And we made from the snowflakes we'd created earlier.

Nothing but the snowflakes.

Warmth spread through my chest as I held it up to examine it. The snowflakes had been sewn together and it was sturdy as I swung it around to look at the back.

Mindy didn't even try to hide the fact that she was reading the card. "Go put it on. Use whatever makeup you want in the bathroom. We'll help you do your hair after."

Honestly, I was too stunned to move, so they shoved me in the door and chattered while I got undressed. There was a small hook at the back that allowed me to step into the dress and pull it up. When I had it on completely and turned to look in the mirror, I sighed.

The dress was strapless and short, but not too short. There was a deep slit on the side and my left leg was visible, but it didn't go up so far as to show my white panties, thank my Soul, I just happened to have them on. The green ones I had on the day before would've looked awful shining through.

Something about the dress seemed familiar, but I couldn't place it. And I don't know how he did it, but it fit perfectly. There were gaps due to the holes in the snowflakes, but the strategic placement of the bigger snowflakes Yeager had made covered my nipples and lady bits. The dress was sexy, but not slutty. Sweet, but not kitschy, and standing there looking at myself in the mirror, I didn't remember when I'd felt more desirable.

Years.

When I was finished putting on a little makeup, I went back out and found a pair of shoes—the silver heels I wore last year—on the bed. Mindy said Hart had popped them in and disappeared again. Which meant he'd popped into my closet back home to get them. I wasn't upset about that because those things were killer.

While Mindy and Monday did my hair, Mandy shoved something in my hand. "This is nymph fuel. It works like a protein bar as far as giving you carbs and protein for stamina, but it's got a special formula designed to keep you from farting. Don't laugh, it happens when you eat high fiber. When that hot Elf is between your legs, you don't have to be holding in a fart."

True. True. I'd never thought specifically about that before, but she had a great point.

When I was convinced, I looked as good as I could, I texted Hart. He popped in seconds later and I was not ready for it.

He wore a white suede jacket with a tight—oh my soul, so tight—white t-shirt under it. His white jeans were slung low over his hips and his hair was a little curlier than normal. He had on his trademark silver rings that were stupidly sexy for some reason that I couldn't define. And his smile? His smile was screaming 'Come and get me.'

He wasn't just sexy. He was magnificent. "Hart." My voice was a whisper. He'd already made me breathless, and he hadn't said one word yet. I had dozens of things bouncing around my head to say to him: thank you, I want you, you're amazing, what have you done, you're making me feel things, just to name a few. But beyond his name, I couldn't choke anything else out.

"I didn't think you could top last year, but you have. You look dazzling."

I took a step toward him. "This dress. I don't know what to say."

"Maybe you'll think of something later. Shall we?" He offered me his arm, like a freaking gentleman caller from the fifties. I took it and we popped out of the nymph cabin and into mine.

Though it took a second to recognize it.

Twinkling white lights were hanging around the entire cabin. They were everywhere and the only light in the room other than the fireplace. The rest of our paper snowflakes were hanging from the ceiling, giving the room the feel of the Snow Ball without being there. I was light-headed as I took them all in. "You did all this too?"

"Not exactly, but we'll get to that in a minute. Right now, we're going to dance, Ginger."

He plugged his phone into speakers and scrolled until music floated around the room. Couldn't even tell you what song. I was so overwhelmed by him, by everything he'd done to give me our own little Snow Ball. So, when he put his hands on my hips, I reached up to circle his neck. And we danced.

It might have been awkward in a room with just us in it, but it wasn't. He was so focused on me and took command, moving me how he wanted, pressing our bodies close, I didn't feel strange at all. His presence just took up the entire cabin and I stepped into the shadow of him willingly.

He leaned in to kiss my neck, moving from one side to the other, nipping and biting in a way that had chills erupting all over me. "Thank my Soul, you didn't turn me down again."

"Again? What do you mean? I've never turned you down."

"Yeah, you did. I asked you to dance last year, and you said no thanks. Crushed my soul like a lovesick prepubescent boy with a crush on the out-of-his-league girl, if I'm honest, but I punched a guy in the bathroom and it helped to make me feel better."

Why did I find that inappropriate action so attractive?

He bit my earlobe, then spun me around so that my back was to him. His hand slid to my stomach as he pressed me against him. I groaned at the feel of his aroused cock as it brushed against me. "I don't think I did that."

Had I? I didn't remember, but it was hard to imagine saying no to him in any way. Not when he made me feel the way he did. Strong. Sexy. Confident. If I *had turned* him down, I shouldn't have.

"You did. But that's okay, I'm going to allow you to make up for it shortly." I laughed just as the door to the cabin opened. I gasped and the chuckle Hart made in my ear went straight down south. "Surprise."

Yeager clicked the door closed behind him. My mouth dried at the sight of him. He was wearing a white cable knit sweater that hugged his body and white soft leather pants that would've looked ridiculous on just about any other man in existence. But on him, they looked seductive. All I could do was think about how they'd feel if I ran my hands over them. He toed out of his shoes and socks, which left him barefoot. I didn't have a foot fetish. I hated feet, in fact, but something about a man being barefoot when he was otherwise fully clothed, I found hot.

He looked over at us, clocking Hart's hands on my stomach and hip, before flicking his eyes up. "Hi Bunny, you look edible. Nice work on the dress, Jingle Bell."

Then it hit me why the dress had seemed familiar. It was the second dress Cupid had sent, only in snowflake form.

The one Yeager had pegged as being the perfect combo of sexy and demure. And Hart had made it from our team's snowflakes.

I opened my mouth, but nothing came out. I couldn't process anything.

Yeager cocked his head, tracking our movement because Hart had started to sway against me again. Damn, he could move. "I see you started without me," Yeager drawled. He didn't sound mad, he sounded turned on. The husky rasp of his voice was the clue.

"Look at her. Can you blame me? I was just reminding Vixen how she'd crushed my heart last year by refusing to dance with me."

"She's dancing now."

"She is. So, are you going to stand over there with your hand in your pocket playing with yourself or are you going to join us?"

I froze.

Did I want this to happen—the two of them together? One-hundred percent. Was I nervous about it? Fuck yeah.

Yeager turned to throw a log on the fire, giving me a nice view of his ass in leather. When he finished, he took one step. One. I found myself wishing for him to eat the rest of the distance up with his long legs. "Like I told you earlier Jingle Bell, not unless I know for certain she's okay with it."

Hart pulled one of his candy canes of truth out of his pocket and unwrapped it with his teeth. Then he trailed it slowly over the swell of my breasts as he asked the question. "What do you want, Ginger? Me, him, or both of us together?"

"Both."

The answer came quickly and without hesitation. I'd never wanted two men more in my life, and while I was nervous about the mechanics of it, I knew I was safe, and beyond that, I knew I owed it to myself to explore this with them. They were more than just hot guys ready to bang Rudy out of my head. They were starting to mean something to me beyond that. Despite it.

So yeah, I wanted them both.

Yeager looked at Hart for confirmation. "Is it true?"

"Yep. Now put one foot in front of the other and get over here. Let's make a fucking dirty girl out of her."

# CHAPTER 29

Didn't have to tell me twice. I went over to them and got as close to her as I could, snaking my arms around her waist as I joined in their seduction dance. Because that's what it was. The way they moved together, their closeness, the grip of his hands on her hips—it was all foreplay.

She backed up and leaned her head back against Hart's shoulder as she looked up at me through her lashes. He dove in for her neck, kissing, nibbling, sucking his way down her throat. The two of them looked good together. And the soft sigh escaping her plump lips had my cock straining against my fly.

This woman was going to kill me.

Us.

Never before had I felt such a raucous desire. It was like she was made to taunt me, and I gave zero shits about it.

Hart still had his candy cane truth-teller in one hand. When he not-so-innocently slid it down Vixen's arm, then over to mine, I stopped moving. I knew what he was doing, what he was fishing for. His question and my answer to it would have to wait. I snatched it away and snapped it in two with one hand, then I raked my hands into his hair and pulled him off her neck so I could look right into his deep blue eyes. "Tonight's about Vixen. We're here for her pleasure. You feel me?"

Probably not the right choice of words, but whatever. He got the message. "Got it. But you know I'm only going to let you Dom for so long." He laughed, then went right back to where he'd been, kissing her neck. She looked up at me with wide eyes. There was so much in that gaze. Curiosity, excitement, desire, apprehension. Even though she was into what Hart was doing, her posture was rigid, and her hands were fidgeting at the hem of her snowflake dress.

I took her hands and kissed each fingertip one by one. "If you want this, Bunny, then you're going to have to let us give it to you. Relax." Before she could protest or disagree with me, I pressed my lips against hers. Softly at first, but it took no time for the fire to light inside me. She groaned as I ran my tongue along her lower lip, then inside her mouth. She was so eager, matching the stroke of my tongue with hers. When she opened up for me and let me fully explore her mouth, it was Hart who made a noise. "Souldamn, Yeager. That tongue."

Breathless, she laughed. "You have no idea."

Then it was on. All it took was one little chip of the ice and she went from stiff and frightened to pliable and fuck- ing willing. She threaded one hand into my hair and kissed me again. It was hot and needy, all tongue and teeth and longing. Hart, unwilling to wait any longer, pulled her chin away and dove in for his own dirty kiss. Her other hand went into his hair and though we were no longer dancing, her body was arching up at me, then back at him behind her. Like she was fucking the space between us.

That wouldn't do. Not on my watch. Not when there were so many other ways to enjoy this.

I slid my hands over her ass, down her leg, then back inside the dress, feeling her ass, then reaching down and finding her pussy. I wasn't even inside her panties yet. "Our naughty girl is soaking wet already. Your panties are dripping, aren't they Bunny?"

She nodded, unable to tear her mouth away from Hart's. I stroked her wet panties and watched as Hart moved his hand between her legs and began stroking from the front. Our fingers touched as she writhed between us. Thank fuck he wasn't one of those guys who had a strict no-touching-while-sharing policy. Like I'd told Jack before, we were a team. And I was man enough to admit, I dug the feel of his silver rings against my fingers as we worked Vixen up. She must have too based on the whimpering we were getting.

"Turn around, Ginger. I want to see those perky tits up close and personal." Hart whipped her around and pulled the top of the dress down.

She gasped. "Don't. You'll tear the dress. I want to save it."

He smirked. "I'll make you as many snowflake dresses as you want. This has got to go now." He ripped the front of the dress, exposing her tits and stomach, and damn near salivating at the sight of her. "Besides, just because something is beautiful, doesn't mean it's meant to last forever. The next dress I give you will be better."

I was impressed with his ability to be wise and horny at the same time. And we all knew he wasn't just talking about the dress. He was trying to help her rip Rascal out of her life like the dress.

It wasn't the moment to stop and consider emotional ramifications, however. It was the time to make Vixen come. I was staring at her beautiful backside, but I was tired of it being obscured. So, I took the hem of the dress and ripped it up the middle, all the way to the top. Then the two of us were groping and ripping and growling as the paper remains fell to the floor like snowfall.

That was just the beginning.

Things got a little frenzied after we had her mostly naked. Vixen alternated between kissing us and pulling at our clothes. She managed to get Hart's jacket off his shoulders but had trouble with his t-shirt because she was trying to get her hands on his chest at the same time as pulling up his shirt. I helped her out by reaching over and peeling his shirt over his head. Then he did the same to me because Vixen's hands were rubbing all over my ass and legs and she couldn't be bothered to stop. My sexy girl liked the leather.

Noted.

And she was eyeing me in a way that had me so fucking hard. Though Hart protested for a minute I picked Vixen up and carried her over to the double lounge chair by the fireplace and deposited her on the soft white blanket. Hart popped over the next moment and we stood there looking down at her with her swollen lips, hooded eyes, and drenched panties.

She dug her fingers into the fur on the blanket. "Wait, this wasn't here this morning."

Hart smirked. "That's the remains of the polar bear I fought off. Had a blanket made. It was a rush order. Gotta say, Ginger, you look good sitting on it. Knowing it's going to smell like you when we're done is even better."

I agreed. "Mm-hm."

She smiled up at us and shifted, spreading her legs apart just enough to let us know it was intentional. Fucking toying with us and I loved it. I knocked Hart with my elbow. "If that's not an invitation, I don't know what is."

He slung an arm over my shoulders. "Right. How do you want to do this? North Pole or South Pole?"

"You're from the North, so you go South. I'll do North. For now, anyway."

A battle plan established—because make no mistake, we were in a war against the idea that Vixen didn't deserve happiness and satisfaction—we went to work. I grabbed a couple of pillows from next to the fireplace and shoved one at Hart. He threw it on the floor and went to his knees. The look of admiration on his face when he got close to her pussy was amazing. He wanted her just as much as I did.

"Take her panties off." I wasn't trying to Dom him like he'd implied earlier. I was just fucking eager to see what lie beneath them again.

She lifted her hips, and he slid the panties down her legs and threw them somewhere behind him. Should've tossed them into the fire as far as I was concerned because I never wanted her to cover that delectable pussy again. "What are you waiting for elf? Make her moan."

He lifted one of her legs and perched on the armrest, then he did exactly what I said by running his tongue over her hot seam and back down again. Her hips bucked and that juicy lower lip of hers went straight between her teeth.

My soul, so damned sexy.

Hart wasted zero time getting down and dirty. Within seconds he was sucking her clit into his mouth as she arched for him. It was mesmerizing really. Her hips bucking and his mouth tasting her. I couldn't help it. I rubbed my cock as I watched them. "Taste good?"

"You fucking know she does. Tell me what the fuck are you doing playing with yourself again? This is a two-man job."

He was right.

As he went back down on her, Vixen managed to crack open one eye. "I love those pants, but maybe take them off for now." Hart chuckled and the sensation drove her to buck her hips to meet his mouth.

I did as I'd been commanded and shucked my pants and underwear too. Vixen sighed at the sight of me and yeah, that felt good. Hart stopped his tongue long enough to glance up.

His eyes went wide as he took in my size. "Respect."

Okay, that was good too. He smirked and I didn't miss the slickness on his lips. "What do you say, Ginger, do you want that beast in your hot mouth?"

She nodded; her lower lip still caught between her teeth. So, I went over and rested my knee on the opposite armrest so I could angle toward her mouth and also get an unob-structed view of what Hart was doing between her legs. She reached out and took the base of my aching throbbing cock in her hand, then ran her tongue along the length of me.

"Sweet mother of my soul."

Hart managed to keep licking her pussy and looked up at me with a look that said, 'right?'

She made a few more passes up and down my length, before she circled the tip, her pink tongue and flicking over my slit had my balls ready to burst open. Finally, she took all of me in her mouth. The pleasure from the groan she made—whether from the taste of my cock or what Hart was doing with his teeth now—did not matter. The sensation rolled through me, and I was lost in it.

In her.

I curled my fingers in her hair, taking some of the weight off her neck as she took more of me in her mouth. The ribbon was still there, and I wanted to pull that thing out so much, but I didn't. I needed to wait for Hart to witness that. He was too fucking into her pussy to pay any attention at that moment.

I was into it too. "Give her more. Fuck her with your fingers. I want to see those rings disappear."

He stopped long enough to shoot me a wicked grin, then went right back to sucking her clit as he slid two of his fingers inside her and started pumping. Sure enough, those rings were gone inside her within a matter of seconds.

Vixen groaned. Or growled. Or some kind of sound that went straight through me. Never once did she act like her jaw was hurting or that she didn't want my cock all the way to the base. She just kept on sucking, and I kept on rocking and pushing inside her. Hart was below me pumping his fingers in her and curling them just right to hit that spot.

Goosebumps broke out on her skin. "She likes that."

When she nodded, I almost came.

Needing to cool myself down a little because I was nowhere near ready, I pulled my cock free of her lips. Her cheeks were pink as she glanced up at me. The woman was fire and it split me into pieces. I leaned down to kiss her. Really kiss her. Slowly, purposefully. The taste of her was what my dreams were made of. I gave her everything that was in me and when we broke apart, she was gasping. "My soul, Yeager. Where did you learn to kiss like that?"

No idea. As far as I was concerned, she was the only woman I'd ever kissed. Or would kiss again. I bent down and sucked on her lower lip and Hart took my hand at the same time, dragging it down to meet where his fingers were pumping inside her.

Message received. I could do that.

I dropped to my knees next to him, swiveling the chair toward me. I took a couple of seconds to admire his technique. Two fingers inside, his thumb stroking her clit. I wanted in on that action, so I pushed two fingers inside her with him.

Her reaction was immediate. "Oh. Fuck. Yes. Both of you."

I winked at Hart then bent over to run my tongue in the junction of her pelvis and thigh. It made her squirm, so I did it again. This time Hart did too. We spent the next few minutes kissing and licking her thighs in tandem while our four fingers were inside her wetness. The scent of her arousal was making me fucking dizzy. And Hart was huffing panting as loud as she was.

Damn, it was hot.

I felt Hart's eyes, so I looked up and found his glazed expression focused on me. He nodded once as if to tell me he was going to do something different, so I slowed down my pumping as he pulled his fingers out of her. Her wetness was all over them, down to the rings and I'll be damned if I didn't have the desire to put them inside my mouth and suck it all off. But I didn't have time because he slid them back inside her pussy, and when he pulled them out again, he skated them along that sensitive area between her pussy and her asshole.

She bucked.

It was a good buck.

Hart laughed. "You want this, don't you? Right here." He didn't wait for her to answer. He just started stroking and slowly inching back until his middle finger was flicking against her hole. I managed to mutter a 'fuck me' as I drove my fingers inside, grazing her g-spot as he played with her ass. The rhythm we found was instant, making Vixen groan and curse and rock against our fingers.

I'd done group things before, but I had never been so in tune with a person as we worked to bring a woman to oblivion like that.

It didn't take long. Vixen gripped one of my shoulders in her hand and the other one held onto Hart. Her fine ass came off the polar bear, which was soaked now, as she came.

Eager to wring as much out of her as we could, we kept our hands where they were and dove for her tits. I took one in my mouth, flicking my tongue first, then sucking as her nipples hardened underneath it. On the other side, Hart had the diamond peak of her tip in his teeth.

She came hard and fast.
And we hadn't even gotten started yet.

# CHAPTER 30

Hearing her come again was blaring music and fire and wind hitting me in the face as I peeled down the highway on my bike. It was beyond everything.

When she finally came down, I kissed her, needing to drive my tongue inside her mouth like I had her pussy. She lapped at me, meeting each thing I did with shameless lust. I tasted the zing of her pleasure zipping through my veins.

Needing more himself, Yeager angled her chin toward him and took his own kiss from her.

With both kisses, she sighed.

She was into the sharing.

So was I. And Yeager too. We'd worked well together, and I figured we'd do well with the next part too. Because, of course, we weren't finished by any stretch of the imagination. Not until we'd fucked Rudy out of her mind and heart for good.

I pulled my red boxers down. Vixen immediately sat up and zeroed in on my piercing. Her grin was wide.

Yeager, meanwhile, let out a cackle. "Now I get it. Jingle bells." He paused for a second to fully examine the bell studs on the ends of my bar, maybe considering how one might use it for pleasure or just plain amusement. He turned to Vixen, who was still staring at my dick. "I've got to hear if it jingles when he's inside you."

It would, but I wanted to let him experience that for himself, so I kept mum about it.

Vixen was there for it too. She scooted up to the edge of the chair and I swear my cock knew it was about to have her because it became fatally hard at the thought of it. I gave her my hand so I could pull her up, but the Yeti with the massive cock had other ideas.

"Here's how we need to do this." He pulled Vixen up and turned her around facing the chair. "Knees up."

She did as she was told because she was a good fucking girl. Yeager pulled the chair out from the fireplace so he could stand behind it. I was starting to see where he was going, so I positioned myself behind her. I took a second to reach in front and map her body with my hands, raking them over her tits, down her stomach, between her legs as Yeager tracked the movement with his lust-filled eyes.

He reached into her hair and plucked on the ribbon, drawing it out slowly, then wrapping it around the back of my neck with a smirk. Her hair tumbled down over her shoulders, and it was everything I expected and more. It was ridiculous to think, but after everything we'd done or would do, that sight would be what haunted my mind the most. He shot me a look that said, 'You're welcome' and threaded his fingers through her locks as he pulled her up to kiss her.

Yeah, I'd need to find a way to thank him for that.

Tension was coiling through me, and I didn't think I could wait much longer, so I put my hands in her hair too, then pressed between her shoulder blades, lowering to meet Yeager's stiff cock. "There you go. Now you can take that California Redwood over there all the way in."

Yeager winked, but all his giddiness flew out the window when she ran her tongue over this tip. "Have mercy," he rasped as she wrapped her hand around his base and went to work, sucking and drawing him in as far as she could get him. The way she was going down on it made it seem like it was nothing. It was not nothing. It was the biggest cock I'd seen, and she was loving the shit out of it.

I probably should've asked before that moment, but I assumed Vixen and Yeager had already had some sort of birth control conversation since they'd banged before. Santa had some policies about that, so I knew there was no way Vixen could get pregnant without checking in with him first. Still, though, I didn't want to assume anything. "I'm about to fuck you into oblivion, Ginger. Do you want me to glove up first or can I do this bare to really feel that pussy?"

She paused her cock sucking and looked back at me. "Not really, but I..." She glanced back at Yeager, and they shared a look I couldn't read. It went on for a couple of seconds and I was starting to wonder if I'd messed up somehow. But I wasn't a dick. I may have had my fingers and tongue inside her, but I wasn't going to do anything else if she wasn't comfortable with it.

After a few more minutes of staring, Yeager kissed her cheek, assuring her it was fine, then placed his hands on my chest.

Okay.

So, there was the answer to the question I wasn't sure I wanted to ask. I raised an eyebrow as he skimmed his large hands down my ribs and my stomach. Warmth spread through my chest. I wasn't quite sure what to do with that. If that wasn't enough to make me pause, his tattoos morphed in front of my eyes.

I thought I might have been having a stroke after all the intense pleasure, but Vixen was watching with awe, so I knew I wasn't imagining it. "The fuck, Yeager?"

The swirling pattern of his sick tattoos lifted off his skin, then vanished in a breath, reappearing a few seconds later on his chest and arms.

Yeager pulled his hands off me and glanced down at her. "It was a good idea to be safe, but he was clean. By the way, you won't be needing cold medication tomorrow. You're welcome."

I had no idea what was happening. I was not used to that feeling at all. I was the man who had fingers in every pie. Intel was the key to everything I did. Being out of the loop on whatever this one didn't sit well in my soul. "One of you want to explain that to me?"

Yeager clapped my shoulder. "Could it wait until after we're done? Because you and I are both hard as stone and she's salivating. Priorities, Man."

Right. I nodded, then pressed Vixen back down to Yeager's cock and she went right back at it. He looked over at me. "Now, what are *you* waiting for? Her hot pussy is right there."

It was.

I shook myself out of the stupor Yeager had caused and got back into the game, taking my shaft in my hand, and running it over her wetness. Then, just for Yeager's amusement, I tapped it against her, ringing the bells. She groaned and he let out a laugh. "My soul, that's the best sound." Vixen nodded, cock still in her mouth. Then she arched back a little and I didn't want to make her wait any longer. I pushed into her, and it was a chain reaction. All three of us grunted in unison.

This was going to be good.

I drew myself out slowly, then slammed into her again. And then again. With each thrust, the bells jingled, and my cock leaped for fucking joy. "Your cunt is like velvet. I can't get enough of you."

I couldn't. Wouldn't. I didn't expect it to be like this. Yeah, I knew it would feel good, but it was deeper than that. She was a surprise at every turn. For someone who always knew everything, that was unfamiliar territory.

Territory I needed to explore.

She whimpered against Yeager's cock as I drove into her. His hands were playing over his spine as he watched her take him. The sheer pleasure on his face was obvious. I knew I had the same look on my own. "Give it to her harder. How do those jingle bells feel, Bunny?"

She backed off long enough to answer him, all the while twisting her hand over his shaft to the sound of his hungry panting. "They feel unbelievable." I thrust harder, angling sideways to give her a different sensation. And make them ring more. "My soul, oh, yes, that's... more of that, please." She swished her hips, making the bells rub against her walls, meeting my thrusts and giving them more friction. I almost came right then.

Yeager glanced up and smirked. And I got what he meant with that look. Felt it down deep in my soul. This was no ordinary woman, and we were fucking lucky. With that thought alone in my mind, I went faster.

The rest was hazy. There was dirty moaning from all of us. My thrusts got downright deadly, but she was leaning into it and asking for more, while she took Yeager's Redwood like she was designed for it. How that damned douche canoe Rudy looked at any other woman was beyond me.

"Fuck. I'm close." Yeager huffed. When Vixen didn't shy away from his warning, he gripped her hips, pulling her toward him and fucking her mouth with abandon. I put my hands on his to help stabilize her and keep her in the rhythm that would help us all. It didn't take much longer for him to come. Hey, I'd been right about his come face. He'd been growling all night, but the sound out of his throat then was beastly.

A second, maybe two, later, Vixen clenched. My bells went into overdrive. "Yes, Ginger, Come on my cock, just like that." I tried to hold off a little longer, but I couldn't. Not with her wet pussy squeezing me like that. I looked over to Yeager as he pulled out of her mouth. Just imagining his cum dripping from the corners of her mouth did it. I came so hard I saw stars.

She collapsed on the back of the chair and the sight of her spent was at the brink of being too much. We'd done what we intended, which was to give her the night she deserved last year. The night she deserved always.

Yeager scooped her into his bulging arms, walking her to the bed. When I'd brought the Snow Ball idea to him, I'd also told him about what I knew was happening at the Pole. Sure, we'd wanted to fuck her together for obvious reasons, but the idea of the mini Snow Ball was to distract her from the real one. There was something I had to tell her. And maybe I was an asshole for getting to the good stuff first, but I wanted her to feel good because the next part was going to feel like shit. I glanced at Yeager as he strolled by me. He nodded. It was time to give her the news.

# CHAPTER 31

Every bone in my body was jelly. I didn't realize it was possible to feel like I did. The second Yeager had eased my nervousness about the sharing by literally kissing it out of me, I was all in. Being with both at once had been next-level amazing. They had their similarities, but their differences were what made the experience better.

Hart was full-tilt. Ardent and aggressive, though not in a way that made me feel unsafe. He kissed me with fire and fucked me in a no-holds-barred kind of way that made me leave part of myself behind. I had no choice but to keep up with him. And I *did* want to keep up with him. He was a force I wanted to be a part of. And the jingle bells? Sheesh. They made me want to go around asking every woman I met if their dude was pierced so I could give them a high-five and an understanding nod. Damn. Huge fan of the jingle bells. As much as a fan of their owner.

Yeager, on the other hand, was patient. He seemed to slide into my mind and pull exactly what I wanted out and give it to me with affection. I didn't have to ask, he just gave.

The way he touched me felt like years of feelings cultivated into a warm sunny day kissing my skin after a long frigid winter. It seemed like I'd known him my whole life. Like I'd cared for him my whole life. His kisses were born of infinity and history rolled into one remarkable explosive moment. That was to say nothing about the sensation of his tongue and the taste of his cock. Everything about him was hot.

And they'd planned this whole thing together.

Hart used a warm washcloth to clean me up while Yeager held me cradled in his arms patiently. They were a good team. I couldn't fathom why I'd been nervous to be with them together. I wouldn't second guess that again.

After they were satisfied I was comfortable, Yeager deposited me in the middle of the bed and pulled the covers over me. He slid into his spot beside me and turned my back to him so he could spoon me while Hart crawled in on the other side. There was no discussion about it that I was aware of. It just seemed like the right thing for us all to lay there together like we were.

Major fan of it.

Hart traced my lower lip with his finger as he spoke. "I need to confess, Ginger. We planned this thing and were deep into hanging the lights above our heads here when I got some intel that you need to hear. Maybe I should've told you before we had our playtime, but I was selfish and didn't want anything to ruin the possibility of how great it could've been."

Yeager's hand slid over my hip. "It was fucking perfect, but you can't take all that on. I agreed with him, so if you end up being mad, you'll have to be mad at both of us."

I didn't want to be mad at either of them. Not after what we'd enjoyed together. Dread settled inside me in the form of a lump in my throat. "Tell me."

Hart got right into it. "My spies told me there was going to be a big announcement at the Snow Ball. I didn't—we didn't—want you to witness it without knowing how it went down. We had the feed going as it happened; while you were getting dressed." Yeager clapped him on the back, urging him to get on with it, so he spit it out. "Rudy proposed to Clare on livestream. They're engaged now. She even had a hashtag locked and loaded, a combo of their names: #Rare, which is stupid AF."

Yeager groaned. Yep, that was bad.

The two of them waited for me to comment. All I could give them was stunned silence.

He'd stood me up last year and this year he was proposing to Clare.

Little pinpricks of light floated in front of my eyes. Probably not a good thing, but I had no control over it. I didn't want Rudy. Not even a little bit. Especially with two insanely perfect naked men lying in bed with me.

Yet.

I couldn't stop the tear that trailed down my cheek.

Yeager pulled me tighter against his chest while Hart used his thumb to wipe the traitorous tear away. Neither of them said a word. They didn't have to. I felt the sympathy coursing from them as I took a shuddering breath. "Gah. Why the fuck am I crying? I hate him."

More tears. Too many for Hart to catch. He pressed his lips against mine for a brief moment. "Maybe you're crying because this is putting a lid on your relationship with him. There's no going back to him now."

I swear, if Yeager could've swallowed me up whole, he would've. He wrapped me in his legs, not caring that Hart came along with me. We lay there, a jumble of tangled limbs and tears. "I don't care. I don't want him in anymore. I promise."

"You don't have to promise anything, Bunny. I can't imagine how you feel right now, but we're here, no matter how you want to deal with this." Yeager whispered in my ear. The low rumble of his voice soothed my frayed nerves.

"Right. If you want to punch or scream or cry or fuck, do it. We're not going anywhere."

Both of them were sincere. I could feel it in their hands, hear it in their voices. And I like a flash of lightning, I felt unworthy of their affection. They were lying there willing to do anything they could for me as I cried over a man who'd cheated on me.

My heart was shrinking in my chest, and I had the sensation of being deep inside a well I couldn't climb out of. "I hate myself for being upset. I can't figure out what's going on inside me. I knew we weren't getting back together. This shouldn't be a big deal, but it is. I guess I'm more broken than I realized."

That was the truth of it. I was cracked into two pieces. The one before him and the one after. Neither of them was whole. The only glimmer I could see on the horizon was that I was wedged between two men who seemed to want to glue me back together.

Yeager kissed my neck. "You're not broken, Bunny. You're not damaged or busted." Hart gripped my hair to angle me so that Yeager could easily swipe his tongue down my neck and over my collarbone. My breath hitched at the sensation of his rippling tongue, and I turned onto my back.

Hart skimmed his hand from my hip, across my stomach, up to my breast. My nipple peaked in response to his touch. "You're not even chipped, Ginger. Maybe you have a tiny little dent on your heart where that dickbag bumped into you, but those things are easy to get out. Let us show you." I groaned when he took my breast into his mouth and sucked.

For the rest of the night, they made me forget everything but them.

# CHAPTER 32

I stood in the middle of the hill watching as Jack rolled the giant snowball toward me. Yeah, it was probably cheating to let the man who'd created the snowballs for our relay race game be the one to roll it, but nobody said anything, so we went with it.

He wasn't even out of breath when he got to me. Annoyed maybe, but not panting like Isaac was as he made it up the hill. As soon as he got there, I went to work, putting a beanie on his head first. I lost precious time, but I had to stop and check him out. It was a different look on him. "Okay, I'm just going to say it," I said, snapping out of it and putting on my beanie and then working to get scarves around our necks. "You should think about keeping the beanie."

He cocked his eyebrow "Seriously?"

"Um, yeah, it looks good on you."

He adjusted the hat, then grabbed the mittens out of my hands. We couldn't move on to the next station until we had all the things in place. "I wouldn't have considered keeping it, but if you like it, maybe I could be persuaded."

I could think of ways to persuade him, but it wasn't the time or place. And I'd been with Yeager and Hart—together—the night before. I didn't think it was right to be thinking about another guy so quickly. Even though he looked fuckable in that hat.

I needed to get a grip.

Maybe I'd been more troubled by *the engagement* than I thought.

Having gotten our winter gear on, we ran as fast as we could to Hart at the next station. He shoved the end of a silvery string of garland at me. "You hold, Jack get on her right side. I'll wrap us."

Hart went to work wrapping the garland around us. He had a little trouble with it at first because it wasn't exactly long enough to go around all three of us as we stood side-by-side. But we couldn't move on until we had it in place. He paused, narrowing his eyes at me and Jack. "New plan. Turn and hug each other. I'll get behind Vixen so we can squeeze in enough for us to all fit."

Jack and I followed his instructions and Hart successfully wrapped us, then got in place behind me to finish up. He leaned down to whisper in my ear, only he didn't bother actually whispering. "Hm, this feels oddly familiar."

My eyes went wide, especially when I looked up and found a questioning look on Jack's face. I grunted. "We need to move."

"I feel like one of us said that last night."

"Hart, I'm going to kill you."

"Yeah, no. I think you mean you're going to kiss me. Like last night." He laughed. "Okay, Redwood is waiting. On three. Three, two, one, go."

We stepped together, heading to Yeager at the very top of the hill. It was tough to manage three sets of legs going sideways in the snow and by the time we got to Yeager, we were all laughing. He smiled at me as Hart unwrapped the garland. "Okay, you get on first, Bunny, then Jack, Hart, and I'll jump on last after I give us a big push.

I glanced down the hill. It was steep. But I was a little excited to sled down it, bobsled style. I glanced over and found Spike, Dracula, and Edward getting close. "We're going to have to be fast to beat the professionals."

"Right," Jack said. "Let me get on first. I can block the wind off Vixen and maybe grease the track with a little ice on the way."

Yeager clapped his back. "I love it. Get on."

Jack got into place, and I slid in behind him. Hart got in next, wasting no time wrapping his arms around me, inching his hands down between my legs. I turned around and smacked his arm. "Not the time for that."

"Got it. Maybe you want to tell the Yeti not to go for my crotch either."

"You wish," Yeager laughed, then started rocking our sled back and forth. "Hold on, here we go." He pushed us forward, then the sled thumped as he got in place behind Hart. Seconds later we were whooshing down the hill.

Jack held up his hand, icing the track like he'd promised, and we went even faster. My heartbeat pumped in my ears as we flew down the hill, laughing and gasping for air. It was freeing and exhilarating and over way too fast.

We won though, just edging out the Frostbite team by a few seconds. Ho Ho Ho Hot came in third and Cherish's team came in last. She didn't much care about that, as she begged to go up and do it again. Isaac tried to contain the happy look on his face, to remain calm and appear like he didn't care that his daughter was actively trying to do something with him. But he failed. Cherish rolled her eyes. "Da-ad, I literally don't even care-uh. Let's just do it one more time."

Jack stood up, but I just fell over, throwing myself in the snow. Hart and Yeager did the same thing. One flick of Jack's wrist and a lump of snow fell on top of them, burying them in one motion. They scrambled up, spitting snow as they emerged. Yeager was laughing, but Hart was doing his best not to. "You motherfucker, you might regret that," He sneered.

"I don't believe I will. What is it they say? Payback's a bitch."

"Excuse me, Mr. Frost? I was wondering if you might assist us." Lestat had approached us in his full gear, black snowsuit, black helmet with black faceplate, protecting himself from the sun. His height was the only reason I could formulate which one of the vampires he was. "As you know, we're practicing for our bobsled events and noticed how you iced the hill to go faster. Could you do that for us? Help us practice more realistically?"

Jack cocked his head. "Of course. I could probably do you one better. What would you say to a real track?"

Okay, that was cool. Cold, I suppose. Lestat agreed with me. "That would be outstanding. How can we help?"

Four hours later, as dusk was starting to break, Jack had created a bobsled run out of ice and snow. Not to be out-done, Yeager had taken down an entire fir tree, stripped it, took out the middle, and created a rudimentary bobsled out of it. Hart, on the other hand, had popped back to the North Pole and gotten a timer system with an infrared finish line so they could see if they were improving timewise. While all that was going on, I was helping Spike pick out new gear to order online.

The afternoon had been fun.

I didn't think about anything but the men in front of me and our goal to help the vampires be the bobsledders they dreamed of.

That was not a thing I ever thought I would do in my life.

But as Hart, Yeager, and Jack stood next to me and watched their first successful run as bobsledders, I couldn't help but note how happy the day had made me. And I wondered if maybe the night before it had anything to do with it.

And I wondered if I could get over my issues and allow it to happen again.

# CHAPTER 33

As I helped Holly clear the dishes from dinner, I caught Hart's eye. He'd been thinking what I'd been tossing around all evening—Vixen and how we were going to spend the rest of the night making her come.

The two of us had clicked on the sharing thing and while it took a couple of tense seconds for her to let go of herself long enough to enjoy things, she figured it out and got into it.

We weren't forcing her. She wanted to be with us, she just experienced a few moments of doubt as we were getting into it. Those little ticks of the clock were mostly thanks to Randall. There was no doubt in my mind that he'd dampened her spirit, and made her self-conscious, not only about herself but what she wanted too.

Hart and I—Jack too—were slowly offering bits and pieces of herself back because we knew the truth: she was remarkable.

And Hart knew what the fuck he was doing in the bedroom.

Win, win, win as far as I was concerned.

As Holly set more plates in the sink, a thump sounded from the dining room, followed by some murmuring and then a woman screeching. I took off, bursting through the door and finding Aaron seizing on the floor. Erin was perched over him, holding his shoulders with tears streaming down her face. She kept mumbling "too soon" over and over.

Jack sprang into action, leaping off the bench and landing next to her. He placed his hands on Aaron's neck, presumably to check for a pulse and see if the cold contact helped. When it didn't, he took Erin's face, bringing it to meet his. His eyes were sharp and not in the least bit cold when he addressed her. "Do you know what this is?" She nodded but didn't give any other information. Shock would do that. Jack looked up at Hart. "Can't you pop him to a hospital?"

Hart was already on his way down to get him when Erin finally snapped out of it. "They can't help him. It's terminal. We've tried everything. That's why we got married so quickly, so we could have as much time..." The rest of her words were swallowed by her sobbing.

Shit.

My stomach bottomed out like I'd swallowed a boulder.

I couldn't imagine how she felt, but as I glanced over at Vixen finding her eyes welled with tears, I had an idea. If it had been her seizing on the floor, I wouldn't have hesitated. Not for a second.

Dumbstruck with the thought of that, there was no way I could just stand there and watch it play out as Erin expected it. None.

I twisted the gold band on my finger. My father was already pissed at me, enough to lock me down. I doubted it could get worse. And the thing of it was, I never agreed with his insistence to hide my gift. True, it could potentially be dangerous if word got out, but I was a big boy and could take care of myself. The idea that my blood had probably sat silently by as someone he could've helped suffered, was unforgivable in my mind.

"Clear the room."

Isaac had already escorted Cherish back to their cabin at the outset. My voice had been commanding enough to move the rest. Hart was reluctant to leave but Jack took him by the arm. I didn't know if he knew enough about my species that he'd guessed or if he could just read the situation. Could've been either with Jack.

Once they'd gone, Holly took her leave, and I was alone with a wide-eyed Erin and Vixen. It took no time for Vixen to wrap her arms around the sobbing newlywed. She knew. "Hey, I know this is going to be tough for you, but I need you to come with me. Let's go to the kitchen and make some coffee. I promise you, you're going to want to stay awake tonight."

Erin looked at her like she'd spoken gibberish. She wasn't going to leave her husband's side without good reason. Vixen wasn't going to be deterred either. It was one of the things I liked most about her. She might have given up on herself, on love, on her Christmas spirit, but she wasn't going to give up on anyone else, including me. And the fact that she'd just known what I was planning without telling her spoke to the trust we'd formed in the past week. "Yeager will be with Aaron. He can help, I promise. Just come with me."

Erin rose reluctantly and I nodded to her. "When you come back, he'll be better." Vixen squeezed my shoulder in silent solidarity— and maybe thanks—then she took Erin away.

I wasted no time stripping out of my shirt and placing my hands on Aaron's head. The cancer was deep, inoperable, and final in a way that seemed tangible. I could see it like a movie playing in my head. Closing my eyes, I grasped the ugly malformed blackness in my hands and lifted it from his brain, feeling my tattoos morph and bend as they dissipated around me.

Aaron's eyes popped open, and I helped him sit up. He looked around for Erin, panic on his face. "What happened? Where's Erin?" He paused, relief radiating from his posture. "Wait a minute, I feel different."

"Yeah, about that." I took a deep breath, realizing it was my moment to define what little part of my life I still had left. Fuck tradition. "Some Yetis are born with special healing abilities. I just took the cancer out of your head. It shouldn't come back."

He gaped at me. "You did what? The doctors all said it was a lost cause, to spend the literal months I had left doing all I could to live while I could. And you're telling me it's just gone, poof?"

"Poof."

"Aaron? My soul, you're awake." Erin came bounding into the room, knocking him back down on the floor as she dove to hug him. "Did I just hear that right? He's cured?"

"Yes. It's a good idea to follow up with your doctor, but I'm confident in saying the cancer's gone now."

The feeling that came with the statement knocked the wind out of me. As the two of them looked up at me with awe and gratitude, for the first time in a while, I appreciated being born as the Chosen One. True, I had obligations surrounding it, ones I wanted out of desperately, but at the moment, I gave no fucks about those.

I had changed their lives.

They scrambled up, practically racing toward the door. I couldn't blame them for wanting to bang the night away. After thanking me more than they needed to, they scrambled out the door, not even stopping for their coats. I laughed. "Young love."

Vixen dropped down, straddling my lap and wrapping her arms around my neck. "What's your dad going to say about that?"

I shrugged, loving the weight of her arms on my shoulders. "I don't plan on telling him, do you?"

"Nope. You're amazing," she whispered breathlessly before diving for my mouth like she was trying to kiss those words into my soul. And I let her because as far as I was concerned, she was the amazing one and I didn't want a moment to go by where she didn't know how desired she was. I grabbed her ass, pulling her against me so she could feel the hardness between my legs. She ground against me, and I tore my lips from her so I could lick her throat, tasting the sweet blush of lust rushing through her.

Yes, my Yeti tongue was quite helpful when it came to reading desire. To tasting it. That's how I knew she was always in with Hart and me together.

As if she'd read my mind, she pulled back, taking me in with her hooded eyes. "We should go back to the cabin."

I nuzzled her neck. "Mm. You know, Hart's probably there already."

"I know."

# CHAPTER 34

We were gathered outside for the next game. The vampires were huddled under a black awning Holly made eager hang for them under some trees at the edge of the forest behind the lodge. Close to where our Christmas trees were. They had all their sun attire on but were successfully staying in the shade.

It had been a quiet morning that started with Yeager curing Crystal of her flu. He'd decided not to adhere to his father's demand of keeping his gift secret and I have to admit watching him do what he did revved my heart up first thing that morning.

The night before, however, had gone exactly like the previous ones. Hart and Yeager and me. And a lot of groping and thrusting and orgasms that made my head spin. I'd expected to wake up feeling remorse or shame or anger based on the roller coaster ride that was my life—smexy men, the engagement, smexy men again, Aaron's seizure, smexy men once more, then the pang of waking up and randomly missing the breakfasts Rudy used to make me. That idea had snuck in like a ninja attack on my soul.

A night or two of good sex, as fun and hot as it had been, wasn't going to solve my issues. That much was clear.

"Woah, shit. What was that for?"

I whipped around to find John Sun laid out in the snow. Jack was striding toward us with purpose with steel eyes narrowed on me. When he made it over, he pivoted slowly and popped his cuffs. "That was breaking the rules, you buffoon."

Hart laughed. "I'm all for taking the fuckhead down a peg—nice shoulder check by the way—but what rule did he break?"

"There are very clear terms and conditions when it comes to negotiating Fae territory. That's why we're here in the first place. But John took it upon himself to assume victory prematurely and started melting the edges of my kingdom, thinking I wouldn't notice. I noticed."

He noticed everything. Always.

"Do we need to ride at dawn, or what? I've got a guy who can supply weapons."

Jack turned his head slowly toward Hart, surprise flickering across his face. "We're not at war. We're in negotiations. Ones I plan on winning."

"Okay. Just sayin'. Give me the word and I'm on it."

Jack continued to gawk at Hart like he had a stain on his shirt. I'd never seen Jack look quite so perplexed. I stood on my toes and kissed Jack's cheek, welcoming the crisp feel of his skin. "Why do you look so surprised right now?"

It took more than a few beats for him to answer and as he did, he eyed Hart cautiously. "I've never needed help, never was offered any. I suppose his proposition threw me off."

Hart leaned over to kiss my cheek too, slapping my ass in the process. I yelped. "Yeah, he's good at that."

Holly clapped her mittens together, but because they had bells on them, they jingled. Yeager strolled up behind me and chuckled in my ear. Yeah, he liked the jingling. Same, Yeager. Same. She fumbled with the pockets in her green puffy coat with snowflakes on it, finally wrestling the card out. "Today we'll construct snowmen.

"Teams will have one hour and can use their own supplies or take items from the buckets I'll bring around. We'll vote based on creativity and execution."

John Sun groaned. "That's not fair, Jack can whip up a snowman with his pinkie finger. How am I supposed to make one if I can't even touch the snow?" He demonstrated by picking up a handful in his bare hand. It melted into water in a few seconds.

"Oh pish. You don't think Santa thought of that Mr. Sun? Please. Let me continue. Because one of the Fae kings has an advantage over the other, I've decided that the two of them should sit this contest out. The other teams should remove a member as well, making it fair across the board."

Cherish used the holes she'd cut in her mittens to thumb her phone. "Thank you, next." She headed straight into the lodge, having made her team's decision for them. From the tent, Dracula did the same action, only he didn't have a phone out.

Okay then.

While Jack whipped up an ice stump to sit on, the rest of us went to work rolling the base of our snowman without much discussion at all. I bent over and sighed as I heaved a lump into the ball the others had made. "No offense Jack, but I hate snowmen and I don't get why people like to make them. It's arduous work that melts as soon as the sun comes out. Well, anywhere but here, but you get what I'm saying. The whole thing is fleeting, so why do it?"

He crossed his legs. "That's the point. To capture a moment and freeze it into place before it melts. Even if it doesn't last, it existed. Think of it as embracing your moments and making them count."

Hart nodded. "Exactly. I don't think Santa gives a shit about what the snowmen look like, or which team wins this game. It's about building the snowman, not what happens afterward."

My chest was tight. They were talking about snowmen, but not exclusively. It burrowed under my skin. I just wasn't sure if it was a bad thing or a good one. "Got any words of wisdom to add to the mix, Yeager?"

He glanced at Hart, then back at me. "Yep. Building snowmen is like building a relationship. You have to start small, adding one little ball at a time, and then before you know it, you've got three big, huge, massive balls to play with. You cannot go wrong with three massive balls."

Jack rubbed his temple. "He's talking about literal balls, isn't he?"

Hart took the snow he was packing in his hand and slammed it down on Yeager's head. "He is." Of course,

Yeager retaliated by picking up a mound of snow which he smashed against Hart's jingle bell region.

Then it was on.

It took a few minutes to break the two of them apart and get back to work. Jack freezing their feet to the ground helped. Finally, we got busy again, making a pretty decent snowman that wore Hart's suede jacket, Yeager's suspenders, and Jack's red tie. Jack had also kept Yeager from using a second carrot for a dick. He'd looked confused when Yeager started asking for jingle bells to put on it. Hart just slapped his back and added a knowing look.

We collapsed around Jack. Before I could protest the cold on my ass, Yeager pulled me into his lap. It was sweet and neither of the other two said a thing about it. Seconds later, Hart popped away and came back with hot chocolate for us all.

As we waited for the time to be called, something snagged in my mind. "Can you really create a snowman with your pinkie finger, Jack?"

"I can. Do you want to see, Flame?"

I nodded and he flicked his little finger in my direction. The snow at my feet began to swirl and swoosh around us. A few seconds later we were staring at a snow replica of me. I was wearing the snowflake dress Hart had made and the look on my face was, well it was exquisite. He'd captured a rapturous moment because my lips were parted, and my head thrown back. It looked like I was seconds away from release. He'd seen me come before. I supposed he could've committed it to memory.

I was haunted by the look in my snowman eyes. "Did you show him the dress before you gave it to me, Hart?"

"No, I didn't."

"Then how—?"

Yeager let out a belly laugh. "You dog. You watched us. You had your nose to the fucking window, didn't you, Ice Man?"

Jack shrugged.

Hart threw his head back and laughed with his whole body, shaking so much I heard his bells jingle. "I'm not sure if that's a violation or a turn-on if I'm honest. What do you think, Ginger?"

I didn't know what to think. I knew Jack liked to watch and even though I'd had my concerns before the three of us ended up naked, I wasn't going to apologize for enjoying what happened after. The thought of Jack seeing us, well, that was sending a warm pulse through my body. I loved the way his steely eyes tracked everything.

He was looking at me now with hesitation. "I apologize if you think I took advantage. I should've revealed myself, but honestly, it was...I was...I didn't want to take away from your experience with them."

I was honest in my response. "I don't feel violated, and I don't know that it would've taken anything away. Maybe next time..."

"Join in, Ice Man." I looked at Yeager, thankful he'd said what I was thinking.

"I'm not certain that's for me."

"Suit yourself. You're missing out." He glanced at Hart who nodded his agreement. "What else do you remember from that night? Show us more."

With the flick of his finger, the snowman swirled away, only to come back as the three of us dancing, with Yeager and Hart's hands between my legs. Again, I had an expression on my face that I'd never seen before. It was full of joy and strength, and I ached with longing at the sight of it. I wanted to be that version of me all the time. But I knew in my soul I couldn't. That wasn't me, it was just a blip of time. Like a snowman.

"Oh my," Holly squeaked on her approach. Jack quickly melted the snow, mumbling that it was for us, not anyone else. "Okay, time's up. You can go around and check out the others, then go cast your vote."

As we walked around checking out the snowmen, Jack grabbed my hand. "It would kill me to know I upset you."

"I told you; I don't mind what you did. Not at all."

"Good. I can't go into this meeting today focused on anything but defeating John. I would've been distracted if you were hurt by what I did."

"What can I do to help with the meeting? I'm with Hart—fully ready to ride at dawn."

"I don't think that will be necessary. Perhaps I can steal some time with you after I'm done. Though sometimes these things can go on for days."

"You'll pause for the games, right?" The thought of competing without him made my gut clench. He was part of our team, and I knew the others would miss his presence if he wasn't there too. They were all starting to warm up to each other. "We can't win without you."

I got his half-smile. "You've come a long way in a week. You're not so against the competition any longer? Something must have changed."

Damn it. Leave it up to Jack to elegantly deliver observations that pierced my soul. Yes, something was changing. He was a part of it, but I had so much farther to go.

I shrugged. "Maybe. Whatever. Yes, just let me know when you're out of your big meeting." I went up on my toes, intending to kiss his cheek, but he caught my chin in his hand and turned my innocent peck into a pulse-racing kiss that made my insides melt, even though his lips were like ice.

Where Yeager was languid and tender and Hart was aggressive and greedy, Jack was possessive and meticulous. The way he took what he wanted from me without doing anything more than moving his mouth against mine made me weak in the best way.

Behind us, both Hart and Yeager cleared their throats. Jack didn't stop kissing until he was good and ready. My head was spinning when he dropped my chin. "I'll see you later. Now I'm off to wipe John Sun off the map."

# CHAPTER 35

It was unfathomable.

I had lost.

Almost everything.

I'd been confident. Maybe too confident. However, I'd been certain my kingdom wasn't in any real danger from John Sun. He was arrogant and brash and had no nuance at all, but he'd walked away from our meeting with all but three provinces. I still had my palace, my court, but most of my kingdom was going to melt in his hands.

It would be years before I could challenge him again.

Time was nothing to Fae, but still, my heart was raw at the thought that I'd let my people down. Let myself down. I didn't know how I was going to tell anyone. Though my kingdom likely already knew, at least those affected any-way. They'd have to go through the complicated process of changing form because frost Fae could never survive in the Summer court. Many of them—more than I could have imagined—were already on their way, having been part of the plan that took my world from me.

That's what hurt the most. Not that I was beaten, but that scores of my people had abandoned me for him. Long before I set foot in that meeting.

I would be more isolated than I already had been.

My head pounded as I blindly stomped through the camp. I didn't know where I was going, what I needed, I just hoped I could garner some strength from the crisp snow at my feet, but I was thrown off as the infectious sound of her laugh as it echoed through the camp, tickling the icicles in the trees above my head.

I stopped pacing.

I may have stopped breathing.

*She* is what I needed.

Turning on my heel, I stalked around the lodge in search of the one shining light that could erase the stain of my mistakes, at least for a while. Beyond the grove of Christmas trees we'd decorated, there was wooden gazebo nestled into an outcrop of trees. I hadn't paid it much attention because it housed a hot tub. I couldn't think of a worse form of entertainment for a frost Fae, but I skulked toward it like a moth to a flame.

My Flame was there.

She was not alone.

It shouldn't have come as a surprise, yet when I heard Yeager's deep baritone laugh, it was like yet another punch to the gut. He and I had a few differences in the beginning, but after I'd studied his actions for a couple of days and got to truly see how his mind worked, and his character, I found him to be warm-hearted and giving. He was quick to laugh and tease others and always first to see a need and fill it without question or expectation. It was hard to deny the feelings for Vixen he wore so clearly on his sleeve. He cared for her deeply. Probably more deeply than he realized.

And she was so at ease with him. Had been from the start.

To think I'd thrown them together the first night when I didn't allow him to bunk in my cabin. I'd given a false excuse because I didn't want to be bothered by some cumbersome oaf in suspenders. It turned out that he wasn't that. And their closeness grew out of my misstep that night.

Shit. I had been fucking things up for myself the whole trip.

Unable to keep myself from it, I angled toward the gazebo and found protection in the dark copse of trees beside it. I could hear them, see them, but I remained hidden, away from the light of the lanterns he'd hung around the perimeter. That's what I did, how I operated. Silent, observing, outside of everything.

"I can't believe they're making Hart do more sexy Elf press. He's going to be miserable the whole night." Vixen huffed.

"Yeah, he is. Maybe we can make it up to him tomorrow."

She turned her head toward Yeager, who was stripping out of his clothes at the edge of the hot tub. I didn't miss her eyes widening at the sight of him peeling off his shirt. His tattoos *were* remarkable. "What do you mean, *we?*"

Clever girl. She picked up on it too.

He threw his shirt at her, and she caught it in one hand. "You know what I mean. Until then, we'll just have to find something else to do without him." He dropped his pants and underwear. I had to admit the size of his cock was intimidating. Vixen did not look intimidated at all. She looked hungry. A sliver of icy desire ran through my bones at the sight of her eyeing his shaft.

He slid into the hot tub; a sharp intake of air hissed through his teeth at the temperature. "Are you going to stand over there and tease me or are you coming in?"

She giggled, then whipped her head around. "Are you sure no one can see us?"

"I told you, I checked. The staff are all asleep in their cabins. So are Isaac and Cherish. The newlyweds are boning. The vamps have gone out in the forest to be in the cold or something weird and vampirey, I don't want to know. The nymphs are on their second bottle of wine waiting for John Sun to finish his meeting with Jack. We're on our own. Let's take advantage of it."

She hesitated for one second longer, decision flashed in her glacially blue eyes and she was sliding naked into the hot tub. I would've preferred that to go much slower, but I wasn't angry about the results. Her body was made to worship. And I was going to enjoy the hell out of watching Yeager do just that. He leaned against the back of the tub, watching her inch into the water. At least he recognized the need to gaze at her beauty like I did.

She took a seat across from him, stretching out her arms so that her breasts were right at the water line. I was mesmerized by the way the water lapped against her dusky nipples. It took no time for my cock to grow hard. Especially because she was squirming on the seat due to something Yeager was doing under the surface of the water.

"I'm worried about Jack." The sound of my name on her tongue made that erection pulse. "I don't get how Fae negotiations work, but he seemed, I don't know, more intense than normal."

Yeager laughed. "His whole mood is intense. I don't think you have anything to worry about with him. He's shrewd enough to best John Sun. Then he can go back to creeping on us like the good little peeper he is. Isn't that right, Jack?"

Of course, his Yeti ears picked up on my presence. I couldn't pretend I wasn't there—I'd been caught. Yet another fail.

"If you're going to watch, might as well do it from a closer vantage point. You don't want to miss the good stuff. I'm going to need you to make this in snow form for Hart tomorrow. Don't want him to feel left out."

I climbed the stairs into the gazebo, stepping into the light. It was difficult to do. I was already so vulnerable from what had happened and while Yeager had invited me, I wasn't sure how he would react when he was faced with the prospect of me not only watching but joining them. Because I wanted to join. I needed her. She needed him. We needed each other as I was starting to understand.

One look from Vixen and all the anxiety in my mind melted. "How did it go? Did you get what you wanted out of the meeting?"

"I don't want to talk about it right now." Concern crossed her face, and I hated I was the cause of it. It was yet another thing I'd done wrong. That, however, I could fix. "I don't want to talk at all."

Yeager smirked. "What *do* you want then?"

My hands flew up and I untied my tie, whipping it from my collar. Then, I shed my jacket, my shoes and socks. Then

I began unbuttoning my shirt at a snail's pace as Vixen's lips parted. Angling my head, I said one word. "Her."

The look of mirth on Yeager's face was positively manic. "You good with that, Bunny?"

She nodded, taking her plump lower lip between her teeth. The sight of it undid me in ways I couldn't explain. My entire body lit as she tracked my hands, inching closer with every button I wrestled free. Though it was difficult, I tore my gaze away from her, leveling it on Yeger. "What are the rules here? What boundaries do I have?"

He let out a bellowing laugh. "This isn't a negotiation."

"Everything is a negotiation."

"Okay. Look at it like this: You get to do anything you want as long as Vixen is good with it. The only boundary you have is that no means no. Other than that, knock yourself out. The only fuck I give is that she's spent when we're finished. Team sport. You feel me?"

I nodded, turning back to Vixen, knowing she understood what I was about to say. Hoping she'd smooth it over with Yeager. "There are things about my genetics, about what I need to enjoy sex."

She leaned over the ledge of the tub, lowering her gaze on me as I whipped the shirt from my shoulders. "It's okay." She turned to Yeager. "He can't get in the tub because of the warmth. Although, I feel confident we can find our way through this. It might even be fun to figure out the boundaries as we go."

That was the best thing I'd heard all day. In a lot of days.

"You'll get no argument from me, Bunny." He leaned down and kissed her, his tongue slid between her lips.

When he'd finished devouring her mouth, he looked up at me. "Okay Ice Man, how are we doing this?"

Even though my head was already in a lust-filled haze, I had to stop and appreciate Yeager's willingness to let me take the lead. I was going to make sure we all got something from this. "Kiss her again. This time, like you mean it."

"Oh, my fuck, I'm going to like this." He dug his fingers into her hair and dove for her neck, running his long tongue over the column of her throat before pressing his mouth against hers. I couldn't say if he kissed her like this all the time, but he made certain he used that tongue where I could see it, flicking over her lips and darting inside as she gripped his waist. It was sensual, slow, and consuming, and her tongue met his with a fervent need I felt from where I stood.

It wasn't enough.

"Lean back, Flame. Give him access to those beautiful breasts." She moved as I commanded, turning to perch against the back of the tub. He responded by giving me what I asked for—his tongue raking over her nipples. I had many Yetis in my kingdom. Stories of their tongues were rampant. The sound of her sighs told me the stories were true. When he drew her right nipple into his mouth to suck, she arched up to meet him, digging her fingers into his hair.

I wanted to get closer, but I had to work up to that. To do so, I raised my hand and picked up some snow with my magic, depositing it at my feet and all around the tub except for the portion where the stairs descended, and their clothes were hanging. I sank my feet in, relishing the chill it gave me as Yeager moved to the other side, flicking his tongue over her other nipple, then moving between her breasts so that I could see the pebbled results of his work.

I sat on the edge of the tub, watching him suck and nibble her tits as she clutched onto him with closed eyes. I was close enough now to see she'd lifted her hips and wrapped them around his waist as he rubbed himself against her pussy. The thought of that made my heart thump heavily in my chest.

Reaching down, I ran my index finger over her other nipple, knowing the temperature would compete with the warmth of the water. She cursed. "Fuck."

As I toyed over the peak, I looked down at her glazing blue eyes. "Do you like that, Flame?" She nodded. "If you want more, you're going to have to convince me. Use your words."

Yeager paused his sucking long enough to look up and smirk, then he went back to her hard nipple again. "I...I want hot and cold. I have to know what your tongue feels like on my nipple. Please, Jack. I'm aching for you."

Yeager was glassy-eyed when he looked up and shifted to the side to give me room. "That was pretty fucking specific Ice Man."

"It was. She's a good girl."

And because she was, I leaned down and flicked my tongue over her peak, just a touch, nothing more. She yelped and arched into me, so I threw all restraint to the wind, and took her whole nipple into my mouth, sucking and biting, losing myself to the feel of her warm flesh in my cold mouth.

Before long I'd flattened myself against the top of the tub and trailed my tongue up her throat, finally finding her lips and taking what I wanted from them. Everything. I wanted it all. I was too close to the steaming water, but I failed to care. She was a life raft I could cling to. One who was taking my desperation over losing my kingdom and turning it into desire. Into hope. Because as long as she was under my fingertips, relishing the feel of my icy tongue, I had more than enough.

"Not to be a buzzkill, but Jack, I think you might want to take a sec. My Yeti is fine with cold, but I'm freezing my nuts off here and I plan on using those in the very near future."

I forced myself away from her luscious lips and found the water in the tub icing over. Yeager was standing there with a grin, but I knew it had to be uncomfortable for him. For her. "I told you things are sometimes difficult with me. I apologize." I stood up, rearranging my hard dick in my pants, then placing my hand over the water to draw the ice away. Within seconds the water was steamy again and Yeager was looking at me with a 'what now' look.

Vixen beamed. "Oh, that skill would come in very handy at bath time."

I shrugged. I didn't take hot baths. I took cold showers, and I liked it that way.

Yeager went over to Vixen, pulling her up, then scooting behind her and encircling her waist with his massive arms. "Again, not to bring us down here, but if you did that just from kissing and playing with her tits, can you actually, you know, fuck her? It would be so tragic if you couldn't. I'm pre-disappointed for you."

That *would* be tragic. "No, I can. It has to be a slow process. I got carried away."

"Good. So, let's resume then. We've left our girl wanting."

The term 'our girl' hit me. While it rang true, I wasn't sure what it meant. I didn't have time to consider it further because Yeager had snaked his hand between her legs, toying with her clit as she stared at me with so much thirst I nearly combusted.

Slow. I needed slow.

"Give her those fingers like she deserves. I want to see you light the flame."

He winked, then placed one of her legs on the bench, giving me more of a visual as he touched her. He leaned in and ran his tongue over the shell of her ear before whispering, loud enough for me to hear, "Do you see what you do to him, Bunny? Show her Jack. Lose the pants."

I bristled at being told what to do. I gave the orders. Always. Yet, the look on her face when he uttered that phrase, and I was in. If she wanted to see me, she would see me.

I stepped out of my pants and shorts, my bare feet crunching over the snow as I got as close as I dared to go. She damn near salivated at the sight of me taking my cock into my hand. She'd seen it before, but this time we were closer in proximity. And otherwise. She was etched on my heart in some way I had yet to determine. And it seemed like I was in hers too.

Yeager looked incredibly pleased with himself as he placed a sweet kiss on her temple. "There you go, Ice Man. You're going to get this group stuff yet. Now tell us what to do. And make her call you Daddy."

# CHAPTER 36

That quarter-grin stretched across his face. There had been some hesitation in him, but I couldn't blame him. I'd been cautious the first time with Yeager and Hart. But as he stood there gazing as Yeager touched me, his shift in attitude was like water going from freezing to boiling.

"What does that feel like, Flame? His fingers stroking you?"

"It feels like magic. I'm hot and throbbing and it's not enough." I reached behind me and grabbed Yeager by his hair, pulling him down to kiss me. He obliged me by stroking faster and kissing me dirty, growling, and pressing his erection against my ass.

"Now give her more, Yeager. Put those fingers where you know she wants them." It was the only warning I got. Yeager sild around me and sat on the bench with his back to Jack, but also to the side so Jack could watch. Then he thrust two fingers inside me, and I yelped at the force of it. My knees buckled and he put his hand on my back to keep me upright. Jack groaned. "What does she feel like?"

"Like silk. Wet, hot, needy silk. Jack, her pussy is so perfect and so tight. You should feel her clench when I do this." He opened his fingers and curled them at the same time. The feeling cascaded through me and yeah, you bet I clenched. Yeager smiled. "You're going to want to get in here."

"Trust me. I will. You just keep that up until she comes all over your fingers. That's what you ache for, isn't it?"

I was panting, so my answer came out jumbled and breathy. Yeah, I wanted that. I mean, who didn't? And watching Jack run his hand over his cock as Yeager went back to sucking my nipples was going to make it happen sooner rather than later. "I'm sorry, I didn't catch that answer."

Yeager paused to smirk at me as I tried to regain enough composure to answer him properly. Which was hard as he'd added a third finger "Mm-hm. Yeah."

Yeager, still pumping, by the way, looked over his shoulder. The two of them shared a look. I could only see Jack's part of it. And it was devious, also smoking hot. He nodded and a second later, Yeager cracked his free hand across my ass. I was momentarily stunned, but then the sting of it sent icy shivers all over my body. Oh, my soul, did I enjoy that. Yeager? He enjoyed it too. "Wrong answer. Try again, Bunny."

Jack's eyes were a volcano of lust, and I was coming unhinged in my need for him to draw closer, putting his cold hands on my body as the steam of the hot tub curled around me. He slicked his tongue over his lip. His "Yes what?"

Torn between giving the answer I knew they wanted and suffering the very, very appealing consequences of withholding, I was at a crossroads. I looked down at Yeager. He'd taken his own cock now and was pumping it as hard and fast as he was me. Then stealing a glance at Jack, I found him twisting his hand over his shaft too. It was all very well and good, but I wanted more. Of them. By them. "Yes, Daddy. I want to come."

"Fuck me," Yeager gasped. "You weren't even talking to me, and I almost blew my load on that, you dirty girl."

The support that Jack leaned against crackled as it froze. Icy frost crawled up and through the beams above us, forming icicles that dripped into the hot tub with a hiss. Within moments the whole gazebo was encased in ice with the flickering glow of lantern light casting slick shadows around us. Somewhere in the back of my mind, a tiny voice said, "Oh, it's on now."

Jack prowled over to us. There was no other word for it. His chest was heaving as he cocked his head and devoured my body with his eyes alone. "Bend her over the edge of this tub and fuck her from behind."

Yeager glanced at me for confirmation which I was all too happy to give. "Yes. Yes, please do it. My soul, I want you inside me, Yeager." He slid behind me and ran his hand over my spine, pressing me down over the tub. He slicked the tip of his cock over my entrance, and I gasped at the feel of it.

The next moment, he pushed inside me and hissed. "I'm never going to get used to how you feel, Bunny." He ran his hand over the curve of my ass, but this time kept it light and gentle.

Jack, however, took a handful of my hair and pulled my face up to meet his. He looked behind me to Yeager. "Tell me how good she takes that big cock."

"So fucking good."

"Great. Then she can have mine too. Open up, Flame."

I was so turned on that my head started to swim. But I wanted Jack as much as I wanted Yeager, so I opened my mouth for him. He took his cock and slid it into my mouth, inch by inch. Yeager growled behind me, shifting his hips upward, his long cock reaching that perfect place. "Oh, my soul, lick that popsicle."

These guys and their cock names.

Though this one was accurate.

It was a strange sensation to feel the coolness as he slid himself into my mouth. It was pleasant and different, but because it tasted like him, I was eager to take it. I used my hand to guide him back out, then licked my way down his shaft and back up again, running my tongue along his tip, then taking the whole thing into the back of my throat. He exhaled. "Your mouth is so hot. So wet."

His hands flew to my hair, and he started to pump. And because Yeager was nearly as observant as Jack was, it didn't take long for him to match the rhythm with his thrusts. We were grunting and groaning together in no time.

When Yeager reached around and started toying with my clit again, I hummed my satisfaction. Jack bucked wildly. "Make her hum, Yeager. Fuck. Please." So he did, using his fingers to pinch and play with my swollen clit as he railed into me. When he smacked my ass again, I lost all control of myself. I couldn't warn them because I had my mouth full of Jack's frosty dick, but my release cascaded from me like an avalanche. "That's it. Come for us, Flame."

Seconds after his command, Yeager let go of my clit in favor of my hips. He pulled me hard against him as he came, growling and cursing into the night. It was all Jack needed. His head flew back as his release poured down my throat. Surprisingly, it wasn't cold. Chilly, at most. I did what I could to take it all because I knew he wasn't just coming into my mouth. He didn't do this much, if at all. This was a far more intimate thing for him than for Yeager. Or me even. On top of that, something bad had gone down at his meeting. He needed this.

Not that I was in the habit of giving pleasure because someone was sad. But with Jack, it was deeper than that. I was giving him a part of me to fill something he'd lost in his negotiations. I didn't even know what happened, I just felt his need and knew I could fill it.

When we'd all come down from the height of our orgasms, Jack laid flat on his back in the snow beside the hot tub. Yeager and I slipped down into the warm water in the tub and took a few breaths. The experience had been as intense as Jack was.

Yeager put his arms around me, pulling me close to him. I loved the safe and protected vibe I got with him. He pressed a kiss to my temple. "Please tell me his cum tasted like ice cream."

~~~~~~~~~~~~~~~~~~~~~~~~~~~~~~~
~~~~~~~~~~~~~~~~~~~~~~~~~~~~~~~

The next morning I sat on the couch between Yeager and Jack, sipping my coffee and trying to look cool. Everyone in the place was focused on us. I wasn't ashamed. Not at all. I was simply confused as to why suddenly everyone but the two of them was either avoiding my gaze or blatantly staring.

Maybe we'd not been as stealthy as I'd thought in the hot tub.

Yeager slung his arm around my shoulders protectively as Jack angled toward me. "It seems that the rumor mill has been churning this morning. I wonder if John Sun has been running his mouth about what happened in our meeting."

After we'd, well, after, he told us what had happened. Fae didn't wage war against each other. Instead, their negotiations were like a strange mix between the old game of Risk and betting. Battles were fought and won on the game board, only the board represented real territory. Jack had bet on what he thought his kingdom was, but John had conspired behind his back, so when he bet the territory of Glacierfloe, he thought he was wagering land with twenty thousand people on it. Jack had made two or three or more territories band together, so he'd bet—and lost—nearly three hundred thousand. When I questioned the legality of that action, Jack had said everything was legal when they played with their special board in the special case. The one that he'd gotten the day I'd first traveled to his kingdom.

Jack tried to tell me it wasn't my fault, but I knew he was hurting and I wondered how much of an inadvertent role I played in it.

A sudden pop reverberated across the room and Hart appeared in front of us. He looked tired, but the cut of his white Henley shirt and black jeans boiled my blood.

He was breathtaking in his hotness. It made no sense to me because I'd been in the hands of two very skilled men, I felt his absence the night before.

Yeager grabbed him by the buttons, pulling him close. "Pop out behind our cabin for a second. We'll wait."

Hart glanced in my direction first but popped away. I was baffled by Yeager's request. Then it hit me. "Jack, did you—"

Hart popped back in with a grin so wide it hardly stayed contained to his face. He leveled his eyes on Jack. "I can't believe you fuckers didn't wait on me to get back. That's cruel and I will be taking my anger out on you by stealing her away from you. You won't know where, you won't know when, but trust me one day when you're balls deep inside her, I'm going to pop in and poof. You'll have to jerk each other to finish."

He bent down and kissed me hard, fast, and so gluttonous it drew my breath. After that, he plopped down on the armrest Jack usually occupied.

Okay then.

Cherish mumbled something about thirsty adults and the room broke out in mumbles. At least everyone had stopped staring.

Holly came into the room with her magic card from Santa and a box of supplies. Her OOTD, a term I'd learned from Cherish, was an understated red jumpsuit with white-tipped pockets and cuffs, no doubt a nod to Santa, and a wreath was hung around her neck. Not a necklace wreath. A. Wreath. This woman and her Christmas 'fits.

"Today's game is going to challenge how well you know the members of your team.

"We'll be playing 'Hide the Coal.' Each team will choose one person to do the hiding and the others will each get a turn at seeking. Once the seekers are outside, the hider will take a piece of coal that matches a card with the same color. They'll hide their coal somewhere in the lodge, kitchen, or dining room they think the seeker will find. Alternatively, players could put the coal where another team might assume it's theirs and pick it up. Whichever strategy you pick for each round is up to you.

"The seekers will find a lump of coal and bring it outside. If it matches the card in the hider's hand, the team gets two points. If you try the fake out and are successful, you'll get one. The team with the most points at the end wins four candy canes, and so on. I knew them very well. Very. At least parts of them. I liked our odds for this one. "It's also going to make you use critical thinking and strategy."

Jack shifted uncomfortably. I took his hand in mine and squeezed it. He'd lost more than part of his kingdom. He'd lost his confidence.

Holly adjusted her wreath before asking, "Any questions?" When none of us spoke, she declared we had thirty seconds to pick a hider.

I immediately went in for Jack. "I think you're the best choice in terms of being able to lay out a good strategy in there. You see things nobody else sees."

He shook his head. "I might be able to guess some things, but if any of the other teams are smart, they'll stick their lumps of coal on this couch for us to assume you'd done it because this has been our spot since the beginning. Don't do that, by the way.

"We don't have time to strategize or come up with hiding spots beyond that. So, the way to win is to use what you know about us. You're the only one with intimate knowledge and experiences with the three of us."

He was so smart. And right. Hart huffed, still mad about being left out the night before, but he and Yeager both agreed. The timer went off and the guys were ushered outside while Cherish, Mandy, and the vampire I called Edward picked up our coal and cards.

We had one minute to hide each round. First up to seek was Hart. It was probably the easiest one I'd do. I waited to see where everyone else was putting their coal before I made my move. Edward stuck his on the mantle above their stocking. After seeing that, Mandy did the same. Cherish thought about it, but after a second, she placed her coal right beside Mandy's. Clever. She turned to me and shrugged. "I don't know anything about Aaron and I can't put the coal in his wife's hoo-hah, so..."

Wow. I liked that inappropriately naughty kid.

As the last seconds ticked down, I hustled into the kitchen and put my coal on the kitchen counter, right next to the wall where Hart and I had, to use one of Cherish's words, smashed.

When the time was up, we went outside, and the seekers ushered in.

# CHAPTER 37

No sooner than the hiders had sat down in front of the Christmas tree grove to wait, Hart popped in carrying a piece of coal with a swipe of blue paint on the bottom. I pulled out the blue card from my pocket and waved it at Holly, who scribbled it down on her score notepad she'd forbidden anyone to touch since it was a gift from Santa.

It didn't take much longer for the others to come out of the lodge. Cherish's gamble had paid off for her, successfully confusing Mindy. I held my hand up for a high five. Which she begrudgingly reciprocated. Hart shook his head and stuck out his fist to her for a fist bump. I guess it was the more on-trend congratulations. They shared an eye roll.

It wasn't lost on me that he just seemed to get her. For all his sexy exterior, he was good with her, and I could tell by the way his eyes lit up when he spoke to her, that he genuinely enjoyed her company as a person. He had layers. It was unfortunate that most people saw only one. It wasn't his fault, but his sexiness was just so encompassing it was hard for anyone to go beyond it.

After Holly had recorded all the points for the round, we were ushered in for round two. I had to hide for Jack this time. It was another no-brainer. However, having round one behind us, all four of us stood in the center of the lodge waiting until the last second to place our coal. Cherish shook her head. "I'm on Christmas break. This game is too extra, and I literally don't even care-uh." She plopped her coal down on the counter and strolled outside.

"Why do I love her when she tries so hard to be unlovable?" That was so true. I shrugged and Mandy placed her coal on the fireplace mantel next to our stocking. At that point, I was failing to care-uh too, so I went over and placed my coal on the window sill where Jack had first kissed me. I knew he'd get it immediately.

Outside as we waited for the seekers to find their coal, the four of us sat in a circle on the stumps by the trees. I realized I'd been with these people for a full week, and I knew little about them. That was wrong. I'd been too focused on myself and my misery to open up to people. That wasn't in the spirit of the games Santa had worked so hard to devise. I needed to change that. "Hey, Mandy. I know you just graduated. What is your degree in?"

"Forensic Science."

Cherish looked up from her phone. "Like on those shows where you figure out blood spray patterns and angles of entry and study fingerprints? For real?"

"Yep. Those things are part of it. I'm waiting to hear back on a couple of good leads on permanent jobs. Looking for a big city but haven't found a good fit yet."

"That is so fire. I bet I'd be good at that." Cherish was beaming and she'd left a text unfinished on her phone, I noted. "Dad always says I'm his I.M."

I glanced over at Hart since the players that had already gone were waiting around too. He shook his head. "I don't know that one. What does it mean?"

She slapped her hand to her forehead. "Ugh. I made my Dad promise not to do that and here I am pulling it out myself. I.M. means inquiring mind."

I was confused. "Okay, but what did you make your dad promise?"

"It's just this weird Dad thing he does. When I was in second grade and the teacher tried to teach us about acronyms, I had trouble with it. So, Dad started using them all the time to help me get it. I'd wake up and come downstairs wearing my favorite pajamas and he'd said Good morning P.P. meaning purple pants. Or he'd randomly point to me and say I.L.Y. I figured out what acronyms were pretty fast, but he just never stopped doing it. Really, it exploded onto everything in his life. He even does it to rando strangers who have no clue what's going on. That's why I made him swear not to embarrass me on this trip by acronyming all over the place. And I was the one who did it. S.M.H"

"I know that one," I shouted. "Shake my head!" Hart squeezed my shoulder like he was proud of me for getting it.

"Aw. That's adorable and I think it's cool of your dad to keep his promise. I haven't heard him use an acronym once." Mandy slid over to get closer to her. "I imagine it's pretty hard for him not to come up with some creative acronyms for Holly's outfits."

"For real, for real. Her fits are extra." She angled toward Mandy. "Is it weird that I was so against Dad doing that, but now I kind of miss it?"

"No. I don't think that's weird. My brother had a habit of turning the lights off twice. He said he was making sure the lights would come on when he got home, which was dumb if you ask me because what if you just clicked the last bit of juice out of them that time? It drove me crazy. But you know what? He moved halfway around the world as I entered college and I missed him and his dumb habit so much, I started doing it myself. To this day, it's how I leave a room." Mandy sighed. "I think it says a lot about someone when their annoying habits become part of your psyche. It's like having the shadow of someone you care about there with you."

She was right about that. The ghost of my ex was still lingering in my condo back at the Pole. "Yeah, Rudy used to leave his shoes right inside the door. Not to the side or in some specified place out of the way. No. he'd come in, and take off his shoes right there in the entryway where he knew I'd be walking. After tripping over them a hundred times, I learned to just jump over the spot where I knew they'd be. His shoes haven't been in my way for months, but I still do that little hop every time I go inside a door from the outside. Probably always will." I laughed. "I guess that's Clare's problem now."

All four of the seekers came out of the lodge. I waved my card at Jack, and he showed me the matching coal. As Holly took down the results, Hart snuck up behind and wrapped his arms around me. "Interesting story."

I could hear the question and concern in those two words. I understood it too. He was responding to me speaking about Rudy in a somewhat civilized manner. Probably the first time I'd done it the entire time I'd been there. The thought had just sneaked up on me based on what Mandy had said. As I was telling it, I was picturing Rudy rolling his eyes as I leaped over his ratty old sneakers. I didn't hate him in those split seconds of the moment. Not really.

But I didn't forgive him either.

"Yeah, just something dumb I put up with. No big deal. What about you? How did it *really* go last night?" I turned and put my arms around him. I could tell from the glassy look in his eyes he was out of it. "We missed you."

Jack slid in behind me, running his hand over my spine. "Speak for yourself, Flame. Maybe Yeager did, but I was content without him. You were too, if I recall."

Hart laughed. "Whatever. I'm not falling into that trap. I told you I'd retaliate, and I will. Mark my words. But to answer your question, everything sucked last night, including but limited to the untimely arrival of Sass Cleavenshire showing up unannounced at my loft where I went to grab some shut-eye. Had to revoke her key privileges. And that got me thinking, so I decided to go pop around and collect all the wayward keys to my place that were floating around the Pole."

"How many keys did you collect?" Jack asked, his eyebrow artfully cocked.

"Let's just say I didn't get a lot of sleep last night." An odd flash of white light flashed across my vision. I had no right to be jealous—I'd been with two men the night before —but I was. That awful gut-churning feeling in the pit of my stomach at the thought of him passing out keys to women all over the place bubbled within me. It reminded me of how I felt when I found Rudy balls-deep in Clare on our bed. My face grew hot, and I was certain my jaw was clenching. "What's the matter, Ginger, you jealous?"

"No. I mean, well…"

"My soul she's cute when she blushes. Look at that, Jack. She's damn-near edible."

Jack stepped around so he could see. "Definitely."

Holly called us to go in for the last round. I took a deep breath of relief as Jack strolled away, leaving us to have a private conversation. Hart tucked me against his chest. "I like that you're jealous. Why do you think I went and got my keys back from all those women? I've got it bad for you, Ginger. I don't see any reason to hide it, even when I know there are two other guys in the mix.

"I don't know how this works, I just know that the visions of sugarplums in my dreams last night tasted of gingerbread and starred me racing down the road on my bike with you clutching me from behind with the wind whipping through your hair, and my name tumbling from these juicy lips."

This time when he kissed me, I felt it all—the gingerbread, the wind in my hair, clutching him as we raced somewhere together. I even heard the jingle of bells. When we pulled apart, Jack had come back across the courtyard to be close to us. He slid his hands in his pocket with that quarter-grin on his face. He gave Hart an infinitesimal nod.

I didn't know how all of it would work either, but if they didn't care about each other, why should I?

"Vixen, you coming, Love? We're starting as soon as Cherish gets out of the restroom." Holly broke the magic that was spiraling between the three of us. I wanted, no I needed to say something back to Hart. He'd just laid out his heart for me and my own was thumping against my chest to an erratic beat as I stood there with tingling lips from that kiss. And tingling nether regions as Jack looked on.

"I'm coming."

Oh, my soul. Wrong choice of words.

No, right choice, wrong time. Both laughed as I turned on my heel. "See you later."

I barreled into the lodge and grabbed the last lump of coal. My mind was spinning. Not only about Hart and Jack but about Rudy too. I tried to pinpoint the moment that I'd stopped being angry at him, but I couldn't. Because I was still angry at his betrayal, but it didn't hold the same sting as it had before. The only conclusion I could conceive was that I had Hart, Jack, and Yeager taking too much of my time and attention to think about what Rudy had done to me.

I didn't have time to think further about it because Cherish, Mandy, and Edward were all standing in the middle of the lodge waiting for my move. Edward was squinting at me but Cherish had a strange look on her face. It looked a bit like fear. Maybe confusion. I don't know, but I smiled at her and squared my shoulders, glancing around the room. Where could I hide the coal for Yeager?

The two of us had never had a significant interaction in the lodge, other than our meeting and all the games we'd played and meals we'd eaten here. He'd always just been there with me from the beginning of this madness. And that just described him so well—he was present, all-encompassing in his generosity and warmth. He was a blanket. A big, warm, comfortable blanket that I enjoyed wrapping myself in.

But thinking about his biceps and the way he used his tongue wasn't going to help me win this game.

After a few more seconds I came up with a plan, strolling over and depositing my coal on top of the logs Yeager had cut and brought in earlier in the morning. He was a lumberjack. Made sense.

The others quickly did the same thing, putting their coals on the same pile of logs, forcing Yeager to pick the right one. It might have been a sound strategy, but they were gambling. If Yeager got mine, we'd get two points, but if he happened to pick the wrong out of the batch, the other team would gain only one point.

I needed Yeager to pick the right one. That was another idea that had crept up out of nowhere—I wanted to win these games.

I did what I needed at the very last second, snatching my coal from the pile and throwing it into the comfy chair by the fireplace. The one where he pinned Hart down to keep him from hurting himself the day he'd found out about the Sexy Elf contest.

Yeah, that moment was still living rent-free in my head. If they'd known how they looked there locked there together with chests heaving and bodies coiled tight? Yeah, I don't know what they'd think about it, but I damn well liked remembering it. Going into my 'pet the cat' visual rotation.

"Vixen tryin' to slay at the last minute. I love that for you." Cherish said as she strolled out of the lodge. I noted that her phone was tucked away in her pocket, and she was worrying her bottom lip between her teeth. She'd never cared about the game, so it was more than that. Something was eating at her.

I jogged to catch up with her. "Hey, are you okay Cherish? You seem off."

She paused midway to the courtyard, taking a few seconds to look around. Mandy and Edward had stopped alongside us. She winced up at Edward. "Um, I'm finna have some girl talk."

He blinked. In rapid succession, not even getting close to understanding her. I tried to help. "I'm sorry, I don't know your name."

He made a move like flipping his hair only his hair was slicked away from his place and didn't even budge. "It's vampiric. You couldn't pronounce it."

"Okay, what do you go by when you speak to non-vampires?"

"I don't go by anything. What would you like to call me?"

"In my head, I've been calling you Edward. The tall blonde is Lestat, the unpredictable one is Dracula, and the sailor is Spike. I'm sorry if it's offensive to call you fictional vampire names."

He laughed. "I love this. I'm Edward from now on. He was the best vampire, I think."

No, he wasn't, but I didn't want to get into a debate over Twilight versus Buffy. "Great, but if you don't mind, I think Cherish wants to talk to Mandy and me privately."

"Sure, sure. I understand. I'll just go over there and re-introduce myself to all as Edward."

The three of us shared a look until he was way out of earshot. Mandy put her arm on Cherish's shoulder. "What's up?"

I expected her to unload another monologue about which boy she liked or what girlfriend betrayed her, but she didn't. She toed the snow for several seconds before finally looking up. There was the fear again. "Um, do one of you have some of those pad things? You know, for the thing."

I was tempted to call Hart over and ask him to interpret but something told me this wasn't the time for Hart. "I'm not following you."

She huffed. "I think I just got my period, and I don't have any kind of supplies and I would die D.E.D before I asked Dad to go get some because he's the CEO of overreacting about life stuff. I mean I thought about asking Erin, she's Gucci, but I am not stuffing a wad of cotton in my hoo-hah. No cap. I won't do it. Besides we used her things on the stocking. But I think there are some pads or something, maybe adult diapers would work. I don't know. I thought I was down with this because my bestie got hers last year, but it hits different when it's you, ya know? Can you help me? Please. And don't tell my dad."

This girl was in serious distress. I couldn't blame her. It was a big deal. I glanced at Mandy, unsure what to do. "Don't worry. We've got you, girl. I've got some pads back in my cabin. And we won't say a word to your father. Though I think it may be something he'd want to know. Eventually."

"Maybe. I'm concerned about the vampires scenting blood, so I'm finna dip."

I gave her a little squeeze. "I don't think it's like that for them."

Mandy agreed. "I can go into the science of why, but you'd probably be weirded out. Let's just go take care of this now and we can talk later, huh?"

Relieved, Cherish nodded. The three of us turned to go back to Mandy's cabin as Yeager strutted out of the lodge beaming and waving his green coal in the air. "I know what you did, naughty girl."

Cherish groaned, so I told them I'd catch up and walked over to Yeager. "I don't know what you're talking about."

"Yeah, you do. You put this in that chair for a specific reason."

"No. I just chucked it in, so you'd know not to pick one from the logs. I didn't give it any real thought." Of course, I had. But I wasn't sure he wanted to hear exactly why. He was pretty open about things, his pack life, but I didn't know if he was *that* open.

Jack's eyebrow was arched as he and Hart approached. "We won. What are you two discussing so intently?"

"I'm telling Vixen that I think there's a reason why she put the coal in that chair by the fireplace. She's feigning ignorance and if she doesn't come clean, I may have to spank her again."

Hart put his hands on his hips and stopped mid-laugh. "Wait. Again? Did you spank her last night too? I hate both of you fuckers so hard right now."

"Hard is the operative word in that sentence, I believe." Jack grinned. "Why did she put it in the chair?"

Yeager glanced at Hart, who was still glaring at him, pretending to be mad about the spanking he missed out on, but I knew him. He'd just spank me himself whenever he wanted. Probably the next time we were naked together.

When I'd decided I was full tilt going to get naked with any of them again, I had no idea. But this wasn't about me. No, Hart's glare was something else entirely.

Yeager gave me a fake snarl that went straight down to the fun-times zone. He put two fingers to his eyes, then pointed them at me, the gesture for I'm watching you. "She knows. And now that you're here, you can have the honor of first spank." He winked at Hart, who grinned as wide as I'd ever seen.

While the thought of what he was suggesting was appealing, I wasn't going to let Cherish down. She needed adult female guidance. "Okay, hold your horses, boys. I have to go take care of something important right now. I'll meet up with you later and maybe we can discuss the logistics of spanking."

Yeager slung one arm around Hart and the other around Jack. "Horses will be held. I've got a little errand to run first anyway. We'll see you later, Bunny." He pressed a kiss to my temple and before I knew it, both Hart and Jack were kissing my cheeks. We stood there together, the four of us, and I became hyperaware of everything around me. The snow at my feet, the feel of Jack's cool lips on my skin, the warm cedar smell radiating from Yeager, Hart's breath tickling my eyelashes as he moved to kiss my closed eyes.

It was too much and not enough at the same time.

I dislodged myself from their embraces and scurried toward Mandy's cabin my pulse skyrocketing. Those men and what they did to me. It was overwhelming to feel such respect and affection radiating from three separate places, three different hearts and minds. I didn't hate it.

# CHAPTER 38

Yeager's errand involved Hart popping him somewhere to get copious amounts of alcohol. The two of them came back from wherever they'd been laughing and joking about doing body shots. It took them a good three minutes to get around to saying Vixen's name in relation to these shots. I thought they were talking about each other. Who knows? Maybe they were. I couldn't care less. My mind was elsewhere.

News of my tremendous loss had reached all the Fae kingdoms and the North Pole too, according to Hart. He'd gotten word from his spies and the word wasn't good. I had to rectify my situation somehow. I couldn't even figure out how to address my kingdom, much less plan a retaliatory attack. So many of my people had betrayed me and I didn't understand why.

"Earth to Ice Man, where is your head?" Yeager set a glass of bourbon in front of me. They'd made me come back to the cabin they shared with Vixen, and as much as I didn't feel like socializing, I also didn't want to be alone with my thoughts either. It was the first time in my life I could remember wishing away the solitude. "Sometimes when things don't go your way, you need to take a minute to regroup. This is us helping you regroup." He raised his glass to clink with mine, as did Hart.

I had to admit the burn of the bourbon on my throat was like my misery in liquid form. I downed the whole glass, then held it up for him to refill. Yeager laughed. "That's what I'm talking about."

I took a little more time nursing my second glass as Hart and Yeager both settled back on opposite sides of the bed, leaning against the headboard to face me as I straddled the chair. "It's not that I don't appreciate this, but I don't see how alcohol can fix my problem."

"Spoken like a man who's never gotten wasted." Hart waved his glass at Yeager, indicating he should pour him another. "Have you ever been drunk before Jack?"

"I drink wine at essential functions, but I've never seen the need to get *wasted*, as you say. I need a clear head to run a kingdom."

Hart shrugged. "Okay, I can see that, but tell me this: is your kingdom going to fall apart more than it has in the next few hours? Nope. Might as well drown your sorrows. It won't make your issues go away, but if you give that calculating brain a break, it may come up with some good ideas. Never know. It can't hurt, right?"

He wasn't entirely wrong. The idea of shutting my brain off for a time did have its appeal. I tipped the glass to my lips and consumed the entire thing. Yeager was quick to pour me another.

When I was halfway through this one, Hart tilted his head toward Yeager first, then turned to me. "So, are we going to talk about the attractive reindeer in the room? Not that I don't appreciate the company I'm in, but I've got to be honest, I keep looking at the door with anticipation of her walking in. Just wondering what's going to happen when she does. In my humble opinion, I get to go first, considering you jerkoffs left me out last night."

Last night had been earth-shattering. I never expected sharing her time with another man would've been as satisfying as it was. Not that I was attracted to Yeager, per se, I was into the way he'd made her moan, the way she moved at his ministrations. They were so in tune with each other, so comfortable. And like he'd said, we were like a team, and I savored watching them together. I suspected it would be the same with Vixen and Hart. The four of us with her together? It sent a warm and swirling feeling through my gut. For once the heat didn't bother me.

Still, though. I was in favor of the spontaneous with Vixen, not of the planned rendezvous with us each taking a number. I usually planned everything. Always. With Vixen though, her eyes lighting in surprise was one of my favorite things about her. While I'd stumbled into last night and wanted more of her, of us, I didn't feel like planning the pecking order was the right way to go.

Yeager put his hand on Hart's shoulder. "I don't feel comfortable talking about this when she's not here. She's not an object to pass around."

"You think I don't know that? Of course, I do. I'm just saying there's one chick and three dicks. I don't want any dumbass male posturing to get in the way of her enjoyment.

Hart belted the rest of his drink. "I don't know if you two have noticed because you haven't known her as long as I have, but she's starting to get back to herself. That's a beautiful fucking thing and I don't want us to ruin it by us throwing elbows because we each want her."

I raised my glass. "On that, we can all agree."

Yeager nodded as he finished off his drink, then pulled his phone from his back pocket. "Shit. I have to take this." He slid off the bed and went outside to take his call. It was a matter of seconds before we heard his loud protests through the cabin walls. "No. No fucking way. It's not happening. You force me into a corner and I'm going to fight back. You don't want that, Dad. Nobody does."

I raised an eyebrow at Hart. He shrugged. Yeager continued to yell. "Let it go. We'll do it our way, and everyone comes out a winner. We don't need to be *together* together. I'll still be involved in raising the kid." Another moment of silence. "I don't give a fuck about the flurry. I didn't choose this, and I won't be chained. Don't force me to make a choice. You won't like the decision."

There was another moment or two of silence, and then out of nowhere came a loud nasty growl. The anguish in it echoed across the hard-packed snow outside and I felt the depths of the despair like it was my own. Hart slammed his drink on the bedside table and popped away. It took me a few more seconds to go over to the door and open it. When I did, I found Yeager pacing back and forth, his hands tearing through his hair, and cursing under his breath.

Hart was poised next to the door, watching each footstep as it ground into the snow. His body was locked tight as he took in the Yeti's actions. "Do you know what that was about?" I whispered. "Never seen him remotely bothered like this."

"It's the ring he wears. Some kind of arranged marriage thing that he didn't want even before he came here. And now with Vixen? It's infinitely more complicated for him, I think."

"Fuck," Yeager growled. He took his shirt in his hands and tore the buttons off with one yank. White Yeti fur rippled over his exposed torso as his warm breath came out in a burst of white. "Fuuuuck."

Hart sprang into action, popping over to him and grabbing him back the back of his neck to pull their foreheads together. "Reign it in, Redwood. It's going to be okay. Breathe with me now." He took several deep breaths which Yeager ignored. He tried to twist out of Hart's grasp, but the Elf was standing firm. A feat for someone facing down a Yeti.

He was a couple of inches shorter and lither than Yeager, but it was in his posture: he wasn't going anywhere. After a few more growling outbursts, Yeager clasped his hands behind Hart's neck too. Their breaths mingled together in a cloud of steam that drifted into the night. "You good?"

Yeager nodded. They stayed that way for another few seconds and in those seconds, I was an intrusion. I made my move to go back into the cabin to give them some space, but they stepped away from each other and pushed past me as I held the door open.

Hart eyed Yeager cautiously as they resumed their previous positions on the bed. This time, a touch closer than before, I noted. Yeager let out a breath. "Sorry. Lost my shit there. I guess I'm going to have to make good on my threat to leave and it fucking kills me to think about being away from my family, but I'm not going to marry Camilla and have a little special Yeti baby with her. I can't do it. It sucks that my father is trying to force me."

I swiped the bourbon bottle from the bedside table and poured him a drink this time. "Take a minute to regroup. Then tell us how we can help." He drank the whole glass and after I poured the second one for him and resumed my position on the chair, he filled us in on everything. Including his special Yeti gift. I have to admit, I experienced a deep measure of kinship with him for sharing something so personal and important. "There are many Yetis living in my kingdom. What if I could get another one with powers like you? Maybe they'd be willing to take your place in the arrangement. Is your intended beautiful in any way?"

His look of surprise and appreciation was genuine. I shouldn't have been shocked by the warmth in it. "Yes. She's pretty, really sweet, but nothing even close to Vixen. The issue that my close-minded father who has a husband on top of my mom and two other wives, by the way, is that he insists on the two of us being married and raising this hypothetical child together. Camilla? She's in love with my sister. She doesn't want any dick near her. Besides, I don't think it would get my father off my back. This is what he deems as my responsibility. I just can't get him to understand all the reasons why something that worked for him might not work for me. I need a fucking miracle to get out of this." He swallowed his drink. "I'm fresh out of those."

Hart bit his lip. I could see his wheels turning as he listened to Yeager's misery. A look I couldn't decipher crossed his face. It quickly passed and before long we'd finished the bottle of bourbon and opened the second.

"Okay, Jack, you're being too stiff. Loosen your hips a little. Make believe like you're thrusting inside Vixen's hot cunt." Hart was behind me, forcing my hips in odd directions. I had to have been drunk to allow them to sway me into recreating the latest dance craze on NickTock. "That's better. Now, do this four times, then the turn."

Yeager had set his phone on the mantle so we would all be in the shot as we danced to Hart's sister's newest song, "Yule Be Sorry."

Even *I* had heard of Brandy Bliss before, and to borrow a word from Cherish, her song slapped. We'd been working on the dance, sporadically taking time to drink, or throwing out solutions to our problems. Like a drunken springboard of ideas, we'd yet to come upon a good one, but I was hopeful based on the brain break hypothesis.

The two of them had successfully brought me out of my funk and I'd like to think I'd helped, in some small way, to bring Yeager and Hart out of theirs. They were good guys. And their camaraderie wasn't lost on me.

Yeager spun in the wrong direction, to which Hart grabbed his hips and spun him the other way before slapping his ass. "Hey Jack, what about the other two kingdoms? What do the queens of Spring and Fall think about what happened?"

I scrubbed my hand down my face. "Don't even ask. Jane Bloom and Jill Harvest might have a thought or two about what happened, but John and I aren't allowed into their kingdoms to ask. They hate us, plus they're too concerned about their harems of men and regular orgies to be concerned with Fae politics. It's a shame. They hold land and power, but all they're concerned with are decadent desires."

Hart sat on the edge of the bed. "What would you say or do if you could get to them?"

I swirled it around in my head, which was a touch hard thanks to all the bourbon, but I'd already given it thought and had an answer to dig out of my brain. "I'd point out that allowing John to have a massive portion of the entire Fae realm is a bad idea for all of us. It's only going to end in all our kingdom's demises if he gets his way. I'd ask them to team up with me, pooling our lands and resources into a challenge he couldn't refuse. At least then I'd have a chance at regaining some of my land and they'd have an equal say in how things happen. It's how it was meant to be."

"If they won't let you in, could you send an emissary in to do your bidding and approach them?"

"It's hard to refuse never-ending orgies. The milder climates bring it out in everyone. I couldn't find any Fae strong enough to resist the pull of their hedonistic magic, so I stopped sending proxies after I lost four Fae to their wanton lust. No other beings in my kingdom cared enough to be put in that position, so I let it die years ago."

Yeager sat on the bed next to Hart, winking at him in a conspiratorial way. He slung his arm around his shoulder and made a big, exaggerated sigh. "If only you knew two strong non-Fae whom you could send instead. Say, one who has the reputation for being the sexiest motherfucker on Earth."

Hart smirked. "And one strapping Redwood who could charm the pants off your great granny with his smirk alone."

I blinked. What were they saying? "I don't follow."

"Don't be a dumbass, Jack," Hart began. "Let us do it for you. We can go in, work our magic, get these queens to see the logic of your proposal, and get out. I promise neither of us will be swayed by their hedonistic Fae magic. We both have too much here to want to come back to."

Yeager glanced at him, displaying the trademark smirk Hart had just mentioned. "Yeah. We could do it. Just tell us how to get there and back."

"Let me get this straight. You want to go to the Fae realm and present my proposal to Jane Bloom and Jill Harvest, knowing you might have to put your bodies on the line to get in?" It didn't compute in my head. Why would they be willing to risk that for me?

"I don't think it will come to Yeager and I having to sleep with these women," Hart said.

The door slammed and we all turned to see Vixen standing there with her hands on her hips. She wasn't even out of her pink coat yet, but she looked like a goddess with her winter-flushed cheeks and fire in her blazing eyes. "I'm sorry, what now? You and Yeager are sleeping with what other women?"

Hart popped over to her, pulling her coat off her shoulders and kissing her cheek. "Keep your panties on, Ginger. At least for now. We've offered to help Jack with his problem by going into the Fae realms for him and proposing a deal with the queens of Spring and Autumn. I have full faith in our persuasive abilities to do this without bodily fluids being exchanged."

Yeager swiped his hand down his torso, his shirt still opened from his tirade earlier. The heat radiating from him, just at the sight of her, was palpable. It caught like wildfire, setting Hart and I both ablaze. "Speaking of bodily fluids..."

# CHAPTER 39

I had no idea what I'd walked in on, but the mood in the room had shifted from light and playful to downright electric as the four of us stood there exchanging glances. I hadn't thought that Hart and Yeager were itching to sleep with anyone else, but the shock of hearing it out loud had thrown me for a loop.

I didn't want them to have anyone else.

They were mine.

All of them.

The trouble was, I didn't know how to go about saying that without feeling like a total psycho slut. *I get to have all three of you, but you get only me.* It wasn't fair to any of them.

Still.

Deep in my heart and other various lady places on my body, that's what I wanted. It was a want I hadn't experienced in years.

I took a second to check the room, eyeing two empty bourbon bottles and glasses strewn all over the place. They'd had a day. And some of the night. The thing with Cherish turned into something bigger than I intended, but she was not someone I wanted to ditch in a moment of crisis. But she was fine, resting with a heating pad after taking some ibuprofen. Mandy had concocted an excuse to give Isaac. I could do no more for her, so I headed back to the cabin with breathless anticipation equated to a kid opening presents on Christmas morning.

The feeling made me smile.

When was the last time I'd smiled like that? I couldn't recall.

The feel of a candy cane scoring down my face brought my thoughts back to the room. "Now that we cleared that up, tell us what you want, Ginger. Don't hold anything back."

I knew he could read my thoughts from the candy cane of truth he was now tracking down my neck. Maybe it was a cop-out to let him drag it out of me like that, but I simply didn't have faith in the words I wanted to say to get my convictions across to him. To them. I was in a freefall, and they were the cause of it. I wanted desperately to cling to all of them. I never expected this to go the way I did, but there it was resting within my thumping heartbeat.

Feels.

For each one of them.

Hart skimmed my collar with the candy cane, then stuffed it back in his pocket. "Redwood, you know that thing you were talking about where you can make us sober? Do it. Now. Our girl wants us to claim her. All three of us."

*Our girl.*

Didn't hate the sound of that.

Yeager jumped off the bed, stripping his shirt off, giving me a view of his panty-melting chest and tattoos as he stalked toward Jack. "Lose the shirt and tie, Ice Man. We'll kill her in the best way possible, but we're not going to a funeral."

Jack rolled his eyes. It was the oddest and best thing I'd seen all day. He'd come out of his shell and gotten relaxed around Yeager and Hart. Jack needed someone outside of his kingdom and they seemed to have formed a bond on their own without me. But with me too. It was heart-warming and I could feel the brotherly affection coming from Yeager and Jack. Hart too.

Without hesitation, Jack whipped out of his tie, and then his shirt. Seconds later, Yeager put his hands to his rib cage. Hart and I watched in awe as Yeager's tattoos did their work and Jack's expression went from glazed to steely in an instant.

Yeager strolled over to where Hart and I stood in the doorway, leaning down to press a quick kiss to my temple before angling at Hart. "You next, Jingle Bell."

Ignoring Yeager's looming presence, Hart pressed his mouth against mine, stealing a kiss that was more posses-sion than anything. It was like he had to get to me first. Payback for leaving him out of the hot tub shenanigans, I guess.

He moved his mouth against mine, releasing a groan like I'd never heard come out of him before. I pulled back to see what I'd missed, to find Yeager's hands inside Hart's shirt, sliding over his ribcage to remove the alcohol from his system. He went to kiss me again, but Yeager began to strip his shirt off for him from behind and got in the way of the kiss. Hart grunted, throwing a look over his shoulder. "I thought we weren't throwing elbows, Redwood."

"I'm fucking helping you, Man. Teamwork makes the dream work. Unless you expect to do this fully clothed."

Did not like the sound of anyone being fully clothed.

I glanced over at Jack. While Yeager was working to strip Hart's shirt, he'd slipped out of his pants and folded them neatly over the back of the chair. He shook his head at their antics. "You could always come over here and leave them to whatever that is, Flame."

That brought their attention back to me. Having successfully stripped out of his jeans and unwilling to wait for Hart's permission, Yeager pulled me to him for his own kiss. It was the same sensual crawl I'd come to crave from him, and a slow burn rose in my belly. Hart's belt buckle rattled across the floor, then then, he was kissing me too, wild and desperate and full of desire.

That kiss with the three of us together? It was all tongues and teeth, and heat. One moment, I could mostly feel Hart, then the next it was Yeager and the groaning and nipping of lips was overwhelming in a way I'd never felt before. I could barely breathe through it. Especially because Yeager and Hart were kissing each other as much as I me. I gripped Yeager's back, only to find Hart's hand already there holding on to him like he needed him to stand up.

It was a lot and not enough at the same time.

All the while, Jack was watching with a cocked eyebrow and arousal pressing against his gray boxer briefs.

Yeager pulled away, groaning as he slid his tongue along the hollow of my throat. He liked doing that as much as I liked feeling it. Hart lifted my sweater, breaking the contact. "I can cockblock too, Redwood."

It wasn't lost on me that they were calling each other by their dick names.

Both of their heads jerked back and I eeked in surprise as I found Jack standing there gripping their hair and pulling them away from me. "You two need a lesson in teamwork. Daddy's going to have to send you to the corner for time out." He shoved them away from me.

The two of them chuckled as I experienced the closest thing to spontaneous combustion I would ever get. Yeah, the Daddy thing was going to kill me. The other two encouraging it meant I'd never survive. It suited Jack on a deep level and I was all in on the Daddy.

I lunged forward, kissing Jack like I never had before. I knew I should be careful so he wouldn't overheat, but I couldn't stop myself. I had to kiss him. His lips were soft and cool, like a fresh breeze on a winter morning and I loved the goosebumps erupting all over my skin as a result.

When he pulled away from me, his pupils were blown out, deep dark desire coloring the silvery gray. He bent over whispering in my ear so only I would hear him. "Get on the bed. I want to watch them take you."

I turned to find both Yeager and Hart completely undressed now. Yeager was leaning against the headboard, his muscular body on display while Hart had his knees on the bed facing me. It was like a buffet of hotness. I couldn't decide which of them to look at first. But in the back of my mind, I told myself it didn't matter. I didn't care and for some reason I'd never be able to define, they didn't either.

This was not a normal situation.

Although normal had hurt me to my core. It was time to embrace something different.

Jack swung the door to the cabin open the flicked his wrist to gather up some snow, which he deposited in an empty trash can. He set it down in front of his chair and dipped his head toward the bed where Hart and Yeager were poised and waiting. I stepped out of my jeans and tiptoed to the edge of the bed, raising my eyebrow to ask how we were going to go about things.

Hart's piercing sounded as he jumped up, taking a spot behind me as Yeager slid down the bed. Hart found the waistband of my panties in the next second. "Look at that fucking wall of muscle and hardness. Do you see how badly he wants you?"

I nodded, swallowing as Yeager began stroking himself and Hart's fingers dipped inside my panties, finding my clit and circling with his expert fingers. I loved the feel of his silver rings grazing against my hot flesh. My knees started to buckle under the contact, under the desire for them.

Jack slid in on the other side behind me. He pressed a kiss to my cheek before rasping with a voice laced with hunger. "What are you waiting for, Flame? Go ride that big cock like a good fucking girl."

Didn't have to tell me twice.

I crawled up to Yeager, putting my knees on either side of his muscular thighs. I was salivating with the need for him to fill me up with his thickness. Taking a deep breath, I positioned myself over him, and he ran the head of his cock over my entrance, as he peeked behind me. "She's already wet and hot for me."

Yeah, it was insane how ready I was for this. He put his hands on my hips and gently eased into me, giving me time to adjust to the feel of him. I hissed, loving the stretch as I lowered myself, pressing down against his pubic bone.

"Look at me, Bunny."

I hadn't realized I'd closed my eyes, but I popped them open and investigated his emerald gaze, feeling warm all over. He rose to a sitting position which would've probably been difficult for anyone without his stomach muscles. I got a sweet kiss then he grazed his thumbs along my jaw. "We don't have to use this position. I'm fine with whatever way you want."

For a second, I was confused. I noted movement behind me, Hart and Jack pressing toward the bed with concern.

Then it hit me. The first time with Yeager I'd told him I couldn't be on top. Rudy had always insisted, and I was so bored and over it. The thought of it seemed so silly to me at that moment. It hadn't even crossed my mind. I just wanted Yeager and he was lying there waiting for me, wanting me, looking at me like I was the most desirable woman in the world.

I had to take a deep breath to stop the tear from falling. He was incredibly sweet to remember that, to want so desperately to make me comfortable. I wanted him even more for it. "No, it's fine. I like this. It feels fantastic." I rolled my hips to show him. That was all it took. He grabbed my hips again and raised his to meet me.

We got into a smooth rhythm as I arched and moved against him, his big cock filling me and making me moan. He was into it too. "Fuck me. Okay. Fuuuck. You're not playing, are you?"

Nope. I was not.

"Are you ready for more, Ginger?" Hart, his hands sweeping my body like he couldn't find where to light. I nodded because I was eager for Hart to join the party, but I could barely breathe with the way Yeager was grinding against me. The presence of the other two behind me was like a steady forceful heartbeat working its way through me. I wanted them all. At once. I didn't give a flip or a fuck if it was wrong or selfish. Not one.

I was so into the feel of Yeager's big cock, I didn't even answer Hart. Yeager was on it though. "Yeah, she needs more. Get in here and help me bring her to ruin, fellas."

Hart bit my earlobe as his hand slid between my breasts, down my stomach, finding my clit and circling it in that expert way that had me trembling. On the other side, Jack's hand grazed down my spine and down between my cheeks. I arched in surprise but soon found that I didn't hate the cool feel of his fingers as he ran them along the crease.

"Hold it. BRB." Hart popped away, then came back another second later, holding something in his hand which he passed to Jack. "Peppermint flavored, in case you're interested."

I looked over my shoulder in time to see that quarter-grin creep across Jack's face. He held the lube between his thumb and forefinger, giving it a little shake and arching his eyebrow. Asking permission. My answer was, "Yes."

Yeager grunted, still thrusting inside me as he spoke. "What has he told you about that? Yes, what?"

They weren't going to let it die.

Not that I minded. "Yes, Daddy."

# CHAPTER 40

The feel of Vixen's pussy was going to drive me insane. Never in my life had I wanted anyone more than her. Throw in her willingness—no, her eagerness—to have all three of us at the same time. I was hooked beyond measure. Her being open to the idea of shared lovers was the single best thing I'd heard in a long damn time.

Not everyone could handle it.

She wasn't everyone.

And I was damned lucky to find two other guys who seemed to be good with it too. It was damn near a Christmas miracle.

The sight of her rocking against me, knowing she'd been bothered by the position thanks to the idiotic Radicchio and his demands on her body, but willing to look past it now? It was everything.

*She* was everything.

I was falling into the notion of her as much as my cock was falling into the hot wet dampness of her pussy as it clenched around me. If I didn't stop myself, I was going to come way too fucking fast. Especially as I watched Hart take one of her pink nipples into his mouth as his fingers swirled around her clit, rings knocking together like the drumbeat to her writhing.

I don't know what it was about those fucking rings.

Something.

She gasped but kept riding me like a fucking cowgirl. Jack had positioned himself behind her and I couldn't be sure, but it looked like he was working his fingers into her ass as he kissed her shoulder and neck. The desire on her face, with those pink lips parted and her eyes glassy with want, it was too fucking much. Too much. I managed to rasp out, "I've got to tap out for a second."

Hart's mouth popped off of Vixen's tit with a wet sloppy sound that went straight to my cock. "Trying not to blow?" I nodded, eyeing the way his fingers toyed with her clit and noting the distinct feel of his rings touching my skin as he did so.

Those fucking rings.

"Let's switch it up, shall we?" Hart gently pulled Vixen off my dick. She sighed, disappointed, which made me feel pretty fucking superior. She perched on the bed, waiting to see what would happen next. I fell for her even more. Rising, I cupped her face and kissed her like she deserved. Slow, aching, searching, searing with heat. Hart huffed. "I love watching you kiss her with that tongue, Redwood." She nodded while I kept on going.

The distinct crunch of snow as Jack stepped into the trashcan he'd filled the room. He was getting as hot as the rest of us. That wasn't the best for him, but I don't think he cared. While I didn't know the specifics of what they'd done together, I got the feeling at the hot tub that he'd never actually had her fully. Out of all of us, he might have been the one who needed her most. "Ice Man, you want a piece of that hot pussy next?" I glanced at Vixen to check if I'd overstepped—I'd die if I had—but she was nodding with her lip between her teeth looking at Jack like he was her next meal.

Fuck.

Jack's voice came out as a plea. One word. "Yes." I slid off the bed to give them room. Jack laid on his side where I'd been and patted the spot next to him. "Here."

A man of few words.

She complied, lying on her side next to him as Hart and I stood near watching to see how it was going to go before we got back into the thick of it. Because we were getting back into it. Jack ravaged her mouth with a blistering kiss I didn't know he had in him, then pulled her to him, positioning her leg over his to get a good angle. He hissed as he pushed into her. In the next moment, they were both bucking wildly like animals. Hart put his hand on my shoulder. "My soul, look at her. Perfection."

It was hard to argue with that.

It was also hard to ignore the way Hart's hand skimmed my neck as he watched.

Those damn rings were starting to fuck with my head. Because I liked the feel of them against my skin. I turned to look at him. His eyes were glued to the action on the bed, but when he felt me looking, he angled toward me. There was a moment of electric spark there between us, but it dissipated as quickly as it came. "I'm going in."

I was imagining things. Not good in the middle of a fuck fest.

Hart grabbed the lube from the bed and popped the cap before he lay on the bed behind her. "What do you say, Ginger? Did Jack get you ready for me?"

She peered over her shoulder. "Yes. Please, Hart. I need you too." The need in her voice was like the sound of sirens singing. He spread some lube over his dick, his bell ringing as he did so. Then he pressed against her, rubbing himself in her crack as he reached around to play with her tit and kiss her neck. He was all over her, and I could only imagine the sensation of it as Jack railed into her with deep guttural thrusts. Fuck, it was hot.

"Give it to her now Hart. She wants that jingle bell." Jack had the Daddy voice down. I don't even think Hart minded being ordered around. Not when the command was going to give his jingle bells a rock. He poured a little lube down her crack and moved Jack's hand to help him spread her cheeks apart. Jack lifted her a little so that Hart could easily slide into her. The smell of peppermint permeated the room and if I thought I was hard before, the sight of his bells disappearing inside her made my balls ache. "Fuuuuck me."

Together they stilled when Vixen moaned as she adjusted to the both of them inside her. "You like this, Ginger?"

Her response was a whimper. "Mm-hmm, move, please. My soul, you have to move."

Hart chuckled as he pulled out of her ass, then slowly back in again. It took a few seconds, but Jack found the rhythm and they started working in tandem to give her what she clearly wanted. It was incredible. The groaning and grunting and begging out of their mouths. It was filthy and beautiful and so raw. My chest constricted and I didn't want to wait anymore.

Moving around behind Jack and perching one knee on the bed, I leaned down to steal a quick kiss from her panting mouth, then I offered my dick to her. Hart grinned. "That's what I'm talking about. Have a little taste of that Redwood." Her tongue reached out and she licked all the way up my shaft and back down again, making me groan. Then I'll be fucked if she didn't open her mouth and beg for me to give her the whole thing. So, I did.

The feel of her hot mouth was excruciating and perfect. It didn't take long for me to find the rhythm too. I dug my hands in her hair and leaned forward so when Hart pushed into her, she inched a little further and swallowed more of my cock. I locked eyes with Hart. He was watching her take my length and biting his lip like he was in the best kind of pain and agony. The heat in my chest flared. "Yes. That's, yeeaah. Shit. Feels good. You like all three of us like this, don't you, Bunny?"

I was starting to see spots before my eyes, and I needed to be sure she was okay. I mean, by the way she moaned with my cock in her mouth, it seemed like she was, but I had to know for sure.

When she didn't respond immediately, Jack who was still gripping her ass in one hand, gave her a quick slap. "He asked you a question."

"Damn." Hart and I said in tandem.

She released my cock, looking at me with her hazy blue eyes in full lust mode. "Yes, I like it. A lot." Reaching behind, she pulled Hart down so she could kiss him. Then she went to Jack, giving him a dirty kiss that he groaned all the way through. She shot me an expectant look and I gave her exactly what she was asking for by leaning down to take her mouth, sliding my tongue inside, and then back out again, nipping at her lower lip, then sucking on it.

"Shit, I could watch you kiss him all damn day, Ginger." Smiling, she looked back at him for a second, then proceeded to take my shaft in her mouth again. Hart pumped into her as he reached between them and found her clit. She bucked as his fingers worked against her. All of us groaned in unison. We sounded like a herd of rabid wildebeests, but that was just fucking fine with me.

Vixen hummed against my cock, and I almost lost it again. But what kind of gentlemen would I be if I came first?

Hoping to give her everything she wanted and more, I kept one hand in her hair to support her neck and I snaked the other one down to her rosy hard nipples, toying, pinching, and playing as she started panting. There were tears in her eyes from taking my length, but she never let up. Not once.

Not until Hart grabbed her hair and pulled her off me. "Sorry Redwood, but I want to hear her when she comes all over Jack's cold cock."

She wailed, "Yes," as she spasmed, thrashing against Jack's pubic bone while Hart bore down in her ass and kept fingering her clit.

Jack huffed. "That's it. Come on my cock like a good girl. My soul, I can feel you clenching around me." The next second, he came. Hard. Brutal. Shoving into her for relief. And she did take it like a good damn girl.

I couldn't help it. I started pumping my dick in my hand. Hart glanced up and shot me a smirk before he unloaded too. Then he collapsed on the bed beside her, as Jack slid off and stuck his feet in the snow again.

She looked up at me with utter desire. My turn to come.

I didn't get the release I was needing because a piercing howl broke through the night. It was so anguished and mournful there was no way to ignore it. Something was wrong.

# CHAPTER 41

Hart sat up, eyeing Yeager as he stopped mid-stroke. "The fuck is that?"

Jack stepped out of his bucket of snow. "Nothing good. Go check." Hart grabbed the nearest pair of shorts—Yeager's red ones—stepping into them and popping away while Jack climbed into his pants. He raised an eyebrow toward Yeager, who groaned.

"I guess I get the blue balls this time, huh Ice Man?" He bounded off the bed, searching for his clothes. "Did that fucker take my underwear? Ass." He ran over to his bag and grabbed some sweatpants, pulling them on, commando style. They did nothing to hide his still erect shaft. I sighed, like a deep audible sigh because as mind-bending as our night had been, I still yearned for Yeager in the worst way. He grinned down at me. "Don't worry, Bunny. We'll get back into it when we find out what's going on."

He was right to put a pause on it. The howls were getting worse.

I slipped back into my jeans and grabbed Hart's sweater. I guessed we were all sharing everything at this point. It smelled like peppermint and vanilla, and I momentarily got lost in it. But when he popped back into the room with a frazzled look on his face, I stopped cold. "What is it?"

"It's Isaac. Cherish shifted for the first time tonight and freaked out. She took off into the woods and Isaac was trying to track her, but her wolf scent wasn't strong enough yet apparently. Mandy said that was common for young wolves. Don't know how she knew, but that's not the point. It seems like he's having trouble locating her."

Yeager handed Hart a hoodie from his bag. "Let's go. I can track. You can pop and get her, bring her back to Isaac."

"Yeah, but we have to find her first." They shared a wary look. Werewolves were unpredictable. Even those we could call friends at this point. Cherish didn't know what was going on and I had no idea if she would attack Hart and Yeager or not.

Cold dread coated my heart. I should've known her shift would come with her period. And we should've told Isaac. I had to get out there and help. "I can shift. Look from above."

"Good call, Flame. If she gets past the temperate climate barrier, I can push back the cold long enough to keep her safe."

Yeager swung the door open. "Told you. Teamwork makes the dream work."

He wasn't wrong.

Shedding the clothes, I'd just put on, I steadied myself for the shift. It wasn't a painful process, but I normally didn't do it in front of anyone. And I had three sets of eyes watching me with interest. And the thing was, they weren't looking at me with passion because I was naked again. No, it was awe. I didn't feel worthy of it, but I appreciated it anyway.

I got down on all fours and let the shift take over. Fur rippled over my body as my arms and legs morphed and my neck elongated. My antlers were the last thing to erupt. I shook my tail out and raised my head to balance the weight of my eighteen-inch span. It wasn't a flex, but I did have the largest antlers out of all the females on Santa's fleet. After they settled into place, I shook my whole body.

Yeager stepped toward me, running a hand between my antlers. I don't know if he realized the intense sensation it would cause, or if he just happened to find the perfect spot. Whatever, it was amazing, and I snorted at him. He chuckled. "Oh, you like that huh? I have to say, you're just as stunning in this form."

Hart pulled his arm away. "Please don't tell me you want to fuck her like that, you beast."

"No, dumbass. You've seen her like this, I haven't. I just think she's beautiful."

"She is, but we should go. Cherish needs help." Jack strolled out of the door, directing us to follow him. Yeager dropped his sweats and shifted himself as he stepped out into the snow. His Yeti form was as imposing as his human one. I couldn't help but notice the kind concern in his green eyes as he pointed to the edge of the woods, where pretty much everyone had gathered.

Mandy was agitated, pacing back and forth. Yeager took a second to sniff the air, then nodded at Hart and they took off into the woods. I reared back on my hind legs and took flight, following them. I looked below as Lestat pulled up on a snowmobile. Jack slung himself behind him and they took off into the trees.

I concentrated on finding Cherish, letting the wind whip over my body as I swooped over the trees. It was so good to be back in reindeer form. Though it was weird that I didn't have my partner Prancer at my side. I was definitely lighter and moving faster without the sleigh behind me, but I found I missed the pull of the reins.

I spotted Yeager's Yeti form weaving through the trees. I dove down and found Hart popping in beside him as Yeager tracked forward. It went on that way for several miles. Yeager would bound ahead, and Hart would appear at his side like a shadow. Isaac was keening in the distance, closing in on Yeager's location too. I guess a big furry white body was easier to see in the dark.

Nerves swirled in my gut as I realized we were all getting too close to the end of the forest where the boundary kept the South Pole weather at bay. There would be nothing good beyond the trees. I didn't know how long a young wolf could survive the frigid temps.

My eyes were peeled ahead of Yeager, but I almost fell from the sky when a deafening roar broke the winter silence. I shot ahead, breaking past the barrier and shivering a bit as my magical reindeer body adjusted to the plummeting temperature.

The freezing air wasn't the only thing different beyond the barrier. I was at the true South Pole now. All ice and frigid water and snow-packed wasteland. And below was a celebration of polar bears closing in a small dark dot. Cherish.

She was nipping at them, growling and backing away as the four big beasts advanced, backing her into a snow-drift. When two of the bears crashed forward, there was the groaning crack of ice breaking. Another bear came out of nowhere, leaping over the snow drift and landing behind Cherish with a thud forceful enough to dislodge another section of ice. It tipped, dipping forward and she slid, paws scrambling, into one of the bears. It moved to swipe her with his massive claws, but she ducked under his legs, and he barely missed her.

I didn't think. I just shot downward, flying around the bear's head to distract him as the ice dislodged fully and started drifting. There wasn't enough room for it to go far, but yet it was enough to create a glacial ice floe between Yeager and Hart, who'd just arrived, and Cherish.

Making another pass, Yeager growled at me, waving his massive hands, directing me away from the five polar bears. He had a plan.

When I landed next to them, Hart shivered but started giving directions. His lips were blue already. I didn't know how he was standing the temperature, but he managed to grit out some words. "I'll pop over and distract the bears long enough for you to go get her. She's going to have to shift and climb on your back. I don't know how to tell her that though. She's probably too scared to understand any-thing at this point."

A sudden warm wind whipped around us. Hart visibly re-laxed. Jack and Lestat pulled up on their snowmobile. Jack slid off, taking in the scene and calculating. He pulled Hart and Yeager to his side "Can you two distract the bears?" Hart nodded. "Vixen can get her out and as soon as that

happens, I'll crack that ice and send them into the deep."
It wasn't lost on me that he'd basically come up with the
same plan as Hart, only with an added step to it.

Yeager roared and lunged forward, easily leaping over
the small barrier of rushing water and landing on the floe
beside a polar bear. He kicked the legs out from under the
bear in a ninja move if I'd ever seen one. The bear fell and
he shoved him over the edge of the ice with his massive
strength. Hart, on the other hand, popped over and landed
on the back of the next bear. Taking a knife that I had no
idea how he got and slicing the throat of the bear in one
quick stroke. It fell with a thud and the blood gushing from
his throat froze as it hit the air.

Two bears down in less than two minutes.

These men.

That was hot.

Didn't have time to ogle though. I nodded at Jack and
took to the air, sailing over and landing on the ice in front of
Cherish. She had the same dark eyes in her wolf form, with
chocolate brown and black fur and menacing teeth that
dripped saliva. She shivered, whether it was from terror or
cold or both, and I ached to talk to her, to calm her down,
but I couldn't in reindeer form.

Sensing what was happening, Hart shouted at Yeager,
then he strolled over and stood beside me like there weren't
three polar bears still advancing. He bent down and produced a candy cane from his pocket, waving at her so she
could see it. "Hey Cherish. You know me, so you know there
is no cap here. Listen, I know this is scary AF, but I need
you to shift back into your human form so Vixen can get
you back to your dad, okurrr?" As insane as he sounded,

the use of her terminology got her attention. She growled low but cocked her head to the side.

Behind me, another polar bear fell into the icy water. Yeager was truly a beast. Hart glanced over his shoulder to check before he continued. "I get that you're salty over all this, but Vixen is ready to swoop you right out of here. You just have to shift back." He looked over to where Jack stood waiting. "We need a blast of heat if you can. Now."

Jack paced uncomfortably, then stuck his hands in the ice to leach the cold as warmth swirled around us. It took another few excruciating seconds for Cherish to respond, but she finally did, shifting into her human form. Her panicked face lit up when she spotted Hart. "What happened? Welp."

She wilted in front of us, but he popped over to catch her before her knees hit the ice. He carried her over to me, placing her on my back then removing Yeager's hoodie and covering her.

I could feel by the way she lay on me, she was in no position to hold on. Hart spied it too. "I'm going to have to ride you too, Ginger. She won't be able to stay on." His eyes twinkled and I snorted at him for the inappropriate comment. The girl was about to die. Not the time for sexual innuendos. But Hart was Hart and I kind of dug that about him.

He slid behind Cherish and wrapped her up in his arms. As soon as he grazed my antlers, I turned to look back at Yeager. Jack slapped my butt, not hard, but enough to get my attention. "Don't worry about him. We've got him. Get her to Isaac."

Trusting him, I reared back on my hind legs again, gaining strength for the heavier cargo. Though the two of them combined were nothing compared to what I usually carried. Then I took off into the night sky with the warmth at my back and the trees on the horizon.

# CHAPTER 42

Vixen landed gracefully in front of Isaac. I'd expected nothing less. She was as elegant in reindeer form as she was as a human. In other words, breathtaking.

Isaac let out a pained whimper at the sight of his daughter lying against my chest unresponsive. He'd changed back into his human form and put on some clothes, but the man was freaking out one hundred percent. "She's okay. Just a little shook. The bears didn't touch her."

His eyes went wide. "Bears?"

Oops. Probably should've left that for another conversation.

But they were in my head.

Probably—definitely—because I'd left Yeager to deal with them on his own.

A clawing pang gnawed at my insides at the thought of him battling those things solo. Sure, Jack and the tall vampire were there too, but as much as I liked Jack, I wasn't sure he could do much to help outside of freezing them. That might work, but neither of them knew what I spied as

Vixen took flight: the rest of the celebration bearing down on their location.

There were at least ten or twelve, maybe more. I'd discovered the group earlier in the week and while I took one of the smaller ones out easily, they weren't the docile shifter kind of polar bears, who chilled in bear form and left everyone alone. They were vicious and aimed to protect their perceived territory. That made them lethal.

As soon as I got back to the North Pole, I was going to have a little chat with Santa. His barrier wasn't working the way it should. He needed to beef it up. I would've popped away and told him the second after I lowered Cherish into her father's arms, but I had something way too fucking pressing to deal with first.

"Hey, Ginger." She turned to me, lifting her snout so I could stroke it. I knew she could understand what I said while she was shifted. Part of the reindeer magic. "If you've got it from here, I need to—" I paused, unsure what I was about to say. Panic was rocketing through me. I fucking hated that feeling. I took a deep breath to steady my pounding heart. "I need to get to Yeager."

Her eyes went soft as she nodded then pushed me forward by putting her snout on my ass and shoving. When I didn't immediately pop away, she chomped down with her teeth. It was just a little love bite, but it revved my pulse anyway. I turned, grinning. "I promise, we'll get back to that as soon as I get our man-beast back."

I popped away, realizing I'd say *our* man-beast, not *hers*.

Fuck. That idea was starting to be a problem.

A big Yeti-sized one. But I did what I'd been doing for days and stuffed that idea in my ass where it came from. I needed to make sure he wasn't dead before I addressed it.

I landed near the ice floe where I'd last seen him. Jack and Lestat were mounting their snowmobile and I scanned the area, checking for Yeager. There were a few dead polar bears, frozen and otherwise, but Redwood was nowhere in sight. I popped over to Jack. "Where is he?"

Jack put his hand on my shoulder, to steady me maybe, I don't know. "The rest of the celebration surprised us. We got a few, but they took to the woods. Yeager was afraid they'd encroach on the cabins, so he went off after them. We're going to use the snowmobile to try and break them up, make them easier to manage."

I slid the knife from my pocket, gripping it with white knuckles. "I'm in. Which way?" Lestat sped off and I popped along behind them. As soon as we breached the woods, the vicious sound of bear growls hit my ears. It was damn-near deafening. And I hadn't even spotted them yet.

The vamp veered in the direction of the growls, and it took some weaving through the trees, but we came up on the backs of five polar bears as they prowled toward something in front of them. My heart thudded and I tasted bile in the back of my throat. They weren't advancing on something.

They were advancing on Yeager.

He was giving a good amount of growl back as he tussled with a massive polar bear, wrestling style. The bear was bigger, but Yeager in his Yeti form was an equal match. He had the added advantage of critical thinking skills, which made it easier for him to duck, maneuver, and subdue. Still, he was fighting a fucking polar bear with his bare hands. I had to help.

I slapped the vamp on the back to get him going again. He zoomed forward right between two of the bears. Jack held out his hand and froze it mid-swipe. The three bears beside it seemed to have the good sense to run at that point, taking off toward another group in the distance. How many of those damn things were there? We had to take them all out.

I pointed for the snowmobile to pursue. When they took off, the sound of the motor spooked another bear and he lunged at Yeager.

Two on one.

I didn't plan my attack. I just popped onto the back of the second bear and started stabbing. As its strength ebbed, I reached around and slit the throat, popping off as he fell to the ground. As soon as that was done, I popped over to the bear tussling with Yeager. His eyes widened. It was strange to see those sparking green gems set against the white fur of his Yeti face. That smirk laid within them as he threw the bear back with a shove. I took that time to stab the polar bear's eyes, one at a time. It wailed and started whirling around, but it didn't have a chance against us together.

I popped down to the ground as Yeager attacked, shoving the bear into a huge tree. He reached out and plucked the knife from my hand, claws and all, then plunged it into the bear's skull. The only thing left in him was the whisp of breath escaping into the cold as it sank to the ground.

"Fuck. That was hot, "I rasped.

Yeager made a Yeti sound that I couldn't interpret, but I didn't have time to ask because he pushed me away with a swipe of his hand just as another polar bear advanced from behind. I'd never seen it coming.

Saving my life? What was beyond hot? I didn't know.

Shitballs, I had a problem.

While Yeager was dealing with one bear, another one prowled over to me. Scrambling, I went over to the dead bear to grab my knife. As I was tugging it out like it was Excalibur, the advancing bear whacked me, and all the breath left my lungs. I stood there gasping and choking as the bear came at me again, this time going for my head and finding it. I swear my brain jostled as my head hit the tree. The next second it was lights out.


I didn't know how much time had passed when I woke. All I knew was that my head was fuzzy, and I was still alive. I shot to my feet, checking for Yeager and the bears. The area was coated in muddied snow and a lot of blood.

Too much blood.

I took a few staggering steps. My whole being was consumed with the aching need to find him and I didn't give a shit if I was concussed—I'd survived that lots of times after fights—I just had to make my feet go.

Doing my best to suss out which tracks were his, I stumbled forward, my head pounding from the bear's attack. I walked more than a couple miles through the trees—toward the Inn—before the unmistakable sounds of a growling fight broke the night.

I bolted.

Careening toward two huge blurry white figures, my pulse rocketed, and I popped forward even though I was near hurling from the pain. I landed on top of the polar bear with a gasp, wincing and groaning in an effort to stay attached to his back while I fumbled for my knife.

My vision swam as the bear I was riding lunged at Yeager, swiping his throat, and tearing it to pieces in one slash. Yeager fell on the pristine snow, coating it in a thick redness that made my stomach roil.

White, blinding rage took over my whole body. I couldn't see. I couldn't breathe. All I knew was I was going to kill that motherfucking bear for taking him from us. From me.

It took too damn long to get my knife in hand, but I was certain I had one shot to get the fucker before I passed out again. With Yeager lying dead feet away, I didn't even care if I died in the snow. I just wanted to take my violent revenge, so I went for it. I stabbed, hitting air the first few times, but finally finding purchase. Clenching my legs together to hold on, I took the soft fur of its neck in one hand, then pushed my knife against its throat, preparing to slice. Before I could plunge it in, I fell to the ground with a thud.

"The fuck are you doing, Jingle Bell? Trying to kill me?"

I blinked, hoping to make the swirling vision in front of me—nope, underneath me—come into focus. It took a few seconds for me to reconcile what had happened, but when it did, a flood of adrenaline washed through me, and I woke the fuck up.

I'd been too out of it to realize I was on Yeager's back, not the bear. When I went to stab him, he must have shifted, and I'd fallen on top of him like this.

The polar bear was dead. Not Yeager.

Not Yeager.

I glanced over at the bear. Just to be sure.

Not Yeager.

Nope, he was lying underneath me, naked in the snow as I straddled him. He put his hand in my hair, tilting my head down to make me look at him, not the bear. His green eyes searched mine with rough concern. And maybe something else. When he didn't immediately let go, a soft roll of desire swept through me.

Fuck.

Had to fix this compromising position we were in.

Soon.

In a second.

Not yet.

"I didn't realize I was riding you. Are you okay?" Did not like the choke in my voice. It said way fucking more than I wanted to say to him.

"I'm good. You?" The hand in my hair moved, grasping in a way that I'd seen him do to Vixen. She always liked it. I now understood why. That soft play of his long fingers in my hair, skimming my scalp, it burrowed inside me. My cock twitched despite my efforts to remain calm and ignore the feelings racing through me.

"Think I have a concussion, but yeah, fine."

Was I fine? Yet to be determined.

His hands went under my shirt, playing along my ribs in a way I now recognized was him using his healing powers. His fingers were cold, but I found myself liking the way he mapped my torso, the sharp intake of breath he made as his tattoos lifted from his body. The way his hands drifted along my skin long after my fuzzy head cleared, and his tattoos settled back on his hard body.

I didn't mean to do it. It just sort of happened. I shifted slightly and the sound he made went straight to my cock like a bolt of lightning. His lips parted in surprise when he realized how fucking hard, I was. For him.

My soul, that smirk was like a lethal weapon. I whipped one of my candy canes from my pocket because I had to know. *Had* to. Was this thing building in me a one-way street? Or did that look on his face mean something?

I traced the candy cane over his shoulder, down his bulging tattooed bicep, but before I could figure out how to formulate the question I so desperately wanted to ask, he jerked it from my hand and broke it between his fingers. "None of that candy cane bullshit. If you want something from me, ask it."

He applied a little pressure as his fingers gripped my hair, forcing me down so that I was close enough for the warmth of our exhales mixed in the frigid air. He glared at me with a challenge written in his expression. "Better yet, Jingle Bell. Just take it."

# CHAPTER 43

He just needed was a little encouragement, a nudge in the right direction to let him know he wasn't wrong about this. Yeah, I wanted him too. Pretty fucking bad. So, after I all but threw myself at him, he did the one thing I admired most about him—threw caution to the fucking wind.

He slammed his mouth to mine with a guttural release of relief and desire and it wrapped around me like those damn rings of his. Fuck me, he was relentless.

Pressing my cock against him so he'd know what he did to me, I took what I needed from him, matching his kisses with the deep probe of my tongue, nipping and sucking his full lips as we groaned our way through the push and pull of this thing. Together we were like fire and oil. We were combusting into an inferno of lust and want and need and I simply didn't know if I could get enough of him.

This had been brewing from day one, for both of us if I read things right. It would've happened eventually, but the adrenaline rush from our night fighting the polar bears had ramped us both up. As far as I was concerned, that was an exceptionally good thing, but we were two alpha types who usually took charge—in the bedroom and beyond. I didn't know how that was going to play out without Vixen between us. I was damn sure interested in finding out though.

Vixen was always in my mind, regardless of the huge boner I was sporting for Hart. I couldn't just dismiss the thought of her. I didn't. She was there in my head though my body was fully lit with the taste of Hart.

He bit my lip and pulled away, giving me a heated look before he took his kisses south, pressing them along my neck, down my chest, over the ridges of my abs, and then further, trailing his tongue along the V in my hips. I arched up to meet his eager lips, desire sweeping through me. Just as he got to the good part, I reached down and pulled his hair to get his attention—not hard enough to hurt, but enough to make him look up. Panic crossed his face. "Shit. Too far, too soon?"

Though I could see where the confusion came from, I had to laugh. "Negative. I'm so into you I'm about to melt the snow underneath me. Maybe you could pop us somewhere inside, so I don't have to do this with snow in my ass crack. No shade on Jack, but I'd like to have all nerves fully thawed when you suck my cock like I know you want to."

He threw his head back, laughing. "Yes sir."

The telltale pop sounded, and my ass hit a soft bed and warmth crept over my body. Hart was still on top of me, stripping off his coat.

We had to be in his loft. There were exposed pipes and brick everywhere, with metal accents old boxing posters, and vintage metal signs on the wall. There was a huge desk in the corner with papers all over it. And a framed gold record hung above it. It was so *him*. I wanted to ask about everything, but the sight of him yanking his t-shirt over his head from behind brought me back to the idea of other things taking precedence.

He was insanely fucking sexy, and I made a move to sit up, but he took my wrists and pinned me down to the bed. It smelled like him, warm peppermint and something sweet too. "Just to be clear, that's the last time I call you sir." He dove for my mouth, laying me out with a dirty kiss that was mostly teeth and tongue.

And I gave it as well as I was getting, I hoped anyway, meeting his strokes with my own grunting desire and moving in a way that forced our cocks to grind together. He gasped, loosening his grip on my wrists and I took the chance to flip him over, so I was on top of him. "You'll call me whatever I say if you want this big Redwood, Jingle Bell."

"Damn," he rasped. "I thought Jack was the bossy Daddy." I licked up the middle of his defined chest, using my retractable corpuscles. He shuddered. "Fuck, yes. Do that again." He pressed me down and this time I went as slow as I could, sliding between his nipples, savoring the sweet taste of him as he moved beneath me. I couldn't get enough of his skin, the scent of him, the way he squirmed underneath me.

Yet.

Something snagged at the back of my mind.

Sensing some hesitation rolling off of me, he pushed up, grabbing my face in his hands and running those rings along my jaw. "I lost you there. Are you having second thoughts?"

I put my hands on his wrists, squeezing and looking into the dark blue storm of his eyes. "No, you didn't lose me and I'm not questioning this. It's just when you mentioned Jack, my brain sailed straight to Vixen." His eyes softened at the mention of her name. She did that to both of us. "You've got to understand, this thing with us, I want it. So fucking much I can't see straight right now, but it feels like cheating on her. I can't do that. I won't. Not after what Rascal did to her."

Desperately hoping he'd understand, I waited for him to say something. Anything. My head was a whirling pit of emotion over wanting him and not wanting to hurt Vixen. It took more than a few ticks of the clock for him to respond. When he did, I was shocked.

He pressed his lips to mine. This time his kiss was tender, quakingly beautiful. Not only did it stir my cock, but it got my heart a little bit too. "You're right. We need to pause and figure out how this works. Because here's the deal Redwood. You're correct, I don't want to do that to her either, but at the same time, I don't feel like I can compromise on this either." He gestured between us. "You're both important to me and I want you both equally. Just like she wants all three of us. There are a lot of complicated angles involved in this, but we might be able to untangle it in a way that makes us all happy if we lay it all out for each other. Starting here with us. I'll go first."

He put his hands on my chest, maneuvering us so my back was against the headboard, then he sat on my thighs and took a deep breath. "I've been in Elf orgies you wouldn't believe and yes, parts have touched, and my lips may have wandered to places I didn't expect—no big deal— but with you? I have a raw throbbing desire that scares the shit out of me. It won't go away. I don't want it to go away."

I scrubbed my hand through my hair. "It was that three-way kiss, wasn't it?

He chuckled, tracing my pecs with his hands. "Yeah. And the night with the snowflake dress. And that time you held me down in the chair didn't go unnoticed either."

"True. That chair thing was something else. Don't know why. And the look on Vixen's face when I let you up? She was into it."

He shrugged. "Of course, she was. Look at us."

I laughed, then closed my eyes, trying to find the depth of what I was trying to say. "Do you really want me to be honest right now?"

"Yes. No candy canes. Just tell me how you feel."

Gripping the back of my neck in both hands, I laid it out the best I could, hoping I wasn't fucking it up. "I'm chained to a woman I don't want, in love with another and I want to fuck the man looking at me so badly that it burns. I feel like I'm screwed and charged and in brutal love at the same time. It's intense."

He searched my eyes, finding the truth of it there, I guess. "You love her?"

"I realize it might seem insane considering we just met a little over a week ago, but when I walked into that lodge and saw her, it was like being swallowed by an avalanche. I was under her spell and I'm not going to apologize for being hopelessly in love with her."

"You don't have to apologize. Not to me. I've been circling her for years, biding my time and hoping. I even considered doing something extreme to get her attention, but I decided against it because I wanted things to be real between us. If there ever was an us. And the weird part is that I didn't *know* her until now. I can't say for certain, but I suspect it has everything in the world to do with you and her together."

We were supposed to be talking our way through it, but I couldn't help it. I took his hands off my chest and threaded my fingers between his. The rings made my pulse kick up. "My feelings for her are knotted up with my feelings for you too."

He slicked his tongue over his lower lip, and I wanted to kiss him again. Especially when a nervous expression washed over him. "Really?"

He was teetering, searching for confirmation and I had no issue giving that to him. This was make-or-break-it time for the two of us. I could stop it now, friend zone his ass, and move on with Vixen, whatever that looked like, or I could convince him we could work too. "Look. I'm a product of pack living, I'm used to the geometry of polygamy for lack of a better word. I've been with men before, not many, but some, and when I fooled around with them, it was fleeting and something I did because they were there and asked. Never once have I sat around and thought of ways to get close to a guy. Not until you. So, if you're asking if this between you and me is more than sex, then yeah, it is. It just has to be on top of what we have with Vixen. Not in competition. Do you feel me?"

His relief came out in his sigh. "Yeah. It's more than that for me too. With both of you. I feel like I should fear it, but I don't. Maybe we should wait until we're with her to explore our connection fully."

There was so much more to him than being sexy. He was wise and in touch with his emotions in a way, I'd rarely seen any man be. I wish everyone could get his depth like I did. Like Vixen did. "Agree. At least until we tell her about this thing with us and get her response. We can go on from there."

He slid off of me, knowing it was the right thing to do. We still ached with need for each other, but we knew what we needed to do first. The whole thing had packed a punch and while it was new and thrilling to think about, we had to go cautiously or there would be some damaged feelings. The last thing I wanted was for either of them to hurt because of something I'd said or done.

After a few minutes of silent contemplation that didn't feel awkward at all, he spoke up again.

"Where does this leave Jack, because we know Vixen wants him as much as she does us. I think she's convinced herself it's okay to be with all of us. Are we going *there* with him too?"

It was damn near cute the way he waited for my answer. While I dug his alpha bad boy persona, the part of him that was open, and questioning was especially heart-warming.

"You're right, she has. And I like Jack. I don't mind sharing with him—be that Vixen or you if that's what you want —though what I feel for him is different. I think it's just as powerful in a way, but not sexual."

At the sound of the last word, Hart's eyes heated. We understood each other better and the crawling desire we shared earlier was there inching to the surface again. "I admire Jack, but I don't want Jack. I want you, Redwood."

The desperation in his voice was insanely hot. I reached over and pulled him to me so I could kiss that need out of him, pulling away again before I took it too far. "Then go get Vixen and fucking have me, Jingle Bell."

# CHAPTER 44

With everything handled and Cherish safe, Jack and I went back to the cabin where our night had started. I changed into Hart's shirt and slid into the covers. It was past midnight and while I was tired, I couldn't sleep knowing Hart and Yeager were still out there battling polar bears.

"They'll be fine, Flame. I've never seen two more resourceful and capable men in all my centuries."

Jack curled up on the bed beside me, being careful to stay on top of the covers so he wouldn't get too warm, but he pulled me to him and wrapped me in his arms. He'd laid out a pretty bold statement and I couldn't let it go. If this thing with the three of us was going to continue, I had to get a read on all of them. I was starting to care way too much about each of them and that spooked me. Just a little. "You admire them?"

"Yes, I do. They're willing to help me when most in my kingdom has abandoned me. Though I might be too stubborn to admit this to others, I know that I come across as distant and cold. Perhaps that's what caused my subjects to be swayed so easily, but I intend to change things, starting with taking cues on how to be thoughtful from Yeager and how to be likable like Hart. All of you have influenced me in ways I can only touch on. I've never been a part of something like this before. I hope it doesn't alarm you, but I figured after the night we've had, it's time to make sure you fully understand how I feel about you. And they come along with you."

His voice was so warm. It was like I could feel the change in him. I leaned up and pressed a quick kiss to his cheek. "I didn't know I could feel like this again, but I do, thanks to all three of you. I don't know what it means or how it ends, but I know at this moment, I'm content. Or I will be as soon as they get back."

He shifted. "Let me fill your mind with other things while we wait." Jerking the covers down, he lowered himself until his head was right between my legs. With no warning whatsoever, he pushed my panties to the side and licked straight up my core.

I yelped at the feel of his chilly lips. The sensation was intense and amazing and within seconds, I was rocking against his mouth and moaning. "My soul, Jack. That's good." He hummed his response as he pulled my clit into his mouth. I gripped the sheets, grinding my hips as he sucked and licked and played with me.

"You taste divine, Flame. Daddy likes."

I doubted he'd even heard the term Daddy before Hart and Cherish joked about it, but he certainly picked it up and ran with it. Thank my soul. He truly was smart and a very quick learner.

A pop sounded in the room, I looked up in alarm and found Hart standing there looking down at us with a smirk. He was shirtless and didn't appear to be hurt, but the absence of Yeager made my heart race even more than Jack's lips on my pussy. "Oops. My bad, but I'm going to have to take Vixen for a little while. You understand."

Jack didn't even look up, he just kept on working me over as he spoke. Honestly, it was a skill to speak and eat pussy at the same time. "I do *not* understand. Surely whatever it is, can wait until she's come so hard, she needs oxygen."

Gulp. Seriously, gulp.

Hart walked over to the head of the bed, getting a better view of what Jack was doing. I couldn't help myself, with his heated eyes on me and Jack's tongue, I bucked and gasped. "Mad respect for that technique, Popsicle, but this can't wait. And I told you one day I'd whisk her away from you. This is that day. Consider the payback complete. Let's go, Ginger."

I didn't even have time to protest. He just lifted me in his arms and popped away. We landed in a dark room covered in brick and metal. I was more than relieved to find Yeager leaning against the headboard of a bed I didn't recognize. He seemed to be fine too. He had the covers over his hips, and I couldn't help but notice the tent between his legs.

What was this about?

Something more than stealing me away from Jack as promised.

Hart laid me in the middle of the bed beside Yeager and slid next to me. My heart was still knocking against my ribs from what Jack had been doing. And I was confused as fuck. I could only imagine what Jack was thinking or feeling. I slugged Hart in the arm. "Why did you do that? He was just saying some genuinely nice things about the two of you and you're going to steal me away from him while he was..."

Yeager's head cocked to the side. "While he was what?"

Hart grinned. "Oh, he had his head between her legs, giving her that cold tongue. She was into it."

"Is that so? Well, if she was all worked up, I suppose we should make sure to finish what Jack started. The least we can do." His tone was all joking, yet he wasn't even looking at me, he was looking at Hart with an expression I recognized. Desire.

Yep. They were up to something. Something beyond sexing me up. I wasn't afraid or threatened. If anything, I was more aroused by the way they looked at me, at each other, the way the air was thick with tension.

"You could've both come back and joined us."

That's what I wanted after all. The three of them.

Yeager slung one arm behind me, trailing his other hand over my collarbone. Hart leaned in, gripping the hip that was wedged against Yeager. Suddenly I was encased between both of them. I didn't hate it, not at all, but there was something in their movements that was different. "What am I missing here?"

Hart kissed my neck. I released a soft sigh as he inched up to that spot behind my ear that was so sensitive it made me wiggle. I leaned into the feel of Hart's lips and Yeager dragged his tongue along the hollow of my throat, forcing my eyes to close. Hart pulled away to watch him, groaning. "I'm finding it hard to find the right words to tell you why Jack has to wait. Just this once." He sighed. "Give me a second."

There was uncharacteristic questioning in his voice. Whatever he wanted to say, it was important enough to make the cockiest guy I knew tentative.

Yeager reached out. I expected to feel the sensation of his hands somewhere on my body, but I didn't. "Maybe we don't need words for this." I opened my eyes and found his hand trailing up Hart's chest, moving to wrap around his neck, and when the two of them locked eyes, I got it.

Like a bolt of lightning came down from the sky, I got it.

I'd already seen them inching toward each other with the play fights and tussling, with the teamwork they fell so easily into, with the odd glances and ways they touched me when they were together. And that three-way kiss? Fire. I didn't know if they'd realized they were kissing each other more than me during the duration of it.

Still, they'd tumbled into each other, because of the bear fight or something else, I wasn't sure. All I knew was that I needed them to know I was one hundred percent there for it if this was what they wanted. Not because the thought of the two of them together was as hot as whatever the hottest thing on earth was. Damn, it was. But because I could feel what they had between them wasn't just about sex. How could I deny them when they were so clearly aching for each other as much as I ached for them? It was beautiful really.

"You're right, Yeager. We don't need words." I pointed between them. "*You* don't need words. Show me."

I leaned back as far as I could and nodded. Not a second later, they collided with each other, kissing and groping like they couldn't get enough. Watching them kiss like that, with desperate passion, set my blood on fire. Yeager had his hands on Hart's face, while Hart gripped Yeager's hip with white knuckles as their mouths moved together, nipping and biting, and yeah, growling. While it looked a little like they were fighting for dominance, it also looked like they didn't care who won it.

I slid down, hoping to inch out and leave them to what they wanted, but before I could even get flat enough to do that, Yeager reached down and put his massive hand on my chest. "Where are you going, Bunny?"

"It feels like you two don't need me right now. It's okay, I'm not upset or offended. I just want you two to have this time to work out what you want. I'm cool with this. Really."

Hart released Yeager and pulled me up, tracing my bottom lip. "No, no, no. We *have* worked it out. This isn't an us and another us and then another us back at the cabin." He gestured between them, then included me, and then used his thumb to indicate Jack. His eyes were blazing blue and so clear it almost hurt to look at him. "It's all one massive thing together. And yeah, I'm about to suck the life out of that Redwood over there, but you're a part of it too. Let us show you how fucking tremendous this will be. I doubt all of us will be breathing when it's done."

There was the Hart I knew and loved.

Liked, a whole lot.

Went a little crazy there with the L-word. Must have been the intense hormones from watching them together.

Yeager chuckled, then pulled my shirt over my head. "You look good in his shirt, but things are about to take a turn, Bunny. You need to be naked for that." He glanced over at Hart with a smirk, pulling the covers down to reveal his arousal. "Don't make me wait any longer, Jingle Bell."

When I say Hart dove for Yeager's cock, I mean he might as well have been bouncing on a springboard and wearing a speedo.

I was pinned beneath him when he took Yeager's shaft in his hand, pumping a few times while Yeager hissed his approval. Hart had landed on top of me at just the right angle for his cock to line up with my core, so when he went to lick all the way down Yeager's cock, he pressed against me with his own hard arousal. I lifted my hips in response. Yeager chuckled when he looked down and realized what was happening. He dug his hands into Hart's hair, pulling his head up. "You think you can hump her while you suck me off, Jingle Bell?"

Hart took the head of Yeager's cock in his mouth slowly, sucking loud enough for me to hear it. Yeager released a deep guttural groan at the feel of it. At the same time, Hart pressed against me, and I gasped. "The answer you're looking for is yes, he can."

There was something so intimate about watching the two of them. Yes, I was into Hart's grinding, for sure, but watching Yeager's face and Hart's lips around his cock? It was a step forward in a relationship I didn't even realize we were in.

But we were. It was clear to me at that moment.

I wanted their satisfaction as much as my own and I wanted their happiness and I wanted to feel all of it wrapped up together in a big bow. The only thing missing was Jack.

Yeager grabbed the back of the headboard as he tilted into Hart's mouth. "Fuck me. How did you learn that trick?" Hart looked up at me out of the corner of his eye as he grazed his teeth from the bottom of Yeager's cock, then when he got to the top, he brought the whole thing in his mouth again. Yeager began thrusting and grunting uncontrollably. After a few more minutes of that, Hart pulled his mouth off with a sloppy pop that I felt way down in my lady parts.

He sat up, wiped his mouth, and then pressed me down against the mattress, turning to Yeager. "I need to rest my jaw, you fucking man-beast. Besides, you're not getting off yet. Her turn."

Yeager had no issues with that. Before I could say anything, I was flat on my back with each of them licking a nipple. I sighed when Yeager moved over and began licking along with Hart, using both their tongues at the same time. They moved my body together, kissing and nipping until they got between my legs. Yeager ripped my panties; Hart pulled the tattered remains off of me and together they used those tongues to make me moan and gyrate in a way some might consider embarrassing.

I wasn't embarrassed though. It was overwhelming to have both of them lapping at my pussy, kissing each other in the process. When Yeager pushed two fingers inside me, I gasped, grasping at his shoulders at the sensation. Not to be outdone, Hart slipped two in with him and together they pumped and watched me fall into a blissful state of oblivion. Yeager raised his head. "My stars, would you look at her? That feels good, doesn't it, both of us giving you what you want."

I nodded. It was all I could do at the time. And when Hart used his teeth on my clit and Yeager leaned down to kiss the top of his head, I lost it. Lost it. I came so fast I got dizzy and saw those stars Yeager had mentioned.

They were not done.

With each other, or me.

I was lying there gasping for air and waiting for the room to stop spinning when they sat up and started kissing again. This time, Yeager grabbed Hart's belt, wresting to get it off. It seemed like it took forever, but he finally got it undone and his jeans off in the next second. He pulled back from him, grinning like a wild man. "If you knew how many times I'd thought about these fucking jingle bells..." He didn't finish his thought. Couldn't, because Hart had grabbed his hand and put it down there for a little jingle while he kissed him like crazy again.

These two were explosive.

And the sound of those bells as Yeager fisted Hart's cock would probably live in my head for a lifetime.

As I was getting my second wind, Yeager pulled away, slowing down his strokes and looking at Hart with mad desire on his face. "Can we, maybe, try something? No pressure. But I'm about to go psycho with need here."

"Sure, what do you want, Redwood?"

He glanced at me first, then back to Hart. "I want to be between both of you. I need to fuck her, and you need to fuck me, got it?"

Hart jumped off the bed. "I love that for us." He started rummaging through his bedside table, cursing when he didn't find what he was looking for. "Shit. I left the only lube I had in the cabin. Be back."

He popped away, naked and hard. I could only imagine what Jack was going to say when he arrived to swipe the lube. While he was gone, Yeager crawled over to me, cupping my face in his hands before he kissed me, slow and with purpose. I was breathless when he pulled away. "Are you sure you're good with this? I'd rather be with no one than to hurt you. That's the truth of my soul."

Yeager. He would always be the first person to genuinely want me after Rudy. Yet, he didn't feel like a rebound. He was a reason to let love in again. "Yes, I want this. More than I can express."

"That's good because I'm about to do something I have never done before, and I'm stoked you'll be a part of it with me."

I was overwhelmed with gratitude. For him. And for what he had with Hart. Hart needed someone to look past his body and while Yeager was about to enjoy said body very much, he *saw* Hart like I did.

The pop in the room drew our attention. Hart was already opening the lube. "We're going to have to find a way to make this up to Jack. He's livid he's missing out, but I promised we'd explain tomorrow. For now, though, come here man beast. I'm about to show you what these jingle bells are for."

Deck the Holy Halls, that was smoking hot.

Yeager pulled me down to the edge of the bed as Hart watched, rubbing lube over his shaft. "You get inside her first. I want you to go slow and describe how that pussy feels while I warm you up."

Yeager wasted no time climbing into place, then rubbing his cock at my wet entrance. He paused to look over his shoulder. "You've never done this before with a man?"

"No, why?"

"Because it sure as fuck sounds like you have. That's okay. I'm glad to be the one to pop your cherry."

"Um, look around. I'm about to pop yours first, Redwood." We all laughed, but as soon as Yeager pushed inside me, my mouth clamped shut.

"My soul, she feels so wet, so hot. She is taking my big cock so good, aren't you, Bunny? She wants it so bad she's clenching when I pull out."

Hart peeped over his shoulder. "She doesn't want to let that massive cock go."

"Mm-hm." He started thrusting, slow and steady, going deep and hard as Hart sidled up behind him. He hissed when Hart drizzled the lube in his crack, but it took about two seconds for him to howl like a wildebeest when Hart inserted his finger or thumb or something.

Part of me was disappointed that I could only guess what was happening, but based on the way Hart was biting his lip and Yeager was groaning, it was all good. And the more they worked together, the more heated I got. The more I fell for them.

After a few more seconds, Hart stepped in close, pressing kisses along Yeager's shoulder. "You ready to make my dick jingle?"

"Fuck yes. Please. Do it now before I come inside Vixen's hot pussy."

These two and their dirty talk.

Hart needed no other encouragement than that. He re-lubed his shaft then went over to Yeager, pushing inside him with a grunt. Yeager stilled long enough to get adjusted to the feel of it, but it didn't take long for him to start moving again.

From there, it was all groaning and kissing and thrusting. We were a feverish pile of limbs and every sound, every scent, every light touch of Yeager's fingers on my skin or Hart's rings grasping Yeager's shoulders sent me soaring.

"Fuck me, Jingle Bell. I didn't think...oh shit."

"You feel perfect, Yeager. Damn, I've wanted this for days and I don't know how long I'm going to last."

"Don't you dare fucking stop?"

Hart looked at me, rolling his eyes. "Like I could stop now." He ran his hands over Yeager's back, gripping his hips to steady himself. He pressed harder and it tumbled through me. I reached out and gripped Yeager's biceps as he held himself up enough to not squash me as Hart panted his approval. "You are both so sexy. I'm desperate for both of you."

The rest was too hazy to even recall. We just worked together, and I knew the thing between them had only grown during this. Between all of us really. The thought of it made me tear up. It was kind of ridiculous that I would get emotional over good sex, but I had to own it. It was true.

"I can't hold off much longer. Get ready Bunny, I'm about to come inside you."

Hart panted. "Yeah. You better get ready too, man-beast."

It was all it took. I exploded as Yeager did, arching and moving my hips from side to side so he would go as deep as I wanted him. Hart cried out a few seconds later, throwing his head back and laughing as he came too.

We collapsed into a heap, sweaty and spent. Satisfied.

After a bit of time passed, Yeager slid out of me, and Hart did the same. He rolled over, using his stupidly strong muscles to pull both of us to rest on his chest. "I wonder what the game will be today.

*Vixen*

# CHAPTER 45

After Hart stood in the middle of his loft and pointed in the direction of the bathroom and we took a few minutes to freshen up, we collapsed on his bed—me in the middle—and fell asleep. There had been a lot going on the past day and night and we needed to rest. At least for a few hours.

I'm not sure who stirred first, but with us all wrapped together in a big bundle, it didn't take much for us all to wake. It was nearing dawn, and I couldn't keep myself from thinking about Jack all alone in the cabin. True, what happened without him needed to be fleshed out, but now that it seemed Hart Yeager and I had a feel for the logistics of it, it was time to get back to Jack and bring him into the fold. "Guys, last night was next level, but I'm worried about Jack being all alone."

Yeager sat up, running his hands through his hair. It fell back into place like it always did. "Yeah. Let's head back so he doesn't burst an artery over us being gone with you."

Hart groaned his displeasure but slid out of the bed and went over to his closet and started rummaging through a massive chest, looking for clothes for himself and Yeager, who I'd learned left his clothes where he shifted. He put on his jeans and sweater as he stood in the closet, then tossed Yeager some sweats and a t-shirt, which ended up being a little snug. Not that I minded. Hart had probably done it on purpose. "I don't think the surprise attack reveal will work on Jack like it did Vixen. What do you think he'll say about us...crossing candy canes?"

That was one way of putting it. I laughed. "He'll start with cocking one eyebrow for sure."

"Yeah, I bet he'll claim to have known it was going to happen all along," Yeager said as he slid into some socks.

"I'll take that bet. The winner gets the next blow job. I think he'll make a smartass comment about us keeping our dicks away from him."

It was hard to say for sure, but I had the urge to loop him in on it as soon as possible. Especially since the two of them were going to visit the queens of Spring and Autumn soon. How they were going to bring it up, I didn't know. I wanted to leave it to them. It was their news to share.

"Alright, let's get out of here." Hart wrapped me in his arms and pressed a kiss on the top of my head as Yeager stepped behind him and put his muscular biceps around the both of us. Hart did his thing and we popped into the cabin where we'd left Jack.

He was lying on his back on the bed, fully dressed in a gray suit, white shirt, and pale green tie, hands behind his head, staring at the ceiling. I couldn't read his mood, but a growing concern laced through my mind. What if he was really pissed about Hart taking me from him? I couldn't handle him walking away from me. From us. "Hey, we're back."

Jack sat up, his steely eyes squinting at Hart. "Explain."

Hart took a beat, then gave him the explanation he asked for. "It's like this: Yeager and I are fucking now. We thought it was best to tell Vixen since we both have it bad for our saucy little reindeer. We took the night to work it all out between the three of us. I didn't exclude you, we just thought it best to do it in layers. It won't happen again. Though I do still owe Redwood one time of swiping Vixen from him. TBD. Anyway, that's why I took her. If it helps, she definitely wasn't left wanting."

One eyebrow shot up. Ha. Called it. "It's about time. Honestly, I don't know what took you two so long."

Yeager perched on the edge of the bed, eyeing Hart and grinning because he'd predicted that response. I could see his wheels spinning at the thought of winning that blow job. "You say you knew?"

"Of course, I did. At any rate, I don't care what you and Hart get up to as long as you keep your cocks on your side of the bed. I'm only interested in Vixen and if she wants to include you, I have no issue with it. As I told her last night, I feel a kinship with you two, though not one that includes sucking either of your dicks."

Hart cocked his head, having gotten his response too. "We were both right about his reaction, so no one gets the blow job. Damn."

Yeager laughed. "Or both of us do."

"Oh, that's a much better solution."

"Please not now." Jack slid off the bed and strolled over to me, placing a cool kiss on my cheek. "We've never slept in the same bed overnight, yet I missed you anyway. I'm glad to have you back."

"I'm glad to be back."

Everything seemed pretty peachy in my world. Yeager clapped his hands together. "I'm famished. Need to replace calories. Let's go eat."

~~~~~~~~~~~~~~~~~~~~~~~~~~~~~~

Later in the afternoon, we were all gathered outside in white snowsuits, courtesy of Santa of course. Holly's had a huge photo of Santa giving two thumbs up on the back of hers. The woman strutted all over the place in that thing. She, Karl, Jasper, and Frank had spent most of the day out there prepping for the game, pulling Jack and John in about an hour before it started.

When he came strolling back into the courtyard in his snow suit—which looked strange on him—he was shaking his head and huffing like Cherish on her worst day. "Kill me now," he muttered under his breath, just as Hart popped back beside me to hand me the sunglasses, I'd ask him to get from my condo.

His brows were knitted together that said something was off with him, but didn't comment other than to tell Jack, "Nice use of phrase there. What's the game?" Jack didn't even answer, he just shoved his hands into his pockets as Holly sing-songed for us to follow her.

Cherish looked perkier than normal. She said something to Isaac and then ran up to our team, taking turns hugging
~~~~~~~~~~~~~~~~~~~~~~~~~~~~~~

each of us. "You saved my skin, Fam. TBH, that's def Gucci. I.L.Y." She ran back to Isaac, jumping on his back.

"What did she just say?" Jack asked.

"Thanks for saving her, basically. I.L.Y means I love you." It wasn't lost on me that she'd used an acronym. I guess getting the life scared out of her went a long way in changing her attitude. I wish it hadn't happened, but in a way, good came from it. She was obviously ready for the game and smiling, with no phone in sight.

Yeager smiled. "She called us a family."

That, she did. While I knew it was just more slang, the idea of it, well it hit different.

I was getting rather good at Cherish-speak too.

None of us said anything, but based on the way I was turning that phrase over in my mind, I knew they were too. All of us.

We rounded the corner and gasped. Huge blocks of snow and ice were laid out over a large patch of open ground. Not only that, but there were stacks of hay, what looked like fishing nets strung between open tents, large drainage pipes, and four flags whipping in the breeze. A course of some kind.

I turned to Jack. "You helped make this?"

"Yes. That was the easy part. Wait until you hear what's next."

Holly whistled for us to gather. "Today's game will be Snow-Paint Ball. Each team has three buckets of snowballs colored by Santa's elves using dye from the candy shop. There will be one player from each team moving through the course at a time. When you're marked by a snowball, you're out and must leave the course. The goal is to have the last member standing, who will get four candy canes, the second to last one gets three, and so on and you know the drill. Fae cannot cheat by altering the snow in any way. Hart, you can't pop around the course. Now have fun. Time starts in one minute. Each team please take a starting position next to a flag."

Now I could see what Jack had grumbled. This didn't seem like his kind of thing at all. I bet he was even uncomfortable in his snowsuit. Hart and Yeager, however, were practically giddy with excitement. I took Jack's hand as we got in place under the blue flag, hiding behind a wall of snow. "You can go in the course first and get it over with."

"Thanks. I won't try to get caught, but I have to admit, I won't be mad if I do."

Yeager started passing out snowballs as Hart took up a position at the top of the wall so he could scout. The timer counted down and Holly shouted for us to begin. Jack took off running, faster than I dreamed or expected, making his way to a big drain pipe and diving down in it just as John Sun's yellow snowball pinged against it. Meanwhile, Erin took a spin, trying to dive over a haybale and Yeager pinged her with one of our snowballs. "Sorry," he shouted. "Hope that wasn't too hard."

She waved back at him and headed off the course. Using the distraction Jack slithered out of the drain pipe, beelining for the same bale of hay as Hart laid down a volley of snowballs toward the tent where John was throwing, narrowly missing the Sun King. The string of words out of John's mouth was impressive, but he started lobbing balls in every direction, pegging Spike in the ass as he sailed toward a wall of ice.

The action only heated up then. It took another few minutes for Edward to hit Jack with his red snowball. The relief on Jack's face was obvious. He strolled calmly back to our fort, shedding the snowsuit and sighing. "Well, that was fun."

Hart jumped down from his elevated position and pulled Jack to him, whispering something in his ear. Jack nodded and they both popped away. I looked back at Yeager, and he shrugged. A few ticks later, Hart popped back without Jack. "Were you cheating by popping around?"

"No, I just took Jack somewhere he needed to be. Your turn Ginger. Make us proud." He ushered me onto the course as Yeager sent another spread of snowballs to occupy the players while I weaved to the closest hay bale.

Less than ten minutes later, Mindy got me as I crawled toward the same drainpipe Jack had used. I thought I'd last longer, but at least it had been fun to get some fresh air in my lungs and work out my limbs. Trekking back to our fort, I unzipped my snowsuit and took off my shades. Hart wasted no time grabbing me and popping me away too.

I let out a yelp when we landed in the bedroom of my condo. Jack was there and had taken off his jacket and stood looking out the window with his sleeves rolled up. I turned to Hart. "Why are we here?"

"There's a couple of reasons, the main one being is I owe him for last night. So do you want to go back and wait in the snow for us to finish or do you want to stay here in the comfort of your own home and maybe get a little naked with Jack?"

Jack turned, his eyebrow cocked.

I grabbed the hairbrush from my dresser and held it up like a microphone. "I'll take option number two please."

"That's what I thought." He smacked my ass which I couldn't feel through the jumpsuit, but still. "We'll join you after we annihilate the rest of the teams. Have fun."

Jack glided over to where I stood at the edge of the bed, using his icy fingers to grab my chin and kiss me like he meant it.

Like he really meant it.

# CHAPTER 46

I pelted John Sun as he deserved. I'm talking about wasting half a bucket of snowballs on him alone. The dude was covered in blue balls by the time I finished with him. Hart shoved me playfully as we celebrated our victory. I shoved him back. Then it was a thing. I backed him against the snow wall and kissed the fire out of him.

When we finally broke apart, we were both panting. He grabbed my ass, pulling me closer than we had been. "You want to go join them at her condo now?"

I nodded. "Yep. But first, tell me why you took them to her place instead of our cabin."

Hart scrubbed his hand over his jaw, his rings glinting in the sun. "I don't think this was a mistake—shit, maybe it was—but when I went to get her shades, there were signs of Rudy being in her place. Dirty dishes that I know she didn't leave, an unmade bed, and a couple of pairs of nasty sneakers at the front door. According to my sources, he's been living with Clare, so I thought she should know he's invaded her home without her consent."

"You could've just told her. It feels like an asshole move to let her be blindsided."

"I know it does, but Jack and I agreed that it may just be the thing she needs." He let out a breath. "I'll come clean and apologize if it backfires, but she's going to need to face him soon. What better way to do it than when we're with her? Preferably after several mind-blowing orgasms. So, should we get to it or are you going to slug me?"

I'll admit I was nervous, but at the same time, he wasn't wrong. She was already moving past Reynaldo, but things might be different when he was right there in the room. Hurting her, intentionally or not, didn't sit well with me. "I don't know. I'm either going to slug you or fuck you. Let's test the waters, see how it's going, and I'll let you know."

We popped into her place to the sound of her moans. Jack had his head buried between her legs, lapping at her pussy like a fiend. Finally getting to finish. They were alone and so into each other, that they didn't notice us there. So, I took the chance to strip Hart from his snowsuit and he did me a solid and helped me out of mine. Then we saddled behind Jack, watching as we both grew harder. I angled my head toward the bed and we each took a side, lying next to her.

She sucked in a deep breath in surprise, but we both just went at her mouth, taking another hot three-way kiss to the next level this time. I would never get enough of the two of them like that. Kissing them together was like being whole.

Jack must have done something particularly amazing down below because she gasped and threw back her head. "My soul, I'm going to come." Hart and I shared a glance, and he went straight down, sticking two fingers inside her as Jack lapped at her clit. I sat up so I could watch her fall apart, getting tugged by the sight of those rings disappearing inside her. But she was having none of it, pulling me down to kiss her. I gave her what she wanted until her breathing slowed and her head fell back on the mattress. Her eyes were the dreamiest of blues when she finally opened them. "Told you. All three of you," she panted.

Who was I to deny her? "You've got it, Bunny. Guys, we need to switch it up."

Jack peeled off his pants as Hart pulled Vixen off the bed, looking down at her with a twinkle in his eye. "When you say all three, do you mean at once, because I'm doing the math here, three cocks, three holes..."

"Yes. I'm not saying it has to be that way all the time, but right now, that's what I want. Now are you going to stand there naked and solve algebra equations or are you going to put those jingle bells to effective use?"

"Message received and understood. Please tell me you have lube somewhere." She pointed to the side table and Hart ran over to grab it. He had a manic look in his eye, and I loved it, but this time it was going to go a different way. I snatched the lube from his hands. Cinnamon scent and flavor. "FYI, I'm not slugging you."

He laughed. "Ah okay, fucking it is."

I looked over at Jack. "Are you sure you're okay with this? With us together when you're involved? Because I have ideas about a position that might work, but I don't want you to be uncomfortable."

He narrowed his gray eyes on me, huffing. "That's been settled. So, either tell me what you're thinking or I'm going to take her as I want. Daddy's as stiff as an icicle over here."

Vixen sighed. Man, she loved the Daddy thing.

And I loved her for it.

For more than that. It had only been half a day, but once I'd admitted it to Hart, it had become easier to accept myself. Not that I had any ideas on what to do about Camilla, but this wasn't the time or place to think about her. My ideas at the moment involved a whole bunch of getting off.

"Get on the bed. Hands and knees, Bunny. Let us see that sweet ass in the air." She smirked, liking how I was taking charge, then positioned herself like the good girl she was. I nodded at Jack. "Get in front, Ice Man. Let her have a taste of that popsicle." After he got on the bed in front of her, she wasted no time taking his cock in her mouth.

With that distracting them, I pulled Hart over to me, kissing him while I took both his shaft and mine in my hand and pumped enough to make his jingle bells sing to the sounds of his growling approval. "Shit. That's good." It was. So fucking good. And when he pushed the two fingers that had been in Vixen's pussy moments prior into my mouth, all I could do was suck and appreciate the taste of them combined.

But we were just getting started. I hated to do it, but I wanted Vixen as much as I wanted him, so I dropped his cock so I could turn him around, pressing his back against my chest and running my hand over Vixen's cheeks to spread them. "You go in the back door."

He huffed. "I know what I'm doing, stop trying to Dom me."

"You love it when I tell you what to do and I'm not Domming, I'm orchestrating." I ran my tongue up his neck and grabbed that jingle bell and he shut his damn mouth quick.

He climbed up on the edge of the bed and I passed him the lube, then I took my cock and lined it up with her glistening entrance. She hissed her approval as I pushed into her.

Hart used his fingers, slowly at first, getting her ready to have us both at the same time. I kissed his back as I grabbed his hips. I had to be as close to him as I was to Vixen. And when he finally lined up after lubing his cock and her ass too, I was at Defcon five levels of turned on.

Vixen moaned her way through the whole thing, taking Jack's dick and mine as Hart pressed into her tight hole.

It wasn't surprising that it took no time for us to find the right rhythm. Hart reached behind, grabbing my hair and taking my mouth like it was his, which it was. We thrust into her, sending her body rocking forward and making her take Jack deeper into her throat. His head fell back as he cursed his way through it. "Fuck, yes." He looked like he might be overheating. He also looked like he didn't care.

I trusted that he'd do what he needed to get through this. We all would. This, the four of us together, was more than just sex. I doubted that I was the only one to feel it too. The closeness, the trust we exhibited with each other, between all of us, made the physical feel even better. I wanted to breathe it into my lungs and live in it. All of it. Hart's ass against my pelvis, as we drove into Vixen, made me see stars. I gripped his hip with one hand and hers in the other, ramping up the pace, going hard and deep inside her wet pussy as it clenched around my cock. I could barely breathe through it. The scent of sex was all around me, not to mention the slapping and grunting. It was so much and not enough at the same time.

She tightened around my cock, so I shifted to reach that spot she liked, moving Hart in the process, taking on a new angle and feeling the fire of it in my soul. "Our girl's about to come." At the sound of my voice, Hart released a guttural grunt. Vixen clenched even tighter. "That's the way. Let me feel you come, Bunny."

My soul, it was life-altering the way she came hard and loud, unapologetic about any of it.

I guess it wasn't just me about to blow because Jack grunted, and I heard the strangled sounds of her throat taking his load. In the next few thrusts, I was coming inside her too. Not to leave Hart out of the mix, I pulled his cheeks apart, inserting my thumb in his hole as I bit his earlobe, forcing him to explode in the next instant.

It was several minutes before any of us could move. The breathy panting around the room was almost enough to make me hard again. I was seconds away from suggesting round two, when the squeak of a door made us all pause.

"What the fuck is happening here? Vixen?"

She scrambled out from underneath us, grabbing one of her pillows to hold in front of her as she sucked in a deep surprised breath. "Rudy, what are you doing here?"

# CHAPTER 47

I clutched the pillow like a life vest. Maybe it was. It was certainly a buffer that I needed between the two of us as he stood there, mouth gaping as his deep brown eyes moved from me to the three men standing—buck naked—around me.

Something in my mind told me to act. To go over and push him out of my room, my home, my life, but my limbs were suddenly too heavy to move and the little tingling spots of white on the edge of my vision were interfering with my ability to calculate my steps without falling.

So, I stood there like a statue, as Hart sing-songed "Awkward," behind me.

That seemed to snap Rudy out of his stupor. He sailed over, breezing past the immovable force that was Yeager like he hadn't even truly seen him, and bumped chests with Hart. "You," he seethed, drawing air between his perfect gleaming teeth. "You're fucking *my* girl?"

Hart popped out of sight only to reappear behind Rudy, grabbing his arm and twisting it behind his back. "What in the ever-loving fuck did you just say to me?"

Rudy tried to get out of Hart's grip but failed. Still, though, he wasn't giving in. "You heard me, asshole. I don't know what I just walked in on, but you three dickbags need to get out of this house. Now."

Yeager pivoted. All he did was slightly change position, but it got Rudy's attention. He looked up and finally registered Yeager for the first time. I swear he gulped. I don't think it was Yeager's size that got him either. It was the smirk on his face that was terrifying. He leaned down, almost bumping his nose with Rudy's brand-new one. "Who are you to make that demand?"

Of course, he knew who Rudy was, but he'd never, ever, give Rudy the satisfaction of admitting it. Instead, he folded his arms over his sculpted chest and did the best impression of Jack's raised eyebrow I'd ever seen. It made a manic grin cross Hart's face.

Rudy was not aware of the danger he was in. He shook his head, testing Hart's grip again, but finding it like steel. "You know who I am. I'm the most famous fucking reindeer of all. This is my home. Get the fuck out so Vixen and I can have a chat."

Hart leaned in, whispering in Rudy's ear. He was caged between the two of them and while I usually got all hot and bothered by that, in the moment I recognized it for what it was: trouble. "And if we don't?"

"The giant here will go to prison for assault or breaking and entering, not sure which yet." He nodded toward Jack. "I know who you are, Jack Frost. You're ancient and irrelevant and I can take your kingdom from you with the snap of my fingers. As for you, Elf?" He spat, like the word Elf was an insult. "It would be so easy to get you canceled with Santa. You know I have his ear. Where would you be then? A North Pole Elf with no skill other than making candy and being a low life. Who'd hire you? You'd have to rely on your hot sister's income just to get by. None of you have anything on me. You're nothing."

There were three ticks on the clock. Ticks where I should've stepped in and said or done something. Ticks that I would never get back. But as soon as those three seconds were over, Hart exploded.

He dropped Rudy's arm and shoved him away. He hit the wall next to the window with a thud and then Hart was on top of him, pounding his face like it was a punching bag. It *was* a punching bag. Rudy fought back, going for Hart's gut and mostly missing. No one could fight like Hart. Not only could he hit, but he knew how to twist to protect himself against Rudy's fists.

They grappled, growling, scuffling, and bumping into my dresser and vanity as they traded swipes in a mad, chaotic free-for-all that landed Rudy on the floor with Hart on top of him, railing him punch after punch after punch after punch after punch.

When Rudy landed a lucky blow a little too close to Hart's eye Yeager shifted toward them, glancing at Jack, who was still on his knees behind me. Jack snaked off the bed and nodded to Yeager who bolted forward and wrapped his massive arms around Hart, pulling him off Rudy as he cursed and kicked his annoyance.

Then Jack strolled over to Rudy, offering him a hand to help him up.

I knew Jack well enough to know this wasn't a gesture of kindness or a deferral. It was a calculated move, designed for a specific reason. He smoothed the wrinkles out of Rudy's shirt, adjusted his collar, and made sure he was standing upright without help before cocking that eyebrow. I loved that eyebrow. "As you pointed out, I'm ancient, so I'll share what I've come to learn in my lifetime of vast experiences. When one shouts about their dominance in favor of demonstrating it, one doesn't actually have it."

Rudy huffed, clearly discounting Jack's take on the matter. Jack didn't even blink. "This is how the next few minutes will go. Listen carefully." He left a long dramatic pause hanging in the air while he picked a book from my shelf and examined it like he was considering sitting down to read it at that moment. He continued only he'd read the blurb and restored the book on back on the shelf. "If—and only if—Vixen wants to chat with you, I suggest you sit with your hands folded in your lap and talk. If she doesn't want to hear a syllable out of your mouth, then you *will* leave with your dirty shoes in hand."

He smoothed a stray strand of Rudy's hair. It looked close to a loving gesture, but I knew it wasn't. He was demonstrating his dominance over Rudy instead of shouting it. Southward, my pet kitty purred. "If you're ignorant enough to attempt a third scenario, I'll unleash the two of them to do their worst." He stepped to the side so that Yeager and Hart were in Rudy's line of vision. Hart had chilled some, but they were both coiled and ready to strike like vipers.

"You won't survive it." He patted Rudy's chest twice, finally releasing that quarter-grin. "No cap."

All of this was said and done with all three of my three guys completely in the buff.

Ovary explosion in five, four, three, two…

I hadn't intended to talk to Rudy ever again. If I'd had my way we'd email about the condo sale specifics, and I'd only have to deal with him on Christmas Eve flights each year. The rest of my time would be spent ignoring his existence and pretending we'd never happened. However as I glanced at Jack and then back to Yeager and Hart, I realized ignoring Rudy would not help me deal with what happened between us.

No, the help I needed was in the room with me, all of them waiting for me to choose what I would do. Never before had I felt safer, calmer, more confident in myself. It was time to face this head-on. "Rudy, go wait on the couch. I'll be out in a few minutes."

When he didn't immediately move, Yeager took a half-step forward. Rudy bolted out of the bedroom so fast I was sure I'd need to check for skid marks. Hart grinned. "I'd run too if that Redwood came at me."

All three of us at once said, "No, you wouldn't."

Hart shrugged. "Okay, yeah. Are you sure about this Ginger? We can forcibly remove him for you. I'm down to pound the guy until he's unrecognizable."

"It's okay. I need to do this. But first?" I kissed each one of them, one at a time, purposefully, and with such conviction that I was certain my heart constricted in the process. It wasn't about heat or sexual attraction in that moment, it was about gratitude and respect. Something more than that.

I wouldn't be able to unlock what lie beyond those kisses until I dealt with the demon sitting on my couch.

I went to my dresser, pulling out my black yoga pants and pink oversized t-shirt, the one that Rudy said I should burn because it wasn't tight enough. Did I choose the shirt as a dig to him? Maybe, but when Yeager whistled and Hart knotted it right under my boobs, I knew it was the last time I'd ever consider Rudy in any of my actions.

Jack took my hand, lacing our fingers. "We're a shout away if you need us."

Yeager pressed a kiss on my temple. "Yeah, but go do what you need to do, then we can leave together and never look back."

It sounded like the best plan ever. "Okay, but maybe you guys should put some clothes on first."

# CHAPTER 48

I inched into the chair across from the couch where Rudy sat sulking. He wasn't used to being challenged by anyone, but to have three different men go at him like that? He was agitated but trying hard to look aloof about it. "Why are you here, Rudy?"

"This is my condo if you recall."

Nope. It wasn't.

"About that. You'll get a call from a realtor soon. Either you buy my half from me or sell me yours. I don't care which, but this place was never yours, or even ours. It was mine and you invaded it." I glanced at his shoes on the threshold of the door, and I hated myself because I'd allowed it.

How could I have been so blind?

Seriously. What about my life had been so awful that let someone like him into my heart? I'd had good, loving parents, awesome friends, and a job I was happy in. My shit was fully together.

Then he happened and I turned upside down.

He didn't acknowledge anything I'd said about the condo. "Since when are you into group sex? And Hart Brandywine is a scumbag. I can't believe you'd be so desperate to get over me that you'd go to the gutter to get dicked."

I closed my eyes, centering myself in a way I'd seen Jack do when he had a problem to solve. Taking a slow steady breath first, I glared at his forehead, not daring to look into his big brown eyes. I wasn't going to give him any more of me than I already had, including a glimpse into my emotions. "Number one, you don't know shit about Hart and I'm keeping it that way. You don't deserve to know him. He's so far beyond you that you're not on the same planet.

"Number two, I'm not going to discuss my love life with you. You lost the privilege when you cheated on me. Where is Clare, by the way? Does she know you're here?"

I wasn't sure when I'd decided to feel sorry for Clare. She'd been complicit too, but I couldn't hate her, not with Rudy sitting there like the smug ass he was. How could I blame her anyway? I'd let him into my life just like she had.

"She doesn't care where I am. She trusts me."

"She shouldn't."

He snarled, crossing one leg over the other. I'd hit a nerve with Clare. Of course, he didn't respect her any more than he respected me. He was only concerned with himself and his reputation. "I guess she's out planning her dream wedding while you're here, what, hiding or hoping to sleep with me? Tell me why you're really here."

"I didn't come expecting to find you, though I'm glad I broke your little party up. Now that we're here though, let's get one thing straight: what happened with us, it never was cheating. It was me being too much man for one woman to handle. Clare will be fine when I tell her how I want things to go. She's docile and accommodating like that. More than you ever were. If you had just been smart enough to realize what you had, you'd be happy now."

I clenched my fists, hoping to find the resolve in me to keep my cool and say what I needed to say to him without bursting into tears.

I don't know where it came from, but as I curled my fingers, I imagined Hart's rings and felt the strong steadfastness of them as if I were wearing them. I went from wanting to cry to wanting to punch him like Hart had, but he kept on talking, not even noticing the anger radiating from me. "Now that I know you're into group stuff though, it's a good time for us to get back together. You, me, Clare, one big happy family. Before you protest, remember you can't have a beef about sleeping with more than one partner at a time, not when you were taking three cocks at once. Besides, I know you miss me."

Did I?

Yes, I'd missed him.

That was the hard truth of it. After he dumped me, it was like walking outside in the afternoon sun and finding no shadow beside you. Though now that I had the warmth, I craved from the three men sitting a room away, accepting me, flaws and all, it occurred to me that shadows were overrated. I hadn't missed him specifically. I'd just noticed his absence. "I'm not getting back together with you. The idea that you think I'd even consider it shows how self-centered you are."

He stood suddenly, crossing to my chair and leaning over me. "You will. I'll let you have the rest of Santa's forced sabbatical. It'll help you get your mind straight so you can ditch the tools in the next room. Then as soon as Christmas is over, we'll take our relationship public again. It'll help you get over the stink circling you that says you're too emotional to handle a real man. It'll be a good look to be seen with me. That'll give me time to bend Clare around to our threesome scenario. It's win-win-win." He paused, looking around. "I like this condo. It's close to work and comfortable. We'll keep it and dump Clare's tiny place. Just you wait, we'll be the most popular throuple in the world. It should revolutionize group relationships. You might even get mentioned in the next song they write about me."

I didn't know what was worse: the fact that he was dead serious or the fact that I'd ever given him even one beat of my heart. Nothing was redeeming about him. Nothing. I couldn't help it; the tears came hot and fast. I wasn't upset, I was livid. At him. At myself. The audacity of this man to propose a three-way with the two women he cheated on and think I was just going to jump on it and thank him for it.

He suddenly jerked away. I yelped and discovered it wasn't of his own volition. Yeager had him by the back of his neck, holding him up so his feet were dangling. Behind him, Jack was standing in the open door. Hart thumped the center of Rudy's chest with the back of his hand, making him gasp and wince. "Conversation done. Bye now." He put his hand on Yeager's shoulder. "Yeet." Yeager smirked then literally threw him out as Hart picked up his stupid shoes, throwing them at him one by one, shouting," Yeet, yeet, yeet, yeet."

Jack punctuated the scene by slamming the door and locking it. "I don't know about you guys, but I could use a drink."

# CHAPTER 49

Too rattled to talk about anything when we got back to the cabin, I had the urge to curl up in a ball in the bed and never come out. However, I overcame that when Yeager scooped me into his arms and carried me to the hot tub again. To my surprise, it wasn't sexual, it was therapeutic. He always knew what I needed before I did.

Jack leaned against the supports as Yeager, Hart and I simmered in the tub.

Not once did Rudy's name come up.

I would talk to them about it. Eventually. They knew that instinctively, which spoke volumes about the relationship I shared with each of them. And with us as a unit.

I needed time. They gave it freely.

Instead, we discussed getting Yeager away from his arrangement with Camilla again. It made him uncomfortable to talk about it with me and Hart, but at the same time, he was desperate for a way out of it that wouldn't end with his total alienation from his family and flurry. Not to mention the guilt I knew he had over it.

Hart slung his arm around behind me, skimming Yeager's bicep with his fingers. "Real talk. If you could fix it in any way possible, no holds barred, no bad ideas, even if your solution isn't physically possible, how would you do it?"

"I can't have what I want. The laws of physics and distinct lack of time-traveling ability forbid it."

"Humor me, Redwood."

He took a deep breath, throwing his head back and closing his eyes. "Okay, throwing the impossible aside, if I could change the world, my half-brother Ivan would have this gift too since he's wanted it his whole life. He'd get with Camilla long enough to produce offspring and my Dad would be fine with whatever way the two of them and my sister worked out for themselves on how to raise the child. I'd be a fucking great uncle, by the way." He really would. It was so easy to picture him swinging a tiny Yeti around in the air, making airplane noises.

"But I'd keep the gift too. Don't laugh, I know it sounds preposterous, but I enjoy getting to help people, so even if I could give it up, I wouldn't want to do it. I just can't be shackled to a woman and life I don't want." He fingered the ring on his hand, sighing first, then shoving it under the water where he couldn't see it.

I squeezed his thigh. "That's a bit of a relief because I'd hate to see the tats go away."

From the other side, I got a hearty, "Same."

Yeager sighed. "Like I said, it's impossible and I'm still stuck. Because there's more that I want, but I'm not ready to share that yet."

He and Hart exchanged a glance. I couldn't read it, but based on the way Jack shifted positions, coming over to the side of the hot tub, gathering with them for lack of a better word, they all knew what was in Yeager's head.

I wasn't ready to hear it any more than he was ready to share.

Hart finally broke the silence. "Do you trust me, Yeager? Really trust me?"

"Yeah. No question."

"Then I'll get you out of this."

"Thanks, but I don't see how it's possible."

"Leave it to me. I'll let you know when it's done." Yeager shrugged, leaving Hart to whatever he was scheming. Deep down I knew if anyone could help Yeager, it was Hart. "Now that Yeager's mess is settled, we should talk about Jack's dilemma."

Jack raised that eyebrow. "Yes, exactly how are you two Casanovas going to help me get my kingdom back?"

The strategy meeting was intense. There were lots of protocols and rules and Jack was insistent that neither one of them sleep with the queens. I know he did that for me, for them too. It could've cost him his kingdom and that spoke volumes about how he really felt about all three of us.

After they'd dressed to kill—oh my soul, Hart in a red tie-black shirt combo with Yeager's red and gray suspenders and Yeager with his white leather pants and red sweater that made his eyes pop—Jack ushered us into his palace using his snow globe. We were greeted by Burl, whose eyes almost squirted out of his head at the sight of us. Jack really never did have visitors. "Sir. I was getting worried you wouldn't come back for the most important day of the year."

"Don't be silly. I'll be here tonight, but first, I need you to take the big guy to the Autumn court and the one who looks like he's going to attack the next thing that moves to the Spring. Tell them how to get back too."

"Sir? This is highly unusual."

"I'm aware Burl. Please just do it. I'm running out of time here. This is my last gambit to save the kingdom and they're going to help me."

Burl gave him a curt nod and motioned for Hart and Yeager to follow. "Be back in two shakes," Yeager called over his shoulder. "Don't do anything we wouldn't do."

Hart slung his arm around Yeager. "Nah, go ahead and do exactly what we would do."

They disappeared through a door, and I turned to Jack. "I know you're nervous, but they won't let you down."

"It's hard for me to give up even a small modicum of control. I'm grappling with the idea that it makes me a weak ruler to need their help."

"Are you kidding me? It makes you a wise ruler who knows how to delegate and play to others' strengths. You can't do everything by yourself, no matter how badly you want to, Jack."

"You know, the same could be said for you, Flame. You seemed to be battling yourself trying to get past what happened to you, living in your grief and anger for months. I think you're starting to see that you don't have to do that alone." He took my hand in his, lacing our fingers together. "In a way, we learned the same lesson."

He still wasn't mentioning Rudy by name, and it hit me why.

It was not about Rudy.

It never was.

It was about me and when I thought about it, I realized I hadn't experienced the sting of aloneness since Santa had started the silly games. With that idea in my mind, another swirling pang hit my gut. We had three days left. What would happen when the games were done? Would I go back to the fleet, leave Jack and Yeager behind at the South Pole while Hart and I went back to the North?

Didn't much like the sound of that.

Thankfully Jack distracted me from going too far into a freak-out spiral. "We need to go back and start the next game without them. Burl will bring them back when they've finished."

~~~~~~~~~~~~~~~~~~~~~~~~~~~~~~

The game of the day had made Jack nearly tear up. While he'd known that he and Santa were somewhat friends, he'd told me that Santa usually stayed out of Fae business. When Holly announced the game of finding and decorating the best Yule log in preparation for the Winter Solstice celebration that night, Jack was utterly gutted. "I didn't realize he knew how important it is to me."

"Santa knows everything."

Or almost everything. I liked to think if he knew about Rudy screwing around on me, he would've done something about it.

Jack and I were in the woods searching for the perfect log as he explained about the Winter Solstice. "It's meant to celebrate the rebirth and coming of the sun, as a catalyst for resilience to get through the dark winter days ahead, so
~~~~~~~~~~~~~~~~~~~~~~~~~~~~~~

John Sun always mocks me with his part in the rituals for my people."

"Um, he's a first-class jerk and I don't like him. Maybe you should've launched Yeager and Hart directly on him instead of fooling with the queens. It would've solved your problem much faster if he was just dead."

I got the quarter-grin I'd learned to love so much. "Hart seems to be rubbing off on you, Flame." He wasn't wrong about that. I stepped over a broken log as Jack continued talking about his traditions, "The Solstice, to me, is about the freezing away of the past, looking to the future and the warm times to come. I'd like to share that with you tonight. Yeager and Hart too, if they'll come. You'll have to be outside in the snow for the night, but I'll make a warm igloo for us. For anyone that wants to participate."

"That sounds lovely. You can count on me and the others. But we have to find the perfect log first, right?"

"Did someone say log?" I swung around and found Yeager and Hart gripping Burl's shoulders having swished back to our world some way. His green eyes were twinkling as he addressed Jack. "I mean, I've already saved your kingdom, but if you need a wood expert too, here I am."

Hart let out a laugh. "Trust me, he knows about wood. And just so you know, we had to refuse a four-way—multiple times—but when we each presented your plan, the queens stopped fucking their concubines long enough to have a powwow. They're both on board. You're welcome."

Jack paused mid-stride, branch in hand. "Explain. Leave out the four-way business."

Yeager strode over and grabbed the branch out of Jack's hand and tossed it deeper into the trees. Not suitable in his expert opinion. "Each queen agreed to give you one-quarter of their kingdoms to push John Sun and his encroaching Summer temps back. Neither of them wants to lose crops and if he's got the majority of the land in the Fae realm, that's exactly what would happen. As long as you allow them to plant and harvest as normal, these lands will be officially Winter lands. Any Fae who want to turn into frost Fae will be granted permission as long as the planting and harvesting continue as normal."

Jack stood stock still as Yeager rummaged in the brush for a log. Hart continued the report. "Those bitches be crazy, by the way, but they seemed to get the danger allowing John to take over. They trust you to challenge him again, this time with their backing. Only John won't know what he's betting for, or against, which is the exact position he put you in last time. All you have to do is come out on top and you'll be sitting exactly where you were with one-quarter of the Fae realm at your feet." He swiped his hands together, indicating it was done.

They'd done it. Truly remarkable. "So that's it?" I asked. "All he has to do is challenge him and play the game again? That's amazing."

"Not so fast, Flame. It's not a matter of playing the game, it's a matter of winning. If I fail again, I truly am done."

Hart put his arm around Jack. "Oh, Daddy Jack. You aren't going to lose. I'll be sure of that. Trust me."

"Aha! Here it is." Yeager came strolling out of the trees carrying a branch. "All I have to do is chop it up and we've got a perfect Yule log. Now, let's go win another game."

# CHAPTER 50

Yeager had crafted the perfect log, cutting holes for the design I suggested. The task was to decorate the log to represent the team, so Vixen and Hart scoured the bag of game-specific supplies, coming up with four dented silver napkin rings that held four candles, one to represent each of us. Yeager had even gone back and gotten real cedar garland to decorate the log as well. It was rustic like Yeager, edgy like Hart, sleek like me, and fiery like Vixen.

Looking at it as it lay in the snow in front of the igloo I'd made us, stirred something in me I thought had been long dead.

These people meant something to me.

I did not want to lose them.

What lay ahead for us was unknown. A concept I struggled with in my life. I was the one who made plans to make plans. Flying blind wasn't in my nature. Though I was willing to feel my way through it if Vixen were even remotely a part of it. Whatever would be, would be. But that was three days away.

After we'd voted for the Hot Chocolate with Marsh-mallows team who'd crafted a log by tying two small dark branches and two branches of white bark together with twine, we'd gathered to participate in the rituals of my kingdom.

Not just the people on my team, but all of the guests at the inn. Save for John. He'd lit their log on fire and stomped away to his kingdom, leaving the nymphs alone. He didn't like the Winter Solstice, even though he was a big part of the reason for it. He just couldn't take me being front and center.

For the first time in my life, I felt sorry for him. Sure, at least two of the nymphs were sleeping with him, but it seemed the minute the games were over, they'd head back to where they'd come from, leaving him to go back to his kingdom alone. I knew the loneliness that came from ruling an entire Fae kingdom and I wouldn't wish it on anyone. Not even him.

Still, I was determined to beat him in the challenge the next day.

Holly nodded for me to begin, so I stepped forward. "Thank you for celebrating the Solstice with me. It means so much that you all agreed to take part in the ritual to-night. I've crafted igloos for each team with a fire inside for warmth. There is a magic barrier in place to keep the tem-perature comfortable, so don't be concerned about freezing overnight.

"The object of the ritual is to write the things on the walls that you wish to rid from your life. It's up to you if you want to write one word or many. Just inscribe what your heart tells you and go to sleep thinking of what lies ahead for you after the troubling things melt away. The solstice is about contemplation and reflection. It's about casting away that which froze us and moving beyond these things in the warmth of knowledge that they're truly behind us."

I glanced over to Vixen, who was biting her lip. She was all in for the ritual, but I knew it would the night would be difficult for her after her confrontation with Rudy. She needed this and we'd help her through it.

"If everyone is ready to begin, please enter your igloos now. They'll melt overnight and when you awake at dawn, all your demons, your troubles, and failures will be cast into the past."

With no further instruction, the guests began crawling into the igloos. It made me feel good to see them dotting the horizon as the sun set behind them. I went in first, followed by Vixen, then Hart. Yeager had a little tougher time squeezing his broad shoulders through the entrance, but he pushed through and landed on top of Hart with a grunt. "Maybe make a bigger hole for the man-beast to get his cock through next time."

Yeager laughed, but I held up my finger, shushing them both. "Can we leave the dick jokes out for one night? This is important." My tone was effective enough to make them straighten up.

Vixen inclined against the wall of the igloo, tracing it with her finger. "So, we just write whatever we want to get rid of on the wall?"

"Yes. You don't have to write big enough for us to see. You're doing this for yourself."

She still looked tentative, so I took it upon myself to demonstrate, etching one word into the frozen blocks of ice.

*Alone.*

She glanced up with questioning eyes as I tried to put my feelings into words eloquent enough to express them. "I've recently come to realize I spent a lot of my life isolated from others, trying to do everything in my kingdom and my life without help. It was slowly killing me. I don't want to do that anymore, so I'm looking forward, with the help of everyone in this igloo, hoping that time in my life is done. I don't know what may come, but I know I'm not alone in it."

Yeager patted me on the back. "No. You aren't, Ice Man." I gave him a nod and he took up my mantle, glancing down at Vixen before he scraped his sentiment next to mine.

*Chosen One.*

He moved his hand to Hart, gripping his shoulder as he spoke. "I don't know how you plan to get me out of my sentence, Jing—Hart, but there's no way I can come through these twelve days of Christmas games and settle for anything less than what I want. Whom I truly want." He looked at Vixen, the love in his eyes potent enough to fill the whole igloo. "I won't give up any of myself due to something I had no control over. Though, if I knew what you had planned, I'd feel more confident right now."

Vixen curled in his arms, and he dug his hand into her curls. On the other side, Hart smirked. "Well said, and I'll let you know when I'm good and damn ready. Now..." he crawled over Yeager, purposefully I might add, and wrote his sentiment in the ice below his.

*Labels.*

"No more labels. I'm not the Sexiest, you're not the Chosen One, you, Vixen aren't the Rejected One. None of it. The only label I'm accepting going forward is Daddy. Right, Jack?"

I had no idea why everyone was so infatuated with the Daddy thing. To me, it was weird and bordered on pedophilia, but it had taken me a manner of moments to discover Vixen was turned on by it, so how could I not embrace it? I was starting to feel pretty Daddy among the group anyway. I'd use it at the appropriate times, that was certain. "Fine. Daddy's good with that."

"I bet you are," Hart chuckled, then looked down at Vixen, cupping her face. "What about you, Ginger? Are you ready to write your thoughts?"

She nodded, still biting that lip. I had the deepest desire to wrestle it from her teeth for her, but it wasn't the time, nor place. This portion of the Winter Solstice was for re-flection, not sex. "You don't have to do this now," I offered. It wouldn't be meaningful unless she was ready and none of us wanted to push her.

"I know. I'm ready." She took a big breath and stood, as close to standing as she could get in the igloo, then reached up and scrawled *Rudy* along the entire ceiling of the igloo, then plopped into Yeager's lap, curling into his chest, then reaching out to take my hand.

Yeager cocked his head. "Who's that?"

# CHAPTER 51

I woke up to the sound of jingle bells and the feel of a tongue on my cock. I had to do a quick check to find out if I was dreaming.

Nope. Not dreaming.

I was being sucked off as I slept.

That was a first.

I liked it on a level I found hard to express.

Or simply hard.

It wasn't quite dawn, so the igloo was still intact. Though the warm glow of the lantern was flickering against the ice so I could tell most of the words we'd written had melted away. A sense of euphoria crept over me at the sight of the smooth walls. Maybe there was something to the Winter Solstice idea.

Or it could've been the tongue flicking over the head of my cock. Hard to say.

I moaned, angling up so that...Yeager? would take it deeper.

Okay, nope. Not Yeager. No bumpy goodness scraping over my dick.

Vixen then. Good girl.

I went to grab a handful of her auburn curls as she did exactly what I'd wanted, going deep into the back of her throat.

Only, there were no curls to grasp.

The fuck was happening down there?

I reached back, snagging the lantern and angling it to see who, exactly, was going to town on my cock.

"Jack? What the fuck are you doing?"

Instead of answering me, he ran his tongue down the length of me and back again. I hissed in pleasure.

Beside me, Vixen stirred. "Is it time to get up?" She sat up which caused Yeager to wake on the other side of her. Before I could formulate a full thought about how cute Vixen looked with sleepy eyes and wild hair, the two of them were stretching and yawning. Meanwhile, Jack was still having a field day on my cock.

So conflicted.

His frigid tongue made my heated dick even harder. "Um, I don't know what to do here."

Never said that before where sex was concerned, but one thing was for damn sure, Jack hadn't reacted to one word, one tiny tug of his hair. He was a focused machine bent on getting me off.

"Jack? What in the name of the moon and the sun is happening?" Yeager grabbed the lantern out of my hand, moving it so he could confirm what I already knew. "Hart, he's sucking your cock."

"I'm—" I hissed, couldn't help it. "I'm aware. And I'm sorry to both of you but I'm finding it hard to be pissed about this if I'm honest. That cold thing he has going on is nice."

Vixen nodded. "Yes. Thank you. But I didn't realize he..."

None of us had realized. He'd been so adamant that he was into Vixen alone.

Yet, there he was with his tongue gliding over my shaft, making my bells tingle and ring. I needed a minute to process this new development. While I hadn't wanted Jack, not like this, I didn't want to deny him if he'd decided to jump all in on our thing. Like I said, it was a fucking phenomenal sensation.

Yeager put his hand on Jack's shoulder, shaking him and trying to get his attention. It did nothing. I shook my head. "Guys, I think Daddy might be having a stroke."

Vixen jumped up, coming around behind me. Was she getting a little jolt out of seeing Jack go down on me? Probably. Still, there was soft concern in her expression. "Jack, can you stop long enough to talk about this? If this is what you want, we can work it out. We just need to discuss it so we're all on the same page. Please."

For the first time since it started, he flicked his eyes up. Just his eyes. His tongue was still licking me like I was an ice cream sandwich. It was like ninety-nine percent wrong, but I groaned anyway. He had some talent. I mean, he was no Yeager, but if he didn't stop soon, I was going to be the vanilla cream in the middle of that ice cream sandwich.

The look of terror in Jack's eyes was instant and intense. It was like he'd suddenly awoken to a tongue stroking his shaft. He truly had not realized what he was doing. "Is there such a thing as sleep head? Because he just woke up."

Yeager growled, grasping Jack's hair. "For fuck's sake, Ice Man. Give it a rest." He went to pull him off me and I winced because Jack didn't move at all. In fact, he groaned along with me as Yeager yanked.

A weighty sense of dread thudded in my body. Jack grunted as he tried to pull away from me, only he couldn't.

His fucking tongue was frozen to one of my jingle bells.

More specifically, to the skin around the bell.

Frozen. To. My. Cock.

"Shit. Jack, get off me right now."

"Ah caht."

"You can't?"

No. Fo-then."

Yeager chuckled so loud I thought the igloo would fall around us. "Let me get this straight. His tongue is frozen to your dick. I can't. I cannot handle the fuckery. You two are messing with me, right?"

"I swear on my soul, I'm not. If I were going to mess with you, I'd be down between your fucking thighs, Redwood. This is legit and I'm high-key about to go postal."

Vixen ran her hand over my spine to calm me. Her voice behind me was a whisper. "Oh, my soul. Jack, just unfreeze it with your magic."

He huffed and his cold breath rolling over my business made me shiver. "Caht. No-gobe mith ing."

"I can't understand him. What do we do?" I asked, fear rising in my throat. Setting aside the chilly blow job, something was off, and I didn't care for the manic look in Jack's normally level gray eyes.

Vixen hugged me from behind, sensing the rising tide of panic from both of us. "I can go get some warm water to—"

"No!"

Everyone got that response. Thank fuck because the thought of pouring anything near hot on my dick had me shriveling. Only, I wasn't shriveling at all. I was still hard. "A little help here. I think he's freezing my cock. I'm losing the feeling and I don't want to know what happens if it gets all the way frozen. And I swear to fuck if you call me Popsicle right now Redwood, I will throat punch you."

I pictured my dick falling off or shattering into a million icy pieces. It made me shudder.

Below me, Jack started waving at Yeager and Vixen. "Mo tug."

Yeager dropped to his knees beside Jack. "You want us to tug."

"No! No tugging. No tugging at all. The goal is for my dick to be intact when this is done. I think you both can agree on that, no?"

Yeager grunted and Vixen dropped to her knees. "He said more tongue. I think if maybe we join him, our body heat will melt the ice without the extreme of pouring hot water on it."

Jack nodded his agreement and I swear my cock skin started to peel off, setting my panic button on eleven. "Do it. Please both of you."

Yeager shrugged, then got busy, running his long tongue along the side of my shaft, which was a fucking shame because I couldn't feel it. I was going to kill Jack when this was done. Vixen did her part on the other side, flicking her tongue over my frozen jingle bell and Jack's tongue at the same time. He moaned into it as she licked and sucked. Meanwhile, Yeager was working his way to my balls.

And suddenly, I was hot again.

Thank fuck.

It didn't take long before Vixen's actions turned into a sloppy kiss with Jack, but it did the trick to melt his tongue enough to slide off without skinning my cock in the process. They fell into each other and while he gripped her harder than I'd ever seen and stuck his hand in her pants, Yeager went full beast on me, sucking as the feeling came back into my cock. He used a cool hand to play with my balls and I came hard and dirty in his throat the next second. Vixen finished off shortly after.

That only seemed to set Jack off again. He jumped up, gripping his hair in his hands like he had the most tormented headache ever. He paced back and forth, mumbling for a minute, then rummaging through our sleeping bags and supplies we'd brought with us.

He was out of control.

It was not a look I liked for him. It was fucking unsettling.

Yeager managed to grip his shoulders. "Tell us what's wrong."

Jack's eyes were crazy, though his tongue seemed to be functioning. "My snow globe is more than just the gateway to my kingdom, it's the source of my magic. I couldn't get back to my kingdom at the peak of the Solstice. That's why I—" he paused. "I apologize, I truly was out of my head there. I can't even imagine how you must feel, but I need to get to my kingdom before it's too late."

I pulled my pants up finally, hating the look on my friend's face. Wait, were we more than friends now? Unsure. "That sucks. We'll find it and get you there. Just try to breathe."

He gripped the lapels of my shirt. "You don't understand. I may not have a kingdom at all anymore. And there's only one person in the world who knew I needed to be there at the precise moment."

John Fucking Sun.

# CHAPTER 52

Yeager had made Jack promise to stay with me when he and Hart went to get his globe back. He'd calmed down some but was nowhere near his normal self. It was bad enough that John had tried to take his kingdom with his sneaky negotiations, but to outright steal Jack's only way to get to his people was beyond reproach.

I put him in the category with Rudy.

"Hart will never forgive me for this," he rasped as he paced around the perimeter of the igloo. "None of you will."

"We already have. You're not in your right mind. And for what it's worth, Hart kind of dug it. He'd probably not turn you down if you offered to give him another blow job."

He stopped, looking up into the lightening sky and releasing a frustrated scream. It was disconcerting to see him like that. "No, I have no desire to suck anyone's cock again. I think when I was overcome, he was just the closest body."

"Yeah, maybe don't tell him that."

His stress came out in the sound of his tight laugh. "I should explain that the peak of the Solstice brings out the basest instincts and urges in Fae. It's why the queens of Spring and Autumn are in a constant state of arousal. They don't experience the full Solstice moments. In my kingdom, as it has been since the beginning, the king gives the signal to give in to the urges. My people won't act without my blessing. And it's nearing several hours now. If you think what I did with Hart was bad? I promise you it's much worse in the Winter court right now. Only they will be trying to fight the urges becoming more violent and unpredictable with each passing minute."

I had no clue how serious this had been. And John had been so casual about it.

Movement caught my attention. I looked up to find Yeager and Hart strolling over the snow with John Sun in tow. That had not taken long. His hands were bound with motorcycle chains and his face was a bloody wreck. I couldn't help but notice the ripped skin on Hart's knuckles and Yeager's heavy panting as they pushed him to his bare knees in the snow in front of Jack like an offering.

Hart pulled Jack's snow globe from his pocket, handing it over to him. Jack sighed, then lunged at Hart, hugging him close, then bringing Yeager in on it while John grunted on his knees between them. "I'll never be able to repay you for this. Or to make up for—"

Hart slapped his back. "Listen. There's no payment or apology needed. Go do what you need to do to set your kingdom right. But first, John has something to say, don't you?" He yanked John up by the chains and waited. "Excuse me, I can't hear you, you overbaked, crispy-ass sun chip."

John looked through the trickle of blood that flowed from a rather significant gash on his forehead. When he said nothing, Yeager squeezed his shoulder hard enough to make him wince. "I guess he's not in the talking mood, so I'll go ahead and let you know, Ice Man. Your kingdom is intact. All of it, the same as it was before you got here. John has agreed that it's a stupid idea to force anyone to play games with the lives of living, breathing individuals, so you won't even need your game board any longer. Instead, you'll rule over your kingdom as you see fit, never having to worry about this colossal waste of space invading or manipulating again. I think the queens will agree to this arrangement, won't they John?" He put his hand on the back of John's head, forcing the nod he wanted.

"Thank you both. I'll never—"

Yeager shook his head. "Stop. Nobody fucks with this family and comes out unscathed. Nobody."

Hart released the chains from John's wrists, shoving him with his boot, then turning his back as if to show he no longer considered him a threat. "Go fix your kingdom. We'll handle the next game." Jack nodded, gripping his snow globe, then whishing away just as the ice on the igloo melted.

If there were turning points in life, that would be one I'd remember.

We started as a team, but we were so much more than that.

~~~~~~~~~~~~~~~~~~~~~~~~~~~~~~~~~~~~~~~~~

"Would either of you be angry if I said I kind of want Jack to suck my dick now too?" Yeager mused as he folded homemade Christmas cards in the next game. We were
~~~~~~~~~~~~~~~~~~~~~~~~~~~~~~~~~~~~~~~~~

making as many as we could for kids in the hospital at Christmas and I couldn't fathom how he'd gone from 'let's put cute puppies on the covers' to having his dick in Jack's mouth, but that was Yeager for you. "I feel left out."

I whacked his thigh with my card as Hart feigned shock and horror. "You know what, I'll give you that because it was amazing. Not that I want it to happen again, but I'm going to give credit where it's due."

I laughed. I loved those guys.

I mean, I liked having them around.

"Yeager, Dear?" Holly called from the doorway. "When your game is over could you help me bring some things up from the basement? I need to figure out which things to donate to charity and which to store before..." She trailed off as a sad look passed over her face. She quickly righted it, smoothing her hands over her pleated red-and-white candy cane skirt. "I just need to go through some things."

He jumped up. "I can do it now. I suck at glitter." He winked at me as he followed her out of the side door. Before long he'd made several trips carrying more than ten huge boxes of things and depositing them along the edge of the room for her to go through. As soon as she pulled out the first item, she teared up.

Erin went over, squeezing her. "Is everything okay?"

"Yes, yes. It's just been a while since I looked at this box. This is my dear departed Cornelius' t-shirt collection. I know I should part with these old things, but I can't bring myself to do it. I don't know where in the world I will store these things when I leave."

"You're leaving? For how long?" Yeager was backing into the door with another huge box. He might have sucked with glitter, but he was good at toting heavy things with bulging muscles and suspenders that cradled his ass.

"Well, permanently, I'm afraid. My old human bones don't like the cold so much anymore, even with Santa's magic. You'll understand in a few centuries, I suppose. At any rate, Santa said he'd buy the property at a fair price because, of course, he'd do that. I just have to weed through my things and find a warm climate to light in, then I'll be taking my leave."

Yeager dropped the box he was carrying. Holly had been a permanent fixture in his life, like a mom really, and her suddenly springing it on him was unsettling. "I can't believe this."

"I'm afraid you'll have to. Rest assured; we'll stay in touch." She gave him a sad smile, then went back to her boxes, oohing and ahhing over every band t-shirt and thrift store find Cornelius must have ever worn.

When Yeager settled back into the couch, he said nothing. He just leaned over and put his head on my shoulder. All I could do was run my hands in his silky hair. "Change sucks, huh?"

"Yep. Sometimes it does."

# CHAPTER 53

Holly's news had come as a big blow. Especially in the wake of knowing I had two days left before Vixen and Hart would leave for the North Pole. For good. Vixen had gotten her Christmas spirit back, despite herself, and I knew she'd go off on her Christmas Eve flight and never look back. As she should.

The clock was ticking.

And I still had the issue that was the clusterfuck of my binding to Camilla.

Holly retiring to parts unknown was like the bitter icing on a shit cake.

However, I couldn't let on how devastated I was about it. My team, my family—yeah, I fucking said that—deserved me at my best. So, when Jack came back and announced his kingdom was fine and dandy, that's what I gave: my biggest smile, my heartiest laugh, and I damn near glittered the entire lodge.

For them.

Still didn't make cards as nice as the vampire ones which I suspect they used their fangs to chew the fancy edges, but whatever. Ours had puppies. We should've gotten at least some of the votes.

A pop went across the room I sucked in a deep breath. I was going to miss that sound.

I was going to miss more than that sound.

I glanced over at Hart, finding him questioning me with his eyes. I shrugged it off.

He was feeling it too.

So was Vixen based on the way she'd gotten quiet.

Even Jack was more pensive than usual.

Holly giggled as she read the note from Santa. "Oh, listen to this one, friends. I think it's the perfect one to end our game.

"I've given you lots of fun and laughter that I hope drew you together and renewed your belief in Christmas and sparked your belief in each other. As a result, I want the twelfth and final game to be up to you."

Immediately murmurs broke out. Holly shushed everyone with the shake of her jingle bell bracelet.

Never in my life had I considered the thought of missing sounds, but that was two on the list in under three minutes.

"It's time for Santa to Hand over the reins for the last game. You've been working together and competing for eleven days and I want to see how far you've come in that time. All teams should gather together to design the last game. You are in charge, you call the rules as long as everyone agrees on the final rules and voting methods. I'll come in before my Christmas Eve run to tally the results of the game. Have fun!"

With that having been announced, Holly excused herself and her staff to prepare dinner.

Vixen squirmed in her seat on the couch. I couldn't tell if she was trying to get closer to me or Hart, or maybe Jack who was sitting across from her on the coffee table. Probably all of us. Santa would be doing more than tallying votes. He'd be collecting Vixen. None of us knew how to deal with that. Instead of dealing with it outright at that moment. she cleared her throat. "I have an idea for our last game."

We spent the rest of the day working on Vixen's idea. It had been a stellar one. Even John Sun had stumbled into doing something remarkable during our game prep. I'd like to think Hart and I had something to do with his change of attitude. Maybe he was just faking it until he could get away from us forever, I couldn't say. But I knew what he proposed was going to be the perfect cap for the game.

And hey, he'd had to give his suggestion through a busted lip, so there was that.

Once we put everything away, we enjoyed the amazing feast Holly had made for us. Traditional Christmas ham and more sides than I could count, along with a fantastic chocolate trifle made with Oreos. I swallowed down every morsel she put in front of me because I knew I'd never eat any of her cooking again. I might have eaten two portions of trifle.

After dinner, the mood was quiet in the lodge. Everyone lingered around long after it was over, just chilling and sipping Holly's mulled cider as we talked. Everything was subdued until Cherish squealed, drawing all our attention. Hart leaned over the couch. "What's up, buttercup?"

She angled her phone so he could see it. "Sophie R. sent me this pic of the new boy in our class, Xayden. He showed up at the school's Christmas concert, thank my soul I didn't have to attend, points Dad and quote, unquote Santa, and he was scrolling through her Insta and found a pic of us together and asked about me. He said I was fire and he wanted to swoop by. She told him I was on vacay and gave him my insta and he just liked my last seven pics."

I smiled, damn my soul if I wasn't going to miss her squealing chatter too. "That's good right?"

"It's so slay, Yeager. You don't just go back and heart old posts unless you mean it, okay? Look at him." She showed me her phone and I had to assume he was good-looking for a twelve-year-old kid. He was trying to give off that broody, I-don't-give-a-shit vibe that reminded me of Hart. "He has rizz and he said he wants us to meet up as soon as I get home. Meanwhile, Aiden is posting on his comments saying he's not down for that, telling him it's my finsta and he doesn't want to mess with me because I'm trash. He's jealous, TBH. So, Sophie R. and Sophie G. and Lilly are reassuring him it's not my finsta and shipping me and Xayden and Xayden is like, bruh, get over yourself, don't come at me when Cherish is my next crush, no cap. He said Aiden has no drip and if he didn't stop messing with me, he'd bust him up. Gah. I think I'm in love."

Isaac sighed. "Maybe you should meet him before making declarations of love." She rolled her eyes at her Dad and went back to thumbing her phone with a big smile on her face. It all seemed very normal, and I had the urge to run over and hug the silly girl and her long-suffering father, who could not stop eyeing Mandy across the room. If she didn't pick up on his signals soon, she was not the nymph I thought she was. And as if I willed it into being, she looked up from her book and smiled at Isaac. That was the smile of promise if I ever saw one. Good for Isaac. Good for both of them.

Hart stood up suddenly, whispering to Jack with a conspiratorial look on his face. Could've been asking for another 'fro job' as he was now calling it. He glanced at me. "Will you two be okay without us for a while? We have an errand to run."

I shook my head, layering some mock sadness in my voice. "Leaving me alone with Vixen. Whatever will I do?"

Jack pulled his cuffs down, snapping them in place under his jacket sleeve. "I'm sure you'll think of something."

I did manage to think of a few things, so after Hart and Jack left, I tugged her into my lap, giving her the rundown of my thoughts and she agreed to come with me back to the cabin.

Holding the door open for her, she stepped over the threshold of our cabin and did her little hop thing. It took me back to the first night we met when she was sad and angry and trying to drown her issues in Jingle Juice. She'd changed in our time together—no longer bitter and struggling—but in some ways, she was exactly as she was when I first met her: spunky, smart, and kind, always making others feel comfortable and pushing herself to be more. I admired her for so many reasons.

My heart was pounding at the idea of her leaving, wailing against my chest like a jackhammer. I couldn't let her go without telling her.

She'd already peeled out of her pink coat while I was in my own head thinking about how deep my feelings for her were. She sunk into the chair by the fireplace and looked up at me with a smile and I couldn't wait any longer. The thought was inside me, fighting to get out, so I opened the dam and let it.

"I love you, Bunny."

The gasp she released went straight to my cock, but more than that, the warmth in her eyes zeroed in my heart and I would never, as long as I lived, forget that look.

Crossing the floor in long strides, I threw myself on my knees in front of her and took her sweet face in my hands. She opened her mouth to say something, but I ran my thumb over her lip so she wouldn't. "I love you more than I thought possible, and I just wanted you to know. Don't say anything right now. I don't want to talk about what it means or what happens after Santa arrives or how you feel because I expect nothing in return but the privilege of letting me show you how much you mean to me."

A single tear tracked down her cheek, but she did as I asked and kept silent. Seconds after I swiped her tear, she dove for me, wrapping her arms around my neck and kissing me with so much enthusiasm, we fell backward on the floor, on top of the polar bear blanket. When she finally pulled back, she was panting with a needy look in her pretty blue eyes. "Show me."

I needed no other encouragement. I stripped her out of her shirt and bra first, leaning up to take her nipples in my mouth, one by one, growling as they pebbled under my tongue. I couldn't get enough of it, but I wanted so much more. "Lift up for a second." She placed her knees on the floor so I could undo her jeans and push them down over her hips as she wrestled with my belt and jeans too.

It took a few ticks, but when we'd gotten our pants out of the way, she climbed back on top of me, grabbing my cock in her soft hand and centering it over her pussy. She was already soaked for me, and I didn't even bother to warn her, I just lifted and sank into her warm softness. She groaned in pleasure. "My soul, Yeager, your cock does things to me. I love it."

I'd take her loving my cock all damn day and night.

Wanting, no needing her to feel more, I reached between us, turning my hand so I could take her clit in my fingers and pinch it hard enough to send a jolt of pleasure through her. She squeezed my shaft tighter as she rode me. "You like that, don't you?"

"Yes," she panted. "Don't stop."

I laughed. "I wouldn't dream of stopping. Not until you come all over my cock." She arched back, giving me the best view in the world, which was to say her tits bouncing as she rode me so good. Things truly had changed for her. I suspected she'd started to love being on top. She slapped her hands on my chest, needing to find purchase as she came. "That's it. Come for me like a good girl, Bunny."

She was a beautiful goddess, gasping and moaning as she rocked through her fierce orgasm. I reached up to run my thumb along her jaw, stilling inside her to give her a moment of peace before I railed her so hard, she was going to see stars.

The pop in the room was unexpected, but not unwelcome. I craned my neck to find Hart standing there watching with a smirk. I had no clue where Jack had gone. "Did she just come on that big cock?"

I curled my fingers in her hair, stroking as she rode out the last of it. "Mm-hm, she did. I'm next."

He strolled over to us, taking up a position behind her and running his hands over her chest, down her stomach, and back up again, as he eyed me. It sent a punch of lust through me. "Afraid not, Redwood. Consider this your payback. I'm taking our girl for a little spin. If you want to join us, I suggest you get dressed and come outside in two shakes of my jingle bells." He grabbed her sweater in his hand, then popped her right off of me. I was left alone in the cabin with a glistening hard cock.

# CHAPTER 54

Jack was right outside, holding back the frigid temps while Hart threw my sweater over my head. "Are you guys really going to leave him in there with a stiff cock?"

Jack raised his eyebrow. "He could masturbate. It would only be fair since that's what I had to do when Hart took you from me."

Hart laughed. "Nah, he's coming."

Yeager pushed out of the door, fully dressed, and handed me my coat. "No, I am, in fact, *not* coming apparently. Not now, anyway." He slugged Hart on the arm, then wrested him closer so he could stage whisper in his ear. "You'll be making that up to me, Jingle Bell."

Hart slapped him on the ass. "That's what I'm doing, Redwood. Let's go." He offered me his hand and together we all strolled around to the back of the cabin.

The night had turned out to be full of surprises. Not only had Yeager said he loved me—I'd decided to put a pin in that— but when I rounded the corner, my mouth flew open. Shock and a twinge of fear rattled through me. "Hart, what have you done?"

Yeager let out a chuckle at the sight of Santa's sleigh. *The* sleigh. It was sitting behind our cabin having been towed to the Inn by eight reindeer crafted in ice. "Jack, you're complicit in this...theft of Santa's most prized possession?" I screeched.

Hart being involved was not surprising in the least, but Jack? Not the level-headed, cool, smart king I knew and...lo—liked a bunch. Putting another pin in that one.

Hart dropped my hand and turned me to face him. His stormy blue eyes were full of mischief. "I didn't steal the sleigh, I borrowed it. Once we're done in a few hours, it'll go right back to the garage below my loft for the final inspection tomorrow. Nobody will be the wiser. We need it tonight. I've got a list of things to accomplish, so what do you say? You two with us?"

I glanced at Jack, then Yeager. "Where are we going, exactly?"

"That would be a surprise, Ginger. But first up, we need to go get a feisty little buttercup and give her the flight of her life." He popped away, leaving Yeager and I gaping at the sleigh.

It took Yeager roughly three seconds before he climbed in the back and held out his hand to me. Here's the thing: I'd never—not once in all my years as Vixen—had been *in* the sleigh. Santa didn't have a rule against it, it just wasn't something that was done. I'd always wondered what it would be like to see the world from above with human eyes, but I never dreamed I ever would. And here Hart was offering it up to me like he'd known one of my deepest wishes.

Hoping it wasn't a mistake, I climbed into the back of the sleigh, taking a seat next to Yeager. We were in the back portion where Santa kept his sack, leaving the driver's seat open. Yeager pulled me to him. "All aboard, Ice Man."

Jack squeezed in next to me and took my hand. "I know how this looks, Flame, but when you find out what he has in store, it's going to erase all your fears. I'd even venture to say that if Santa knew about this, he would've approved and handed Hart the key himself."

I couldn't imagine.

When Hart popped back with Cherish, she rolled her eyes. "Seriously, Hart? I'm not a baby. I don't need a photo in your fake sleigh. This is a little cringe for you, if I'm honest."

"Is it though?"

"Yes. I know Santa is just some guy Holly hired to get us all hyped up on Christmas. I get it, I played along but this is taking it too far. Like, the CEO of too far."

Hart gave her his most charming grin. "Come on, humor me. Take one little trip, then I'll take you back to your cabin if you're not convinced Santa and this sleigh are real." She reluctantly climbed in, and Hart followed suit. He peered over his shoulder. "Fire up the reindeer, Jack."

Jack flicked his wrist and the ice reindeer sparked to life, running together in unison just like the real fleet did when we lifted. Moments later, my stomach—and Cherish's too based on her squeal—bottomed out as we took to the air.

It was so different in human form. It took effort on my part not to squeal in delight as we soared above the cabins and beyond. I closed my eyes and let the wind whip my hair and blister my cheeks pink. It was so awesome.

Once we'd cleared the South Pole, Hart clicked on the GPS—the one I learned *he* supplied Santa with to help find the kids on the nice list homes in record time—clicking on something and we swooped away into the night. Using the sleigh's magic, it took only a few minutes to arrive at our first stop, landing on the roof of a house on the outskirts of Pittsburgh if I read the screen correctly. "Where are we?"

"Xayden Alexander McMillan, age twelve, four-fifty-seven West Crimson Peak Ave, lion shifter, nice with occasional naughty tendencies, loves his mama, stands up to bullies, expert-level gaming skills, currently needing help to catch up on his history assignment over the break thanks to his sudden relocation." Hart turned to Cherish. "I have it on good authority that you're an expert in Mrs. Perry's class."

He was good. He knew everything.

Her face lit up. "Really? I can just go in there and help him write a history paper, no cap?"

He pulled out a candy cane from his pocket and handed it to her. "Your dad and I had a convo. You can go as long as you keep this candy cane on you. If either of you try any shenanigans that might even lead to any action with this bae that would not be approved by your father, this thing will alert me, and we'll swoop so fast it'll make your head spin. Not only will I take you back to your Dad for certain punishment, but you'll have to deal with Uncle Hart, Uncle Yeager, and Uncle Jack first, no cap. Bet?"

She nodded. "Bet."

"Okay good. Scurry on over. His bedroom is in the converted attic, which is dope, by the way. We'll be back in two hours."

She scrambled out of the sleigh, rushing over to the window and knocking. A blonde head popped out. "Cherish? Why are you here? *How* are you here on my roof in the middle of the night?"

She pointed to the sleigh. "I'm tight with Santa and his peeps and if you don't believe Santa's real, that's on you."

He took a long look at us. I waved, hoping to convey that we weren't crazy, but honestly, I wasn't even sure at that point. He gave her a crooked smile that I know melted her insides. "Goals. Come on in. Nice to meet you in person."

She climbed into his window, and I was speechless. Yeager was on top of it though. "That was fun, but do you honestly think they'll behave with no supervision?"

"Yep. No doubt. I've used my canes on both and they're good kids. I figured she needed a little help believing in Santa and after what she went through with the polar bears, giving her a chance alone with her crush before Sophie R. or Sophie G. decided to get their claws in him, would be the least I could do. Sophie R. is not a nice kid, by the way. She's on the naughty list."

Yeager patted Hart on the back. "Despite the fact you try to hide it, you're a pretty nice fucking guy."

I nodded my agreement, leaning up to give Hart a quick kiss. He was beyond nice, and I loved that about him.

Ugh. Three pins weren't too many, right?

I forced myself to focus on the present instead of the ever-looming future. "Where are we going while Cherish is occupied?"

Hart clicked on the GPS and Jack's reindeer sprang to life. "Surprise number two. Yeager's going to like this one."

# CHAPTER 55

Despite the thread of nervousness running through me, I veered the sleigh to the next destination with determination. For once, I'd left my candy canes of truth at home, and I didn't know how Yeager was going to react to where we were headed. In the deep recesses of my heart, I hoped he'd understand and take it for what it was: an act of unselfish, dare I say, love.

No, I wasn't in love with him. Or Vixen either. But I damn sure knew what I felt for both of them would turn into love if we kept going as we were.

If the next thing I'd planned worked, we'd keep going.

And I was fine with that.

More than fine. I was actively trying to make it happen. For all of us.

Jack too.

When Jack and I first met I never dreamed I could open up to someone so different from me. But we'd gone through some shit—fro job notwithstanding—and I had developed a brotherhood with him like I'd never experienced before, not with other Elves or friends I'd ever had.

Yeager had pointed out we were a family, not a team. He was right. Jack was like my brother. The other two were something else. Before we could figure out what exactly our future looked like beyond the next couple of days, I had to do something about his OG family and the unfair demands placed on him.

Jack made his ice reindeer float down to the ground. Yeager had already seen where we were, and he was eerily quiet about it. It set me on edge. After everyone was out of the sleigh, his boots crunched over the snow leading to his brother's wing of their massive chalet stuck in a snowy mountain. "Why are we at Ivan's door?"

We were there—the moment of no return. Vixen curled her arm in his, sensing his trepidation, poised for my answer, so I gave it to them. "Remember when you told us exactly what you'd wish for to get of your Chosen One situation? That's what we're going to do now. Make it happen, exactly as you said."

He shook his head, the blonde bits falling right into place. "Oh, so I'm just going to walk in there and transfer some of my gifts to Ivan and my father will be magically okay when Camilla pops out his child in nine or ten months that will carry on the Yeti line? Come on, man. Don't be an asshole. This is my life, not a joke." I raked in a huge breath, letting the chill hit my lungs to erase the sting of his words. He had a point, and I could see why he was bothered, but he didn't know what I knew.

I pulled a tiny vial of glittery gold liquid from my pocket, slapping it in his hand. He cocked his head. "What is this?"

I shrugged, forcing the lump that had appeared in my throat down by swallowing a few times. "It's a Christmas miracle. One of four I obtained by winning the Sexiest Elf at the North Pole contest each year. I used the first miracle I won for my sister, making her a success, but none of you can ever tell anyone you know how that happened.

"This is my second miracle and I'm giving it to you, Redwood."

He shook his head. "I don't understand."

Vixen let out a little breath of air that I wanted to catch and hold in my hand. She was so beautiful and when she looked at me, I felt seen like I never had before. She knew. Not only the truth of what it was but the emotion behind why I was giving it to him. "Yeager, this is huge. I've only heard rumors about specific Christmas miracles before—due to the nature of them—but if he's giving this to you, you absolutely will get what you want out of it. One hundred percent. Even if it is impossible. Christmas Miracles override the laws of nature."

Jack stepped in, placing a hand on his shoulder. "If it helps, I can confirm there will be no repercussions or stipulations that go along with the miracle. I've seen this happen many times in my life. It's the truest form of gift anyone could ever give another."

My legs started to tremble, which pissed me off to no end. If he didn't want the miracle, then fine. He didn't have to take it.

I wanted him to want it though. The moment understanding sparked in his emerald eyes, I realized I wanted it more than I'd realized. He stepped away from Vixen and Jack, getting right up in my face, so close that his cedar warm scent wrapped around me. He was gripping the miracle in his hand and searching me, looking for something in my soul as he did. He said one word. "Why?"

"You know why."

I glanced over his shoulder because I couldn't look directly at him anymore. Jack had his arm slung around Vixen, who was doing her best to hide the tears that fell from her eyes. I saw her belief in them, her relief too. Her utter need for this to work out for all of us. The miracle we needed to end one chapter and turn to the next one.

It couldn't work out if he didn't accept it though.

"What do I do?" His normally boisterous voice was a haunting whisper that dug into my soul.

He was going to use it.

"Drink it while you think the exact things you want to happen. Picture transferring the tats to your brother, picture him with Camilla, picture that fucking sperm hitting the right spot at the right time. Then picture your father's face as their child is born. All of it, everything you want. It'll go down exactly as you see it."

He uncorked the vial with his thumb, looking directly at me with such a fierce, raw gaze that I started to grow hard. I knew it wasn't the time or place, but dick's gonna do what dick's gonna do. I had no control. When he downed the glittery liquid, he shoved the vial into his pocket and closed his eyes. We all stood there in silence while visions of sugar plums danced through his head.

Okay, the man had to picture his brother and a chick he didn't find sexy getting down, so probably not sugar plums.

It took more than a few moments, but he finally opened his eyes and pulled keys from his pocket, unlocking Ivan's door and strolling in like he owned the motherfucking place. I glanced at Vixen. "Damn, that was sexy."

# CHAPTER 56

Yeager strolled out of Ivan's door, and I swear he looked lighter. Relief was written all over his handsome face. He grabbed Hart by his jacket and slammed him against the door, kissing him like he'd been given a new life.

Which, he had.

We all had.

What Hart had done was bigger than the miracle swirling in that little vial. We all knew it. The air was thick with it.

Jack cleared his throat to get their attention. "One more stop, Hart."

Hart tore himself off Yeager, whispering something in his ear. To which Yeager grinned like a maniac. They both bounded over to the sleigh in the next second. Yeager slid in next to me and tugged me in his lap as Jack said, "Better hang on, Flame. The next part might get bumpy."

Hart turned around to face the three of us. "Vixen gets to choose our next destination. A, B, or C?"

"Okay, I need some details before I decide that. Where are each of those locations?"

"You don't get to know yet. Just pick a letter."

Well, that was annoying, but I was willing to play along based on the looks on each of their faces. "I pick C for Christmas."

Hart answered with a maniacal cackle and punched in something to the GPS. "Number one, Yeager, take off your shirt. I want to make sure those tatts are still there."

Oh, that was a good point. I turned to help Yeager unbutton his shirt, then practically tore it off his shoulders for him. All of his tattoos were still there. I gave each one of them an appreciation kiss as I ran my hands up and down his body while Hart and Jack watched with rapt attention. Finally, he ran his hand over Yeager's ribs, then pushed him back down on the seat. "Thank fuck you still look the same. Now, you two keep her busy back there. Don't want to spoil the next bit."

Jack was quick to wrap a protective barrier around the sleigh, locking in warmth and then he took my chin in his hand, pulling me to him and kissing me while Yeager wrapped his hand in my hair and kissed my neck.

I shifted against him. The hard ridge of his cock pressed against my ass. He groaned and Jack pulled back with heat in his steely eyes. "I dare you to make her come before we get there."

We were daring now?

Couldn't say I hated it.

Especially when Yeager started rubbing against my clit. "Lift your hips, Bunny. I want you grinding against my hand like you fucking need it."

I did. I needed it.

Jack stood and removed his jacket folded it neatly along the back of the driver seat and watched as I lifted my hips to the tune of Yeager's hand and tongue along my skin. "Fuck, yes," Hart groaned. I lifted my eyes and found him turned completely around and stripping out of his shirt. With he and Jack watching what Yeager was doing, I heated up real fast. I don't know what it was about having all their eyes on me. I couldn't imagine doing things like this in public with anyone else watching, but with them, it was arousing on levels I didn't realize existed.

They'd unlocked something in me and as I let myself get carried away with the thought of it and Yeager's skilled hand driving against me, I started to sweat.

Though maybe it wasn't entirely the touching and viewing that was raising my temperature.

I realized we'd stopped. As much as I was enjoying the feel of Yeager's hand against my jeans, I was very curious, so I looked around and tried to pinpoint our location. When Yeager realized what I was doing, he let up. "Okay, I get it. Look first, fuck second."

Jack's barrier dropped with a rush of air and I was slapped with a warm balmy feeling. Sitting up I peered over the side of the sleigh. We were about twenty feet up over a deep blue ocean with a beach directly below, and a jungle beyond that. Toucans were cawing in the distance. "Where are we?"

Hart was dropping his pants as he spoke. "C was Costa Rica. We knew how much you wanted to visit someplace tropical for your vacation but ended up at the coldest damn place on earth. The least we could do was give you an hour or so in a location you'd enjoy."

I giggled. I couldn't help it. The setting was beautiful, with white caps cresting in the moonlight and the sound of waves hitting the shore. It was everything I'd thought about when Santa had told me I was going to have a little break. It was perfect. And these men had delivered it to me on a platter of sand and waves. "This is amazing, but..." I couldn't quite figure out how to express what I was feeling. Not because it was hard, but because it was too easy.

"I love this, it truly is a gift, but if I hadn't gone to the South Pole, this wouldn't have happened." I gestured around the sleigh, touching each of them. "Thank you, but I think our thing, however it can be defined, is the bigger gift to me."

Hart pulled me to him. Yeager let go willingly but kept his hand on my back. "Remember, we left labels behind the night of the fro job. This is what it is, no definition needed."

Jack huffed. "Will you please let fro job die? I explained what happened."

Yeager nuzzled against Hart's neck, taking his hand inside my sweater, and squeezing my breasts from behind. "Uh-oh. I think Daddy's mad."

I glanced over to gauge Jack's reaction, shocked to find him ripping the buttons off his shirt as he tracked Yeager's hands and my squirming beneath them. "I'm not mad, but Daddy wants his good girl on his lap right now." He tore off his shirt, revealing his toned body, then stepped out of his pants and underwear like a professional stripper.

My soul.

Hart took the opportunity to slip my sweater over my head, exposing me to the warm air, and then he reached out and shoved Jack down. As soon as his ass hit the seat,

Yeager plopped me on Jack's lap. He took his cock in his hand and ran it over my core, making me squirm Yeager wrapped his hand in my hair, tugging to get my attention. "Better not keep Daddy waiting, Bunny."

Good point.

I lowered myself onto Jack's shaft, reveling in the frigid feel of his skin. That was all it took. From there it became a hedonistic experience. I rocked into Jack, grabbing his neck and kissing him while Hart and Yeager went at each other like they'd never been together. They groped and groaned for a minute, and I had to turn away from Jack long enough to watch. They were so hot together the freedom they enjoyed when it was just the four of us only made me want them more. Made me appreciate what each of them gave not only to each other but to me as well.

Yeager went on his knees and did what he could to make Hart's bells jingle, taking him all the way in his mouth and back out again as Hart hissed and cursed at the feel of it.

"Eyes on me, Flame."

Jack was actually smirking when I turned back to him. It made me laugh. He'd opened up in the time I'd known him, gotten bolder, and I was there for it. "Yes, Daddy."

"Good girl."

Hart grabbed my shoulder. "Oh shit, he is not good girling her without us."

Yeager popped off his cock and I had to take a second to fully appreciate the sound of that. "Nope. Not happening. No solo good-girling on my watch. Switch up. You two stand up."

Jack looked at him like he was delirious, but eventually slid out of me and helped me to my feet. "I got this," Hart declared, making sure to put some authority in his voice. I guess it was his turn to Dom, I mean orchestrate. "Over here with me, Redwood." Yeager stepped over the back seat of the sleigh and Hart turned me so that I was facing Jack. "Back at it, Jack. You know that warm pussy is aching for that popsicle."

True. True.

Hart helped me wrap my leg around Jack's waist and he spent zero time being cool and calm about anything as he thrust into me again. At the same time, the signature click of lube being opened did some serious things to ramp my temp. Yeager hummed his understanding "Oh, okay. I'm into it."

Yeager kissed me on one side of my neck as Jack kissed the other, and then he plunged inside me, and my senses swirled with the scent of peppermint lube and tropical air. The next thing I knew, the telltale jingle sounded as Hart's cock thumped against my ass, and the gooey drip of lube went into my crack. He paused to ask permission, which I gave him without hesitation. I wanted him and I'd come to learn those jingle bells were fun, no matter where they ended up.

I gripped Jack as Hart slid into me. It took my breath away to feel both at the same time, especially when they got into immediate rhythm, pumping in and out of me as I groaned loud enough to scare a couple of toucans below.

Just when I thought I was going to combust, Hart hissed behind me. "Shit, Redwood, give a guy some warning next time. You're a big boy."

Yeager laughed. "Glad you noticed. Now you're going to shut up and take my cock while we make our girl come so hard the tide reverse. Got it?"

Jack lifted his head from my neck. "You better say yes sir to that if you know what's good for you."

Hart laughed. "Never." The smack Yeager gave his ass was loud. "Fuck. Do that again." Yeager complied, and then he slid that same hand around Hart, snaking it over my stomach, then in between my legs, doing what he loved to do, which was driving me loopy with need based on two fingers alone.

I truly don't know how the rest of it went because I was in a hazy fog of lust and passion, and I was lost to us. The feel of us, the geometry of us, the honesty brewing between each thrust and throaty huff, the truth beyond the kissing, the depth of our feelings. It was all there, lying under a blanket of stars. It was too precious to even consider giving up.

# Jack

# CHAPTER 57

The warm breeze against my skin didn't faze me. True that I'd need to get back to a colder climate sooner rather than later, but I was content to lie against the seat of the sleigh with Vixen in my arms. Her legs were stretched over the back of the driver's seat where Hart and Yeager were inclined, Hart sweeping her calf with his fingers while Yeager twisted their hands together. The serenity in all of us didn't go unnoticed.

Yeager finally broke the silence. "Did we really just have a fuckfest in the air above a beach in Santa's sleigh?"

Hart laughed. "Yep, we did."

Vixen turned so she could face me. Her eyes were blazing, and I felt the warmth of them as she looked at me. "Do you still think Santa would hand over the keys?"

"Maybe not for that part." I glanced around, checking out my creations. They were starting to melt. "I hate to be the bearer of bad news, but if we don't take off soon, the reindeer aren't going to be able to pull us back and I'd hate to ask Vixen to do the job after what we just put her through."

428

She leaned up. "You say that like it's a negative thing. I enjoyed what you just put me through. But yeah, I'm spent. Let's get out of here and go pick up Cherish."

Having seen reason, we all dressed. Well, Hart made Yeager keep his shirt unbuttoned, but the rest of us got presentable and I used my magic to get the reindeer moving.

Hart declared he was taking the long way home, then he and Yeager began talking quietly in the front, so that left me in the back with Vixen. I wasn't going to squander the opportunity I'd been given. While I wanted to start my own round two with her, there was something more pressing weighing on me. Something we'd all been avoiding. It seemed like my responsibility to get it out in the open.

Whether that was my thinking, or I'd picked it up from the others, I didn't know. I just wanted to address it before the night ended.

"I'm not asking you to make any commitments at the moment, but I'd like to know where your mind is concerning this thing between us." I gestured around the sleigh. "Between all of us. We can all see how far you've come concerning Rudy and what he did to you. Your Christmas spirit is practically ringing from your pores. You've come back to yourself and I'm so pleased to have been some small part of it. At the same time, I fear in overcoming your demon, you've become a person who no longer needs us. What are you thinking right now?"

Her smile was soft, and it melted a piece of my heart that I would never dare to freeze. She had changed me. They all had and for once in my long life, I was okay with myself. It was a gift I never thought I'd ever receive. She took my hand. "My mind is a jumbled mess, if I'm honest."

"You've had a whirlwind twelve days."

There it was. Midnight had come and gone, and we were riding into our final day at the Holidays Inn, our last hours together. The finality of it was hard to digest.

"I have. Thank you, all of you. I feel like myself again and it seems like it's been twelve months, not twelve days. That makes no sense, but that's what it feels like to me. I know each of you and care deeply about each of you. And I respect you enough to give you nothing but honesty now, so I'll say I am looking forward to seeing Santa and joining the fleet tonight. Beyond that, I don't know."

"Fair enough. Thanks for your candor. I may be speaking out of turn, but none of us has been in this type of situation before and for what it's worth, we're here because of you. We are three men used to getting what we want who are willingly sharing our time—our hearts—with you and each other because you're worth it. No matter what happens beyond today, I share a bond with all of you that won't be severed by time or distance.

"For what it's worth, my kingdom travels with me, so my location in this plane of existence is irrelevant. Furthermore, there's plenty of space in my palace if you need it once you sell your condo to Rudy."

She raised, swinging her legs over my lap so that she was straddling me. Her voice came out as a screech "Did you just ask me to move in with you?"

"Whoa, whoa, whoa there Daddy." Hart twisted in his seat. "What's that again? You don't get to cockblock us. We have rules."

I looked over Vixen's shoulder. "This has nothing to do with our cocks and I remember asking for rules and being denied them. I'm just offering her a place to live after she sells her condo. You two can come as well if you want. My palace is gigantic."

Yeager snickered. "Are you sure we're not talking about cocks?"

I huffed. "Forget it. You two aren't allowed anymore. You're banished." They both laughed because they knew I wasn't serious in the least.

Vixen, however, was chewing on her lower lip. "Jack, you're amazing and you've given me a lot to think about."

"I hope not too much. The last thing I intended was to make your mind more jumbled."

She leaned down and kissed me, her lips soft and warm against my cold skin. There was a lot in that kiss, and I knew she wasn't denying me or saying no to my suggestion. She was making sure before she made it.

Rudy may have made her more hesitant, but that wasn't necessarily a terrible thing. We had only known each other for a short while. If she needed more time, I would give her every clock in existence, as long as at the end of it, she was there with me.

# CHAPTER 58

We managed to tumble into bed after picking up Cherish, who was in lurve—that's how she said it. Well, Jack didn't tumble into bed, he laid on top of the covers in his underwear while I snuggled into Hart who snuggled into Yeager under the covers. All three of them had their hands somewhere on my body and I decided I would never sleep as well as I had that night.

We slept past breakfast, but I bolted up like a child on Christmas morning to go play the last game, which wasn't so much a game as it was a parting gift.

There was some groaning, but after I forced Hart and Jack to clean up at their places and Yeager to go after me in our cabin so that there would be no shower shenanigans, we didn't have time for, everyone was dressed and ready to go.

When I say dressed and ready, I mean it. Jack swooshed back in from his kingdom wearing his normal crisp white shirt and black pants, but instead of a jacket, he wore a green and black plaid vest with a freaking pocket watch. Hart popped in right after him having put on his faded ripped jeans and light blue V-neck cashmere sweater that I couldn't wait to feel. He took one look at Jack and said, "Daddy's got drip." I'd learned that was a good thing.

Not to be outdone, Yeager pulled a pair of black leather pants from his bag and topped them with a black and blue plaid shirt, leaving several buttons open enough that his chest tattoos were peeking out.

They all looked edible.

What I wore didn't much matter since I'd be removing my clothes to shift, but I went ahead and pulled out my favorite hot pink sweater and dark jeans. I felt like my old self. No, I was a better version of myself. Vixen two-point-oh and I was ready for the last game.

Yeager escorted Holly to the comfy chair by the fireplace. She was wearing her most subdued yet telling outfit ever: red jeans with a gray t-shirt that read 'Christmas is' in red scrolling script font.

A lump formed in my throat.

It was perfect and she didn't even know why.

"Well, I must say, I'm anxious to hear what you all have come up with for today's game."

Yeager squeezed her shoulder, and I began, considering how everyone had deemed me the spokesperson. "Holly, our last game is simple—it's what Christmas is about. Each team was tasked with finding the perfect gift for you as you embark on the next part of your life."

She gripped the armrests. "Oh my. How kind of you, but I fail to see how this is a game."

"We'll give you our gifts, and then each team will vote for who came up with the best one." What I didn't tell her was that we already worked out that each team would get one candy cane from another team, making us all tied for the win this time. I knew Santa, therefore Holly, would be a stickler for the rules and make us vote, so we worked it out ahead of time.

"Hot Chocolate with Marshmallows, you guys are up first."

Cherish ran over to the Christmas tree got the bag they'd wrapped their present in and gave it to Holly, who pulled it out and gasped. "Oh, my word, I can't believe this." Cherish helped her unfold the quilt Erin had sewn using a bunch of Cornelius' t-shirts.

Tears started to flow as Holly lovingly ran her hand over the quilt. "Dad and boy Aaron picked which shirts and cut them, girl Erin sewed them together and I made the knots in the fringe. We thought you could take some of his shirts with you and not have to worry about storing them where you'd never see them or throwing them out. I hope you like it."

Holly hugged Cherish, who had the biggest smile on her face. "I love it. It's so thoughtful. Thank you all."

Yeager swallowed over and over. He was already having a tough time keeping it together. Hart went over and rubbed his back as I called the vampires up to give their gift.

Dracula carefully picked up a wrapped box that had holes all over it. They'd been secretive about their gift and part of me was an eensy bit worried about what was inside. Letstat bowed to Holly like she was royalty. "We would understand if you'd rather not have this sort of present, but as we thought about you leaving this place, it felt, to us, like leaving your homeland. As vampires, we carry Transylvanian soil with us everywhere we go, but your soil is buried under snow right now, so we took the next logical step and got you a living breathing reminder of your life here at the South Pole."

As Holly tore the paper and opened the top of the cardboard box, Cherish got on her knees to see what was inside and squealed in delight. "Vampires are the CEOs of gift giving."

Yeager leaned in over her and laughed. "Hey Bunny, it's a bunny."

Holly reached inside and pulled out a beautiful white snowshoe hare. I'd seen several hopping around, thanks to Santa, and this one was already sniffing Holly as she snuggled him to her chest. "It's adorable. How sweet of you to provide me with my first friend away from home. Is it a boy or girl and what should I call it?"

Spike scratched between the hare's ears. "It's a male. We thought he should be named Cornelius. Last night we called him Corny."

Holly held him up in front of her face so she could look into his eyes. "Hello Corny, nice to meet you. How about you and I going on a grand adventure together?" Corny's ears twitched at the sound of it and everyone—and I mean everyone including John Sun—cooed and aww'd.

I took a breath. We were up next.

And with everything I had, I wanted Holly to love and appreciate our gift. When we'd devised it, Hart had been vague about how his part was going to work, but now that I knew what he did for Yeager, I had a feeling he'd used another Christmas miracle. He popped over to the tree, swiped the gift he'd wrapped in white glossy paper and a big red bow, and popped back and handed it to her with a kiss on the cheek. She immediately blushed.

Yeah, there were no more labels, but that didn't mean he'd lost his sex appeal.

She unwrapped the box and pulled out the gift, her eyes welling with tears before we could explain it to her. I found myself tongue-tied and unable to speak due to the intense emotion swirling in my heart. I hadn't seen the finished product before that moment. And eyeing it like Holly was, I was just overwhelmed with feelings for these men.

Sensing my troubles, Jack stepped in for me. "I made the ice sculpture from the wedding photo Yeager showed me. It's enclosed with magic, like your own personal snow globe, it will never melt, no matter the climate. You can take it anywhere you want as a reminder of your love."

Yeager bent on his knees so he could be eye-to-eye with her. "I made the base from a branch in the tree outside your cabin window. I know Cornelius loved to sit and have his coffee looking out at that tree. Maybe it'll help to remember him when you look at it."

I could not keep my tears inside.

Hart bent down on the other side of the chair. "See that button on the base? Push it."

I bit my lip as a loud raspy voice floated from the sculpture. "*How's Holly? Well, she's the love of my life and makes me a better man every day. I couldn't ask for more, now could I? She's perfect.*" Merry Christmas Darling by the Carpenters started and as soon as it did, the sculpture of the two of them spun as if they were dancing.

Holly tore her eyes off the sculpture long enough to ask Hart, "How did you do this?"

He patted her knee. "When kids visit Santa and tell him what they want for Christmas, the candy canes serve as recorders. The wishes are transmitted back to the North Pole and stored there for the toy makers to use as they prep for Christmas.

"I never met Cornelius myself, I remembered Santa talking fondly of you two and my mind just went back to several years ago when I was working an event and Santa was on a break talking to this huge red-haired guy who laughed when he spoke like he was so full of joy. I'd later asked Santa if it was his brother. He responded by saying not biologically, but he was a close friend who ran the Holidays Inn cabins with his wife.

"All I did was go back through the candy cane records until I found this. The kid had wished for a Barbie doll and a GTA game, but Cornelius' voice was loud and clear on the recording. I just copied it and put it in a drive in the base. It's a bit magical, so it'll never stop working."

I sucked in a breath. He'd done more than just search an old recording, but as Holly watched the two of them dancing to a song with the perfect lyrics, I knew if he'd used a miracle, he'd never regret it in a million years. It was beautiful. And I suddenly felt awful for not having created any part of the remarkable gift.

Jack snuck in behind me. Whispering as he pulled me to his chest. "Why do you look so sad?"

"I didn't do anything to help with the gift. I should've contributed something."

"Oh Flame, you may not have made anything with your hands, but your heart is solely responsible for every bit of this gift. Do you think any of us would've created such a meaningful present if we'd never met you? I'd probably given her a random snowflake, while Yeager might have whittled an ornament and Hart probably would've shoved a bunch of candy canes at her. But you? You made us feel, and you made us appreciate the value of what Holly shared with Cornelius. You are every bit of this gift and more."

I turned to hug him and when he let me go, the song was ending, and Holly was a sobbing bucket of tears. "Thank you so much. I've never seen such treasure. I love it."

It took a few minutes for all of us to compose ourselves. Finally, it was time for team Ho, Ho, Ho, Hot to present their gift. I nodded at John. He stood and handed Holly a pair of rainbow-tinted, cat-eyed sunglasses. "We'd like to invite you to the Summer Fae Court. The weather is always warm, and the beaches are plentiful." He side-eyed Jack and I had to laugh when both Yeager and Hart took a step in his direction. It was a warning that nobody but us picked up. "My kingdom now is a fixed point and there will be nothing but sunny days ahead. You're free to live as long as you want anywhere on my land. If you don't find a home suitable for your taste, I'll construct a new one."

"John, how generous of you. I have to admit, I've always wanted to visit the Fae realm. What better place to start my new journey? What do you say Corny?" She looked down at the hare in her lap and he responded by wiggling his pink nose. "That seems like a yes!"

Everyone cheered like we'd all won something. And I guess we had. Jack looked down at Holly. "I'm sure you'll be happy in the Summer court, but if you ever get lonely for snow, feel free to visit the Winter court anytime you like."

"That would make me so happy, Jack. Thank you. As soon as I'm settled in the Summer Court, I'll take you up on it, I'm sure."

# CHAPTER 59

Everyone had allowed us some space, clearing out of the lodge as soon as we'd finished dinner and drinks. They all knew Santa would be coming soon. As a result, I was jumpy and pacing between the couch and coffee table, chewing my lip and thinking.

Really thinking. About the run I'd soon be making and what happened beyond it.

Yeager reached up and pulled me into his lap. "Are you nervous about seeing Rustin again?" He threaded his fingers through my hair and did that thing he always did by massaging my scalp and sending shivers through me.

"Who?"

"Ryan, Rayden, Ratatouille? The asshole who cheated on you."

He hadn't even entered my mind in over twenty-four hours. He'd just vanished from my brain like he was nothing.

He *was* nothing.

At least he was at that point.

Oh, Rudy? Nah." I put on my best Cherish. "I literally don't even care-uh."

Hart snorted, yanking me off Yeager's lap and into his. And yes, he lifted his hips and yes, we heard the jingle bells. "Including all the dirty things you've ever said to us, this is the best thing you've ever uttered."

"It is," Jack agreed as the door to the lodge opened. Santa walked in with a blast of chilly air behind him.

"Ho, ho, ho, Merry Christmas! Vixen it's great to see you again." He eyed my collar that I'd put on. It didn't feel the same around my neck now. I'd chalked it up to not wearing it for twelve days, but I couldn't even lie to myself about that. I'd changed and my feelings had changed along with me. I don't know what was beyond this night, but I was excited to get back into action, as long as Santa allowed it.

"Hey, Santa. Merry Christmas Eve. How are you?"

"I'm dandy." He looked around the lodge and spotted our stockings lying empty next to the fireplace. "Well, I came early thinking I was going to tally the votes in the game, but it appears someone beat me to it. Tell me, who won? Was it the vampires?"

Hart finally let me up from his lap. He went over to shake Santa's hand. "They did have the best odds in the gambling pool I was running, but I'm going to have to take a loss on the payouts. We don't know who won and never will."

Santa cocked his head. Yeager pointed to the big pile of candy canes on the desk behind us. "Yeah, we decided that we all won, so we dumped the candy canes out without counting them. Feel free to take some when you head out."

"That's an unexpected event. One I can get behind. Who knew?"

Jack cocked his eyebrow. "You did, of course. You had the whole thing rigged to come out this way. Not only that, the visitors at the lodge, weren't random guests that just happened to appear at the same time as we did, were they?"

Santa unbuttoned his coat and went over to sit by the fireplace. "You've got me, Jack. You were always a smart cookie. Yes, the people at the lodge weren't random. Each one needed something. Something they got from you, and you got things from them. I couldn't and wouldn't have predicted how it turned out, but in the end, I'm comfortable saying it went well."

It was true, even if it had been orchestrated. Yeager had cured Aaron, Cherish had gotten closer to her dad with our help when we saved her. Mandy had broken away from her trio of mindless nymphs and found real potential love in Isaac. Even the vampires had gotten practice in on their bobsled track Jack had made them.

Then there was us.

Santa continued, "I do hate that Holly needs to give this up, she was a great caretaker and always ready to help me help others, but I understand her need to move on. We'll find someone else to help my little side project move along. She told me what you all had done for her and I'm so pleased. Which is why I want to discuss something with you, in particular Hart."

Yeager angled toward Hart, a protective move. Hart shook his head. He didn't need protection from Santa. "What's up?"

Santa took a deep breath. For the first time I'd known him he looked unsure of himself. It made me nervous. "Holly isn't the only one retiring."

I froze. We all did. Santa just couldn't decide not to be Santa. The world would be in chaos.

"What?" I don't even know which one of them said it.

"Yes, it's true. The Mrs. and I are tired. It's been a great run, but I'm comfortable with my decision. Beyond that, I'm certain I've chosen my replacement well. This affects all of you, which is why I'm allowing you to see something only a handful of people who ever existed know. This requires trust. Do I have yours, and you mine?"

"Yes." That, we all said in unison.

Santa leaned back and removed his hat. In the moments that followed, his body morphed, changing from the jolly ole Elf we knew and loved into a somewhat hot silver fox with a shorter beard and deep brown eyes with crinkles in the corner. So, Santa, only sexier.

Nope. I cannot think Santa is sexy.

My eyes. My eyes.

"Fuck me," Yeager whispered as Jack's eyebrow went up.

Not only was Santa an attractive older man, but he was one we knew. Hart shook his head. "Wait, you're Craft Winkleman. You work in Accounting. You sign my damn paychecks. And you're telling me you're Santa."

Santa winked at Hart. I mean Craft Winkleman winked. "I realize this is shocking, but it's the best way to explain. Yes, I work in Accounting most of the time, however, I'm but one of many Santas. There are eleven others including the OG Kris Kringleman. We rotate duties and when we use the magic hats, no one is the wiser. It makes the job doable and so much more fun, but I've been doing this for centuries and it's time for a change."

I was flabbergasted. "Kris Kringleman has been doing this longer though, right?"

"True, he has. Only he's more of a figurehead and source than anything. He does one event per year and the occasional Christmas Eve run when he wants, but the rest of us have taken up the mantle for the other responsibilities that go along with the job.

"I specifically asked to be the Santa who makes this run tonight because I've chosen who I want to be my replacement. I want you to come ride along with me tonight, Hart."

Yeager let out a laugh that rivaled Santa as Hart scrubbed his hand over his jaw. "Me?"

"Yes, you. You act like a badass and do lots of things that would land you on the naughty list permanently, if not for your big heart. A fitting name for you if you ask me."

We all agreed by nodding. It's not like we could speak. We were all stunned into silence.

"If you shadow me tonight and decide you want to go ahead as Santa, you'll spend the next month or two figuring out the job, then you can go back to making candy canes or..." he glanced around the room, eyeing all of us one at a time. "...maybe you'll find some other ways to spend your non-Santa time. But the thing is, no one can ever know who you are when you put on the Santa hat. You'll essentially be invisible. Not everyone can give up their identity for the job."

Hart stood up and started pacing, his mind spinning. "Nobody would know me? I'd just be the guy giving out presents and making people happy?"

"Exactly."

I knew what Hart's answer would be before he said it. We all did. It was the perfect thing for him. No labels, no sexy man who must be sexy on command, no demands, just him doing what he was good at—using his resources to make people happy. I couldn't have thought of a better thing if I'd tried.

And the best part was that Santa had included all of us in it. He obviously knew about our nontraditional relationship and didn't care. He wanted us all to know what we were getting with Hart.

He would say yes. No doubt in my mind.

"Okay, big guy, let's do this. I'm in."

I glanced at Yeager, who I knew was holding in a silent, 'Oh my stars, I'm fucking Santa' in his head. Honestly, I was thinking the same thing.

# CHAPTER 60

S anta turned his attention to me. "With that out of the way, how are you feeling about our run tonight, Vixen?" Now that Hart was coming along, I was pretty ecstatic. But I knew Santa's question had a deeper meaning.

"I'll be ready to go soon, but first, I need to have a conversation with Rudy." Santa nodded and put his hat back on. The silver fox disappeared in favor of the jelly belly and flushed cheek man I'd grown to love and respect. His revelation would take some getting used to, but it had also made me insanely happy to know Hart would be taking over. I couldn't wait to watch him put on that hat.

Santa went out to ask Rudy to shift and I took a second to talk to my guys.

Mine.

All three.

"I have to do this. I'm ready to do this. The last time, at the condo, I wasn't fully prepared to face him. I was too emotional. Now, I'm as steady as I have ever been. He's behind me." I bit my lip, knowing what I was about to say was big. "The three of you are in front of me."

Hart and Yeager simultaneously fell back on the couch and Jack pulled one of the wooden chairs close to the door, straddling it with his manspread and folding his arms over the back of it. "We'll be here when you're done."

I grabbed my coat and went outside. The fleet was all there, Mariah had come into my place as a sub, I noticed. Thank my soul, it hadn't been Clare there. I took a second to rub Prancer's nose before I went over to the sleigh.

Rudy was sitting in the seat, wearing joggers that Santa must have given him. He eyed me with interest. "Where are your bodyguards?"

"They're inside waiting for me. I wanted to talk to you alone."

He hopped out of the sleigh, and I brought him around to the place where we'd put our Christmas trees. He eyed the plaid bows on ours but said nothing. "I want you to understand I'm no longer mad at you. What you did was wrong, and I hope like everything that you won't do it to Clare." He snorted and I kept talking so he couldn't interrupt me. "I'm not getting back with you or doing some kind of joint relationship with you and Clare. It's over. We're over completely. You need to act accordingly and so will I."

"You're going to regret leaving me," he sneered.

"I won't because you left me first. And I'm willing to admit my complicity in it. I should've told you I was uncomfortable with some of the things in our relationship. I should've asked when I suspected things had gone wrong. Instead, I kept my head down and tried to squeak out what I thought a relationship should look like.

"I need you to understand this: we did things together, but we were never together. Not really. You see, now I know what it feels like to be treasured, to be respected and part of a real relationship and I will not settle for anything less. I hope the same for you and Clare. I truly do."

"I doubt that."

"You're free to think what you want. I just wanted you to know. I'm going to go shift now so we can get on the way."

He shook his head, brushing past me and bumping my shoulder. "Have fun looking at my asshole all night."

I sighed. He wasn't going to change. But that was on him.

I veered back into the lodge to get Hart. As soon as I hit the side door, Jack was on his feet. Seconds later Hart had popped up and grabbed me from behind and popped me back down between him and Yeager. Jack came over to the coffee table.

It was so real to see them like this. I'd taken a lot for granted in the past twelve days and I wouldn't do that any longer. Yeager threw his arm around the back of the couch. "How did it go, Bunny?"

"It went well. He's still a jerk but I can't control him. What I *can* control is how I think about him, which is in the past tense. It may sound strange, but as much as I adored him at first, then as much as I hated him later, when I looked at him now, there was nothing there. Not even a hole in my heart where he used to be." I shrugged. "I think that's because of you."

Jack took my hand. "We might have nudged you, but what you feel now is all you, Flame. Don't take that away from yourself."

"Right," Hart agreed. "How about we never talk about him again? He's a ghost."

Jack turned around and picked up our stocking. "Maybe RAR can stand for rest and relaxation now."

Hart took it from him. "Or rock and roll."

Yeager took it next, glancing at Hart with a smirk. "Or rings and redwood."

I groaned. "Hart and I have to go now. We'll see you two when we get back?" I'd phrased it like a question, but it wasn't. Not really. I'd see them later.

A lot of laters.

As Hart prepared to pop me away, I swear I heard Yeager say something about a fro job.

~~~~~~~~~~~~~~~~~~~~~~~~~~~~~~~~~

My hooves hit the snow several hours later. Thanks to Santa's magic, we'd flown the equivalent of several days, but made it back by dawn. It had been great to stretch my reindeer legs and feel the wind in my fur, but I couldn't help my mind wandering as I soared above the clouds.

Hart and Santa had a quick conversation. Details about his transition, no doubt. He patted me on the ass as he walked by on his way to our cabin. "See you inside, Ginger."

Santa came over to unhook me. I took my time before I stepped out of line, nodding to Cupid, who knew I'd be filling her in on everything as soon as I had time. Finally, Santa escorted me inside the lodge where I shifted and threw my clothes back on quickly as he stared at the fire. The second I was done, I walked over to join him. He looked up with that characteristic twinkle. "You're retiring too, aren't you?"
~~~~~~~~~~~~~~~~~~~~~~~~~~~~~~~~~

I held out my Vixen collar. "Yes. Tonight was great. Every moment I've worked for you—for you all—was great. I wouldn't change a second of it, but—"

"But, what? This isn't about Rudy is it?"

"Not at all. He's of no consequence to me. I just realized that my time on the fleet is done. I feel like I'll still be a small part of the team because of my connection to Hart, but I have an idea that I can't shake. I've had it for a couple of days now and before you fully retire, I'd like your blessing."

I took my collar from me and listened to what was in my heart, mind, and soul. I told him everything I was thinking and feeling based on his contest and the results of all the connections I'd made through it. When I was finished, he pulled me in for a hug and said, "That's the most beautiful idea. You should make it happen."

I strolled into the cabin, a spring in my step. Hart and Yeager were lying on the bed, facing each other and Jack was perched on the chair beside them. Hart was telling them all about his night and they hadn't even heard me come in.

Just looking at them, I felt so lucky. So full of emotion.

I didn't think Santa, rather Craft Winkleman who'd been the one to design the games I'd learned, intended to put the four of us together romantically, but it had happened, and I was fully invested in it.

No more questions, no more doubts, no more shadowy reindeer figures in my mind. These three incredible men were devoted to me in a way I'd never experienced before. I was going to treasure it, and them for as long as I could. The future was right there in front of me, and I was going to embrace it.

I cleared my throat and they all looked up, smiling at the sight of me. Warmth crept over my whole body. "So, how do you feel about running Holidays Inn together?"

*** THE REST PROBABLY WENT DOWN IN HISTORY ***

Keep reading for the epilogue.

# EPILOGUE

One year later.

Jack grunted, kicking pool water at me. His aim sucked. "Why did I let you talk me into this? I'm literally dying, and you don't even care-uh."

Yes, the Cherish impressions were still in full force. We'd kept in touch with her via NickTock, Isaac, and Mandy called a lot too. Aaron and Erin sent regular postcards, enough for Vixen to wallpaper the fridge of the huge cabin I'd built on the edge of our Inn property. The only ones we weren't completely sure of were the vamps, but wherever they were, we knew they were making folks scratch their heads in confusion.

I swiped an ice bucket from a passing waiter, giving him a nod and waiting for him to leave before I dumped it on Jack's crotch. "You agreed to the tropical vacations for

Vixen every year, one for each letter of the alphabet. We're on Aruba, Ice Man. Long way to Zanzibar."

"I know. I love the idea of this, it's the execution I'm having difficulty with. Where are they anyway? Shouldn't they be here by now?"

He was losing his cool, literally and figuratively.

Vixen had insisted on seeing Hart off for his first run as *the* real Santa. I'd wanted to come to, but I got nixed in favor of setting up our island destination. It was fine with me anyway. Unlike Vixen, I didn't fancy seeing a bloated version of Hart walking around ho ho hoing everywhere. I preferred him in his natural state. "They'll be here soon. Just cool your jets."

"Easy for you to say."

We were both waiting for that pop to arrive, so I called the waiter back over and asked for two more ice-cold beers while we waited. No sooner than I'd taken my first sip when I spied them walking out of the cabana we'd rented.

They still ripped the breath from my lungs. Both of them.

She was wearing a black bikini with a hot pink see-through skirt draped around her hips and he wore black swim trunks. As the two of them approached, all eyes were on them. They looked like the perfect couple on a honey-moon. His hand was on her back, gently guiding her and she looked at him with a huge smile.

Fuck me. I was one lucky son of a bitch.

A woman behind us gasped at the sight of him, or maybe them. I had to laugh. If she had any idea what was going to be happening to Santa and Mrs. Claus in the cabana later, she would probably clutch her pearls.

Jack stood up. The ice had melted into his blue trunks, making it look like he'd peed on himself. He didn't care. He was careful not to greet Vixen in a way that would be scandalous, but knowing him like I did, his eyes were full of need for our girl. I took the moment to glance at Hart and wink. He could read my winks now too. He chuckled and wiggled his eyebrows. That was a yes for later. I handed him my beer. "I was expecting you to pop in."

"We did, just not out in public where everyone could see." Made sense, but I still loved that pop.

"So, did you have a good night in the seat solo for the first time, Jingle Bell?"

He plunked on the lounger next to me. "It was lit. One of the best nights of my life." As Vixen slid into the chair beside Jack, he cocked an eyebrow at Hart. He scowled, "I said' *one of.*' Don't get offended. You know I'll never forget our first Winter solstice."

Yeah, that joke was still happening too. How could we not rib him forever over it? I turned to Hart to high-five him and was stunned into motionless silence as he held up his hand. I grabbed his arm, tracing my finger over his bicep. I didn't give two shits who saw me. "You got new ink."

He nodded and flexed his bicep and I swear Vixen moaned.

Could've been me.

"Merry Christmas," he said through a devious smirk. Yes, he knew I dug his minimal ink. As much as he loved my heavy ink.

I read it in my head first, then again aloud. "When one shouts about their dominance in favor of demonstrating it, one doesn't have it."

Jack leaned in to get a better look at the scrolled words decorating Hart's arm. His face went through every emotion there was in seconds. "I said that."

Hart took a swig. "Yeah, I have quotes from all my family in ink."

We were all familiar—intimately— with the song lyrics on his thigh and the quotes from his parents on his rib and back, but this new thing had Jack dumbstruck. Seriously in awe. We called ourselves a family all the time and had from the very start, but seeing it written plainly on Hart's body in a permanent fashion, seemed to get to Jack. "That's never going to come off."

"Yes, I'm aware of the permanence of tattoos."

Jack was still speechless when Hart angled toward me in his lounger. "Want to see the one I got for you? I won't show you unless you promise to let me orchestrate later."

"Bet."

He tugged the waist of his trunks down revealing that cut V I loved to lick on occasion. There over his hip was an artistic outline of a Redwood tree. I gasped at the beauty of it, the placement. Still giving no shits at all, I pulled him closer so I could really look at it and my mouth dried. 'Brutal love' was written on the trunk of the tree.

I couldn't breathe. Or speak.

Vixen leaned over, kissing Hart right there in front of me. I had to fight the urge to join in with them because I was too stunned to function properly. "I think he likes it," she whispered.

Finally, I regained the use of my tongue. "We need to go. Back to the cabana. This second. We can lie in the fucking sun tomorrow."

Hart chuckled then pulled Vixen up from her chair. "I'm going to agree with that idea."

"My soul, yes. Air conditioning."

I grabbed Jack's arm. "This is definitely not about air conditioning."

"I'm fully aware of what this is about, I was just stating my agreement." He picked up his towel and started walking toward our cabana, but he paused and turned back to Hart. "What about Vixen? Are you waiting for a more private place to show us that one?"

Hart laughed. "I have a plan for her. I want to get her name tattooed right here." He slapped his chest, right at his heart. I loved that idea. "The problem is that I've been asking for months, and she still won't tell me her real given name. And I tried to make her with my Santa mojo, saying she was Vixen no longer, but she wouldn't give it up. Help me out here guys."

It never occurred to me that we weren't calling her by her real name. We'd lived with her, worked beside her at the Inn—she was the center of our family—and none of us knew her real name. "You could always get Ginger there," I offered. He'd called her that mostly anyway. Just like I called her Bunny and Jack called her Flame, but still, now I had a mystery to figure out.

She was the first to get to the cabana, so I picked her up and carried her over the threshold. "Why aren't you telling us?"

"Because it's embarrassing, and I don't feel like that's who I am anymore. I like it when you call me Vixen or your other nicknames for me. Let's just leave it at that."

I put her on the bed and waited for the other two to get inside. I looked over at Jack. "She's not going to tell us."

And because Jack was smart and had learned a lot from me and Hart, he strolled over to the bed, leaning down close to her. "I guess that means Daddy's going to have to punish her."


Five years later...

Go to my site to read the rest of their story, from the other POV, including what happened to the vampires and Vixen's real name! Just scan the QR code below. The button is on the front page or click on the EXTRAS section!

# A QUICK WORD ON REVIEWS

I hope you enjoyed Fixin' Vixen.

As an indie author, I depend on ratings & reviews to support me and my books. Please take a moment to leave a review for Fixin' Vixen on Amazon my scanning the QR code below. I welcome any and all reviews & ratings from my readers. I believe there are readers for every book & books for every reader. Reviews help other readers like you determine which books might be for them.

I'd be thrilled if you shared any positive thoughts on social media and post your review on Goodreads or other book review sites, as well.

Thanks so much!

~ Cat

# ACKNOWLEDGEMENTS & A NOTE FROM THE AUTHOR

Thanks, first & most of all, to my ARC team who agreed to get into the Christmas spirit early. I appreciate you more than I can express. Without you, this story would just be a weird idea in my head, so THANK YOU for helping me to get it out in the world by reading.

Special shout out to my parents for encouraging me to watch all those Christmas specials each year. Look at what they turned into! (Okay, so maybe don't do that.)

To my readers, I hope I have not ruined all your Christmases and given you an inability to watch that cute little Claymation movies from the sixties. Thank you for reading this book & any of my others. If you enjoyed the humor and spice, check out my Diminishing Magic series!

Mandy O'Dell, I know I dedicated this book to you, but it bears repeating, you are a big part of all of my books. Thanks for stepping outside of your comfort zone for me on this one. You're the CEO of friendship.

To whomever suggested reading "Tangled in Tinsel" on TikTok, special gratitude! I'd been toying with the idea of stand-alone *Why Choose* romance, but until I read that one, I wasn't sure it was possible to get it all (and by it, you know what I mean) in one book. But, I did, and I did. And here we are.

To my family and friends, love, love, love! Thanks for putting up with me when I go on writing binges, which is pretty much all the dang time.

# JEWELS OF CLAY TEASER

If you enjoyed FIXIN' VIXEN, check out my Paranormal Romance stories in the DIMINISHING MAGIC series. The first three books are available on Amazon. Book 1, JEWELS OF CLAY, features an unconventional supernatural creature, a gnome, who gets caught up with a pack of werewolves. Here's the first chapter.

---

I couldn't believe I'd done it: cash-apped a sketchy leprechaun two-hundred bucks for intel on the location of the closest fairy ring. In my defense, I was running out of time and catching fae wasn't illegal by definition; just frowned upon by most Magicals. Good thing I was *half* magical.

I laid my oversized purse onto the kitchen counter, careful not to jostle the contents inside the small carved trunk or scatter the cooking utensils I'd laid out in preparation for this. The food was in the fridge, the recipes picked. I'd even grown and picked the vegetables with my Earth magic that morning and pre-rinsed them for good measure. Rinsing veggies was easy. It was the fairy's job to do the hard stuff.

Taking a deep breath, I removed the box, eager to see if giving up the last of my savings account for the ride-share it took to get to the ring and back was worth it. I didn't have a choice. Not if I wanted a roof over my head. Throw in months of bank notices, unopened letters from bill collectors, and stacks of Gram's unpaid medical bills, and my situation added up to be one big pile of suck.

Nabbing a fairy was the only way I could see out of it.

The lid creaked as the fairy burst out, cerulean wings fluttering as he sailed around the kitchen. He was easy to track because he wore what had to be Polly Pocket clothes from the eighties—bright pink shorts and a neon yellow and green tank. He whizzed by, almost colliding into the antique rack full of banged-up pots and pans before passing behind Gram's lace curtains that were now more cream-colored than white.

He finally flapped toward me and hovered a few inches from my face, coughing in the most exaggerated way as his shaggy mess of blonde hair flopped. "What in the name of the Mage did you let die in that bag? It smells like pig's feet and donkey ass!"

I stuck my nose inside the purse, picking up the scent of leather and breath mints. "No, it doesn't."

He pointed toward his nose. "Trust me. You'll appreciate my overdeveloped sense of smell after you taste what I make for you. That's what you said when you ripped me from my home: I'm here to cook. Right?" His voice was pleading and hopeful, and a nugget of guilt lodged in my gut. I quickly assured myself that Magicals had probably captured fae for much worse things than cooking. "Yes, I need this meal to be perfect." Mage knew I wasn't going to chance this very important meal on my culinary skills, or lack thereof. I could barely make toast.

"Well, you nabbed the right fairy, Babycakes." I raised an eyebrow at the nickname, but it didn't slow him down a bit. "In Aetheria I was known for my skill with the culinary arts. Have you tried roasted strix? I know it's hard for some to stomach eating something that eats human flesh, but once you get past that, they're delicious. Though, I guess I'd have to pop over to the Mediterranean to get some. I could be back in a day, maybe two. Where are we, anyway? I was in that trunk for a few hours. Are we still in Oregon?"

"We're in Eugene. My deceased Gram's house. In a retirement village." I checked my phone, nervous titters swirling through me. Six hours and counting. No time for strix hunting. "I need you to understand: an entire species of Magicals is at stake here."

Not to mention my accommodations, living expenses, food on my table. Or, again, lack thereof. I couldn't survive on tomatoes and carrots I'd grown in my garden. Vegan was more of a dirty word than way of life for me. And I'd had enough ramen noodles for two lifetimes already.

I kept mum about how I was about to be kicked out of my home and had no real job outside of a seasonal gig at the garden center and part-time meal delivery service driver, where I'd skimmed a few fries off the top every now and then. He didn't need to know how desperate I was.

"A whole species? Sounds ominous." He dropped to a lounging position on the counter, crossing his legs and throwing his muscled arms behind his head. "As the humans say, spill the coffee."

Already, he was getting under my skin, and he'd been there less than five minutes.

I shook my head. "Spill the *tea*, not coffee."

"What-the-fuck-ever. I try to steer clear of humans as much as possible."

Same. Which was weird considering I was half human. But truth be told, I stayed away from just about everyone, human or magical. If I'd had a middle name, it would've been hermit. That was mostly due to circumstance. It was hard to form relationships, friend or otherwise, when you spent all your time caring for an ill, unstable person. Once my Gram died, I didn't even know where to start to look for people to socialize with outside of work, so I didn't.

I took a deep breath. It seemed like a point of no return moment, but I needed the fairy to fall in line. "We're petitioning to join the Conclave."

I'd sold Gram's car to Liam for information on the leader and how the petition process worked. Which meant I was no longer going to make food deliveries. Another gamble that could've left me homeless if it didn't play out as I'd planned.

Even at his small size, the fairy's deep throaty laugh filled the entire kitchen. "I'm impressed you got anything on the Conclave, but they haven't let a species join in hundreds of years. The last one was gargoyles. That ended *so* well for them."

Thanks for the reminder about how high the odds were stacked against me.

I grabbed a dish towel and threw it at him, which he dodged like a professional...dodger.

*Douchehead.*

"We've got more to offer than gargoyles and we wouldn't let being in the Conclave go to our heads like they did." I sounded lame, even to myself. I was more worried about my personal stake in this than getting my species in the Conclave. They'd managed millennia without the protection and privileges the Conclave offered. Me? I had another week or two, tops before I was out on my ass.

Helping gnomes into the Conclave was the only way to get to Aetheria, the birthplace of magic—my true purpose for all of this nonsense. In Aetheria, there would be no hiding from humans, no taxes or monetary system to worry about, and oceans of ambient magic, free for the taking. It sounded like the perfect place to be. Besides, I had no ties keeping me in this realm since Gram had died two years ago, leaving me a house I couldn't pay for and no inheritance whatsoever. I couldn't even afford to change the old-lady lace curtains or, Mage help me, the wall-to-wall gold shag carpet.

The fairy took me in with his crystalline blue eyes, which matched his flittering wings. "So, what species are you? No, don't tell me." He surveyed me, trying to pinpoint my species.

My pulse raced under his scrutiny because being in the spotlight was not my thing. It unnerved me. Enough that I went straight to goading him. "What? Your super sniffer failing you now?"

I folded my arms across my chest. Not my most mature moment, but he was wasting my time and frying the last remnants of my nerves. Again, he laughed. Then, he sailed off the counter and made swirling circles around my neck. I didn't have to hear or see him to know he was sniffing me.

Sniffing. Me.

Though, in all fairness, I basically invited him to take a whiff.

In response, he grunted. Not sure if it was a good or a bad kind. I almost grabbed the fly swatter, but I stopped short.

*Slow your roll, Terra. You need him.*

He flitted around my head, picking up a strand of hair before he nearly landed on my nose. "Plain brown hair, so you aren't a pixie; dark eyes instead of gold, so gryphon's out...too small to be Valkyrie...Who else isn't in the Conclave like us lowly fae?" He said with a hint of bitterness in his voice, then landed back on the counter, cocking his head. "You smell of buttery gold and rich soil after a rain. And there's something else, but maybe just your own personal aroma."

"Can we just get—"

"Wait. Oh, my Mage. Are you...no way, you can't be!"

There it was.

He slapped his own knee laughing and nearly rolled into the jar of flour he should've been using to cook my meal. "You're a gnome, aren't you? An elusive gnome. This just keeps getting better."

Among Magicals, not even trolls got the amount of ridicule that gnomes did. We didn't deserve that but having so little magic made a difference in our world. I released a slow breath. I didn't have time for his nonsense.

I slammed my hand on the counter for emphasis, setting my features into a cold stare. Letting him know I meant business. "Yes, I'm half-gnome. You've got three seconds to stop laughing and get busy. Or did you forget? I captured you, so I own your ass."

At least I thought so. Liam was a little loose with the details on that.

"Yes ma'am." He managed to pick himself and assemble what resembled a serious expression, then ruined it by turning and slapping his own butt. "This ass is yours."

What had I done?

I'd gambled the remnants of my savings, not to mention my future, on a flippant, smartass fairy.

To his credit, he didn't even blink at the half-gnome comment. Being half-blood had cursed my entire life. Most Magicals did a one-eighty when they found out about it. And, of course, I couldn't tell any human friends about my magical half. If I'd had any. I guess if you counted co-workers who occasionally ate in the same breakroom and had conversations about last night's tv shows count as friends, I did.

*Yup. Terra Hermit Youngblood had a nice ring to it.*

I turned my back on the fairy. The pressure was getting to me, and I didn't want to lose my shit in front of him. There was too much riding on this.

He pricked my shoulder with his tiny finger. "Oh good, I thought you were turning into a statue. You know, like a garden gnome. Get it? Garden gnome!"

Anger rocketed through me. I grabbed a dirty glass containing the remains of my breakfast milk from the sink and slapped it down over the fairy, capturing him in one swift motion. Droplets of souring milk dripped onto his head, splashing on his shiny hair. He did not like that.

As he flapped and gagged and made a fool of himself trying to escape, I tapped my foot. "I'm sorry, what? I can't quite hear you. Did you need something?"

*Juvenile behavior – two. Maturity – zero.*

I knew I was overreacting. But Gram's gnome pride was ingrained deep inside me. I even refused to sell the garden gnome statues at work. I let my co-workers think I was freaked out by them, so I didn't have to face the insult head-on.

When the fairy quieted down and sat cross-legged on the counter, I let him free. He raced to the sink, hit the nozzle and took a little fairy shower. When he had the milk removed, he shook his head like a dog.

I could've sworn the ancient cuckoo clock hanging in the dining room ramped the volume up to eleven.

*Tick. Tick. Tick.*

If he didn't start cooking soon, it would all be for nothing.

"Sorry about the milk. I'm just nervous," I admitted.

Not that I owed him an apology because from where I stood, he started the whole mess, but I was desperate, and anxious. Though, I understood the big question mark that accompanied the word, gnome. I may have forgotten all about that part of my lineage if not for my frantic need to provide for myself.

To appease some of his questions and get his ass in gear, I went with the simple explanation my dear ole gnome-proud Gram gave me when she told me what I was. "Yes, the cheesy garden gnomes are based on our species. No, we don't all have pointy red hats." Though my favorite beanie was red, but that didn't count. "We're an ancient, cunning, and noble guardian species formed by the Mage to guard the palace jewels for the Fae Kings of Court. We're experts at hiding and protecting valuables."

If it was someone else's, not our own, but he didn't need to know that part. There were other things too, but I wasn't going to share them with a fairy. Before she went loco and died of some unknown disease no human or Magical doctor could pinpoint, Gram had told me fae couldn't be trusted.

She also said trolls were the best lovers and she'd spoken to the Mage many times and he replied because he was her bestie. She was full cuckoo at the end, my Gram. I'd filled an entire journal with her harebrained ramblings because they made me laugh. *Gramisms*, I called it.

"Gnome. Okay." He side-eyed me like he was trying to make sense of my existence. Been doing that for twenty-two years and hadn't come up with much yet, so good luck, Bud. He sailed off the counter, buzzing around my head. "Gnomes are alchemists, right? So, you could make some edible gold leaf for the meal if I asked?"

If only.

Most gnomes were great at alchemy, but I sucked at it.

I assumed I didn't have enough magic in me, thanks to my human mother. Not that I could've kept the gold for myself anyway. Magical rules and all that B.S. I *did* have some that Gram had made tucked away though. I nodded at the fairy. "Yeah. How much will you need?"

He rifled through the pile of recipe cards and clapped his hands. "A quarter-cup should work. Now, I have dishes to prepare. Go somewhere else and deal with your nerves, get laid or something."

Not an abysmal idea, but I didn't have the time to dedicate to that endeavor. Besides, who was I going to sleep with? I had no prospects on the horizon. My life had been about prepping for that night, not Terra's personal plan to hook up with the hottest guy I could dig up.

Which was usually how my encounters were. One-night stands or occasional sexy liaisons that lasted a few days or weeks. Because even though I was a solitary soul by nature and by circumstance, I still had...needs. Though getting laid would have to take a back seat, at least until I got into the Conclave. Maybe then I'd find a sexy elf or gryphon in Aetheria that caught my eye. Until then, ix-nay on the ex-say for me.

I tromped down the stairs to my basement suite. The rich brown walls reminded me of the soil when I tunneled. It was dark, cool, and enveloped me like a hug. I was safe there. Protected. Throwing myself down on my comfy and unmade bed, I wrapped my homemade green comforter around me and glanced at my bedside table.

Out of instinct I reached for my Gram's Magic 8-Ball. It was a silly human toy she'd bought for my father when he was young, but after her mind started to go, she used it every day when she wanted to *consult the Mage.*

I had to swallow down the lump in my throat. I missed her so much. So much that I made a point to ask the thing at least one question a day, just to keep her memory alive. Since the fairy had put the thought in my head, I went with the obvious question. "Magic 8-Ball, will I get laid anytime soon?"

*Reply hazy, please try again.*

That's what I figured. I needed to stay the course and see my plans through. There would be time for all the hook-ups in Aetheria as soon as I got gnomes into the Conclave. Obviously Magic 8-ball agreed.

Reluctantly, I set the 8-ball back in its place and pulled myself off the bed. There was work to do. I went over to the tiny water closet where my ever-so-seventies gold tub and toilet were located and started the shower. Thanks to the practically-prehistoric water heater, it would take about ten minutes for the water to heat to a bearable level, so while it warmed, I pulled my Gram's battered old trunk from under my bed.

Inside were the last fragments of my Gram's gold stash. She hadn't made gold in quite some time before her passing, but I'd kept the last of her supply just in case I needed to sell it. Turned out I had exactly a quarter-cup.

I swore when I died and went to Netheria—that is, if a half-magical person's soul were even permitted in the resting place of Magicals—I'd ask the Mage why he'd made gnomes incapable of keeping any treasures or riches for ourselves. That sick trick of nature was responsible for a lot of pain. Though, in fairness, my human side didn't seem to be that great at holding on to my own money either.

After I showered, I dressed in my black dress pants and fitted black sweater, attempting to look as put-together and professional as I could. Out of habit, I reached for the vial that contained soil from my birthplace. It hung from a black cord, and I only took it off to shower. I even slept in it.

Gram was too deep into her delusions to ask where the soil was from when I discovered the vial tucked in her jewelry box with a note saying *"Terra, this is the soil from where you were born. It will ground you and guide you."*

It didn't matter where I was born. What was important was that I had something that connected me to who I was, to Gram. I put it on, feeling the familiar silk cord, the weight of the vial against my chest, and stared at myself in the mirror. I instantly calmed. The vial *did* ground me. But I was still waiting for the guide part to kick in. Maybe it and the Magic 8-Ball needed to get together.

The cord looked fine with my outfit, but something about having dirt hanging from your neck screamed weak and desperate. Okay, I was weak and desperate, but they didn't have to know that, so I pulled the vial off and hung it over my mirror.

I poured the last sprinkles of Gram's gold in a bowl, then headed upstairs, where the fairy forbade me from helping him. Great idea on his part. I almost burned my whole house down making French fries in the oven.

*Teach me to try and be healthy.*

I set the table as best I could, using gold-plated utensils that I hoped wouldn't be too obvious, because it was all I had. The tablecloth and napkins were made of gold silk I picked up at a thrift store and I added a sprinkling of gold leaf down the center of the table. It looked majestic and elegant. That's what I was going for. The Conclave was all about formality, tradition, and sticking to magic rules. It's how Magicals had survived undetected by humans for so long, according to Liam the leprechaun.

I gathered the rest of the gold leaf in a bowl and pushed the swinging kitchen door open. "Here's your go—" The glass bowl slipped from my hands and tumbled to the floor. "Oh, my Mage!"

The fairy was standing at the sink with his back turned. He didn't even react to the shattering glass. "Oh, my Mage, what?"

He'd turned into a full adult-sized man—no wings.

Also, no clothes.

# About The Author

Cat Collins is the #1 bestselling author in her home. No really, her husband wrote a training manual for work once. He sold one copy to his boss. She writes what she likes to read: swoony alphas, witty dialogue, and steamy scenes that make your heart (and various other parts) flutter.

Her Diminishing Magic series has garnered a Readers' Favorite 5-Star critical review and praise from reviewers for its hilarious banter, sexual tension between characters, and turns you never see coming. Described as a "twisty bundle of fun," the series includes elemental magic, wolf shifters, and a main character who's full of sass.

A reading interventionist by day, a reader and binge-watcher by night, Cat lives in the Southern US with her husband as mentioned above, two kids, and two cats who like to help her edit by jumping on the keyboard randomly. Any stray typos must surely be the work of Raven or Poe.

She loves connecting with readers on social media. @CatCollinsBooks on TikTok, Instagram, Facebook & Twitter.

Subscribe to her monthly newsletter at catcollinsbooks.com for behind-the-scenes exclusives, news, book recs, and more. Scan the QR code to see the subscribe link.

# FUN & (REINDEER) GAMES

As I said in my bio, i love connecting with readers on social media. Here are some fun things to talk about to or with me!

- Who was your favorite, Yeager, Hart or Jack?
- Fave spicy scene? Are you a hot tub fan or a voyeur like Jack?
- What team would you join?
- Pro-vampire or too creepy?
- Would you fight a polar bear if you got to hook up with Hart & Yeager after?
- Favorite Christmas song. (Hint: Not Rudolph)
- Do you want the Jingle Juice recipe?  I HAVE IT!
- What tropical vacation spot would you have the guys take you to
- Favorite game devised by Santa is...
- Do you want to read Cupid's story next....??
- Any weird or unusual Christmas/Holiday traditions I can "borrow" for the next book?
- Do you want to read Cupid's story next....??